The Illusionists

Rosie Thomas

HarperCollins*Publishers*

HarperCollins*Publishers*
77–85 Fulham Palace Road,
Hammersmith, London W6 8JB

www.harpercollins.co.uk

First published in Great Britain by
HarperCollins*Publishers* 2014

1

A catalogue record for this book
is available from the British Library

ISBN: 978-0-00-751201-0

Set in Sabon by Palimpsest Book Production Limited,
Falkirk, Stirlingshire

Printed and bound in Great Britain by
Clays Ltd, St Ives plc

MIX
Paper from
responsible sources
FSC
www.fsc.org   FSC C007454

The Illusionists

By the same author:

Celebration
Follies
Sunrise
The White Dove
Strangers
Bad Girls, Good Women
A Woman of Our Times
All My Sins Remembered
Other People's Marriages
A Simple Life
Every Woman Knows a Secret
Moon Island
White
The Potter's House
If My Father Loved Me
Sun At Midnight
Iris and Ruby
Constance
Lovers and Newcomers
The Kashmir Shawl

For my family

PART ONE

ONE

London 1885

Hector Crumhall, known to his legions of enemies and even his few friends as Devil Wix, sauntered up the alley as if he owned every cobblestone and sooty brick. He stepped over the runnel of filth that ran down the middle, touching the brim of his bowler in a mocking salute to Annie Fowler who was seated in the doorway of her house. Two of her girls, torn robes barely covering their shoulders, lounged at an upstairs window with a tin cup on the sill between them.

'Good afternoon to you, ladies,' Devil called.

Annie took her pipe out of her mouth, cleared her throat and spat.

A pair of urchins emerged from the shelter of some crates that had once held fish from the market. They came at Devil with their hands out, driven by desperation rather than any hope that he might drop them a coin.

'Mister?' the bigger one wheedled. They were poised to run in case he lashed out.

Devil stopped. Except for the two brats the only onlookers were Annie and the listless drabs, but he was unable to resist any audience for a trick. He slid two fingers into a waistcoat pocket, displacing the watch chain with his thumb. There was no timepiece on the end of the chain, but who was to know

3

such a detail? He slipped out a bright penny and flicked it into the air. The boys' heads jerked as they followed its ascent and descent, and they sighed when Devil's fist closed on it. He repeated the flick and catch a second time, and then a third, and the fourth time the boys' heads hardly moved. But Devil's fist didn't close again. Instead he spread his palm and gazed into the air as if searching for the penny. The boys gaped and spun on their heels, straining to hear the coin's clink, hunched in their anxiety to pounce on it. No clatter or roll sounded. Thin air had seemingly eaten the penny.

Devil frowned, raising his arm to cuff the nearest boy for losing his coin. The child scuttled off and Devil caught the ear of his slower companion. The boy immediately twisted and yelled at the top of his voice, 'Lemme go, I done nothing.'

Devil groped behind the other ear and produced a red apple. Mouth open, the boy squirmed free and snatched at the fruit but Devil held it just out of his reach. Shaking his head in reproach he bit luxuriously into it. The boy groaned and the girls jeered from their window. Devil continued his interrupted stroll up the alley, chewing with relish and smiling at the thin shaft of sunlight that slid between the overhanging eaves.

The street into which he emerged was hardly wider than its tributary alley but there were more people here. Men leaned against the house walls, dirty-faced children played with pebbles and sticks in the gutters, a couple of shawled women murmured at the steps. The cats' meat man, a familiar figure, trundled his wheeled cart round the corner. Announcing itself with a pungent reek, his merchandise was condemned meat and chunks of ripe offal. It was intended for animals, but there were plenty of housewives in this neighbourhood who were glad to buy a little piece to boil up with half an onion and a handful of potato peelings to make a dinner for a hungry family.

Tossing away the apple core Devil stuck his hands into his pockets and passed on by. The intermediate street led in turn to a much wider thoroughfare. Here there were tall black buildings and glass shop frontages with names picked out in gilt lettering on their fascias. Painted enamel signs advertised tobacco and patent medicines, slate boards chalked with the prices of the day's dinners hung outside working men's eating-houses. It was noisy here with street vendors shouting their wares over the hammering from building sites and the clip of horses' hooves as loaded drays and hansom cabs and a crowded omnibus bound for Oxford Street rolled by. Pedestrians brushed past Devil, some of them glancing at his handsome face.

Let them stare, he always thought. *What's worth looking at must be worth seeing.*

On the opposite corner of the street stood the Old Cinque Ports, a large public house. He hadn't decided where he was heading today, but wherever it turned out to be would be fine because he felt lucky, and his instincts rarely let him down. In any case there was no hurry. A quick visit to the Ports would be a good way to get business started.

The heavy doors had twin panels of etched glass. Devil leaned on a brass handle and pushed open the door. It was the middle of an autumn afternoon but the lamps in the ornate saloon were blazing, and the bevels of the glass split the bright beams into little rainbows. As it always did, the interior of the pub reminded him of a place of worship. The cavernous ceiling arched overhead, polished brass and carved mahogany fittings glowed, and the altar – or in this case the long, sinuous curve of the bar – was the focus of all attention. The main differences were that it was warm in here and the place attracted a more interesting class of sinner, including numbers of women. One of them swayed towards Devil now. She had broad hips swathed in red sateen and a deep-cut bodice that revealed most of a pair of white breasts so heavily powdered that a pale fog rose off them as she moved. He didn't think he had encountered her before, but she linked her bare arm in his as if they were old friends and guided him with a nudge of the hips towards a pair of stools. Devil had no objection. He liked sitting up here against the bar where he could admire the rows of bright bottles and their reflections in the painted glass, or flick a glance

5

sideways at the drinkers' profiles ranged on either side to assess them as potential threat or target. The stools were carved to fit a man's rear, and when you parked yourself you felt that there was no finer place on earth to be than beneath the roof of this brewer's temple, and no more promising day in your life than this very one.

'I'll have a gin, duck,' the woman sighed in his ear. She had hopped up on to the stool next to his. Devil rapped on the marble bar top with a florin, and the barman came with a brief nod of greeting. The Old Cinque Ports was a busy place and Devil didn't come here quite often enough for the man to try to use his name, which was how he preferred it. He ordered a glass for the woman and a pint of Bass for himself, and when the drinks came he put hers into her hand.

She had bad teeth which she tried to hide by keeping her lips drawn taut over her smile. Her hair lay thin and brittle over her grey scalp. She was several cuts above Annie Fowler's wretched girls but most likely she lived in one corner of a room somewhere in the rookery from which he had just emerged, and probably struggled to find the shillings even for that. No doubt she had children to feed.

The woman lifted the glass and swallowed an eager gulp of gin. Her eyes met his, acknowledging that it was a hard life.

Devil leaned forward so their faces almost touched, like a kiss about to happen.

'Now, get off with you and leave me alone.'

Her smile died, but she made no attempt to change his mind. She slid wearily from the stool and moved into the throng in search of another mark.

Devil sat back and made a survey of his companions. Several were familiar, none was of interest to him today. Sighing with satisfaction, he drank his beer and lit a cigarette. All was well. All would be well, at least. Coupled with the gift of an optimistic disposition he had the knack of finding contentment in small things. Current circumstances were unpromising, but this was a pleasant interval and he wouldn't spoil it with dismal thoughts. He might be broke today – indeed, he *was* broke – but that didn't mean that tomorrow would tell the same story. He wasn't like the beggars and thieves who populated the Holborn alleys, immured in poverty and unable to help themselves, nor did he resemble the slightly better-off clerks and drovers and shop workers who gathered under the decorated ceilings of this public house as a break from their menial routines.

He was a man of talents.

Devil had finished his pint and was contemplating the possibility of another when a woman screamed, high and long. This was followed by a burst of shouting and cursing. There were the sounds of a scuffle and breaking glass and Devil idly turned to see two bloodied men in shirtsleeves swinging punches at each other. A woman staggered between them as she tried to haul one out of the fray. There was some jostling for a better view and a few shouts of encouragement from the onlookers, but fights weren't at all uncommon in the Old Cinque Ports. The publican, a muscled fellow with a pugilist's face, was already shouldering his way across the room to break it up. Devil was about to turn his back on the spectacle when he noticed the child. He was sliding between the drinkers, short as a midday shadow, dipping pockets.

The slut in the red dress began hauling at the other woman, shrieking, 'Nellie, Nellie! Stop it now, afore 'e kills the both of you.' Her purse was a leather pouch pinned at her waist and the child had obviously noted that the mouth of it gaped open. With the swirl of the crowd in the path of the approaching publican to his advantage, he pressed close up against the woman and his hand flashed faster than the eye could follow.

He was good, Devil noted.

Amusement, a dart of interest, or perhaps just a sense that he had treated the whore rudely despite having paid for her gin, made him jump from his stool. He leapt through the crowd and caught the boy as he reached the doors. Devil held him by the throat with one hand and grasped his surprisingly sturdy

wrist with the other. The doors swung open and the publican
booted the brawlers out into the street, followed by the handful
of onlookers who wanted to jeer the fight to its end. Devil and
his writhing captive stumbled out amongst them and Devil
whipped off the child's cloth cap so he could get a good look
at his face. He stared in astonishment at the glare that met his.

The child wasn't a boy at all but a man, his own age. There
were furrows at the sides of his mouth and a jaw dark blue
with stubble.

A pocket-picking dwarf. That was a fine thing.

The little man cocked an eyebrow.

'I've seen you in the halls. You're Devil Wix.'

He frowned. 'Mr Wix to you. How much did you get?' The
dwarf tried to look offended but Devil snatched him off his
feet and shook him until his pockets rattled. 'How much?'

The feet in miniature boots swung viciously. Devil's interest
quickened. This was a lively little pickpocket.

'Put me down.'

'Give me the money you nabbed.'

'Why should I? It's not yours, is it? Unless she's working for
you.'

'Do I look like a pimp?'

The dwarf put his head back, pretended to consider the
question, and then shrugged. Devil almost laughed.

The combatants had exhausted their antagonism. One
slumped on a doorstep and mopped his face with a rag. The
other spat out blood and broken teeth while his whore clung
to his arm and wailed. The woman in red stuck her fingers
into her open purse and her mouth fell open in dismay. Devil
and his captive were beginning to attract attention so he lowered
the dwarf to the ground and roughly explored the small pockets
with his free hand. He found a few coins – two shilling pieces,
a threepenny bit and four pennies. He held out this haul to the
drab and her mouth snapped shut again.

'Don't throw your money away,' he advised pleasantly. She
took the coins from him with a blink. Dragging his miniature

companion by the arm, Devil marched out of the circle and made for the nearest corner. Another hundred yards brought them to a cabmen's halt where a sign in the smeary window read: '*Try our champion 4d. dinners*'.

'I feel like I've got a hole in me. Let's eat,' he said.

'Got no money. You just stole it,' the dwarf snarled.

'I'll play you for a dinner,' Devil offered and the little man suddenly grinned, showing pointed teeth that made him look like a wolf backing into the undergrowth.

'Right then,' he agreed.

Inside the eating-house damp steam scented with boiled meat and potatoes rose around them and Devil sniffed appreciatively. A score of hungry cabmen clattered and guffawed as they shovelled up their dinners.

They took their seats at a table towards the back. The dwarf was perhaps three feet tall. He hauled himself into place with muscular arms and then settled on his haunches to bring his chin to the right height at the tabletop. He pushed his cap to the back of his head and Devil took a good look at him. His long-chinned but well-shaped face looked too large to be perched on his stunted body but his expression was alert and his hands were quite clean and cared for. He was no vagrant.

'Cards or cups?' he asked Devil, who only waved a hand to indicate indifference.

The dwarf took three tin cups out of an inner pocket and with a flourish placed a pea under the middle one. Devil was already bored. The dwarf shuffled the cups, elaborately feinting, and as soon as he sat back Devil pointed. The movements had been practised enough, but not so quick that he couldn't follow them. He knew exactly where the pea was, and when the dwarf flipped the cup he wasn't surprised to be proved right.

'You pay,' he yawned.

Slyly his companion lifted the second cup and then the third, and there were peas under those too. Devil grinned back at him. The little man had a sense of humour, and his touch wasn't bad.

9

'All right, my friend. You get a fourpenny dinner for your efforts.'

The cups and peas were tucked away and the dwarf rubbed his hands.

'Are you going to tell me your name, since it seems you know mine already?'

'You can call me Carlo.' The dwarf didn't sound as if he came from London, but neither did he sound as if this exotic label properly belonged to him. He was from the north of England, Devil guessed, although he was hazy about the geography of anywhere that lay beyond Bedford.

'What kind of name is that?'

'The one I have chosen,' his new acquaintance snapped.

A pimply boy leaned over and slapped down cutlery, and at a sign from Devil followed it up with two swimming plates of mutton stew and mash.

'Or is it a half serving for you?' this person sneered at Carlo, making to scoop one plate away again. 'It's only tuppence for littl'uns.'

'You put that down,' Devil ordered. 'And keep a civil tongue for customers.'

Devil and Carlo ate eagerly. The dwarf dispatched his plateful so quickly that he must have been ravenous.

'Now,' Devil said when Carlo belched and wiped his mouth with the back of his hand. 'What's your story, Carlo from Manchester, or wherever it is and whoever you are? What brings you to London with your quick fingers? Richer pickings down here, is it?'

'None of your business.'

'I believe it's at least fourpenn'orth of my business now.'

Carlo pursed his lips. He took a handkerchief from his pocket and unwrapped a toothpick from the folds. Applying this instrument to his teeth, he seemed to weigh Devil's desire for information against his own requirements.

'Morris's Amazing Performing Midgets,' he said at length.

'Eh?'

10

'I said . . .'

'I heard. I'm asking you to elaborate.'

Carlo sighed with impatience, as if he could hardly believe that Devil wasn't already familiar with the Midgets' reputation.

'You should know. I know you, and you're not even first-rate.' He pronounced it *foost*. Devil said nothing, amused by the dwarf's high opinion of himself. 'High-class act, it was. We didn't just play the penny gaffs, although I'm not saying there wasn't times when we were glad to. But we were booked in the better halls, and some private entertainments. We did song and dance, of course, and Sallie had a little piano and a miniature harp, very popular that was, especially with the ladies. Sam and me did a juggling turn, a set of acrobatics, well rehearsed, top-notch costumes. But the meat and taters of the act was magic. Cards, coins, handkerchers. Miniature. And we ended it all up with a nice box trick. *Very* nice. All my own work, that was.'

The little man delivered the last snippet of information in a theatrical whisper, tufty eyebrows drawn together, his sharp eyes peering up at Devil. And as he must have known they would, his words made Devil sit up and pay attention.

'All your own work?' he repeated. 'Inventor, are you?'

'That's right.'

'Well, well.'

Devil snapped his fingers at the serving boy who carried away the empty plates and brought them pint mugs of tea. Devil blew on his and took a swallow.

'Was, you said. *Was* a high-class act?'

'Nowt wrong with your ears.'

Devil reflected. He had heard on the circuit or perhaps read in the trades of a northern touring troupe of midgets. The name that suddenly came to him in this connection was Little Charlie Morris.

'Charlie Morris, that's who you are. What's the business with *Carlo*?'

The dwarf sucked at his teeth to extract the last remnants of food and folded away the toothpick.

11

'New start.'

'I see.' Devil understood that well enough. 'What about your sister and her husband?'

He was almost sure, as fragmentary recollections came together, that Charlie or Carlo's fellow performers had been these two members of his family.

The dwarf's face flooded with such real sadness that Devil was sure it wasn't part of an act, nor any attempt at gathering sympathy for mercenary reasons, but the base note of his being.

'They passed away last year, within a week of each other.'

'I'm sorry.'

Carlo jerked his head. He added, 'In-flu-en-za,' tapping the syllables between his teeth with such finality that Devil didn't want to upset him by fishing for any further information. But naming the illness seemed to unlock the dwarf's tongue.

'My father was like me, my ma's one of you although she's no giant. Of us four children there's two big 'uns and then my sister Sallie and me, and we two always knew we'd have to take care of ourselves because of being small. My dad was a singer in the taphouses. Used to stand him on the counter, they did, and he'd do a ballad and play the piccolo and pass his hat round.

'Our two brothers went in for mill work but for us littl'uns the best we could have got was being sent to crawl under the looms to collect the waste, and our ma wouldn't have that. So we were going to join our dad with the act. Make all our fortunes, he said. He trained us up and made us practise the routines, and when we didn't work hard enough he'd thrash our hides raw with his belt. Poor old Sal used to howl. She was glad to marry her Sam to get away from home. Sam came from Oldham. Just him in the family was small, so it was lonely for him. He was sweet on Sal the minute he saw her. They'd been wed a year when our dad fell off the stage one night when he was corned and hit his head. He didn't last long after that. I had Sam into the act gladly enough, even though he didn't have the talent for it. Sal was the one out of the three of us

12

who had the real stage quality. You should have seen her. Like a shining star her face was, under the lamps.

'We did all right. Then one night Sam was ill with a fever and she was nursing him, and two days after that she was ill herself. Less than a week went by and they were both gone.'

Carlo drank his tea. His mouth tightened as if he regretted having confided so much.

Devil waited. This story would surely lead to a request for money, a bed for the night, a helping hand of some sort, and he was already wondering precisely how much he would be prepared to do for Carlo Morris if the circumstances happened to be right.

The dwarf added, 'I can't be a troupe of one, can I? Can't work the box trick single-handed for a start.'

'And so you've come down to the big city to look for some work in the halls. Juggling, acrobatics, and the magic, I think you said? Just doing some dipping for the practice, were you?'

Carlo smacked his hand on the table so violently that the mugs rattled.

'Don't talk to me like I'm a casual fallen on hard times. I don't need to look for work. I've already got a job. And if I'm hungry today and an open pocket is held out to me in an alehouse, am I going to turn my back on it?'

'I suppose not,' Devil agreed. This attitude rather neatly matched his own. 'You performed well enough. First time you'd tapped a purse, was it?'

This time it was Carlo who shrugged and flexed his strong fingers. He climbed down from the chair and straightened his cap on his head. 'I'd not see Sallie go hungry. Or our ma for that matter, even though she'd slap me round the head quicker than cook me a dinner. Same with you, I daresay.'

'I don't have a sister or a mother. I wouldn't take trouble for them even if I did.'

Carlo tipped his head to scowl up at Devil.

'It's not right to speak of family like that.'

'I'm obliged to you for the sermon.'

13

Devil reached in his pocket for eightpence, and gave the money to the pimply youth. They made their way back out into the street. Now he had eaten, Carlo seemed relaxed, almost genial. He tucked his thumbs into his pockets and looked about him. Devil supposed that from his perspective the scenery was mostly composed of hansom wheels and women's backsides.

'I'm going that way,' Carlo pointed. For a miniature man in a strange city he seemed remarkably at ease. 'Why don't you walk along? You can take a look at my new place of work. You'll be interested in that.'

Devil wasn't going anywhere in particular. 'All right.'

They strolled through the crowds in silence imposed by the three-foot difference in height. They crossed a busy road, with Carlo picking his way ahead. He had to gather himself to spring across puddles that Devil stepped over without checking his stride. They skirted the web of alleys where Devil currently lodged and headed south into the yellow-grey murk of a fading afternoon.

'Know where you're going, do you?' He addressed the button on top of the dwarf's cap.

'Do you take me for a fool?'

Devil was still amused. This dwarf was a lively little person.

After a longer interval of walking in silence Carlo led the way out into the Strand. By this time the lamps were lit, each yellow flare wreathing itself in a wan halo of mist. Devil regularly worked in the taverns and supper clubs lining the nearby streets and he had assumed Carlo was heading towards one of these. But the dwarf stopped only when they reached the Strand itself, at a gaunt building on the southern side that Devil had often passed and never troubled to look at. There was not much to be seen anyway because the front was largely obscured by boards, nailed into place with heavy beams to shield passers-by from bricks or chunks of stonework that might fall from the crumbling facade. Tufts of dried brown buddleia sprouted from the cracks in the lintels.

Carlo dipped into the alleyway that sloped along the building's

14

side. Somewhere further down lay the busy river; the reek of mud drifted up to them. There was a door in the side of the building, the cracked panels just visible in the fading light. The dwarf knocked, waited for a response, and when none came he put his small shoulder to it and pushed it open. The two men stepped into the damp, dark space within.

'What's this place?' Devil asked.

'You ask a lot of questions, don't you?'

Devil grabbed his collar. 'Someone of your size might take more trouble to answer them.'

'Listen,' Carlo said.

There was music playing. It was tinny, so faint that the trilling was almost swallowed by the clammy air. They shuffled towards the sound and the glow of light spilling from another doorway.

In the centre of a hall that lay beyond, its shadowy depths hardly penetrated by a pair of gas lamps, a couple was dancing. The music was louder and sweeter here. It came from a musical box held in the lap of a solitary spectator, a very fat man in a heavy old coat. A silk scarf was knotted under his sequence of chins. When the mechanism wound down the fat man lifted the box and turned a handle until it started up again, and the couple went on waltzing. All three of them ignored the new arrivals.

Devil studied the dancers. Carlo swung on to a stool to give himself a better view.

The woman was very young, with long glossy hair that fell almost to her narrow waist. Her profile was serene, her lips slightly parted in a faint smile. Her partner was an attentive man of middle age, his face partly shielded by steel-rimmed spectacles. He danced with great concentration, his head bent so close to hers that his lips almost brushed the lustrous hair. The precision of his steps and his protective bearing suggested that she needed guidance in some manoeuvre more complicated or demanding than a waltz before an audience of one. Devil saw that the man's shoes were rimmed with the mud of London streets, but the woman's were pale satin and unmarked. She hadn't walked here, or anywhere else, in those slippers.

The music stopped and the fat man turned the handle once again. Devil nodded to himself. The oddness of the scene, the dim light, the abundant hair had all momentarily confused him but now he knew what was happening here. He let his attention slide away.

They were in a derelict little theatre. As his eyes acclimatised he saw that it had been partly burned out. The space where the stage would once have been was a mess of charred wood and fallen beams, and the delicately painted walls of the auditorium had been spoiled with smoke. The ruins of seating had been thrown into the corners, and every surface, except for a circle in the centre that had been roughly swept for the dancers, was layered with soot. Yet even in its decayed state Devil could see that this was a harmonious space. A gallery extended its arms almost to the stage, from which it was separated only by two levels of little boxes with apron fronts that had once been lavishly gilded. The gallery was supported by slim pillars, blackened too but still intact. When he looked upwards he glimpsed the ruins of a once-magnificent plaster ceiling.

The last tinkling notes of the mechanical waltz died away, yet seemed to be still echoing in the intimate sounding-box of the hall.

Devil listened, all his senses heightened as a pulse ticked in his neck. What was this place?

'Thank you, Herr Bayer.' The fat man was barely smothering a yawn.

The dancers stopped but the man's right hand still clasped his partner's, and the fingers of his left rested lightly at her waist. Then he bowed to her and took one step back. As soon as she was released her white arms gracefully descended to her sides. She stood motionless, her eyes glittering. Her faint smile now seemed too fixed.

Devil had seen already that this was not a woman but an automaton.

16

A well-made thing, but still a thing.

'She is beautiful, yes?' Herr Bayer said.

The other shrugged.

Herr Bayer's voice rose. 'We have toured in France and Austria as well as in Switzerland. In Berlin we danced for a niece of the Empress.'

The fat man's chins looked like warm wax melting into his scarf. 'Tell me, what else does the doll do?'

Herr Bayer recoiled. 'If you please. Her name is Lucie.'

'What else does your *Lucie* do?'

Bayer guided her to a seat across the circle from the fat man. She moved in a stately glide, her head turning slightly on her slender neck as if to acknowledge her admirers. He dusted the chair seat with his handkerchief and she folded at the hip and the knee to adopt a sitting position. Bayer lifted one of her hands to his lips and kissed it.

'As you see, Lucie stands and sits, walks and dances.'

'I hear Mr Hoffman has a mechanical creature who plays chess. It will take on any opponent, and it usually wins.'

'Hoffman's Geraldo is hardly bigger than a child's toy.' Bayer swung on his heel and pointed at Carlo. This was the first acknowledgement from either man of their arrival. 'And there is a person like *him* concealed in a box just behind its shoulder, directing the movement of the pieces.'

'Davenport's latest invention tells fortunes and reads minds.'

'He uses a clumsy puppet, a scarecrow, hardly more than that. And the act is a common memory game. Pure trickery.' Bayer almost spat. His Swiss-German accent grew heavier.

The fat man sighed. 'It is all trickery. This is what we do.'

'No.'

Bayer leapt to Lucie's side. He put one arm round her smooth shoulder as if to defend her from insult. 'This is no trick. She is what she is, a work of art. A miracle of precision, perfect in every movement. Look at her face, her hair, even her clothing.'

Devil strolled across the circle. 'May I?' He reached out to stroke Lucie's head. The hair was human, but it felt lifeless under his hand. The automaton's dress was lace and silks and velvet, but there was no breathing warmth within its rich folds. The face was exquisitely moulded and painted and utterly unmoving. He stepped back, faintly disgusted by the doll's parody of womanhood.

Bayer said, 'She is lovely, you see? Mr Grady, you will not find a better or more ambitious model to delight your audiences.'

The man smiled but an imploring note had entered his voice. Lucie might be dressed in the latest finery, Devil saw, but her partner's clothes were worn and mended. The man was another itinerant performer, hungrily searching for a paying audience, just like Carlo and – indeed – himself. For a moment Devil was depressed to think how many such hopefuls there were in London, let alone elsewhere, but he didn't allow the anxiety to take hold. *He* would succeed, because he would do anything and everything necessary to ensure that success. And the rest of them could go to hell. He returned to his contemplation of the theatre's lovely ruin.

Grady put aside the musical box and wrote in a notebook.

'Very well. Come back here in two weeks. We'll be ready to open by then. I'll try you out for a few performances, see whether the crowd takes to you.'

Bayer's face brightened. He bowed to Grady and nodded to Carlo and Devil, but his proper attention was for Lucie. He wrapped a shawl round her shoulders and kissed the top of her head before bringing forward a brass-cornered trunk and undoing the clasps. The interior was padded with red plush and shaped to accommodate a female form. Bayer lifted the automaton in his arms and gently folded the doll into captivity. Then he hoisted the locked trunk on to a wheeled frame like a market porter's, bowed again to Grady and took up the handles of the frame.

'*Auf Wiedersehen*,' he said from the doorway as he trundled Lucie away.

No one spoke for a moment. Then the fat man looked at his pocket watch.

'Let's get on with it,' he said to Carlo. 'What's your name again?'

'I told you. Carlo Boldoni,' the dwarf replied, unblinking. 'And as I said, direct from performing before the finest drawing-room audiences in Rome. And Paris.'

'The finest taphouses in Macclesfield and Oldham, more like. Real name?'

'In our world of magic and illusion what is real, Mr Grady?'

'Pounds, shillings and pence,' the fat man snapped, not greatly to Devil's surprise. Grady looked like a man who would count all three most carefully. What were his plans, and what was the story of this ruined theatre?

Devil considered the possibilities, and the potential for himself, but said nothing.

'Call yourself whatever you like,' Grady went on. 'I haven't got all day to listen to you. Show me what you've got. And who is this?' He pointed at Devil.

'He is my assistant.'

Devil opened his mouth and closed it again. There was a time and place.

Carlo hurried into the shadows, then staggered into view once more bearing a pile of boxes and cloths.

'Here,' he muttered to Devil. Obligingly he unfolded the legs of a small table as Carlo shook out a green cloth covering. On the cloth he placed an opera hat and a wicker birdcage. He stood in front of his table and made a deep bow to Grady, then whipped a silk handkerchief out of his pocket and mopped his brow as if the effort of setting up his stall had brought on a sweat.

'I haven't got all day,' the fat man scowled.

Carlo fanned himself with the handkerchief. His expression was so comical that Devil smiled. Then Carlo clapped his hands and the handkerchief vanished.

'Dear me. Where has that gone? Can you tell me, sir?'

'No,' yawned Grady.

'Then I will show you.'

Carlo produced the handkerchief from his pocket and clapped his hands. Once more it vanished, to be extracted from the pocket again a moment later.

'You see, sir, how useful this is? Especially for a gentleman like you whose time is so valuable. You have only to take out your handkerchief, and never trouble yourself to put it away again.'

Devil knew how this old trick was done, because it was the first he had learned. But he had to acknowledge that it would have taken plenty of practice as well as natural skill to perform it so adroitly.

'Continue, please,' said Grady.

Carlo tipped the hat to show that it was empty but for the smooth lining, then pulled from it a knotted string of coloured silks. He whirled these round his head, drew a pair of scissors from the hat and snipped the silks into bright confetti that drifted to his feet. He scooped these fragments into his tiny fists, balled them up and threw them into the air, where they became whole handkerchiefs again. Devil was impressed. Improvising his role he snatched up the hat, bowed over it to Grady and gestured elaborately to acknowledge Carlo's mastery. This gave him the opportunity to examine the hat, ingeniously constructed with a double interior.

Carlo lifted the birdcage and his sad, long-chinned face peered through the struts at Grady.

'I have a sweet trick with the doves but I couldn't leave my birds here with the rest of my old props, sir, could I? All I have to show you is their pretty cage.'

He wafted his fingers inside to demonstrate its emptiness and latched its door, dropped a cloth over the cage, marched twice around the table and snatched the cloth away again. Inside the cage was a crystal ball. Carlo extracted the ball and peered into the clear interior, rubbing his chin and muttering.

'What have we here? Ah, this is a vision worth seeing, Mr Grady. We have a packed theatre, ladies and gentlemen applauding until their hands are ready to drop off, a heap of guineas, and handbills announcing the Great Carlo Boldoni in letters as high as himself.'

Grady stuck out his slab of a hand. Turning a little to one side Carlo blew on the ball and gave it a polish with his sleeve before handing it over. Inside the glass an orange now glowed.

'Doesn't look to me like even one guinea,' Grady scowled.

'You need magician's eyesight, perhaps.' Carlo retrieved his crystal ball, replaced it in the birdcage and covered it once again with the cloth. He settled the hat on his head and began to gather up his boxes. Almost as an afterthought he whipped off the cloth to reveal that the cage was empty once more.

Carlo tipped the comical hat to one side and thoughtfully scratched his cranium. Then he darted over to Grady, dipped a hand into the man's coat pocket and brought out the orange. From the opposite pocket came a knife.

'You look hungry,' he said, slicing the orange into neat quarters and offering it to Grady.

'Can't you do a beefsteak?' was the reply.

'Not for a farthing less than five shillings a show.'

Grady gave a sour laugh. 'For you and Her Majesty singing a duet, will that be?'

Carlo sucked one of the orange slices.

'I have plenty more tricks. And some new ones, all my own, never performed on stage. You need Carlo Boldoni for your theatre opening, Mr Grady. What do you say?'

Devil returned to studying the graceful pillars and the sinuous curve of the gallery. He longed for a brighter light so he could see more.

Grady puffed. 'I'll think about it. You heard what I said to the fellow with the doll. The Palmyra will be ready to open in two weeks.' He gestured to the gallery. 'Go right through it, we will, get rid of all this old rubbish. Make it look like something.'

'The Palmyra?' Devil interrupted.

No, he was thinking. *You won't destroy this place and turn it into some penny gaff for vulgar music hall, not if I have anything to do with it.*

Grady ignored him. To Carlo he said, 'Your assistant doesn't do a lot to earn his keep, does he? It was named the Palmyra, yes. That's a town in Arabia, you know. Something like Babylon. What a name, eh? What's wrong with the Gaiety, or the Palace of Varieties, a label with a bit of a promise in it? Built sixty years ago as a concert hall, it was. Never did any business, though, and the debts piled up until the poor devil who owned it went under. He died or he topped himself, one or the other, and there were decades of family disputes after that. In the end all the money went to chancery and they had to sell up.'

Grady tapped the side of his nose and Devil almost laughed out loud. The man was absurd. 'The price was keen, I can tell you. Shall we just say that Jacko Grady is now the proud possessor? And under his management the old Palmyra will be the finest music hall in London.'

'Don't change the name,' Devil said.

'What?'

'If I'd been clever enough to buy an opportunity like this, I'd keep the name. It's different. It's got class. More than you could say for the Gaiety.'

'If I want your opinion I'll ask for it. Which is about as likely as our friend here hitting his head on the Euston Arch.' The fat man wheezed with pleasure at himself. 'Who are you, anyway?'

'I am Devil Wix.'

The dwarf hovered in Devil's line of sight, gesturing to him to shut up.

'Is that supposed to mean something to me?'

'Why not? You are an impresario and I am a stage magician.'

Carlo gestured more urgently. Jacko Grady displayed no sign of interest and Devil thought, *Six months. That's about as long as you'll last as the manager of your Palmyra. Money is the only thing that interests you.*

Devil strolled to Carlo's table and picked up the opera hat. He showed the empty interior to Grady, made a pass and

22

extracted the dwarf's scissors from their concealed place. Then he reached into his coat pocket and took out his own forcing pack of cards. He flexed his fingers, expertly shuffling so the cards danced and poured through his hands. He fanned them and offered the pack to Grady.

'Any card. Memorise it and put it back.'

Grady yawned again, but did so. Devil shuffled again and then spun in a tight circle. He flung the cards in the air, brandished Carlo's scissors and snipped clean through a card as it fell. Then he dropped to his knees and retrieved the cut halves. He held them up.

'Ten of diamonds?'

Grady nodded. Devil gathered up the fallen cards and placed the cut card in the middle. He shuffled once more and held out the fanned pack. Grady's thick forefinger hesitated, withdrew, hovered and then pointed. The card he chose was the ten of diamonds, made whole again.

The only sound that greeted this was Grady's chair creaking under his weight.

Devil coaxed him, 'We have some time between other engagements, Mr Boldoni and I. Try us out, Mr Grady, and we'll put our new box trick on for your customers before anyone else in England sees it.'

Carlo's signals grew more imperative but he held still as soon as Grady turned his glare on them.

'What's this new box trick?'

Devil improvised rapidly. 'Ah, the Sphinx and the Pyramid? Mystery, comedy and Arabian glamour all in one playlet. Don't tell me that's not made for the Palmyra. There's a lot of interest from other theatres. You'll regret it if you let another management snitch us from under your very nose . . .'

Grady still spoke to Carlo. 'All right. If I don't see anyone better in the meantime I'll put your act on when we open. Half a crown a performance, and you'll play when I tell you to whether it suits you or not. That's for you and your assistant, Satan or whatever he calls himself.'

23

Carlo ran forward and stood in front of Grady's chair, legs apart and fists on his hips.

'Five bob.'

Grady spat out a laugh that turned into a phlegmy cough. Carlo's face turned livid with anger.

'I said five bob. I won't do it for less.'

Grady finished his coughing into a handkerchief and wiped his face. 'Then don't do it at all. It's no trouble to me, I assure you.'

Devil smoothly interposed himself, dropping a reassuring hand on Carlo's shoulder.

'I am Mr Baldano's manager as well as his assistant.'

'I thought he said Boldoni.'

'. . . And we are prepared to work for half a crown a show, with just one small stipulation.'

'What might that be?'

'For every show we appear in that plays to more than eighty per cent capacity, Boldoni and Wix take a percentage of the box office.'

'What percentage?'

Devil hastily ran figures through his head. Bargaining against calculations of this sort had previously only taken place in his wilder fantasies, but his fertile imagination meant that was fully prepared.

'Ten.'

Jacko Grady looked cunning. Clearly he thought that the likelihood of playing regularly to houses more than eighty per cent full, against all the competition from taverns and music halls in the nearby streets, was sufficiently remote as not to be worrisome.

'All right.'

Carlo and Wix presented their hands and the fat man ungraciously shook.

'I'll bring a paper for you to sign. Just to be businesslike,' Devil said. Grady only swore and told them to get out of his sight.

Darkness had fallen. Carlo and Devil stood with Carlo's stage props and boxes in their arms as the tides of vehicles and pedestrians swept past along the Strand.

Carlo was boiling with fury. Devil thought the dwarf might be about to kick him and he tried not to laugh out loud.

The dwarf spluttered, 'The Sphinx and the Pyramid? What blooming rubbish. What's Grady going to say? We haven't got any Arabian box trick.'

'Then we'd better get one. You talk about your new trick, all your own work. We can dress that up, whatever it is, with a few frills. We'll start tomorrow. Where's your workshop?'

'I haven't got a damned workshop. You had to buy me my dinner. I haven't even got anywhere to sleep tonight.'

Devil looked down at him. The dwarf was defiant.

'You told me you had a job already, starting tomorrow?'

'I knew I'd have one, once I'd shown him what I can do. I'm good. I'm the *best*. Compared with Carlo Boldoni you are just a tradesman.'

It was true. The Crystal Ball and the Orange had been something special, even though Jacko Grady was too stupid and too venal to have appreciated it.

'So I'll be your apprentice, as well as your manager.'

'Boldoni and bloody Wix? What d'you mean by that? And all the gammon about ten per cent of nothing, which is nothing? I want five bob to go onstage. I don't need you to manage me, thank you kindly.'

A lady and gentleman were lingering to watch the comedy of a dwarf squaring up to a full-grown man.

Devil stooped to bring his face closer to Carlo's. He said gently, 'You do need me. And you will have to trust me because I am putting my trust in you. That is how we shall have to do business from now on, my friend.'

'I am not your friend, nor are you mine,' the dwarf retorted.

Devil good-humouredly persisted. 'I've also got a roof over my head, even though it's not Buckingham Palace. You can come back there with me now. I've got bread and cheese, we'll

25

have a glass or two of stout, and we can start work on the box trick in the morning.'

Carlo's fury faded. Devil could see that under his bravado the little man was exhausted, and had battled alone for long enough.

'Come on,' he coaxed.

Carlo said nothing. But after a moment he hoisted his boxes and began to trudge northwards, at Devil's side.

Later that night Devil sat at the three-legged table in the corner of his attic room, an empty ale mug at his elbow. Apart from chests and boxes of props the only other furniture was a cupboard, two chairs, his bed and a row of wooden pegs for his clothes. It was cold and not too clean, but by the standards of this corner of London it wasn't a bad lodging. The landlady was inclined to favour Devil, and he took full advantage of her partiality.

Devil was watching the dwarf as he slept, rolled up on the floor in a blanket with one of his prop bags for a pillow. He twitched like a dog in his dreams.

Devil wasn't ready for sleep. He thought long and hard, tapping his thumbnail against his teeth as his mind worked.

TWO

The workshop belonged to a coffin maker. Coils of wood shavings had been roughly swept aside and the air was fugged with glue and varnish. Carlo stuck his hands on his hips and scowled about him.

'Gives me the creeps, this place does.'

Devil raised his eyebrows. 'We can't be choosy, my friend. And contrary to your dainty feelings it strikes me as perfect for working up a box trick. Shall we begin?'

'Don't try to tell me we haven't got all night,' Carlo grumbled.

The workshop's owner had gone off at seven o'clock, warning them that he would be back again first thing in the morning by which time they were to be cleared out, and not to disturb any of his handiwork in the meantime. 'I'm going to eat a bite first.'

With this he settled himself on the coffin maker's bench, unwrapped a square of cloth, and tore into a hunk of bread laid with cold mutton. With difficulty, Devil held his tongue. After just two days of Carlo's company he knew not only that the dwarf's small body could absorb surprising quantities of food, but that he was always to be the one who paid for it. The end would be worth the outlay, he reassured himself. If

27

the intimations he had already picked up about Carlo's box trick turned out to be correct.

Jacko Grady was not so stupid as not to have an inkling of the potential too, because without overmuch protest he had signed two copies of the contract prepared by Devil. Ten per cent of box office returns, on every house of more than eighty per cent capacity.

The arithmetic ran in Devil's head like a ribbon of gold.

Once the dwarf had finished his meal, they turned to the collection of materials assembled to Carlo's precise instructions and eventual approval. As well as the borrowing of a handcart and the negotiating with sawyers and metal smiths, the procuring of everything had obliged Devil to use almost the last of the sovereigns he kept hidden under the floorboards and in various other niches in his lodgings. The bribe to the coffin maker for night-time use of his premises had taken most of what was left.

'This had better be a dazzler,' he muttered.

To answer him Carlo rummaged in one of his bags and produced an armful of metal. This he assembled to make a knife with a blade as long as himself. He whipped the air with it, then drove the point into the rough floorboards before leaning on the handle to demonstrate the weapon's strength and flexibility.

'In my costume as whoever you please, Pharaoh perhaps, or the Medusa, or Milor' the Frenchie Duke – it don't matter – I will stand, so,' said the dwarf, taking up his position in what might be the centre of the stage. 'For whatever reason it is, you will cut off my head. It will drop into a basket, most like, and my body will fall to the ground.'

'Good,' Devil replied. 'Is that all?'

Carlo glared. '*Wait*, can't you? My headless torso remains. Onstage with us we'll have the cabinet, ornate as you like, on four legs.'

'Or on what appears to be four sturdy legs?'

'Yes, yes. You know what the mirrors are for.'

'And what I paid for them,' Devil added.

'Don't you ever shut up? You will cross the stage to open the cabinet and within it will appear . . .'

'Your severed head. Floating in mid-air, I assume?'

'Aye. So we talk. There'll likely be some pact, and your end of the bargain will be to put my head back.'

'So I close the cabinet doors.'

'You do. There's the mumbo-jumbo and the lights flash. In an eye-blink there is my living, speaking head secure on my neck again.'

'I hold the basket up, empty except for the horrible blood-stains.'

The dwarf yawned. Devil tapped his teeth with his thumbnail.

'No, wait . . . I've got it. A river of gold pours out of the basket. It's alchemy, that's what the trick is. It's all about the philosopher's secret.'

'Theatricals are your department,' Carlo shrugged.

The two men eyed each other. Devil had been optimistic in his first definition of their relationship. In fact their mutual mistrust was not much diminished by the two days and a night they had been obliged to spend together, nor even by the strange liking that crept up between them. Neither would have cared to admit to this last. Carlo stuck his jaw out while Devil pondered the mechanics.

'It's not a new illusion. Monsieur Robin has something similar.'

'It's still a sweet trick, and it can be as new as tomorrow if we choose to make it that way.'

This was true. Devil well knew that apart from endless practice it was audacity, force of personality and the glamour of the stage itself that created magic out of mere mechanics. His thoughts ran ahead.

'As it happens, I know a wax modeller who is employed by the Baker Street Bazaar.' He strode across to their cache of materials and held up two short ends of deal planking. 'Show me,' he ordered.

29

Carlo returned to a squatting position on the coffin maker's bench and indicated that Devil was to hold the boards up to his neck. The little man's head protruded between them as he settled on his muscular haunches. Then he folded his limbs. His knees splayed to the sides and his ankles crossed as he brought his feet towards his chin. His short spine telescoped further, his shoulders rose towards his ears as his arms wrapped round his torso. Devil had to lower the boards, and lower them again as Carlo shrank into a ball of muscle.

'That's good. That's really very good,' he said. He was impressed. The dwarf had compressed his body into a space that seemed hardly more than a foot square.

'Watch me,' Carlo snapped. He breathed in deeply, exhaled, and reduced himself by another inch in all directions.

'Stop,' Devil laughed. 'I am afraid that you will vanish altogether. Can you still speak and move your head?'

'Of course.'

The dwarf's head, which was not undersized, rotated freely above the boards. There was no sign of physical strain in his face and his voice was as smooth as cream.

The ribbon of gold in Devil's head looped and tied itself off into a giant bow.

He put the boards aside and silently admired the way that Carlo unfolded his limbs before stretching his little body upright again.

'There is just one detail.'

Carlo tipped his head. 'What's that?'

'Your size.'

'What? My size is our money.'

'It will provide a significant contribution to our funds, I agree. I acknowledge that. My skills as an actor, as the master magician who will conjure your smallness, will be another invaluable element. I am also our financial negotiator, as you know.'

'Hah,' sniffed Carlo.

'And all my experience dictates that your stature should be our stage secret.'

'What do you mean by that? I am not ashamed. I want the world to know who I am, Carlo Boldoni, straight from performing before the crowned heads of . . .'

'Quite,' Devil said. 'I am only suggesting that to reveal your stature to the public would be to take away some of the intrigue of the illusion.'

There was a silence. Carlo's personal vanity and ambition strained visibly.

'What do you want me to do?'

'For this trick, to appear onstage as a full-sized man. Is there perhaps a way you can do that?'

'Hah,' Carlo sniffed again. He made a return to his baggage and this time brought out a pair of wooden struts with shaped foot-pieces at either end. Devil watched with interest as he sank to fit these stilts to his boots, then used Devil's long leg as a prop to haul himself upright again. Their eyes met almost on a level.

'Walk,' Devil ordered.

The stilt-walk was well practised, tinged with swagger, like everything Carlo did.

'That's good. Very good,' Devil said again. 'You could use those to step out in the world like a normal man, couldn't you?'

Carlo's face went dark. 'I *am* a normal man. My body is the same as yours, bar its length. My feelings are the same as yours and all, except I'm too mannerly to tell you that you're an ignorant numpty. Until you force me to do so, that is.'

Devil kept a straight face. 'I am very sorry, and you are quite right. I was rude and tactless. Will you forgive me?'

He held out his hand and after only a moment's hesitation the dwarf extended his own and they shook. This was a significant moment and they both chose to ignore it.

'So I get a costume?' Carlo persisted.

'Allow me time to work out the details of our drama, and we will have the finest costume in London sewn for you.'

Then Devil unbuttoned his waistcoat and put it aside before

rolling up his shirtsleeves. From the heap of timbers he selected and held up one pair of cheap chair legs, roughly turned and bristling with splinters. He was no master carpenter, but he had built plenty of stage devices in the past. This one would have to be the best of them.

'Let's get to work,' he said.

The lantern light threw up their shadows, large and small, against the dirty wall. For the rest of the night the coffin maker's workshop was as loud with the sounds of sawing and hammering as during the daylight hours.

Dawn was breaking when the two men finally emerged into the street. Carlo was grey with fatigue, rubbing his face and stretching to ease his aching body. Devil looked as alert and handsome as he had done before their night's work started.

'I will need a coffin myself if I don't get some rest,' Carlo grumbled. 'I'm going back to your place for a sleep.'

'I shall see you later,' Devil replied.

He walked through the tiny alleys and the crowded courts of the area that housed timber merchants, furniture makers, metalworkers, printers and block makers, and emerged into Clerkenwell Road. The sky lightened from grey to pearl and the cobbles underfoot glistened with damp. Birdsong rose from the eaves of the houses and the trees in St John's Square, competing with the rumble of carters' wheels. Devil walked slowly, savouring the bite of the chill air and the smell of frying kidneys that drifted from an open window. In Farringdon Road the omnibuses were already crowded and a steady stream of black-coated clerks flowed out of the railway station. Devil was washed along in the tide of men, passing under the florid ironwork of the new viaduct and on down to Ludgate Circus. When he glanced up Ludgate Hill he saw that the dome of St Paul's was rinsed in the glowing light of the rising sun. He stopped to admire the view. It didn't often occur to him that the city was beautiful. In general he thought it was the opposite but today, with the satisfaction of a good night's work completed and the gold ribbon decorating his dreams, he saw its richness and promise reflected in all the domes and roofs and sun-gilded windows.

He was whistling with satisfaction as he paced along the Strand and reached the Palmyra theatre at last.

The frontage looked the same, still boarded up and whiskered with buddleia stalks. Down the side alley, however, there was a change. A heavy new door had been fitted, secured with iron hinges and locks. For good measure a padlock and chain were attached to a massive bolt. That was all good. The threshold and step were spread with sawdust. Devil stooped down and rubbed the damp grains between his fingers. There was work being undertaken here, just as there was at the coffin maker's. Then, not hoping for anything, he put his shoulder to the door and pushed. It didn't yield even by a fraction. He resorted to thumping on the door panels but no response came except from a knot of urchins looking out for trouble at the street corner.

'Ain't nobody in, mister,' they jeered. 'Forgot yer key, did yer?'

They raced away as soon as Devil headed for them. He walked along the flank of the building, running his fingertips over the flaking paint and crumbling stonework. The old theatre seemed to breathe in response to his touch.

'Here I am,' he muttered to it. 'And we'll see what we shall see, eh?'

Recalling the dim interior, he wanted nothing more than to explore the place properly, in daylight, and without the vulgar insistence of Jacko Grady at his shoulder. For one thing, the box trick he and Carlo had in mind would require trapdoors, and other installations beneath whatever kind of stage would replace the ruined one. He needed to inspect the whole area and take measurements for the construction of his cabinet. Clearly, though, this wasn't going to happen today. He bestowed a last touch on one of the fluted pilasters flanking the ruined front doors, and looked upwards to the little cupola surmounting the building. He touched the brim of his bowler.

'See you later.' He smiled almost tenderly.

He had it in his mind to pay a visit to the wax modeller, who happened to be one of the very few of his acquaintances with any knowledge of the days before Devil Wix, when he had been Hector Crumhall. But this craftsman's place of work was in Camden Town, a long way north of the Strand. Devil thought he would go home to his lodging first and snatch an hour's sleep, if that were to prove possible against the racket of Carlo's snoring.

The series of alleys, growing ever narrower, twistier and more foetid as they led towards the rookery, obliterated all Devil's benign thoughts regarding the city's early-morning loveliness. He passed Annie Fowler, already seated in her doorway with a cup of gin, but he ignored her. The low door of the house where he lodged creaked open and Devil stepped inside. A heavy figure immediately placed itself in front of him.

'Good morning, Mrs Hayes,' Devil greeted his landlady. 'It's a fine day.'

Mrs Hayes folded her arms. 'It may well be. For those who don't have to see a blasted midget creeping up and down their stairs, in and out at all hours. What's that creature doing in my house?'

'He is my associate, Carlo Boldoni the famous theatre performer, until recently a member of Morris's Amazing Performing Midgets, no less, and fresh from performing before the crowned heads of Europe . . .'

She came one step closer to him. 'Do I care who he is? I can tell you straight off, I do not. He is a dwarf and I find he's sleeping under my roof without so much as a handshake. I don't care for him. This is a respectable house.'

'It is a temporary arrangement, Mrs Hayes. You see, he doesn't have anywhere else to go at present and I am a kind-hearted fellow. I suffer for my kindness, but I hope you will understand.' Devil's voice grew softer. 'I believe you will, Maria, of all women. You have shown such particular kindness to me.'

Maria Hayes hesitated. She was a large woman in her forties

34

with some of the prettiness of her youth still in her face, her black hair unpinned, and the white folds of her body unconfined by stays. Devil might have assumed she had only just stepped out of her bed, had he not known that she could be encountered in a similar state of undress at any hour of the day. She raised a hand and brushed a stray coil of hair from her flushed cheek.

'I have, Mr Wix. I have been as kind as I could be.'

Devil lifted a matching coil of hair from the opposite cheek. They were already standing close together and the confined space of the vestibule offered no latitude. Devil used his elbow to nudge open the door of the landlady's room. It was not a very much more spacious resort. One glance was enough to reveal that Mr Hayes was absent, as usual, nor was there any sign of the slow-witted son of the house.

Maria's mouth was only six inches from his. He leaned down to close the distance. Her lips obligingly parted.

After the kiss Devil ran his hands over her breasts. He put his mouth to her ear.

'Tell me, is My Lady Laycock at home today?'

Maria smirked. 'I'll have to see if Her Ladyship is receiving visitors this morning.'

'Won't you tell her Mr Devil Wix is calling?'

Maria grasped his wrist and yanked him over the threshold. Devil kicked the door shut and she slid the bolt behind them. He put his arms round her and they half waltzed to the stuffy alcove with the bed concealed behind a curtain. The sheets were far from clean and the bolster leaked feathers from its case of greasy ticking. Devil untied the strings of Maria's chemise and the thought of the golden ribbon came happily into his mind again. His landlady pressed herself against him and her tongue sought his.

'I find she is at home, and waiting for you,' she murmured. Her fingers were tugging at his shirt buttons, then her hand moved downwards. 'It's a good name for you, wherever you got it. Devil by nature as well, aren't you?'

Cheerfully Devil tipped her backwards on to the bed and pulled up her grubby petticoat. He got busy, at the same time tasting the sweat of her neck and the rankness of her black hair.

Afterwards they lay on the mattress with a coil of bedding twisted round them. Maria was an energetic performer and Devil hadn't slept for twenty-four hours. His eyelids were so heavy that he was wondering how he was going to get up the stairs to his own bed. A sudden thumping on the door jolted him upright quickly enough, however. Groaning at the thought of Mr Hayes on the threshold he pulled his clothing together. Maria went undressed to the tiny window and stuck her head out.

'Stop that racket. Get down to Ransome's and bring me back a jug of porter,' she yelled. From this exchange Devil understood that it was her son at the door, not the husband. When she pulled herself back into the room they grinned at each other.

'You'll wet your whistle?' Maria asked.

Devil took her reddened hands and kissed the knuckles of each.

'I have to go to work, my lovely girl.'

The delighted smile she gave him was almost shy, and her blush did make her look girlish. Devil slid out of the room and softly closed the door before she could mention the dwarf again. Aching for rest he climbed the bare flights of stairs, past doorways to rooms hardly larger than cupboards, which nevertheless housed families of lodgers, until he reached the attic. As he had expected he found Carlo lying on his makeshift bed, fast asleep and snoring like an engine. Devil kicked him as he stepped past, but this had no effect at all. Ten minutes later, his own snores provided a counterpoint.

In the two weeks that followed Devil worked harder than he had ever done, and he had laboured for long, bitter hours on plenty of occasions before this. Nights with Carlo at the coffin maker's followed on from late evenings of performing his own

36

act at whichever of the taphouses or small halls would offer him a booking. He took the money wherever he could get it. One evening he arrived at the workshop still in his stage costume, such was his eagerness to resume work on the cabinet trick. Carlo eyed him as he discarded his greatcoat.

'What's this?' the dwarf sniggered.

Devil preened. He wore a suit of red cloth, cut to fit so snugly that it might have been a second skin.

'Ah, my performance costume? It is for a trick called the Infernal Flames. Tonight at Prewett's they were begging for more.' This was not strictly true, but Devil was always good at reinterpreting reality in his own favour. 'But for our grand opening at the Palmyra we *will* do far better than Jacko Grady has bargained for.'

They turned to their work. The cabinet interior was empty except for a double shelf. Tonight's work was to line all the inside surfaces with a seamless layer of jet-black velvet. Devil undid a draper's brown-paper package and smoothed a bolt of fabric on a swept circle of floor. He took a tailor's tape and called out the measurements in feet and inches and Carlo pencilled them on a sheet of paper. Each measurement was taken twice, to ensure accuracy. The velvet had been expensive to buy and none of Devil's techniques of persuasion had achieved even a pennyworth of discount. Carlo set to with a pair of shears. He was a dextrous worker and the first neat rectangle was soon cut to the precise size. Devil had applied brush and glue to the cabinet wall and with some cursing and arguing they succeeded in sticking the light-absorbing material in place.

Halfway through the task they stood back to gauge the effect. The finished walls of the box seemed to melt into black space. Even Carlo the perfectionist was pleased.

'I have some more good news,' Devil announced. 'Tomorrow your head will be ready. I am to collect it after we leave here.'

'At last. So we must begin to work up the beheading. I'll be needing a suit of tall clothing.'

Devil sighed. There was a deal of investing to be done before any return could be hoped for, but still his confidence held.

Devil and Carlo together had visited the wax-modelling studio of Mr Jasper Button in Camden Town, and Carlo had made his way there alone on three subsequent occasions. He had sat patient and motionless on a stool, with the smells of warm wax and linseed oil and turpentine all round him, while the modeller built up sub-layers and then sculpted pellets of wax over a wire frame. On the last visit the modeller had sorted through a basket filled with plaited hanks of cut human hair, holding up one specimen after another next to Carlo's head and muttering to himself as he searched for the best match. He ran his fingers through the dwarf's abundant locks and pulled at the sprouting tufts of his eyebrows.

'Where does it all come from?' Carlo had asked.

'Plenty of people hereabouts are glad to sell the hair off their heads for a shilling or two.' Jasper held up a long plait of rich copper-gold. 'This one belonged to a woman who knew that all her youth and loveliness shone out of it, but the day came when she had nothing else to sell. Her hair was just the start of it.' He dropped the plait into the basket again.

'If this was quality work, I'd be using human hair on you. See? This is the closest for colour and texture.' He brandished a salt-and-pepper bunch next to the dwarf's face and Carlo twisted away from it in disgust. 'Devil Wix won't pay for that, of course. You and your model will be making do with an identical pair of horsehair wigs. What are you supposed to be? The good philosopher, isn't it? Maybe I'll be generous to you both and give you your eyebrows in real hair.'

Carlo stared at the egg-bald wax head on its stand. The coffin maker's was creepy enough, but this shadowy place deep in the wrecked streets surrounding the railway yards more than matched it. There was a box containing dozens of glass eyes on the floor at his feet, all unwinking and all fixed on him.

'You and Wix know each other from back when?'

The other held up a loop of wire, measuring by eye the breadth of skin between Carlo's brows.

'A long time.'

No more was forthcoming.

Without meeting the gaze of the glass eyes Carlo tried another topic on the modeller. 'Odd sort of a job you do, wouldn't you say?'

Jasper gave him a contemptuous glance. 'My waxwork of Miss Nellie Bromley in *Trial by Jury* is the favourite figure in the Baker Street exhibition. I'd not call my artistic work odd. Not by comparison with your own, for example.'

Carlo scowled but said nothing. After that they had posed and modelled in silence.

After a long night at the coffin maker's Devil walked up from Holborn to Euston and thence along the sooty roads that led to Camden Town. All along the way rough tent encampments lay beside the railway lines and under the arches and bridges. The men, women and children who existed here were black-faced and their ragged clothes were black, as were the heaps of brick rubble and even the dead leaves hanging on the few weak trees. Black smoke billowed from cooking fires and smouldering brick kilns, and the occasional threatening figure lurched out of this murk and mumbled at him. By shrinking inwardly Devil made himself seem smaller and darker too, and he passed through these places without difficulty.

By the time he rattled the latch of the studio door Jasper Button was already at work.

'Jas? You there?'

'Where else would I be?'

'I'd say anywhere you could be, if only you had the choice.'

Jasper ignored him. The streets outside might be warrens of decrepit houses and belching chimneys and gaunt sheds but his studio was snug enough. A blanket hung over the doorway to keep in the warmth, there was a coal fire in a narrow little grate and a black kettle on the hob.

'You want some tea?'

'You don't have anything stronger?'

It was a question that didn't expect an answer. Jasper Button never touched a drop, and given what had happened to his mother and father Devil understood why not. The modeller warmed an earthenware teapot and lifted the kettle using a knitted potholder.

Devil was stalking the bald wax head, examining it from every angle.

'What do you think?' Jasper was eager for Devil's approval. More than a decade ago, the two of them had played together up in the green fields and lanes surrounding the village of Stanmore. Devil had been the ringleader in those days, the admired and feared chief of a band of boys who had in common their rebelliousness and their longing for first-hand experience of the world they could see from the top of Stanmore Hill.

Devil pretended to consider. 'I think you have achieved a reasonable likeness.'

'Go to hell. The head's not for sale, then.'

'Poor Jas. What will you do with it, in that case?'

'I'll exhibit it. There's always an audience in the Chamber of Horrors.'

'True enough. Let's have a look.'

Jasper lifted the head off the stand and turned it upside down to reveal a meticulously gory cross-section of severed bone, muscle and artery. Devil whistled.

'I say. That's very pretty. Is that what it really looks like?'

'Like enough,' Jasper said brusquely. 'Enough to satisfy your tavern audiences, at any rate. If I decide to let you have it, that is. I rather liked your midget friend, so I might just keep his likeness beside me for sentimental reasons.'

'I expect you will feel even more sentimental about two sovereigns, won't you?' He put two fingers into the pocket of his waistcoat where the naked end of his watch chain rested.

'Let's see the colour of them,' Jasper insisted, knowing his friend too well.

The money and the model were exchanged and Devil stowed the waxen version of Carlo in a bag with his scarlet stage costume. Once the transaction was complete he was able to give due praise.

'You're a magician, Jas, you know, in your own way. Not in my league of course, but it's a decent skill. Are you going to pour that tea or leave it to stew?'

Jasper passed him a cup and they settled beside the fire.

Once, long ago, the two of them had been amongst a crowd of gaping children who had watched the performance of a few magic tricks in a painted canvas booth set up by a travelling conjuror on the village square. The man had been more of a tramp than a real performer, and the sleights as Devil now recalled them had been shabby and fumbling. But still, here was a man who could make a white rat appear from a folded pocket handkerchief and who could grasp a shilling out of blue air. They hadn't been there an instant before, but the rat and the shilling were definitely real. He could still remember how the sleek warmth of the animal had filled his hands when the conjuror asked him to mind it for him, and he could taste the coin's metal between his teeth when he had tested it with a bite. How had such solid things appeared from nowhere? What strange dimensions existed beyond the range of his limited understanding?

Everything he had known up to that point had been narrow, painful, humdrum, and devoid of mystery. There was his own confined world and then there was beyond, somewhere out of reach, where great events took place. Yet here he was in the centre of the ordinary with the extraordinary somehow taking place right in front of him. To witness the magic had been his first experience of wonder, and it had filled his childish heart with yearning.

All around him his friends and their brothers and sisters were shouting and jeering and trying to grab the rat or the shilling but Devil was silent. All he wanted was to see more magic, to be further amazed and transported, and at the same time he was envious. Why was it not given to him to create wonder in the same way? What a gift that must be, he thought, as he gazed at the grog-faced man in the canvas booth with his tattered string of silks and his hands that shook so much he dropped his shilling, to the great amusement of the crowd.

Ten-year-old Hector Crumhall hardly knew how, but he understood that the bestowal of *wonder* was the ticket that was going to carry him out of Stanmore.

At the end of the scrappy show a few halfpennies and pennies landed in the man's hat. He gathered them up and peered at the skinny black-haired boy waiting at the edge of the booth.

'Mister? Can I do that with the rat?'

The man coughed and spat a thick bolus into the grass at his feet. The wooden struts came down and the canvas with its daubed stars and moons and strange symbols was strapped into a package ready to be hoisted on the traveller's back.

'Only if you learn the craft, boy.'

'How? How can I learn?'

'Ah, that'd be difficult enough. I'd say you'd have to find a 'prentice master in the magic trade.'

The man was ready to leave and Devil looked past him down the lane that led southwards to London. The path through a hollow way beneath oak trees and out across the fields had never seemed so enticing.

He begged, 'Take me with you. If you teach me how to do those things like you did I'll carry your bag for you, mister.'

The man didn't even smile. Devil was surprised that his offer wasn't instantly taken up. He thought he would make a fine apprentice.

'You stay here with your ma and pa. You don't want to be getting yourself a life like mine.'

With that he picked up the last of his belongings and trudged away. Devil stood and watched until the man turned the corner. His body twitched with longing to follow. For weeks afterwards he daydreamed about magic and regretted his failure of courage when the moment of opportunity had presented itself.

Devil's father was the village schoolmaster, a man who had just enough education to be aware of how much he did not know. Mr Crumhall's only child had been intended for the Church, but Hector was barely eight years old before it became clear that he was an unsuitable candidate for the cloth. He stole apples, raided the dairy, bullied children who were bigger than himself, and to his father's constant disapproval only paid attention to what interested him. He was a slow pupil even in the undistinguished setting of the village school. After the travelling performer's visit, what did interest him was the craft and performance of magic. He pestered his father for information. One of the mysteries that intrigued him was the difference between magic and conjuring.

'Why are there two names?'

'Conjuring is tricks. Packs of cards, vanishing handkerchiefs, deceptions of the eye for fools with money to throw away on tawdry entertainments.'

'What is magic, then?'

He wanted his father to acknowledge the transport of wonder, and to give him permission to immerse himself in it.

'There is no such thing as magic, Hector. There is only truth, and God shows us the way of that.' Mr Crumhall was a quietly devout man.

'What is alchemy?'

His mother glanced up from her darning and frowned at him, and his father became impatient. 'Only charlatans ever believed in such a thing. There is no process that can turn base metal into gold, or make any such transformation, and all the business of mumbo-jumbo associated with it is nothing more than the devil's work.'

The child thought he had never heard anything so fascinating, and that the devil's work sounded a good deal more interesting than anything he was required to do, in the schoolroom or out of it.

'Why?'

'Creation is the Lord's, Hector.'

43

Hector continued to talk about magic, and its lowly cousin conjuring (as he thought of it) so incessantly that Mrs Hargreaves of Park House, for whom Mrs Crumhall did some sewing, presented him with a book from her late husband's library. It was small, with worn red covers and endpapers printed with signs and symbols that thrillingly reminded him of the traveller's booth. The title was *The Secrets of Conjuring Revealed*, by Professor Weissman. Hector raced up to his bedroom with this treasure and began to read.

At first he was disappointed. The print was tiny, there were far too many long words like *instantaneous combustion* and *proscenium*, and whilst there were a few intriguing engravings of disembodied heads floating in mid-air, quite a lot of the illustrations were tedious geometrical diagrams showing dotted lines diverging from a sketched representation of a human eye. He persevered, painstakingly consulting the dictionary on his father's bookshelf, only to be further disappointed because most of the secrets that the Professor revealed employed special apparatus – hollow coins, wires as fine as human hair, or something called an electro-magnet. There was one effect, however, that only called for a handkerchief, a piece of string and a coat sleeve, all of which items happened to be available. While his mother's back was turned he took a needle and a piece of thread from her workbox and stitched the end of the string to the centre of the handkerchief. This in itself was difficult enough, resulting in a blood-blotched cotton square and a frayed piece of string.

Next he memorised the sequence of movements described in the book and began to practise bending and straightening his arms and making a sharp clap of the hands. There was a framed looking glass on his mother's washstand, and he stood in front of this for hours.

Then at last, for an audience consisting of Jasper Button, Jasper's two sickly sisters and poor Gabe who didn't understand much, he performed for the first time the Handkerchief which Vanishes in the Hand.

Gabe's jaw fell open in astonishment when the handkerchief disappeared, and he shouted out in his clogged voice. 'Gone! Gone!'

The Button girls' shrivelled faces shone with unaccustomed pleasure and even Jasper was deeply impressed.

'How did you do that?'

'By magic,' Devil said. He had never experienced such power, or so much pleasure in exercising it. And his appetite grew. He studied whatever books he could lay his hands on and practised harder. Every penny that came his way he spent on apparatus.

A bad day came when Devil turned fourteen. His mother had died the year before, from one of her fits of breathlessness in which her face turned grey and then dark blue as she struggled for air. The schoolhouse was cold and comfortless without a woman in it and his father grew silent and morose and even more exasperated by his son's behaviour.

'Why can't you follow Jasper's example?' he would demand.

Devil shrugged, trying to pretend he didn't care that he wasn't clever in the way his father would have liked him to be.

Jasper was Mr Crumhall's favourite pupil by far. He had been a ready learner for as long as he was able to come to school, and he knew how to apply himself. He was working for a saddler now but he was also developing into a promising artist. There was never any money for any of the Button children because their mother and father needed to drink more than they were able to earn and pay for, but Mrs Hargreaves and the rector's wife and a few others helped the boy out with paper and pencils. There was even talk of him attending a school of art.

'I am not him, I am me,' Devil replied.

'More's the pity,' Mr Crumhall snapped.

Fury curled up in Devil like a flame licking the corner of a document. He leapt up and kicked his chair aside so it crashed on the flagged floor.

'I'll show you. I'll be a great man.'

45

'Greatness doesn't arrive by magic, Hector. You won't do it by shuffling playing cards and waiting to be fed.'

Anger was always Devil's stalker.

It burst out of him now in a great wave and the force of it swept him across the room to where his father was seated. His hands closed around his father's throat and he squeezed.

He didn't keep up the pressure for more than two or three seconds before the appalled recognition of what he was doing came over him. He realised that he was shouting, ugly words that were choked with the piled-up frustration of his village days and unvoiced grief for his mother. His hands dropped to his sides and he sprang backwards, shaking from head to foot as if he had a fever. Mr Crumhall had a temper that matched his son's. He leapt up and hit the boy across the face, a blow that sent Devil flying backwards against the kitchen dresser and knocked three plates to the floor where they smashed into flowered shards.

Father and son faced each other, panting and appalled.

'Get out of my house.'

'I wouldn't stay here to save my life.'

Taking nothing but his tiny library of magic books Devil left the schoolhouse. That night he spent shivering and trying to sleep on the hay stacked in a barn. The next day Jasper and one of his sisters slipped in to find him, bringing some bread and apples which Devil crammed into his mouth like a starving man. Jasper advised him to go home and tell his father that he was sorry but he refused even to consider the possibility.

'I don't care,' he insisted to the others. 'I'm going to London. I'll be rich, I'm telling you. I'll have – I'll live in a house bigger than Park House. With a butler and maidservants, and lamps to light all the rooms like a palace.'

Sophy Button sneezed and wiped her nose on her sleeve.

Devil summoned up his determination. He could feel his power leaking out of him and its loss was intolerable, so he pinned a smile across his face.

'Tell everyone to come. Before I go I'll show them a spectacle to remember me by.'

After the Buttons had left Devil sat down to wait. There was silence except for the rustling of rats under the hay.

The news spread quickly enough. As twilight came a little file of contemporaries and smaller children flitted and crept towards the barn.

One of the books in his possession described a trick called the Inferno. Devil loved playing with fire and he had read through the description often enough, although he had never actually tried it out. But now he was ready to do every last thing he could to impress this small world before exchanging it for the bigger one. He had to save his own face by leaving Stanmore on a drum roll and a crash of cymbals.

There were twenty spectators gathered in the darkened barn. Only one of them had thought to bring a lantern, and there was no other light except for the box of lucifers that Jasper had been instructed to provide. Devil's arms ached and his fingers were as stiff as wooden clothes pins. He fumbled with a lit taper, holding the wavering flame poised above a little figure he had made out of plaited straw. It was supposed to be a bowl of golden fish, but desperate times called for extreme improvisation. It was satisfying to think how demonic he would be looking with the taper's light licking his face and deepening the shadows in his eye sockets.

Sophy Button sneezed again and Devil jumped. At the same time a gust of wind caught the barn door and slammed it shut. With the jitters in his blood Devil swung round to see who was coming. The taper spat a stream of sparks into the dusty air and the hay caught fire in a dozen different places.

The audience sat gaping, imagining this was the very spectacle they had been invited to see. Devil threw himself at the spurts of fire but as soon as he had stamped out one another flickered to life with a whisper like an evil rumour spreading. In a matter of seconds a wall of flames roared up to the barn roof. Poor Gabe was laughing, *haw-haw-haw*, and thudding his hands together in raucous applause.

'Good un!' he yelled.

'Get outside!' Devil bawled.

Most of the spectators were on their feet now, staring uncertainly from the fire to the barn door and back to Devil again, expecting him to work some magic that would restore the hay to its original state. Devil ran to the door and threw it open and a great gust of air was sucked in, fanning the blaze and sending a pall of smoke to stifle and blind them all.

'Get out of here.' This was Jasper, who was dragging one of his sisters by the arm. Children coughed and choked as they stumbled over each other. One by one they spilled out into the sweet darkness. Devil ran dementedly through the smoke, thinking of his precious books being consumed by the fire. He knew that there was no hope of beating out these flames, and that his childhood was burning up along with the hay. He was taken by the elemental urge to run, to hide, to escape the inescapable. He found his way out into the cold air and gathered himself for flight.

Then he heard Jasper yelling for Gabe. Staring out of the darkness they could all see that vast black clouds were rolling out of the barn and that the interior was an inferno, no trickery.

Wired with terror Devil ran back towards the blaze, sensing rather than seeing Jasper racing alongside him. They both stopped as a black silhouette appeared against the roaring barn, its margins fretted by flame. Gabe staggered towards them, arms outstretched. The sleeves of his old coat, his breeches, even his hair was on fire. The boy was screaming. He dropped to his knees and then fell prone as the others swarmed about him to try to beat out the flames.

Jasper pulled Devil's collar.

'Run,' he said. 'Run before the bobby gets here.'

Sophy Button howled like an animal.

'My ma said you were the devil's spawn, Hector Crumhall. She did.'

As he ran down the hollow way and across the fields, his feet pounding over the familiar ground, Devil was thinking that he had killed a halfwit boy. The other thought was that Jasper's poor drunken mother, a sodden bag of bones and wet gums and muttered curses, considered that *he* was a devil.

The next night he slept in another barn. The nightmares of fire and Gabe's screaming were terrible, and when he was awake and walking he was so sure the spectre of the burning boy was following him that he had to keep turning and looking over his shoulder.

The evening after that he was in the heart of London. Grand carriages and hansom cabs and handcarts crowded the streets as money and filth fought for supremacy. Exhausted, he sank down at a street corner and looked up to the gable end of a building across the way. It was painted with elaborate curling letters that read:

'Wix's Elixir. It does the trick'.

In his weary, famished state the word *trick* took on great significance. This was a message aimed at him. He was going to be a magician, the best on the London stage. He needed a new name, because Hector Crumhall had killed a boy.

Devil Wix.

The black shape outlined in flame ran at him out of dark places. Even when he was wide awake it came at him. The screams still sounded in his ears, louder even than the din of the city. If he was no longer Hector Crumhall, perhaps he could escape the apparition?

Devil Wix.

'You're going to drop my china cup.' Jasper took it from his hand. Devil woke with a shudder. He rubbed his face and looked at the kettle on the hob, and at the bag beside him that contained Carlo's decapitated head.

'I'll be on my way. You'll come to see the show, Jas, won't you?'

'If you give me a ticket.'

'It'll be worth a tanner or two of anyone's money.'

'Not mine,' Jasper sniffed.

The two of them briefly embraced, like the old friends they were. Neither of them had spoken of Stanmore for years. Mr Crumhall had followed his wife to the churchyard, the Buttons had drunk themselves to death, and Jasper's two sisters were gone into service. In their different ways the two boys were doing their best to better themselves.

THREE

As Jacko Grady had said it would be, the Palmyra was partly restored. The charred ruins of stage and seating were carted away, the worst of the soot was rinsed from the walls and the pillars. The box fronts were crudely repainted, obliterating the ruined gilding, and carpenters sawed and hammered to create a new stage. Grady obtained a set of curtains, well used on some other stage. The cloth was faded and the folds exuded plumes of acrid dust. The owner was out to make some quick money and he invested as little as possible in his restoration. The theatre was still a shabby place, with none of the colour and opulence its structure called for.

The trapdoors Devil and Carlo required were cut and hinged and tested with care. Backstage on Jacko Grady's grand opening night, Devil sat on an upturned bucket listening and waiting.

He was obliged to acknowledge disappointment. That it was a poor audience came as no great surprise, although he had hoped for better. It was true that the gallery was filled almost to capacity, but the crowd in these cheapest seats was composed mostly of rowdy young men. They came in search of novelty, spectacle and vulgar comedy, and they were ready to express their dissatisfaction when these were not immediately forthcoming. The act now on stage, only the second on the bill, was a comic vocalist and before this performer could

51

finish his smirking delivery of 'Kitty and the Old Corner Cupboard' they were drowning him out by bellowing coarser versions of the chorus. As he struggled to lift his voice over the uproar of singing and guffawing the musicians played louder and faster to help him along. An object flew through the air and landed on the boards close to his feet. It was a ripe peach. The pulp sprayed over the cracked toecaps of his patent leather shoes.

In the better seats were pairs and trios of young gentlemen, sitting with arms akimbo and legs outstretched. At the supper clubs, during the acts which did not appeal to them, they could be diverted by chops and potatoes and by the young women who served them, or else resort to their own talk and cigars, but here they found themselves captive as if they had bought tickets for the opera.

Interspersed with these gentlemen and in one or two of the boxes sat a few families and some young fellows who had brought their wives or sweethearts. Two or three of these had already stood up and escorted their womenfolk to the curtained exit.

Devil dropped his head into his hands. Grady had sent out printed playbills, and he had done that well enough. For their act, all that was promised was:

Boldoni and Wix:
THE EXECUTION OF THE PHILOSOPHER.
See it, if you dare to do so.
You will not believe your eyes.

Devil approved. Keep them guessing, that was the idea. But Grady had ordered the distribution of his bills in the taverns and markets and such places, and this had brought in the gallery crowd. All this was quite wrong, in Devil's opinion. The desirable audience was composed of the very people who were now leaving. The Palmyra was an elegant theatre and the show should be an elegant affair, to which a gentleman could bring his wife and daughters, his mother or his sisters.

Devil had tried to point this out to Grady but the fat man had rudely dismissed him.

'It would be of benefit to us all if your act proves to be as big as your mouth, Wix. Anyways, I thought it was supposed to be the Sphinx. What is this monstrous thing? It looks like a damned duke's tomb.'

In constructing their magic cabinet Carlo and Devil had encouraged each other to pile decoration upon decoration, and the piece was ornamented with golden pinnacles and carved finials, paste jewels and panels painted with stars and suns.

'This will be better than anything else you've got,' Devil answered.

The vocalist came offstage, mopping his face with a handkerchief. Despairingly he hurried away to the dressing rooms. The next act was ready to go on. It was a pair of acrobats, one of them a supple young woman. The lower half of her face was covered by a spangled scarf and as she edged past Devil their eyes briefly met. There were tiny bells stitched to her clothing and these jingled a mocking accompaniment as her brother grasped her hand and they somersaulted out into the lights.

Devil resumed the contemplation of his own feet. It was warm in the wings and the close air was heavy with sweat and greasepaint. He needed this interval to concentrate and collect his wits. Beside him stood the cabinet and the mirrors, ready to be placed in position when the curtain fell. It was unusual for Devil to feel nervous, whatever lay in store, but there was no other way to explain the damp palms of his hands and the small impediment in his chest that seemed to catch his breathing.

Tonight was an opportunity, even though the audience was wrong and Grady was a fool.

The opportunity must not be missed.

One act followed another. The acrobats were popular, the musicians and singers less so. The curtain came down as the hem of another costume swept across Devil's line of vision. He glanced up, and then looked higher. Carlo towered over him,

Carlo on stilts that were concealed by a long robe and an academic gown stitched with occult symbols. He wore the grey wig Devil had bought for him, the horsehair combed smoothly back from his brow. Under the stage paint his long-chinned face looked authoritative, even noble. The dwarf was pleased with his appearance.

'Ready?' Devil asked automatically.

Carlo's lips twisted to indicate that he was always ready, that Devil would never find him in any other condition. In a moment of fellow feeling Devil even patted the dwarf's shoulder but all that met his touch was the wicker frame that Carlo wore over his shoulders to increase their breadth beneath the philosopher's gown.

A pair of stagehands lifted the cabinet between them and positioned it on the marks. Devil himself carried the precious mirrors and placed them on the angled lines he had so carefully calculated and measured. When they were aligned the cabinet appeared to stand clear of the stage on its four legs, with no other support or place of concealment visible from the body of the theatre.

The curtain rose once more.

The stage was empty apart from a soot-black basket and the cabinet itself. Paste jewels glittered under the lights. To begin with there had been some tittering and a couple of louder guffaws, but the effect was sufficiently striking to capture attention. Devil swept onstage into an expectant silence, the first real silence of the evening. As the evil philosopher he was costumed in stark black. The lights dimmed, there was a slow roll of the drum and he threw open the double doors of the cabinet. There was nothing in the velvet-lined interior, so much nothing that the emptiness seemed infinite. Devil slid his hands inside and spread his arms to prove that the audience's eyes did not deceive them. As he withdrew there was a flash of light, and a puff smoke rose from the cabinet. Devil came forward to the footlights and bowed low.

'Are you finished?' some wag called down.

54

Towards the back of the stalls Devil spotted Jasper Button, seated with a young woman on either side of him. He was glad that after all Jasper had come to see him perform.

Devil held up one hand. 'I have not yet begun,' he said.

His air of authority was enough to quell the unrest. The audience shifted in their seats. There was another flash of light and smoke drifted across the stage.

He led Carlo out from the wings at the end of a short length of rope. The captive's hands were bound at the wrists. He moved at a slow shuffle, his head hanging like a prisoner's. Devil brought him to centre stage.

Between them, in the past days, they had worked up some lines of dialogue.

Devil was pleased with his own literary abilities and he had composed a declamatory paragraph or two to establish the proper degree of evil exhibited by himself. Carlo's response to the first recitation of this had been to scowl, pinch his own lips between finger and thumb and then jab a forefinger at Devil.

'Keep the jawing short. Tell 'em a bit of a story as fast as you can do it and move on to the action.'

There had been a day or two of violent disagreement followed by a period of coolness, but Carlo had won. The exchange now established simply that Good and Evil were locked in a struggle for possession of the formula for transforming base metal into gold. This was established mostly by sign language accompanied by plenty of smoke, drum and cymbal.

'I shall never yield my secret,' said the good philosopher. 'Never, while breath remains in this body.'

He raised his grey-wigged head and held it high.

Behind him, with relish, Devil drew a long blade from beneath his academic gown.

The audience fell silent.

'Then the breath shall be extinguished,' Devil cried.

He swung the blade in a glimmering arc. There was a collective gasp. Following a loud bang, a second's total darkness and a savage chord from the musicians, the lights flared again. Devil stood alone in a swirl of smoke. The knife dripped with gore and at his feet a huddled outline lay beneath the good philosopher's robe.

Devil reached down to the soot-black basket and slid one gloved hand into the interior. With a flourish he pulled out the severed head and brandished it by a hank of the grey hair.

Jasper had done his work well. The noble philosopher's features were Carlo's smeared with blood, the eyes glazed in death. When the executioner tilted it to show the mutilated neck a woman screamed aloud in horror. Devil bared his teeth in a snarl and tossed the head back into the basket. Once the grisly thing was hidden from view and the shock of its appearance subsided, there was a tide of applause followed by a substantial rising cheer from the gallery. In the wings Jacko Grady stood watching, thumbs in the pockets of his waistcoat and feet planted apart, a cloud of cigar smoke about his head.

Devil passed in front of the ornate cabinet. He caressed the gilded pinnacles and touched the paste gems with the tip of his finger. He uttered some words in an unintelligible language and flung open the doors.

Another gasp rose from the auditorium. The good philosopher's head floated in black space within. It turned from side to side and its ashen lips parted.

Devil demanded, 'Tell me the formula now. You are my prisoner for eternity.'

'I curse you to eternity and beyond,' Carlo's voice answered.

Devil threw back his head and laughed. He stretched out one foot and kicked over the basket. It rolled, empty, towards the footlights. He picked up the sword once more and drove the point into the lower part of the cabinet where the living body attached to the head must surely be concealed. He stabbed the emptiness over and over again.

'My secret is mine,' the head mocked him.

'Die, then.'

56

'You cannot kill me. I will always be here. In sleep, in waking, in daylight and darkness. Wherever you travel, I will be at your shoulder. I shall be always watching you'.

His words echoed in the air. Across Devil's face in rapid succession passed realisation, understanding of what he had done, and then the dawning of a terrible fear. It was a moment to behold, and the audience edged further forwards in their seats.

Carlo Morris had agreed to throw in his lot with Devil just as deliberately as his partner had chosen him. He had done so because he recognised from the outset that Devil Wix was a useful melodramatic actor. All he needed was proper restraint.

Jacko Grady pulled on his cigar.

Out on the stage Devil had closed the doors and taken a step backwards from his magic cabinet. He snapped the blade of the sword. He fell on his knees beside the black basket and dropped into it the fragments of metal and the twisted hilt.

'Forgive me!' he cried.

There was a deafening drum roll and every pair of eyes in the house fastened on Devil as he prostrated himself. The lights flashed off and then burned cold blue and silver.

With his forehead pressed to the boards and dust in his nostrils making him want to sneeze, Devil wordlessly prayed that the sequence would go smoothly. This was the trickiest part of the entire illusion.

Across the stage to his right the tumbled heap of clothes belonging to the good philosopher stirred and grew as it took on human shape. The gown's hood fell back, and the audience saw that the noble grey head rested on broad shoulders again. Standing tall, Carlo held up his arms. The sleeves dropped to expose his bare wrists, freed from the rope.

When Carlo leaned over him Devil shielded his head with his hands, but his rival did not strike him. Instead he picked up the black basket and held it high in the air. More smoke coiled from the interior.

Carlo tipped the basket. There was no broken sword. Instead, a stream of golden coins cascaded over the evil philosopher's body.

'Here is your black heart's desire,' the good philosopher called. 'You shall have no happiness from it.'

The curtain fell as clapping and whistling surged through the Palmyra.

Devil scrambled to his feet and embraced the sweating Carlo. His blood jigged in the euphoria of a successful performance.

'You did well, my friend.'

Carlo swung an extended leg. 'I did better than that. I am a hero. Let me see *you* fastening on stilts and then climbing a ladder into your costume, all in the space of two seconds.'

'Yes, that was excellent. And I performed the sleights to the same standard.'

'You were adequate.'

The curtain swept up, they took their bow and it fell again.

The stagehands ran on to collect the props. Devil and Carlo shook hands, although even this much appreciation was awkward. They hurried offstage together. Jacko Grady picked a shred of tobacco off his thick tongue and cleared his throat.

'Too long,' he growled. 'They were restless out there. Make it faster tomorrow.'

'How many seats sold?' Devil pleasantly enquired.

'One hundred and seven paid for.'

The capacity of the theatre was two hundred and fifty.

'You should give us more stage time, not less. Word travels fast, Mr Grady. Tomorrow everyone will be talking about Boldoni and Wix.'

Figures relating to percentages danced between them. They stood on opposite sides of this barrier of numbers until Grady waved Devil and Carlo aside. The Swiss engineer Heinrich Bayer moved out on to the stage with the beautiful Lucie on his arm. The violinist began to play and the couple danced, Lucie's shining hair curling over her white shoulders and Bayer bending his head as if to breathe in her perfume. Their timing was mechanically perfect, but Lucie's smile was fixed and sadness drifted from her creator like mist rising from water.

A voice called from the back of the gallery.

'What else does the lady do?'

Laughter broke out, interspersed with catcalls and coarse observations. Heinrich gave no sign of having heard them and Lucie continued to smile and rotate her head. The waltz ended and the band began to play a polka. Lucie danced the polka with just the same degree of elegant detachment.

The show concluded with a sentimental soprano. The audience had thinned out, the rump of it was growing ever more unruly, and when the final curtain came down it was to nobody's particular regret. In his narrow cubbyhole of an office Jacko Grady took his seat behind a card table with a cash box set on it. Devil and Carlo waited at the midpoint of the queue of performers, having been engrossed in a card game with the comedy tenor and the male half of the acrobat duo. Carlo had won a shilling. The acrobat's partner looked through her eyelashes at Devil as the press of performers nudged them together.

Miss Eliza Dunlop was also waiting. Her married sister Faith Shaw and Jasper Button were talking together, in the manner of people who did not know each other very well but who are concerned to be pleasant. At the end of the show Jasper had asked her, 'Would you care to meet the good and evil philosophers in person, Eliza? You enjoyed their performance, I think.'

'It was very gory,' Faith shuddered.

'It was the best act in the programme,' Eliza said in her composed way.

'It was, but that is not to say a very great deal,' Jasper laughed.

'And I am sure you know perfectly well that your wax head was the best thing about the best act,' Eliza told him.

In fact, she had been astonished by the brio of the little

playlet. The confident speed of it, and the smoke and flashing lights and drum rolls had been thrilling, and somehow affecting. It had also been macabre and not a little vulgar, of course, but still the illusion – however it had been achieved – was impressive.

'Thank you,' Jasper said, with evident pleasure.

Eliza liked Jasper reasonably well.

Faith's husband Matthew Shaw was the manager at the Baker Street waxworks gallery, and one afternoon when the sisters had called on him there he had introduced the talented modeller to his wife's younger sister. A little time later Eliza had been happy enough to accept Jasper's invitation to accompany him to the opening of the new theatre of varieties, and Mrs Shaw made up the party while Matty stayed at home with their two small boys.

'I am in no need of chaperoning, Faith,' Eliza had protested. 'I am a modern woman.'

'You are indeed,' Faith agreed, but she had come along just the same.

This threesome lingered for a few moments in the Palmyra's foyer as a mob of overheated young men surged in the entrance, shouting to each other about where and how to continue their evening's pleasures. Two of them took sudden offence and they squared up, swaying and jabbing until the theatre's doorman bundled them out into the street. He was seeking to secure the premises, so along with the rougher elements of the audience Jasper's party found themselves outside in the noise and glare of the Strand.

'I think we shall make our way to the stage door and wait there for my friends,' Jasper said quickly. He shepherded the two women a few steps to the alleyway that ran down the side of the theatre.

Eliza was not afraid of a pair of brawling inebriates, but she allowed Jasper to guide her. As soon as they turned the corner they were buffeted by a sharp wind that funnelled up from the river, carrying with it the stink of mud and horse manure and wet straw. The cobbles were greasy with the damp of a November evening, and they reflected the glimmer of a single torch burning in a holder next to the unmarked stage entrance. Jasper was about to knock when the door was suddenly flung open. A line of people emerged, but before she could distinguish them she became aware of more footsteps skidding down the slippery cobbles. Someone fell and loudly cursed, and another voice jeered, 'Get up, Makins. See here, it's the philosopher. Looking to cut off another couple of heads, are you?'

'Whoa, *and* the dancer with the pretty doll. Where is she? In the box? Care to loan her, would you? I'll teach her a different dance.'

'Ha ha.'

Eliza saw a man in a threadbare coat throw himself across a trunk on a porter's wooden cart. Two toughs wrenched his arms behind his back and tried to haul the trunk from underneath him.

More figures scuffled down the alley to reinforce the assailants and seconds later a proper fight erupted.

'Get inside the door,' Jasper called hoarsely to the two women. Faith did as she was told but Eliza stood her ground. She saw how Jasper pitched straight in alongside the man she recognised as the evil philosopher, as if they had both done this sort of work before. They made a useful pair of combatants. The ring-leader staggered backwards from a punch delivered by the philosopher, and Jasper followed up with a series of jabs which obliged two others to abandon their attempt to wrestle open the trunk. Seemingly oblivious to the fighting, the man in the overcoat knelt to secure the catches, his pale hands shaking.

Eliza became aware that a considerable force was operating at a secondary level. She looked down and saw a miniature man, hardly more than three feet tall. He launched himself between the legs of the attackers, pummelling and kicking until one of them stopped short. This man swiped his coat-sleeve across his moustache, gasping in derision.

'Hulloa, who is this? Is the midget your familiar, Mr Conjuror?'

Carlo's reply was a savage punch at the tender spot behind the man's knee. He yelled with pain, at which his nearest accomplice responded with a kick that connected with Carlo's jaw. The little man collapsed like a punctured bladder. Eliza cried out in dismay and ran the few steps to his side. She sank to the cobbles and held his head in her lap as bright blood ran from his mouth.

A whistle sounded at the top of the alley. Instantly the fight broke up and the assailants ran off in the direction of the river. The man in the overcoat took up a protective position in front of his trunk. Jasper and the philosopher dusted themselves down and tried to look inconspicuous as the bobby marched towards them. None of them had the slightest wish to attract the attention of the Metropolitan Police. Carlo opened his eyes and saw Eliza.

He sighed and thickly muttered, 'Don'th revive me. I am quithe comfothable.'

The police officer loomed over them.

'Is this person badly hurt?'

'I don't believe so,' Eliza said. 'There were some drunken creatures who ran that way . . .'

Jasper came to her aid. He explained that they had been to the theatre and had been set upon as they made their way to meet friends at the stage door. He didn't think the attackers were thieves, but they had been threatening enough. 'There are ladies here,' he added.

'What is this?' the bobby demanded, pointing his stick at the pale man's locked trunk.

'Theatrical properties,' he answered in a Swiss-German accent. The policeman frowned.

'Open up.'

Eliza gave her handkerchief to the dwarf. Sitting up he spat some blood and reached a clean-enough finger into his mouth to explore the damage. The flesh over his jaw was darkly swelling.

'Rest for a moment, then we'll take you to find water and a dressing. You will be quite all right,' she reassured him.

The bobby was staring at the trunk's contents. A woman's body, folded in half, was nested into a cocoon of padded velvet. Disbelieving, he ran his hands over the rubber limbs and shone his lamp into the cold glass eyes.

'I am an engineer of automata,' Heinrich Bayer said.

The policeman straightened up.

'Are you, indeed? It takes all sorts. Go home now, the lot of you. I'll see if I can catch up with your friends.'

Carlo muttered a thick phrase and Eliza patted his arm in gentle restraint.

As soon as the bobby had moved off a small knot of performers emerged from the stage door with Faith in their midst. Jasper groaned.

'Faith, are you all right? And you, Eliza? How in the world am I going to explain to Matty that I brought you to an innocuous evening at the variety and we ended up in a pretty bout of fisticuffs?'

'You could avoid any mention of it. That would be the easiest course,' Eliza advised.

In the presence of the policeman the evil philosopher had made himself next to invisible. Now he seemed to regain his full stature, even to be somehow bigger and made of more solid matter than the rest of them. He became the inevitable pivot of their strange group.

'Jasper, you have lost none of your abilities. Won't you introduce me to your friends?'

Jasper muttered, 'Mr Hector, ah, Mr Devil Wix. Mrs Shaw, Miss Eliza Dunlop.'

Devil bowed to Faith, but Eliza was still crouching on the cobbles with one arm supporting Carlo. The dwarf was sitting up, dabbing at his smashed mouth with her handkerchief. Devil folded himself to their level just as Jacko Grady's barrel body and surprisingly diminutive shoes emerged from the stage door.

'What's this?' the manager demanded.

'Mr Boldoni was attacked by some pleasant individuals from your choice audience.'

'Don't let him lie here in front of my theatre. Is he hurt? Wix, you'd better make sure he's fit to perform tomorrow.'

Grady secured the big padlock with much jangling of a large bunch of keys. The performance was calculated to display ownership and Devil hated him for it. Grady picked his way past them and headed towards the Strand. Turning his head, Devil saw Eliza Dunlop stick out her tongue at the man's receding back.

'Of course he's *hurt*,' she retorted. To Devil she said, 'We need warm salt water to rinse out his mouth. And some light to inspect the damage.'

Carlo moaned as the pain in his jaw intensified.

'Shhh,' she told him, and stroked his hair.

Devil noticed that her gloves were blotched with blood and Carlo's spittle. This detail touched him more directly than the prettiest smile or the most fashionable dress ever could have done.

Who is this? he asked himself and his eyes slid at once to Jasper's neat boots, standing only a yard away beside Mrs Shaw.

Ah, is that it? Fair enough, he thought.

To one side of their little group Heinrich Bayer looked as if he had been violated. His face was colourless and he was trembling, his hands still on the clasps of Lucie's box.

Devil put his hands under the dwarf's arms. He scrambled to his feet, staggering a little under Carlo's unexpected weight, but he found that he was able to carry him.

'Follow me. It's only two hundred yards,' he called over his shoulder to the others.

The private room was on the first floor of a public house well known to Devil. The landlord admitted them and put some coals on the fire. Eliza Dunlop took off her cloak and bonnet (she had thick, glossy dark hair) and once Devil had deposited Carlo on a high stool the two women inspected his mouth. Devil gave orders and a tray clinking with glasses and a bottle soon arrived, followed by the pot boy carrying a basin and ewer and a kettle of hot water. Devil mixed a hot toddy and put it into Bayer's hands.

'Drink that up, man. You look as green as a lettuce. Don't faint on me, please. Jas, you will refuse the offer of strong drink, but here is one for me. You shall have a tot, Carlo, when your medical review is completed. Good health, gentlemen. We may or may not have something to celebrate tonight. Unfortunately most of the power to determine such matters lies with Jacko Grady.'

Eliza looked over her shoulder. 'The fat man?'

'The same. He is the owner and manager of the Palmyra theatre. For the present,' Devil added and tipped back his toddy.

'He is an extremely unpleasant person,' she said.

Devil glanced again at her discarded gloves, the emblems of the evening's events. Carlo swilled out his mouth with hot salt water and spat a brownish stream into the bowl Faith Shaw held out for him. Eliza patted his shoulder and gave him a strip of her sister's clean handkerchief, snipped with a pair of nail scissors taken from her reticule, to put inside his mouth.

'Well done. You will heal up in a few days. I don't believe your jaw is broken.'

Carlo couldn't smile, or even speak clearly with his mouth stuffed with linen but his appreciation was plain.

'Are you thuh they ith no boken bone?'

Eliza ran her fingers over his jaw then cupped his large chin in her hands. Carlo gazed up at her with as much admiring awe as if she had stepped out of a vision of heaven.

'I'm not a nurse, but I know a little anatomy. It's badly bruised where that ruffian's toe connected, and there are tooth cuts to your tongue and the insides of your cheeks. You should gargle with salt water to keep your mouth clean, but I am confident that there is nothing more serious.'

'We muth go on tomohoh. Thuh will be nowt to pleathe an audience if *I* am not thuh.'

65

Carlo waved his empty hand to Devil who passed him his tot in eloquent silence. The dwarf removed his dressing, drank, and winced extravagantly as the alcohol stung his open cuts. Mrs Shaw and her sister had declined Devil's offer of a small glass of wine, but they agreed to a cup of tea and the pot boy now reappeared with a second tray.

They disposed themselves around the fire. Faith Shaw presided over the teapot and Heinrich Bayer released Lucie from her velvet casing, bringing forward a chair so she could join them. He placed her hands in her lap, arranged her skirts and straightened her necklace. He was more comfortable now that he could see her and be assured that she was not threatened, and his face regained its more normal degree of pallor. Eliza watched all this with her bright eyes, but when he felt her attention on him Herr Bayer stared at the floor.

Even so, it was a convivial gathering. Jasper stopped saying that he must take the ladies home or else poor Matthew would be frantic with worry.

Faith remarked, 'He will not be worried, Jasper, because he knows that we are safe with you.'

'We can look after ourselves,' Eliza corrected her. 'Besides which we have the security of this lady's blameless company, don't we?'

'Lucie. Her name is Lucie,' Heinrich insisted.

Eliza left her seat and went to take the automaton's hand. If she was disconcerted by its lifelike appearance coupled with the cold touch of the rubber skin she gave no sign of it. 'How do you do?' she murmured.

Heinrich was pleased. 'She is well, thank you. A little tired this evening. Our stage performances are always exhausting for her, and I wish the audience had been more appreciative. They were a rough crowd.'

Eliza returned to her seat. 'Is Lucie your daughter? Perhaps a closer relationship? You dance together so beautifully.'

Devil stared. Miss Dunlop was unusual for looking like a perfectly orthodox young woman and yet being startlingly un-demure. He noticed now that Jasper Button regarded her with admiration that was tinged with possessiveness. How charming, how pleasant for Jasper, he thought.

'Lucie is my life's work. And also my dear companion,' Heinrich was saying. He didn't look at Eliza as he spoke. 'She is the amalgam of art and artifice. Few people understand what it is to have created such a thing. I designed each mechanism that animates her, I made or contrived to have made every separate piece of her.'

'Maybe such appreciation requires an artistic temperament? Eliza is herself an artist, you know,' Faith put in.

Devil liked the sly, humorous mischief displayed by the two sisters.

'I am only a student of art,' Eliza demurred. 'I attend classes in life drawing, sculpture, painting. Of course, I don't have the means to pay outright for my tuition so I make payments in kind by working as a life model.'

The images generated by this information caused Devil to cough into his brandy. Jasper frowned at him.

'You do know thomething abouth anatomy,' Carlo agreed.

'Shall we finish the bottle?' Devil wondered as he stirred up the fire with the iron poker. Carlo held out his glass. Jasper looked at his pocket watch and Heinrich glanced towards Lucie. The sisters seemed perfectly at ease.

Conversation turned to the evening's entertainment, and its strengths and shortcomings.

'Tell us about the Philosophers illusion, Mr Wix,' Faith said. 'We were most impressed.'

Devil bowed. 'I regret that I can't reveal to you how the illusion was actually performed. No professional magician will ever reveal his secrets, even amongst friends. I was helped by Jasper's skills, as you saw. His modelled head of Carlo is a masterpiece. And Carlo himself has certain, ah, invaluable attributes.'

Carlo spat into the wadded dressings to clear his mouth. 'You thaw a bocth trick. It'th thimple enough but thith one

67

can't be performed without a dwarf to do the work. The idea and the thkill in it were mine. Devil and I made up a bit of bithineth to go with it. You get a bigger effeck on a proper thtage like tonight'th, where you've got muthicianth and lighth and thuchlike.'

'But . . . you appeared to be tall,' Faith put in.

The dwarf shrugged. '*Thtilth.*'

'I am relieved it doesn't cause you pain to talk so much,' Devil said to him.

'Devil?' Eliza softly wondered. 'Didn't I hear Jasper call you Hector first of all?'

'Devil Wix is my stage name. It is . . . simpler to go by that in both spheres of my existence.'

'And you and Jasper have known each other since you were boys, I believe?'

The firelight glowed on pewter dishes and the smoke-yellowed walls. From the street beneath the window came the rumble of carriage wheels.

Devil gave a brief nod. The two sisters exchanged a glance and Jasper produced his pocket watch for the last time.

'If we are to have any hope of seeing you safely back home before midnight . . .'

'It has been a fascinating evening. Thank you,' Faith said as she politely stood up.

Jasper put her cloak round her shoulders and then performed the same service for Eliza. Carlo sat fingering his swollen jaw and Heinrich, affected by the two glasses of brandy he had drunk, silently stared into the depths of the fire.

Eliza smoothed the ruined gloves over her fingers.

'Conjurors? Magicians? Is that what you are?' She spoke generally but the question was addressed to Devil.

'You would not call Herr Bayer a magician, I think. None of us would be pleased with conjuror, which sounds to me like some fellow conning for pennies on the street. I prefer *illusionists*,' he said.

Eliza put on her hat. 'The illusionists,' she slowly repeated.

To his surprise Devil heard himself confiding, 'I would like to transform the Palmyra theatre into a palace of illusions. It should be the home of magical effects, of transformations and mysteries and bewitchments. It should be a place of *wonderment*.'

'I think the fat man stands in the way of your dream.'

'Not for ever.'

'I hope not. I like the sound of your Palmyra.'

Eliza held out her hand and Devil shook it, then her sister's.

'Thank you for coming,' Devil murmured to Jasper as they wished each other goodnight.

'I wouldn't have missed my head's grand theatrical debut. I hope the show will be a great success.' Jasper was a kindly man, but he couldn't keep the doubt out of his voice.

'No question.'

Heinrich suddenly jumped up, knocking his chair sideways and staggering somewhat before placing a reassuring hand on Lucie's shoulder.

'Success? Listen to me regarding this if you please. I tell you what you need to put in your act. I tell you what will make all the difference.'

'Yes?' Devil sighed.

'You should have a woman in it. I have an idea for such a thing.'

'Yes, of course. Thank you. You would be the expert on such matters.'

It was Eliza who paused in the doorway.

'He's right, you know,' she said to Devil.

'Come, my dear. We have a matinee tomorrow,' Heinrich told Lucie.

Now that the impromptu party was over and the agony in his jaw came to the forefront, a black mood descended on Carlo. He grumbled to Devil, 'Wonderment, did you thay? How far will the two thilling and thicthpenth we have earned thith evening go towardth *wonderment*? Particularly thinth you have laid out motht of it on brandy.'

Heinrich Bayer was negotiating the doorway with the wheeled trunk. Swaying a little, he let go of the handles and reached two fingers into the pocket of his tragic coat. He held out a shilling to Devil.

'Please take this. I wish to hear no one say that Lucie and I do not stand our treat.'

'Put your money away,' Devil said, against his inclinations. He turned to Carlo.

'Give me time, my friend. Then you shall see.'

FOUR

The young couple walked southwards through the park. Suspended behind bare trees the pale orange sun held little warmth, and the insistence of the wind obliged them to keep up a steady pace. Jasper Button would have preferred to stroll and perhaps to have taken hold of Eliza's arm, but he was compensated for the lack of this opportunity by the way brisk exercise in the chill air brought colour to her cheeks and made her eyes sparkle. He thought how pretty she looked in her neat bonnet and brown coat, and this demure exterior coupled with his awareness of where she was heading only increased his pleasure. She was not just a beauty. She both was and was entirely *not* what she seemed. He had never met anyone whose contradictions fascinated him so entirely. His admiration made him a little awkward in her company, but he was a determined man who did not lack self-confidence. He would win her in the end, Jasper assured himself. Eliza Dunlop would be his wife, and they would have a handsome family together. Aspects of this plan brought a flush to his cheeks to match Eliza's own.

Between the trees ahead there was a flash of gold. Laughing, Eliza pointed to a Gothic spire and a canopy topped with pinnacles that spiked the fading sky.

'The Memorial looks just like the Philosophers cabinet,' she said.

71

'Or rather, Devil constructed his cabinet to resemble the Memorial,' Jasper replied. 'In either case, they are both monstrosities.'

The sun was setting now and the gilt bronze of the Prince Consort's statue glimmered so harshly in the horizontal rays that Jasper lifted his hand and pretended to shield his eyes. They skirted the west side of the structure and stopped to examine the modern frieze and sculptures. Jasper seized the opportunity to link Eliza's arm in his. Her gloved hand rested on his forearm, neither yielding nor resisting. Her chin was tipped upwards as she gazed at the enthroned Albert.

'I am half expecting his head to rotate and Carlo's voice to utter a dire warning, aren't you?' In a mournful voice she quoted, '"I curse you to eternity and beyond."'

'Carlo isn't of a size for it. It would take a giant to work a trick inside that vast thing.'

'You are right. They would have to recruit a suitable one. Then it would be Boldoni, Wix and Cyclops, and that doesn't sound nearly so good.'

Eliza laughed again and withdrew her arm. She turned her back on the Memorial and began to walk so fast that Jasper had to scurry to keep up with her. He was thinking, *Does Boldoni and Wix sound good to her? Why is that?*

'I am afraid I shall be late,' she said.

'You have plenty of time.'

They passed through the traffic in front of the imposing dome of the Royal Albert Hall and set off through the streets of South Kensington. The evening was closing in, and yellow lights shone in comfortable rooms where the curtains had not yet been closed. Jasper admired the handsome stucco residences with their solid front doors surmounting flights of stone steps.

'I would like to live in one of these houses some day,' he said. There was no reason not to be ambitious.

'They're very large.'

'A suitable size for a family.'

72

She turned her head and their eyes met. 'Is that really what you want, Jasper?'

Her directness unnerved him a little but he answered with complete conviction, 'Yes. Of course it is. A wife, a family, a comfortable home and security for all of us. What man wouldn't wish for the same?'

'Quite a number, I believe,' she said in her composed manner.

Jasper persisted, 'And what do you want, Eliza?'

They walked under a street lamp and as the light swept over her face he noticed the sudden bright eagerness of her expression. She looked almost avid, he thought.

'Ah. I want to know the world, and myself.'

Jasper smiled. He sometimes forgot it, but she was very young. Barely twenty years old. He felt the opposite weight of his own cynical maturity, forged by the years in Stanmore as much as by those that had followed. Eliza was quick to follow his thoughts.

'You think that sounds jejune? Believe me, I have considered my future with proper seriousness, even though you think I am hardly old enough to have learned my alphabet.'

'Not in the least. I think you are amazingly aware.'

Eliza almost tossed her head. 'For one so young and so *female*, do you mean to say?'

'Of course not.'

'I do not want to be like my poor mother. Nor do I even want to be like my sister Faith.'

Jasper knew that Faith and Eliza were the daughters of a moderately prosperous greengrocer. Their mother had been a dutiful wife who had devoted herself to the care of her husband and daughters, always putting aside her own quiet interests in choral music and landscape painting, and then had died of a consumption before Faith turned fifteen. Until Faith's marriage to Matthew Shaw an aunt had lived in the Dunlop household, but once that union was accomplished the aunt had grown tired of her role and returned to her own home, leaving Eliza in the care of her father. Mr Dunlop had soon remarried, but Eliza did not hold a high level of regard for her mother's replacement. She had lived next with Faith and Matty, but when their first child was born a nursemaid arrived to help the new mother and the small house had been distinctly too small for all of them. By this time Eliza had declared that she would study art, her determination to do so only increased by John Dunlop's opinion that this would be a waste of her time and his money.

'Nevertheless, it is what I shall do,' Eliza said.

She had a tiny amount of capital of her own, left to her by her mother, and this she used to establish herself in a room in a ladies' lodging house in Bayswater. From here she had only to walk across the park to the Rawlinson School of Art.

'A life model?' her stepmother had gasped, her eyes two circles in her circular face.

'Yes. It is a perfectly respectable job, and I need employment. Would you and my father prefer it if I went into service?'

John Dunlop had plenty of other pressing concerns, and there would soon be a new addition to his family.

'Eliza reads books. She has educated herself out of our understanding, my dear. We must allow her to make her own mistakes,' he said.

So Eliza had got her own way, which was the usual course of events.

Jasper asked too quickly, 'Why don't you want to be like your sister? Matty is a good man, they have healthy children, Faith appears – to me, at least – to be very contented.'

'I hope so. But why do you assume that what makes my sister content would have the same result for me?'

He longed to tell her, Because I want to make you happy. Our happiness together will be my life's ambition.

They had reached the steps of the school. Preposterously, Jasper found himself scanning the area for a spot where he might sink to his knees and propose to her. He didn't manage to do this, or anything except gape at her like a village idiot.

A dark thought quivered at the margin of his consciousness, but out of long practice he suppressed it.

Eliza skipped up the steps and paused with her gloved hand on the massive doorknob.

'You know, Jasper, there are so many places and things I would like to see. There is so much to learn.'

'Yes,' Jasper agreed, sounding even in his own ears the essence of dullness.

'Thank you for walking me here.'

'I'll come back after the class and see you home again.'

'No, please don't do that. I can look after myself.'

Here was the nub of it, he understood. He wanted to protect her, but to place herself under a man's protection went against what Eliza imagined to be her independent principles. He would have to be patient.

'All right.'

She waved her small hand and the heavy door closed behind her.

Disconsolate, Jasper walked away. They had not quite quarrelled, but still the discussion had not taken the direction he had hoped for.

Inside the school's domed entrance hall Eliza took a moment to collect herself. Students on their way to five o'clock classes clipped across the black-and-white marble floor, the double doors to Professor Rawlinson's office stood partly open to reveal a slice of oriental carpet, portraits lining the stairs gazed down at her with welcome indifference. Jasper's unspoken urgency, his sheer *concern*, had ruffled her temper. The school's atmosphere of calm focus on art was soothing. She was pleased to find herself a small – but still essential – component in the functioning of this higher machine.

She untied her bonnet and mounted the stairs towards the Life Room.

'Good evening gentlemen, Miss Frazier.'

The students had been lounging at their boards but they sat up as soon as Raleigh Coope RA, Master of Life Drawing, came in.

'Good evening, Mr Coope.'

The Academician was an admired and respected teacher.

Eliza waited behind the screen. She was ready for the class. When the room fell silent she experienced a small flutter of nerves, but this always happened before she took a pose.

'Miss Dunlop, if you are ready to join us, please?'

She emerged into the room. There was the usual circle of gentlemen, Charles Egan and Ralph Vine and the others, and one lady, Miss Frazier, in her tweed skirt and artist's smock blouse. A mixed life drawing class was highly unusual, but the Rawlinson was a very modern school.

At the centre of the circle was an empty chair. Eliza walked to it, enjoying the snag of tension in the air. She untied the string of her robe and slipped it off, and Mr Coope took it from her and hung it within her reach. Naked, Eliza sat down and found her pose. She turned her head to reveal her neck, eased her shoulders, curled one hand and extended the fingers of the other on her thigh, letting all the bones and ligaments of her body loosen and settle in their proper alignment. A faint stirring of a draught brushed her skin.

Her gaze found the canvas she liked on the opposite wall. It was a blue-and-grey composition of sea, shingle and sky. She let her thoughts gather at the margin of this other place, and then she slipped into it as if into the sea itself.

The only sounds were the scrawl and slither of pencils on paper and Mr Coope's slow tread as he circled the room.

The class lasted for two hours, with a short break halfway through during which Eliza put on her robe and drank a cup of tea. Miss Frazier ate a sandwich and read her book while most of the young men went outside to smoke and talk. The routine was familiar, even including Charles Egan's attempts to engage Eliza in banter after Mr Coope brought the class to an end and left the room. She didn't find any aspect of the work in the least tiring. She felt clean and refreshed after the dreamlike hours of wandering within the sea painting.

When Eliza emerged from the school she found herself

satisfactorily alone, and briefly hesitated. An omnibus route passed quite close to her intended destination, but she noticed a hansom cab waiting nearby. She told herself that she took it on impulse, although at a deeper level she knew that this was what she had intended all along.

It had been a bad night. The house was less than half full and the sparse audience was sullen. All the performers were affected by the poor reception of their best efforts, and Jacko Grady's brandy-fuelled bad temper and curses as they came offstage only added to the atmosphere of despondency.

Devil couldn't see what was happening beneath the concealed trapdoor but Carlo had been slow to perform the demanding manoeuvre leading to his reappearance in the good philosopher's robe, and there were three or four long seconds of delay before the heap of clothing stirred and resurrected itself. Devil lay waiting with his face in the stage dust and silently swore. Fortunately the audience seemed too sunk into lethargy even to notice the mistake.

When they came off Jacko Grady muttered to Devil, 'What the hell's the matter with you two? I keep telling you to go faster, Wix, not the opposite. Get it right or get out of my theatre.'

Devil clenched his fists within the sleeves of his costume. He hated the fat man so much that his fingers itched to close about his neck. In the foetid corner where they changed he took his fury out on the dwarf.

'Grady's right. You were like a dog in a sack out there. This is our chance, this act. Nothing less than perfection will do for Boldoni and Wix.'

Carlo's bruised face turned even darker, but not before Devil saw the flicker of shame in it. He was proud and he would be even more disappointed with the night than Devil had been.

He snapped, 'Shut your sloppy mouth. Where would this act be without me, I'd like to know? Who are you? Nothing but a tuppenny broadsman.'

'What happened?'

'Bloody stilt jammed in the trap.' Carlo thrust out his hand. The heel of it was scraped, and freckled with splinters where he had evidently wrenched the raw wood to free himself. Silently Devil handed him a wet rag to wipe the skin clean. Next to them Heinrich took Lucie in his arms and arranged her ringlets over her shoulders before they went out into the lights. Bascia, the female partner of the acrobatic duo, sniggered and muttered something under her breath to her brother. The tiny bells stitched to her costume tinkled like an echo of laughter.

Devil tried to breathe evenly but suppressed frustration only made his heart knock against his ribs. Tremors ran under his skin and he shook as if in a fever. Failure was at hand, and out of failure fear blossomed.

The old figure of darkness edged with flame took shape and sprang at him. It was as real in that moment as Carlo or Grady. Devil recoiled. He pressed the heels of his hands into his eyes to block out the apparition, but the screams of a dying boy were loud enough to deafen him.

Leave me alone, Devil inwardly howled. *You are gone, I am still here.*

He made himself drop his hands. If he brought his mind to bear on the here and now, he knew that the shape of Gabe would fade away.

He forced himself to think.

The badness of the show was Grady's fault. Like its poor performers the theatre itself was cracking and subsiding all round them. Grady had chased away the proper audience, the front row customers in silk hats and jewels, and in their place he encouraged vulgarians and drunks – and not sufficient numbers even of those. The coarse comedian who now closed the first half was supposed to appeal to Grady's mob, but the man wasn't good enough to make even the lowest people laugh. Without subtlety, without at least giving an audience the opportunity to feign innocence at double meanings, dirty talk was just dirt. Devil was surprised to note his own prudery but he knew what was right: he knew what would bring in the crowds and their money. The failure was Grady's, not his own.

The dark figure was still there, in the periphery of his vision. He was afraid of a *memory*, and a memory couldn't hurt him. He aimed a vicious kick at the inner spectre but his foot connected only with a storage hamper that toppled over and spilled its contents. He slouched forwards to set it upright and saw that as usual Bascia was looking at him. Her black eyes reminded him of ripe berries in the Stanmore hedges. She tilted her head in a gesture of invitation.

Carlo ignored his antics with the hamper. He pulled down his cap to cover his eyes and stalked away. Devil understood that he should go after him and try to set matters straight, perhaps even apologise if he could bring himself to do so. There would not be much of an act without Carlo, whereas the dwarf could always find another front man. But instead he matched Bascia's head tilt with one of his own. The warmth of a woman's body would obliterate Gabe more effectively than brandy ever could.

There was a cupboard in an angle of the dim corridor that led between the dressing rooms and the stage. He took the girl's hand and they slid into the cramped space. The opening bars of Heinrich's and Lucie's waltz scraped the air as their mouths met.

Eliza paid the hansom driver, wincing at the size of the fare. She hurried down the alley beside the theatre and she was at the stage door when the dwarf flew out. He almost collided with her but before she could stop him or call out his name he whirled past and raced towards the Strand. She watched him go, then seized the opportunity to step in through the open stage door. She blinked in the yellow light. The air was redolent of sweat and smoke and there was a hollow echo of stamping feet in the distance.

'Yes?'

A man seated in a cubbyhole looked at her over his newspaper.

She recognised the doorman who had bundled them into the street on her first visit to the theatre.

'Mr Wix. I am here to see Mr Wix.'

The man's grin showed his teeth, or the place where most of his teeth had once been.

'Box office round at the front of house, *ma'am*. I believe there may be some seats available for this performance. Just a handful.' He laughed at his own wit.

Eliza had no intention of negotiating with this person. She marched past the cubbyhole and into the warren of tight corridors and wooden stairways at the back of the stage. A foreign-looking man tried to push past her as Carlo had done, but she caught him by the elbow.

'I'm looking for Mr Wix.'

'Good luck,' the fellow almost spat. He shook off her hand and strode to the stage door. She pushed her way deeper into the theatre. The din of stamping feet now mingled with boos and jeers. A space opened in front of her, except that space was the wrong word for this wild muddle of strewn clothing, trunks and boxes, dismembered chairs, fragments of mirror perched on ledges strewn with face powder, empty bottles, discarded boots, and half-dressed performers jostling for room to clothe themselves. From behind a screen with a broken leaf emerged the soprano who had closed the show on the night she came with Jasper and Faith. The woman adjusted her bodice as a slatternly creature tugged at her laces.

'That will do,' the singer snapped and pushed the dresser aside. She took a long pull at a tankard, wiped her mouth with the back of her hand and set off at a tipsy angle towards the stage. From the opposite direction came a ragged shout of mocking laughter mingled with louder catcalling. Eliza was about to appeal to the nearest performer for Devil's whereabouts when she saw him emerge from a doorway. A dishevelled girl sidled in his wake, accompanied by a faint tinkle of silvery bells.

Devil saw her and his face changed.

'Miss Dunlop? Eliza?'

Eliza kept her head up. 'I have an idea to discuss with you,' she said. 'When it is convenient.'

Before he could offer a response they became aware of silence spreading through the dressing room. Heinrich Bayer had appeared with Lucie in his arms. His face glistened with tears. The performers stood awkwardly aside to let him pass as he carried the doll to her velvet nest. Eliza went to him, putting her hand on his sleeve.

'What is wrong? Can I help you?' she whispered.

Heinrich leapt away from her. He began the work of folding the rubber limbs into their niches. He wept soundlessly as he leaned over to smooth the doll's hair and kiss her forehead. Lucie's glass eyes gazed up, void of all expression. Devil came to his side.

'They are all fools, Heinrich. Ignorant, stupid fools. Make Lucie ready and we'll go.'

The other performers gave up their staring and turned aside to occupy themselves as Grady burst in on them. Hands in his pockets, belly jutting, he glared at the room.

'That was the worst of the bad. You, Bayer, and your dancing doll. Don't trouble to come back tomorrow.'

Heinrich was trembling, but he had stopped weeping. Lines deepened in his worn face. He closed up Lucie's trunk and fastened the catches, then positioned himself in front of it.

'You should please pay me for tonight's performance.'

Grady made a sound like rending fabric. 'Not a brass farthing.'

'We danced for your audience. It is not Lucie's fault nor mine that they did not appreciate the artistry . . .'

'Bloody *artistry*. Entertainment, that's what I want. And I'm going to get it from the rest of you if I have to whip it out of you.' The man's sausage finger jabbed at the silent onlookers.

Devil could suppress his hatred no longer. He dived at Grady and grasping his hands round his thick neck he shook him as hard as he could although the manager's bulk barely rocked.

Behind them somebody, perhaps the coarse comic, gave a low-voiced cheer.

'Pay him what you owe or I will kill you,' Devil growled.

Grady's eyes were watering. He coughed, 'Is that what you are, Wix? A killer?'

Through the fog of his rage Devil glimpsed the dark figure again. He blinked and it was gone, drawing his strength with it. His hands fell to his sides.

'Pay him,' he muttered.

'You can get out of here, as well. You and the dwarf. And stay out.'

The same voice muttered. 'It's them as are bringing in what audiences you do get, Mr Grady. Knock 'em out and you're done for.'

Grady cursed. He caught sight of Eliza at Heinrich's side.

'Who are you?'

'A friend of Herr Bayer's.'

'A living woman? Indeed? Backstage is for artistes only, madam.'

Jacko Grady adjusted his straining waistcoat and stalked away.

'Let's go,' Devil muttered to Heinrich Bayer and Eliza chose to believe that she was included in the command. As they left the room there was no sign of the dishevelled girl although Eliza believed she heard an accusatory jingle.

'Where d'you live?' Devil demanded of Heinrich when they reached the Strand. The Swiss gave an address not far from the coffin maker's workshop.

'It's a fair step, but I'll walk back there with you,' Devil sighed. 'Miss Dunlop, how did you come here? May I find you a cab, perhaps?'

She gave him a look. 'I will come with you. As a matter of fact the idea I hoped to discuss with you was originally Herr Bayer's, so this is quite opportune.'

Devil sighed again. He was disgusted by his failure to get the better of Jacko Grady over Heinrich's money. Getting the better of Jacko Grady was becoming as important to him as the success of Boldoni and Wix, and it was infuriating that the success of Boldoni and Wix was dependent for now on staying with Grady and the Palmyra.

Heinrich Bayer was already walking, trundling ahead of him the cart with Lucie's trunk strapped to it, seeming too unhappy to care whether or not he was alone. He looked utterly beaten, his shabby coat over-large for his thin body. Devil and Eliza flanked him and they moved through the late evening crowds of swells and revellers and street hawkers that surged to the steps of theatres and saloons. London seemed all glitter and celebration, with poor Heinrich Bayer the frayed figure at its brass heart.

They walked in silence, occupied with their separate thoughts. Devil's pace was purposeful and Eliza could only reflect on the differences between this journey and the earlier stroll though Hyde Park. Jasper was forever holding back and taking her arm, asking questions as if he was trying to work his way into her head. Devil was bracingly indifferent to her presence. Eliza was excited to find herself out in these vivid streets with the crowds washing past her, not knowing where she was going or what lay in store.

Beyond St Clement Danes there were fewer people. Street lamps shone on empty stretches of cobbled road and the wheels of Lucie's cart clattered in the sudden stillness. The dome of St Paul's was pasted black against the sky as they turned to the north of it, skirted the heaving city within the city of the meat market, and headed deep into the warren of Clerkenwell. When they finally reached a recessed doorway Heinrich looked at them as if surprised to find that he had company. But he nudged the door open and led them down an internal alleyway to unlock another door, a low entrance leading into a darkened mews at the rear of some forbidding building. They stepped over the threshold in his wake and waited as he lit a candle.

'Oh,' Eliza said in astonishment.

The room was little more than a barn, but it was not a barn

that either she or Devil could have imagined. It seemed as much a charnel house as a laboratory. On a bench lay the lower portion of a leg, the limp flaps of its rubber skin partially peeled back to expose bright metal rods within. On a clean square of cloth a row of silvery instruments, small tweezers, pliers and screw clamps was neatly laid out. A brass microscope occupied the end of the bench, and next to that stood a metalworker's lathe with coils like tiny locks of metal hair littering the floor beside its clawed iron feet. A foot and a hand, each with a piston shaft protruding from the severed joint, rested on a smaller table. This much the light of the single candle revealed as Devil and Eliza silently stared around them. The recesses of the room were hidden in shadow but there was an impression of other implements, tall cupboards, and more strange work in progress.

The centre of the room, where the candle glow was brightest, was occupied by two chairs. In one sat a female doll, wide-eyed, her hands resting in her lap. Her flaxen hair was tied back from her slender neck. Her lower body was clothed in petticoats but she was naked from the waist up. Her breasts were unmodelled protrusions of pallid rubber. Next to her sat a manikin on a square pedestal, an expressionless Chinaman with a round black hat and long, drooping moustaches. With his triangular yellow face he looked like an illustration in a child's picture book.

'Excuse me, Miss Dunlop. My work . . .' Heinrich murmured. He wrapped a shroud of cloth around the torso of the female doll.

'I believe Miss Dunlop did mention that she is employed as an artists' model,' Devil put in.

Heinrich frowned, evidently distracted. The candle flame flickered.

'We need more light,' he said. He pressed a bell push and Eliza thought she heard a distant peal. Heinrich busied himself with Lucie's trunk and a moment later a knock announced the arrival of a servant, in this strange room a surprisingly conventional figure in a dark dress and white apron. She brought in a lamp and placed it on the bench.

'Good evening, Herr Bayer. Shall I light a fire? Will you be wanting some dinner?'

Eliza's eyes met Devil's. His eyebrows rose in black circumflexes but she could see that he was intrigued rather than repelled by this macabre place. The shadows of the room were barely dispelled by the lamp, and dread seemed to linger just out of her sight. A tremor of fear ran down her spine.

Heinrich laid Lucie on a cushioned surface that appeared to Eliza something between a bed and a catafalque. She shivered at the spectacle.

'Yes. Some dinner,' Heinrich said vaguely. He shook out a fine paisley shawl and let the folds drift over Lucie's face and body. The resemblance to a catafalque was heightened.

'Shall I lay up a table over in the house, sir?'

'Perhaps we could stay here.' Devil put in. 'I think this is where our business will lie.' He sounded quite at ease, with a purposeful note under his light tone, and Eliza wondered how he achieved this in so bizarre a setting.

Heinrich waved his hand. Whenever his attention returned to them he seemed startled to discover that he still had company.

When the servant had withdrawn Devil strolled to the bench. He picked up a watchmaker's glass and screwed it into his eye, then examined the dismembered leg. Next he inquisitively turned the bezels of the microscope.

'Whose place is this, Heinrich? Do you work here?'

Heinrich sat down on a stool, then jumped up again and offered the seat to Eliza.

'Thank you,' she said, and sat. She was beginning to feel weary.

'I work here, yes.'

'For whom?' Devil persisted.

'What? For myself, of course. My interests are not so usual. I am a maker of automata.' He gestured towards the flaxen

85

doll and the Chinese manikin. 'But you know that much, Mr Wix. You are acquainted with my beautiful Lucie.'

There was a small silence.

'I thought you were a poor man, Heinrich, like me. If you are rich, as it seems you are, why have you and Lucie danced every night for Jacko Grady and his audience of barbarians?'

Heinrich was still wearing his ruined coat, with his frayed shirt collar protruding. His boot heels were worn to wafers and he looked as if he had not eaten a meal in the last week. Eliza longed to ask the same question, but she would not have had Devil's boldness in coming straight out with it.

Surprisingly the Swiss smiled. The deep lines in his face vanished and for a moment he looked a younger man. 'I am not rich. My family have been watchmakers at Le Locle in Neuchatel for three generations. I am the last son. My care is not for watches, but in what I do there is the same precision. The same love for a device that is intricate, ingenious, unique. I am a craftsman, Mr Wix, not a banker. What is money?'

'I could tell you,' Devil said bitterly. The note in his voice made Eliza look at him with attention.

Bayer said, 'I dance with Lucie at the Palmyra because I want the world to see her. There has to be a debut. A London debut, in your popular music hall. I hoped – expected – this would quickly lead to better things. But, sadly, it seems not. We are disappointed of course.' He shrugged his thin shoulders. It was clear that his brilliance as an inventor was not matched by his knowledge of the world. 'The worst of it all is the insult to Lucie. This evening, I am afraid, I was unable to hide the pain it caused me.'

Eliza was filled with sudden pity for him which only intensified her discomfort.

The servant came back with a young boy to assist her, and together they unfolded a card table and set three chairs around it. On the bench they laid out a china tureen and some covered dishes with a tray of cutlery and glassware.

'Will there be anything else, Herr Bayer?'

'I don't think so, Mrs McKay. Or, wait a moment. Perhaps some wine?'

'Thank you. Yes,' said Devil with distinct emphasis.

A bottle was brought and uncorked. Devil and Eliza helped themselves to soup from the tureen and thick slices of ham with potatoes. The food was plain, but plentiful and good. Devil drank a glass of wine straight off. Heinrich took a few spoonfuls of soup but he soon left the table and went to the Chinaman sitting on its plinth next to the yellow-haired doll. He reached behind it, and its head suddenly flopped sideways with a gasp of exhaled air that sounded like a human sigh. Eliza jumped and her spoon clinked in the bowl. The creature's hands rose from its lap and its head jerked upright with another hiss. The fingers flexed and its mouth opened and closed to reveal two rows of porcelain teeth.

'You see?' Heinrich said.

'I do,' Devil replied. He put down his spoon and fork in order to concentrate on the inventor.

'He is operated by a system of compressed air cylinders, controlled from here.' Heinrich indicated a notched drum with a handle, a simple enough mechanism that reminded Eliza of a barrel organ.

Devil remarked, 'He's of a size with Carlo Boldoni. But this fellow is more biddable, I'm sure. Tell me, Heinrich, what is your creature *for*?'

The inventor frowned. 'I made him. His existence is sufficient reason in itself. But I thought I might have him tell ladies' fortunes? One shilling a time. "Mr Wu knows the secrets of a woman's heart, and will answer the questions you cannot ask." Look at this.' He turned a handle and one of the Chinaman's hands drew a spool of paper from the opposite sleeve. 'What is a fortune? You or I could invent a fine one.' Heinrich laughed then, a creaking sound of rare usage. Eliza found that the palms of her hands were damp.

Devil's concentration intensified and his forefinger rubbed slow circles in the green baize surface of the card table.

'Do you play cards?'

'I am a busy man, Mr Wix. No, I do not.'

'Please call me Devil. If I had friends that's how they would know me.'

Jasper is your friend, Eliza silently corrected him. Why had Devil obliterated the Hector of their shared boyhood?

'I wonder if Jacko Grady plays cards,' Devil mused in the softest voice. The Chinaman's hands descended and once more lay inert in its lap as Heinrich wandered away to his bench. He took up the half leg and held it suspended by its metal arteries.

'Have you ever heard of a false automaton?' Devil asked.

Heinrich did not look up. These questions bored him.

'Of course. Who has not? Even Mr Grady spoke of such a thing. But why would I be interested? They are the province of . . .' There was a pause while he searched for the word. Not tricksters, or even conjurors. 'Illusionists.'

'Exactly.' Devil's smile did not reach his eyes. He poured himself another glass of wine to rinse down a large mouthful of ham and potato. Only when he had cleared his plate did he turn to Eliza.

'Tell me, what drew you back to the elegant and acclaimed Palmyra theatre this evening, Miss Dunlop? Eliza, that is. That is how I think of you.'

He thinks of me? She only nodded. 'How is Carlo's poor face? I was not able to ask about the damage when I saw him earlier.'

'Probably for the best. He would have bitten off your head, if you had done so. Yes, he is mending quite well although he complains enough. You came to the theatre to ask after him?'

'No, not for that reason alone. As I said earlier, I have an idea. You recall the suggestion Heinrich made when we were leaving the tavern that evening? That you should perhaps have a woman in your act?'

Summoning his patience Devil nodded. 'And you agreed with him.'

Eliza said, 'I enjoyed the Philosophers illusion, of course. But so much gore? And to tell the truth, the play as a whole did not appeal to me in the way it would have done had there also been a *female* role.'

Heinrich returned to his automata. He rested his fingertips on the shoulders of the flaxen girl. 'Nor to me,' he agreed.

'Ah. You would prefer a female philosopher. Really?'

Eliza looked at her surroundings. Surely nothing she could propose in such a setting would seem outlandish? 'You are laughing at us, Mr Wix. The role would not necessarily be a philosopher. The time will come for novelty, don't you agree? I was envisaging a more – what? – feminine scenario. A comedy, perhaps. Disappearances, clever materialisations, mistaken identity, laughter closing with a kiss.'

'If I knew any Shakespeare I would say that is what your idea sounds like.'

'Why not?' Eliza laughed.

'And who do you suggest might play this female role, Eliza?' Devil's mouth was curling.

'Not Lucie. I could not agree to that. But Hilde, here,' Heinrich cried. 'When she is finished.'

Eliza said, 'I am an artist, and a model. I have always dreamed of acting, and I do not think it would be such a big leap to make.' Seeing Devil's face she protested too quickly, 'I'm not a fool, you know. You might at least let me try. I will even write you a comic playlet, if you like, and you can tell me what you think of it.'

'That sounds delightful. I am obliged to you. But you are overlooking the sad fact that the Palmyra is owned and managed by Jacko Grady. I have no control over his programme, and I don't believe your tender comic playlet will appeal to his low audiences.'

'That is true,' Eliza acknowledged.

'If I were the owner and manager, it would be a different matter. A sparkling comedy of illusion? Of course. The best tricks Carlo can devise? Certainly. Maybe Heinrich might assist with the engineering of the devices? My stage would be a perfect showcase for Lucie, also. Who knows what fame she might achieve?'

A silence fell.

Between them Devil and Eliza had wiped the plates clean of the last crumbs of food, and the wine bottle was empty. Devil still traced circles on the green baize with his forefinger.

'What is inside your Chinese fortune-teller, Heinrich?'

'Inside him? The mechanisms, of course.'

'Of course.' Devil stood up. 'It is late. You have been hospitable, Heinrich. Thank you.'

Heinrich put out his hand. 'We don't see many people, Lucie and I. We enjoyed our excursion the other evening with you, and Miss Dunlop and her friends. And you refused my money at the end of it, which doesn't happen often. It was also kind of you to notice my distress tonight and to walk all the way home with us. Therefore I believe the thanks are all due to you.' With the strange, sidelong look that Eliza attributed to shyness he shook Devil's hand.

Once they were outside in the Clerkenwell alley Eliza realised how late it was. She was thoroughly relieved to be out of Heinrich Bayer's domain, but the eeriness seemed to extend even to here. There was no sound, and few lights showed in the nearby tenements and warehouses. Damp clouded the air and muffled their footsteps as they hurried to the corner. Devil asked where she was going and she told him.

He said, 'I have to go only to Holborn, but Bayswater is too far to walk. What shall we do?'

Another two turns brought them closer to Smithfield where there was still torchlight and a sullen clatter of activity around the market. A dejected hansom stood at a corner, the horse's head hanging low and the driver dozing under his greatcoat. There was nothing for it, Eliza realised. Two cab rides in one night, and no money left over. At least she had gained a square meal, although the eeriness of Herr Bayer's workshop had depressed her appetite.

Devil followed her thoughts. He was embarrassed that he could not even pay for the girl to ride home in safety, when he would have wished to drive her to Bayswater in his own brougham.

'It is all very well for Bayer to say, *Vat is money?* as if he were royalty. It is always people who have plenty who profess their lack of interest in it. I will get some very soon, and then I will allow myself the luxury of dismissing its importance.'

Eliza thought of the afternoon's walk through South Kensington. It seemed a long time ago.

'Jasper was saying earlier that he intends to buy one of those fine white stucco houses with eight steps up to the front door. He will have a man in livery to open the door for him too, no doubt.'

'My house will have ten steps. And my man will have a finer set of whiskers than Jasper's man.'

They burst into laughter.

As they reached the hansom and Devil was holding open the door for her he asked, 'How long have you been walking out with Jasper Button, Eliza?'

'I am not walking out with him.'

'I think you are.'

He handed her up the step. The sad vehicle reeked of tobacco.

'Will you consider my idea?' she persisted. 'About the role?'

'When I own the Palmyra theatre, I promise I will do so.'

'When you *own* it?'

He stood back from the door, his black face hard under the brim of his bowler.

'Yes. What else did you imagine?'

He touched his hand to his hat and the driver whipped up the old horse.

FIVE

Eliza recalled the backstage realm at the Palmyra theatre as a chaos of casually naked limbs barely concealed by dressing screens, where discarded or not yet assumed costumes gaudy with feathers and sequins hung in wait for the strutting performers. It was a swarming, hectic and self-absorbed space stinking of perspiration and gas fumes, stale beer and face paint, where a half-consumed dinner of bread and cold beef lay on a table under which a bucket of piss stood in plain view. In her waking hours she mulled over the thrillingly disreputable vigour of all this, and the trapped din of the unseen audience reverberated in her head along with the jingle of tiny bells.

But when she slept, it was different. When she slept she became one of the performers. Amongst these creatures, who like a series of violently coloured butterflies had managed the transition from humdrum world to stage glamour, she grew wings and flew, she spiralled in dances, she sank in an exaggerated curtsey to acknowledge the roar of applause.

When she woke up from her dreams, she felt dull.

To be an artists' model had in her own estimation seemed daring, and she had certainly shocked her father and stepmother – this Eliza always found pleasant to contemplate – but now she realised that her own notions of what it was to reject proper behaviour were in themselves staid enough. Up until now she had felt fairly satisfied with the precariousness of her existence, but her spirits sank when she contemplated the stale routines of the day that actually lay ahead. A languid class in water-colour painting at the Rawlinson School did not compare with the seamy adulation she was offered in her dreams.

At this point, with an inevitability that was becoming familiar, her thoughts would turn to Devil Wix. If she wished for closer acquaintance with the theatre, surely it was Devil who could lead her to it? It was true that he had dismissed her barely thought-out suggestion about a female role, but – characteristically – she would not allow that to deter her. Eliza considered matters. The first strategy was to earn Devil's approval, and his gratitude if that were possible. She must find a way to direct paying customers to the box office in the Strand.

To this end, after the next life class, instead of leaving immediately once she was dressed and Mr Coope was out of the room, she lingered for a few minutes to talk to the students. Charles Egan and the others were delighted with this opportunity and they were soon established in a semicircle, with the young men's coats slung aside and their feet hooked up on chair rungs. Ralph Vine laced his fingers behind his head and tipped his seat at a reckless angle. Even Miss Frazier hovered within earshot. For her own part Eliza was enjoying the stimulating contrast between her nakedness of half an hour ago and the polite cadences of the present conversation.

She began by asking them, 'I wonder if any of you have seen the new variety show at the Palmyra theatre?'

'That old place?' Leonard Woolley shook his head. 'My father used to go to concerts there. It has been closed for years.'

'Indeed it was closed, but it has recently reopened as a variety hall. It is not much better than derelict even now, but you should go and see the magic act. The illusion is called the Execution of the Philosopher. I promise you, Mr Woolley, you will not believe your eyes.'

'Whatever you command, Miss Dunlop. May I persuade you to come with me?'

'Thank you. I have already seen the performance,' Eliza smiled at him. Some of the young men were languid and others were bumptious. None of them had interested her, even before her visits to the Palmyra and Herr Bayer's studio.

When she arrived for the next class Leonard Woolley and two others were quick to announce that they had followed her instructions and enjoyed a visit to the theatre.

'It's a rough sort of place, though. Who took you along there, Miss Dunlop, may I ask?'

'My sister and her husband.'

'Not your young man?' Ralph Vine slyly murmured.

'I don't have such a thing.'

'I saw you walking in the park with a chap who looked as if he'd like to be.'

Charles Egan mocked him. 'You might like it too, Viney, but that doesn't necessarily make it happen.'

'What did you think of the Philosophers illusion?' Eliza persisted.

Mr Woolley whistled. 'Top-notch, I have to say. I was astounded. Cutting off his head, you know. A strange person in the row in front of us nearly screamed her own head off. The trick is a waxwork of course. But how is it done?'

'I couldn't reveal any details.'

'But you do know? How come? Do tell us. I love theatrical illusions. They have such a primitive appeal.'

Everyone was interested now. Miss Frazier paused in the adjustment of her smock ties.

'I know in principle. I am acquainted with the performers.' Eliza couldn't resist the little boast. There was another whistle.

Ralph Vine said, 'Are you? Dark horse, Miss Dunlop. Gentlemen, who apart from me has not yet seen this fascinating show? I propose we put matters right tomorrow evening.'

All the male students went in an exuberant group to the Palmyra. Eliza crossed her fingers that Devil and Carlo would give their best performance, but she could come up with no reason for going to the theatre herself. She returned to her lodgings in Bayswater instead. After eating the usual dinner in the company of her two fellow lodgers she left the beef-coloured downstairs front room and withdrew to her bedroom. Laid out beside the oil lamp on the table in the tiny bay window were two quires of blank paper acquired at an advantageous price from the clerk of supplies at the Rawlinson School.

Eliza sat down, picked up her pencil and turned over the pages. She sighed as she did so, but she persevered. The playlet she had envisaged, an airy confection of lovers, a duenna, and cupboards into which people disappeared before comically tumbling out through a different set of doors, remained obstinately buried inside her head. She had tried for several evenings in succession but however hard she stared at her paper before pressing the lead pencil into its creamy whiteness, the actual words defied excavation. Who would have thought the business of writing could be so difficult? She knew the character she would play, had planned her elegant costume and even the way her hair would be dressed, but how did one make any of this happen?

'*Good evening, Charlotte,*' she wrote, the first line to be uttered by the lover, a role that would necessarily have to be taken by Devil Wix.

'*Good evening, sir.*'

Was that really all she could manage? The noise of the Palmyra's brutal audiences in likely response to this insipid exchange was all too easy to conjure. Eliza gnawed her lip and screwed up her eyes until the sheet of paper faded to a fuzzy grey rectangle, but the pencil obstinately refused to move. She listened to her upstairs neighbour's footsteps as they passed overhead, from the washstand to the wardrobe and back again. Miss Aynscoe was the overseer of an atelier specialising in fine beadwork and embroideries for ladies' clothing. She was so poor that her own garments seemed worn almost to the point of transparency, and the sparse evening meal provided for them by their landlady was probably the only food she ate all day. But then Miss Aynscoe lived within her means. Eliza did not, and she was perfectly well aware that her small capital would not last for ever. Or indeed, much beyond the next year. But what was the point of being alive, she reasoned, if everything were to be planned for and measured in advance? That was the way Faith and Matthew lived, and it did not appeal to her.

She shifted her position so that she sat more perfectly upright. It was tempting to let her eyes lose their focus, even to drift into the reverie of her hours of posing – for all her energy, this state of suspension always beckoned her – but there was work to be done. *Why* would a pair of lovers tumble into separate cupboards? To escape from the duenna, perhaps. *How* would the cabinet interiors conceal and then reveal their contents? Whose advice should she seek on these technical matters? Not Devil's, she instinctively knew that. Carlo Boldoni's, perhaps. At the prospect of this collaboration the tight wire that ran between her shoulders loosened a little. Frowning like a schoolgirl, Eliza wrote a few lines of dialogue that she hoped were tender and sprightly.

Reports of the show at the Palmyra circulated at the Rawlinson. The young men visited it a second time, recruiting more of their friends to accompany them, and on this occasion they continued with a long night in and out of the drinking parlours behind the Strand. Someone had narrowly avoided being arrested after snatching a bobby's helmet, someone else had fallen asleep on a porter's barrow in the fruit market and had only woken up when the man threw him off in favour of a few bushels of pippins.

'Viney, poor Viney proposed marriage to a young lady who sat on his knee for an hour and whispered her dark spells into his ear,' Charles Egan crowed.

This riotous evening rapidly became a totemic event for the whole group, and as a result they adopted the Palmyra and the Philosophers illusion in particular as their badge of dishonour. Ralph Vine swept through South Kensington in a long black cloak like Devil's, and the others started calling him Socrates.

Devil had told Jacko Grady that if there was to be no place for Heinrich Bayer in the company there would be no Philosophers either, and Grady had reluctantly agreed to include him again. Now a rival student coterie struck back by proclaiming their admiration for Bayer and the amazing Lucie. Two of them came to school wearing an approximation of his old-fashioned evening clothes, and one persuaded his fiancée to dress up like the doll and smile fixedly to the applause as they waltzed over the black-and-white tiles of the entrance hall.

As a result of this exuberance more and more of the Rawlinson School's students and their friends began to make their way to the Strand, and now they sat through the entire show as a collective demonstration of their commitment to understanding (prior to rejecting) the broadest spectrum of public taste.

A young polemicist from the sculpture school wrote an article entitled 'Art and Every Day. Static Gallery *versus* Mobile Music Hall' for a pamphlet that was read by some of the professors. As a result of this, Raleigh Coope and his current best protégé, a versatile young man of artistic promise, took two seats in the front row at the Palmyra to see the Execution of the Philosopher.

And at the end of the next life class Eliza was surprised when Mr Coope unrolled a sketch for her attention.

It was a lively pencil drawing of Devil in his robes, holding up Jasper's waxwork head of Carlo Boldoni.

'It's a very strong likeness,' she murmured.

Raleigh Coope waved this aside. 'Mr Gardiner knows how to draw.' Unlike some of the present company, he might have added. 'He is much more interested in the subtext, the way that the piece subverts the biblical and classical mythologies. There is a subject here, Miss Dunlop.'

'Yes, I see.' Eliza did not think mythological subversion had been Devil and Carlo's first intention.

97

'If you are acquainted with the performer, you might enquire whether he is interested in sitting for Mr Gardiner?'

'Yes, Mr Coope.'

'The show has its slender merits, as Mr Gardiner has noticed. But it lacks an audience. The house was half empty on the night we visited. Doesn't the management know how to attract paying customers?'

'It seems not,' she had to say.

A development which Eliza could hardly have foreseen now took place at the art school.

Attached to the back of the building was a mews and in this more humble environment – where the windows were not so tall, the north light less plentiful and the heating governed by economy – another establishment was housed. It had been set up as a philanthropic gesture by Professor Rawlinson himself and it was dedicated to the teaching of what he and Raleigh Coope chose to call commercial art.

'For all the world,' Charles Egan had once scornfully remarked, 'as if that were not a contradiction in terms.'

The students at the secondary college were boys and young men who possessed a degree of artistic talent but did not aspire to become artists, and were in any case from poor families unable to afford the much higher fees at the school itself. Those applicants who were fortunate enough to be selected were taught by expert practitioners the techniques of signwriting, illustration for manufacturers, magazines and catalogues, and even of constructing models and mannequins for display purposes. Once they were Rawlinson trained, they easily and quickly found employment. When Eliza told Jasper about this he had sighed enviously.

'If only I had known of such a school when I was sixteen years of age.' Jasper's own studies and apprenticeship had been hard, although easier to endure than his childhood in Stanmore.

Mr Coope had a fondness for lively and ambitious young men and he diligently involved himself with the curriculum of the technical school. One afternoon he addressed the class of illustrators and signwriters on the use of art as a means of selling goods.

'How might you employ a visual image to encourage a purchase?' he asked them. This was not a question he would have put to Mr Egan and his cohorts, who were paying for the chance one day to be able to write RA after their names.

'By making a positive association?' someone attempted.

'Yes. Very good.'

The group dutifully discussed the possible combination of sturdy oak trees with health-giving patent medicines, and of portraits of beautiful young women with face creams. Mr Coope swallowed a yawn. Mr Gardiner and his enjoyment of the Philosophers illusion crept into his head and he was thinking idly of the Palmyra theatre's rows of empty seats as he asked his class, 'What if it were not a commodity to be sold but – say – an event?'

There was some more tedious discussion, this time of hand-bills and posters.

A red-haired boy at the back of the room raised his hand.

'You could do the opposite, couldn't you?'

Raleigh Coope arched one eyebrow.

'I mean, sir, by not telling the people too much but in some way making them want to know more?'

'Please go on.'

The boy's face flushed as bright as his hair.

'Sir, if I'm lectured over and over about, I dunno, who is going to preach in church on Sunday and if I have to listen to parson telling me what I have to renounce so as to save my soul, with my ma always reminding me even on a working day, then I starts saying to myself, I don't care. But if it's kept a secret, say, what really will get me to heaven, then I'm going to try my hardest to find out, aren't I? It's only natural.'

The rest of the class was tittering but the boy said defiantly, 'Well, I am going to. It stands to reason.'

'You have an idea there, Mr Cockle. Continue with it,' Coope said. The boy's forehead furrowed as he thought even harder.

'So, if I wants to get people to come to my meeting perhaps I'd leave a hint they can see everywhere, not giving away so much but making them feel hungry to find out more. The idea is they will be worrying inside their noddles, "Am I going to miss what he's got? Whatever it is?" 'The boy jabbed a paint-splotched finger at his grinning neighbour.

Coope clapped his big hands. 'Make them hungry, as you say, and whet their appetites further by filling the air with the scent of a fine roast.'

'But folk will be disappointed when they get no pig at the end, wun't they?' someone muttered.

Coope looked over the rows of faces, many of them clearly familiar with what it felt like to be denied roast pork. He was a sympathetic man and he wished he had chosen his words and his example more adroitly, so he hurried on.

'Here is an exercise for you.'

He had thought of setting them to the lettering of a handbill, but the young man with the unfortunate head of hair had accidentally come up with a more interesting proposition. So out of a moment's embarrassment and otherwise acting on an impulse, Raleigh Coope began to tell them about the Palmyra theatre and the want of an audience for what he privately judged to be a music-hall turn. It was an audacious and well-executed turn, it was true, but it was mostly George Gardiner's enthusiasm for it that had fired his own.

'What might you do to bring in an audience, using a visual image, gentlemen?'

There was a long, baffled silence. Too audibly someone scratched his head. Then, slowly, the red-haired boy raised his hand.

'Sir?'

Devil left the stew of alleyways and trudged out into Holborn. December's bitter wind made him hunch his shoulders and clench his fists inside his tattered pockets. His belly rumbled with hunger and with the less easily assuaged pangs of general dissatisfaction. He was thoroughly tired of sharing his lodgings with an irritable dwarf of eccentric habits. Maria Hayes's demands were intensifying according to the length of time that Carlo spent under her roof, and her husband had begun to glare at Devil with dull coals of suspicion in his eyes. Reaching a street corner, he hung there with his chest hollowed against the gusts as he tried to decide where to go. There must surely be a tavern nearby with a fire, and a landlord who would take his promise in exchange for a tot of brandy?

But no such place came immediately to mind so his steps tended southwards, towards the Palmyra.

In the distance in an angle of two walls, splashed over sooty brickwork, he saw a painted palm tree. The size of it – three feet tall, if it was an inch – and the insolent brightness of whitewash against the dingy background were what caught his attention in the first place. But then it came to him that its outline was entirely familiar because it was a crisp stencil-cut version of the palm that crowned the theatre pillars. The same palm motif had been taken as an ornament for the head of Jacko Grady's playbills and posters and it also adorned the theatre's programmes.

Devil splashed through the mud to examine it more closely.

The whitewash had been applied haphazardly through the outlines of a stencil held up against the wall. Trickles ran down from the curved leaves and dribbled from the base. It was clearly fresh. Devil ran his thumb over a section of the trunk and scraped the brick beneath. The whitewash was only just turning grey with wind-blown dust. He walked on and passed a dozen more palms. As he drew near to the Strand he noticed arrows in the same whitewash, painted over walls and lintels, on steps and on the stones underfoot, all of them pointing in the direction of the Palmyra. People hurried by, but Devil estimated that most of them bestowed at least a wondering glance on trees and arrows.

He reached the Strand. Here another much bigger arrow

101

pointed from the street towards the theatre entrance. A ragged street sweeper prodded his broom at it.

When Carlo arrived for the matinee Devil asked him what he thought of this proliferation of palms. The dwarf shrugged.

'Grady's doing?'

Devil thought this was highly unlikely. 'Grady? You mean, he's had a selling notion and then paid to have this done? Or is there some third person involved? Someone we know nothing about?'

The dwarf shrugged again. He and Devil were constantly at odds, chafed by too much proximity and downcast after a run of poor houses.

'Ask him, if you're so interested.' He swung away and took the philosopher's wig out of its box. The horsehair was matted with grime from its excursions beneath the stage.

Devil never spoke to Jacko Grady unless it was impossible to avoid him. He undid his buttons and took off his shirt, ready to put on his costume. Next to him the soprano was preparing for the stage by gargling and spitting linctus into a tin bowl. From her other side Bascia darted Devil a thin, complicit smile of disgust.

The next day there were more palm trees, a white forest of them waving all across Covent Garden as far as Trafalgar Square. Devil saw a man stop walking, turn in his path and follow with his eyes the direction of an arrow. That night there was a somewhat bigger audience, and the atmosphere of expectation amongst the crowd raised the quality of the performance. There were some Rawlinson students present, and the Philosophers received by far the longest and loudest applause. Grady intercepted Devil and Carlo as they came offstage. His thumbs were tucked into the pockets of his grease-blotched waistcoat.

'What is this, Wix?'

'What is what?'

'The trees.'

The bustle of the wings might not have existed. Prickling

102

with antagonism the two men appraised each other. From the belligerence of his question Devil understood that Grady was concealing suspicious alarm, and so most probably was not behind the strange multiplying of whitewashed palms. This did not reassure him. It could only mean that some other individual threatened to intrude, one who might be more devious and therefore a more formidable rival than greedy Grady.

'I have no idea,' Devil blandly countered, hoping to convey that he did. 'The question is – is it criticism or applause?'

Grady's mind was working, but the labour did not bring forth any explanation or a reason to blame Boldoni and Wix. He contented himself with a generalised thrust. 'You need to get up some new material. Use the rigmaroles from your audition. Cards, memory, vanishing. Your box trick will be stale by next month.'

'I don't believe it will, but to offer you some of our astonishing new tricks will be a great pleasure.'

The cabinet was carried offstage and they followed it, leaving Grady at his vantage point. As soon as the stagehands deposited the piece Carlo pressed his ear to the mechanism that controlled the hidden doors.

'The hinge is catching. It takes a full second longer for the door to spring. You might pay more attention to the act, Wix, and less to your personal ambitions,' he grumbled.

'You heard the audience tonight. My ambition will pay off, and then perhaps you will appreciate what I have been trying to do.'

'No one will ever appreciate you as sincerely as you do yourself.'

Devil ignored him. The dwarf's carping pessimism and sense of his own importance were irksome, but whenever he thought of reclaiming for himself his lodgings and his act – the two halves of his life, because he had nothing else – he was forced back to the bare truth that he needed Carlo more than the dwarf needed him.

'Ten per cent of every house more than eighty per cent full,' he murmured. 'Tonight we were three-quarters sold.' The ribbon of gold that had shone so enticingly in Devil's dreams at the beginning of the enterprise had drooped and grown tarnished, but in recent days it had started to glitter all over again.

'New hinges,' Carlo bared his wolf's teeth. 'Tomorrow.'

Heinrich Bayer passed with Lucie in his arms, her unmarked satin slippers skimming an inch from the floor. She had a new costume, a narrow skirt of heavy oyster-coloured silk worn over a high bustle in the latest style. But it was the other automaton, the manikin glimpsed in Bayer's studio, which occupied Devil's thoughts.

He was going to need Carlo's cooperation for a trick much more difficult to execute than the Philosophers illusion. The dwarf would have to be kept sweet.

'Tomorrow, my friend, of course,' he agreed in a voice as silken as Lucie's gown.

If the fine art students were piqued by the apprentices' appropriation of their theatre, they did not retaliate by withdrawing their support for it. Stark black cloaks became the preferred costume for a certain section of the house, and each night the swoop of the executioner's blade and the crash of the head into the basket were greeted with a louder roar. The severed head's words from the black depths of the cabinet carried a whispering echo as twenty others mouthed them from the stalls. With the warm swell of approval buoying him up, Devil's snapping of the sword blade and plea for forgiveness found a real pathos that even Carlo could not fault. The smoke coiled with devilish effect in the flashes of blue and silver gaslight that were now, with long practice, perfectly synchronised. The bitter cascade of gold coins at the end drew a storm of applause.

The Execution of the Philosopher illusion had reached its point of perfection. Word of mouth spread from the students to their friends, their families, and their friends' friends and families. The palm trees had caused their own stir, and there had even been a picture and a teasing paragraph about it in the *London Illustrated News*. For an entire week the number of seats sold was greater with each successive night. Devil quickly concluded that the rumbustious youths who had taken to attending performances in costume were also in some way responsible for the street decorations. So long as the business was not a plot of Jacko Grady's, he did not much care what young gentlemen mysteriously did with their time and money. As patrons of the Palmyra went they were on the harmless side, and therefore more than welcome.

Two nights before Christmas Eve, two hundred people took their places for the evening performance.

'Two hundred,' Devil repeated to Carlo as they waited to take the stage. Perched on his stilts, with the wicker cage supporting his gown, the dwarf's enlarged shoulders nudged his. Devil added, 'I may not have a Varsity man's head for mathematics, but I do know that figure represents eighty per cent of capacity. I am looking forward to seeing Jacko Grady's face.'

'You think he'll give you the money, do you?' Under the make-up Carlo's face was flushed and his eyes glassy.

'We shall see,' Devil said simply.

At the end of the show the place where Grady sat to hand out the performers' shillings and pence was taken by his deputy, a terrier of a man who wore his hat tipped on the back of his head like a bookmaker.

'Two hundred seats,' Devil growled when the man passed him the usual two shillings and sixpence.

'What's that?'

'Eighty per cent capacity. Tonight Carlo and I get ten per cent of the takings.'

Grady's deputy sneered. 'Next,' he called to the waiting line and waved Devil and Carlo aside. Devil planted himself squarely in front of the table and leaned over the man.

'Ten per cent. According to my contract, signed by Jacko Grady.'

'Take it up with Grady, then. *Next*.'

Devil's fist smashed down, sending a little pile of coins rolling.

'Contract!' he shouted.

'You can roll up your so-called contract and stick it up your arse. So far as I am concerned,' the man said. Devil grabbed him by the coat lapels and hoisted him out of his seat. Coins spilled all over the floor and the other performers catcalled and jostled as they snatched them up. The deputy's legs feebly kicked in the air and the table overturned.

Carlo sadly shook his head.

'Won't help,' he sighed.

'Give us our money,' Devil snarled into the man's face.

'Not mine to give,' the other retorted. Recognising the truth of this Devil slammed him back into his chair and took up the rickety card table as if he were about to joust with it. Impatience at the delay began to ripple down the queue. Devil poked the legs of the table at the deputy's chest.

'Tell Grady. I want my money. Tomorrow.'

'Tell him yourself. Next, I say, and look sharp the rest of you if you're wanting to get paid tonight.'

Devil dropped the table on the deputy's feet. With the man's yelp of pain to console him he stalked away and Carlo followed. Outside it was bitterly cold, with clots of wet snow swirling through the sepia glimmer of the street lamps. In silence they began to trudge towards Holborn but Carlo walked so slowly that Devil gave up the pursuit of his own furious thoughts to look round for him. The dwarf pressed his hand against a leprous wall for support as he coughed and spat the product into the gutter.

'Are you ill?' Devil asked him.

'Yes.' Carlo was too tired even to attempt a sharp retort.

Devil sighed. 'Come on.' With their heads down they trod the familiar way back through the alleys to the lodging house. When they reached the attic room it was hardly warmer than outside. The squalor of it struck even Devil after he had lit the lamp. He looked around at the mounds of props and boxes, the unswept boards and dirty pots. Carlo's white doves sat in their cage, reproachful black eyes on Devil. He stirred up a fire and the dwarf sank into his blanket. He drank the toddy that Devil mixed for him and then lay in a piteous huddle. He closed his eyes.

'This is how our Sallie went,' he murmured.

'You're not going anywhere. Except to the Palmyra theatre.'

Carlo only shivered.

'We are about to make our fortunes, my friend. Two hundred seats sold, remember.'

'I want to sleep.'

Devil lay in his bed and listened for most of the night to the dwarf's feverish tossing and turning. In the morning Carlo's face was hollow and his eyes were sunk in their sockets. Devil let him rest and went out to buy food that Carlo could barely pick at. As the time approached for them to make their way to the theatre Devil fussed from bed to table, peering at the small heap of skin and bones under the blanket and praying that the dwarf would at least get up from his bed. He was hardly able to hope that he would actually be able to perform. At the last possible moment Carlo dragged himself upright. He coughed fitfully and lurched to his feet.

At the foot of the stairs Maria Hayes was waiting for them. She raised her thick eyebrows.

'Compliments of the season, ma'am,' Devil murmured. Carlo moved like a shadow behind him and Devil believed he could feel in his own bones the shudder of a suppressed cough. The landlady would welcome a sick dwarf even less readily than a healthy one.

'Rent is owing, Mr Wix. For two occupants.' Her voice was like ice in a bucket.

'And it will be paid this very evening, Mrs Hayes. Boldoni and Wix are becoming quite the spectacular success, as you know.'

Devil had taken care to present the landlady with a pair of tickets, and she and her husband had duly visited the Palmyra. For two or three days thereafter relations had been cordial, even admiring, and Carlo had been tacitly accepted as a lodger even though none of the Hayes family ever spoke to him. But when the rent was overdue Mrs Hayes was immune even to Devil's persuasions.

'This evening.' She turned the phrase into a threat, her mouth as yielding as a cut-throat razor. She withdrew into her quarters.

As they walked up the alley Devil grimly said, 'Carlo, we have to work. Tonight and every night. Otherwise' – but there was no need for him to say what *otherwise* would involve. It lay hungry all about them in the ruined houses, even in the meagre shelter beneath market carts, and for the unluckiest in corners where the sleet-laden fingers of the wind dug a little less keenly.

Carlo looked up at him. For the first time in the long weeks since they had met he seemed fragile. Usually his tiny frame was springing with energy but tonight his neck seemed hardly strong enough to bear the weight of his large head. His cracked lips barely moved when he spoke, and he still winced.

'I know.'

He was brave, for such a scrap of a man. Devil felt an urge to pull his cap down and wrap his ragged muffler closer about his throat for him, but these signs of tenderness embarrassed him. He touched the dwarf's shoulder instead, quickly withdrew his hand and turned towards the Strand.

The audience were already taking their seats. In anticipation of the Christmas holiday there was a hum of good-humoured anticipation rising through the auditorium. Devil put his eye to a chink in the curtain. More than two hundred in tonight, that was certain. As soon as the show was over he would force Jacko Grady to an accounting. He made this decision and then put it aside in order to give all his mind to the performance.

Carlo looked like a death's head as Devil led him out into the lights. A cohort of costumed philosophers in the cheaper seats roared at his appearance. The familiar moves of the playlet began. In the third row he was surprised to see Eliza Dunlop's face turned up to the stage.

'I shall never yield my secret,' Carlo said. His voice was hoarse and would not have been audible at the back of the theatre had not the students raised theirs in echo. 'Never, while breath remains in this body.'

The dwarf's body was visibly wobbling atop his stilts. The occult symbols stitched to his robe swayed and shimmered.

Devil swung the blade and crushed the small phial of cochineal liquid concealed in his palm. In perfect synchrony the percussion powder detonated in the wings, the lights went down to the crash of a chord and Carlo fell in a heap at the evil philosopher's feet.

The lights flared again, catching the coils of smoke rising through the vents in the stage. As always the stink of it caught in the back of Devil's throat. Red liquid ran down the sword blade and smirched his fingers.

The trick was wrong. He knew it even before Carlo fell.

Instead of a neat heap of empty robes supported by a wicker frame there was an inert body. Carlo lay in plain view, his wig askew and his robe caught up to expose a rough wooden limb extension.

The audience had quietened. They waited, collective breath drawn in, for the interesting new direction the illusion must take.

A second of time stretched for Devil into a creeping eternity, and Carlo did not stir. From the darkness at the back of the hall came the slow clapping of a single pair of hands and then more handclaps drew out a whispered hiss that swelled in an instant into a wave of jeering.

Devil held up his hand. 'The performer is ill.'

He looked over two rows of grinning heads into Eliza Dunlop's eyes.

'Dead?' someone bawled.

'Dead drunk,' another hollered.

'Must be living. 'E's still got 'is 'ed on.'

Devil waved his hand to the wings.

'Bring down the curtain.'

When they were screened from the booing and stamping he knelt at Carlo's side. The dwarf had fainted. Devil shook the wicker cage and his eyes rolled up in his head.

'God help us,' Devil muttered.

Even the stagehands, the roughest of men, were disconcerted. Between them Devil and one of the men easily lifted the dwarf's body with the dangling stilts still attached, and the others bore the cabinet into the wings. Jacko Grady was seething there.

'Christ Jesus, Wix, what game are you playing now?'

'Does it look like a game?'

The roar of the audience battered the curtain.

'Get the next act on. Where are the bloody acrobats?' the manager yelled. Bascia and her brother ran past, bells tinkling. They somersaulted into the lights as their music struck up. Backstage Carlo was carried into the airless dressing space. They laid him on the floor, took off the costume trappings and Devil stooped to unfasten the stilts. It was awkward enough to do and yet the dwarf had to carry out the manoeuvre in seconds beneath the stage trapdoor before he flew to take up his cramped position in the cabinet.

'Get some water,' Devil commanded but no one in the little crowd of gawping performers made a move. They stood looking down at the unconscious dwarf as if they too could not quite believe that this was not part of a new trick.

There was a movement at the edge of the circle.

'Let him breathe, for God's sake', Eliza Dunlop said. She knelt to place her hand on Carlo's forehead and then lifted his wrist to feel his pulse.

'He is burning up with fever. How long has he been ill?' Her eyes met Devil's again, across the prostrate body.

'Two days.'

'He should not be here. He should be in his bed.' Her rebuke was crisp. Even in his anxiety Devil was irritated by her assumption that he and Carlo had any choice in the matter of where to be.

'Thank you for your opinion,' he snapped.

110

'Not at all.' She leaned closer to Carlo and as if her proximity communicated itself to him the dwarf's eyelids fluttered open. His chest heaved as he tried to cough. Eliza held up her hand and a cup of water was at last passed through the knot of spectators. As she gently supported Carlo's shoulders and raised the cup to his lips Grady appeared, crimson in the face and furious.

'Move, all of you. It's a sick dwarf here, not a peep show. This performance is already a catastrophe. Get on and give 'em their money's worth.'

The other performers slid aside, leaving only Devil and Heinrich Bayer beside Eliza and Carlo. Grady planted his legs apart and his belly jutted over them like a ship's prow. Carlo breathed out a tiny sigh and turned his head away from its shadow. His horsehair wig was forced askew and Eliza removed it, stroking the dwarf's matted hair back from his face.

Grady said, 'I hope whatever plague the creature has is not infectious. Take him away, Wix. And get yourselves back for tomorrow's matinee if you want to go on working for me.'

'Wait one moment,' Devil countered. He stepped across Carlo and brought his face up close to Grady's, although the man's breath was foetid enough to drive him back again. 'We have a contract to discuss. You owe me—'

Grady spat out a laugh. 'After tonight's mess? Nothing.'

Devil was ready to swing the first punch when Eliza spoke his name. He glanced down and saw distaste clear in her face, and it caused him an odd pang to realise that it was directed at him.

'Not now,' she said.

Devil uncurled his fist. Grady shifted his bulk and walked away at a commendable lick.

'I will help you to take Carlo home,' Eliza said to Devil. She eased the dwarf to a sitting position and let him rest in the circle of her arm. Devil thought briefly of what *home* might mean to another man: a tidy fire with a kettle on the hob, a chair drawn up beside it, and a woman looking up with a smile from her work basket. This sentimental picture he firmly dismissed.

'If you like,' he said, made graceless by the rapid procession of unfamiliar reflections.

'Carlo? Might you be able to stand up?' Eliza murmured. The dwarf's teeth chattered with the violence of his shivering. But he clasped Eliza's hand in his burning fingers and struggled to his feet. Between them they took off his trailing cloak, put on his street coat for him and wound the muffler around his throat.

'I would come with you . . .' Heinrich said, but he turned his eyes to the chair where Lucie sat waiting for his attention. Her satin shoes and the pale hem of her skirts were lifted clear of the dirty floor.

'We'll manage,' Devil said.

Carlo did his utmost, but his legs would not support him. Devil grunted, stooped and then hoisted him over his shoulder as he had done once before. The dwarf groaned but he made no protest. Eliza shadowed them in silence, down the passageways that echoed with the din of the theatre, and out into the eternal rain beside the Strand. Pinpricks of driven ice needled their faces. Another ride in a swaying hansom brought them to the head of the lane that doglegged towards the alley with Maria Hayes's house at the far end of it. The way was too narrow for the driver to proceed any further. With Carlo still slung over Devil's shoulder they walked the rest of the way past windows where weak lights glimmered behind the dirty panes, and mute stares followed their progress. Just once a bundle in a doorway roused itself to cackle after them. Devil heard the hesitation in Eliza's steps.

'I am afraid we're not heading for the Savoy.'

'I did not imagine so.'

At the low door of the house Devil held a finger to his lips. He did not want to bring Mrs Hayes out of her lair, although at this time of the evening she and her husband would most likely be sitting at their table with a bottle between them. They

112

climbed the stairs, Eliza feeling her way in the unfamiliar black-ness, and gained the attic room. Devil lowered Carlo's body on to his own bed and groped for matches and a candle.

He felt rather than heard Eliza draw in her breath as she examined their quarters. He pushed past her in the confined space and lit a second candle. There was no lamp oil left. Their shadows briefly reared on the stained walls.

Eliza bent over Carlo. The dwarf was shivering violently enough to crack his bones. Devil took the meagre covers from Carlo's bed on the floor and laid all their spare clothing on top of him.

'Make up the fire,' Eliza ordered.

He did as he was told.

She sat on the edge of the iron bedstead, Carlo's hand folded in her own. She watched him intently, sometimes murmuring a soothing word, her pale skin amber in the candle glow. Devil waited, not looking directly at her, all too aware that without her he would be at a loss for what to do next, and therefore grateful for her presence. After a time Carlo drifted into a muttering doze and Eliza gently released his hand. She took off her outdoor clothes and put them aside, and Devil took this as a sign that she intended to stay and help.

'Will you fetch a doctor?' she said. It was not a suggestion.

'I don't know any doctors.' Rain scratched on the window and Devil stood closer to the smoky fire. He indicated the chair but Eliza ignored it.

'Whose house is this?'

Devil told her about Maria Hayes, warning her at the same time, but Eliza ignored that. She left the room and he listened to her footsteps descending the stairs. It was perhaps fifteen minutes before she returned. There was colour in her cheeks but she was composed as she took her place beside Carlo once more.

'That lump of a boy's run for a doctor,' she said. 'I had to give him sixpence.'

The dwarf's head rolled on the mattress and he murmured

disjointedly. He called Eliza Sallie, and struggled to sit up. Eliza put her arms round him and made him lie again.

Within the hour, footsteps came clumping up the stairs. Following the briefest knock, Maria Hayes's inquisitive face poked round the door.

'Doctor's here,' she sniffed. 'But I don't want dirty diseases in my rooms. The creature will have to go somewhere else. I told you.'

Devil could mollify her, that much at least was within his power. The doctor puffed up the last steps and when he appeared they saw he was almost as fat as Jacko Grady, with a nose like a punnet of strawberries and a smell of alcohol about him. The boy followed and stood gaping until his mother pushed him out. The doctor gave Carlo a cursory examination as Devil cajoled the landlady with promises of money and, without actually speaking of it, other attentions. She refused all his offers and finally Devil was obliged to reach into his inner pocket. A pile of coins clinked into her hand. Eliza levelly observed all this.

The doctor stood back from the bed.

'The fever must be purged,' he said. 'No other course of action will have the proper result.' He opened his greasy leather bag and extracted a glass bottle, handing it with a leer to Eliza. 'A large spoonful of this, three times a day. Keep him warm, and you could give him a tot when he fancies one. Merry Christmas to you.'

Eliza hunted for a spoon amongst the pots and crumbs on the table. The doctor told Devil that his fee would be a guinea but Devil only scowled, and after searching his pockets with theatrical disbelief he produced half that amount. He advised the man that he could take it or leave it, and eventually the doctor wisely took what he could get. Maria Hayes went to see him out. From the threshold she warned, 'I said the dwarf can't stay here.'

Devil suavely promised her that he would soon be gone.

'And you.' Mrs Hayes pointed at Eliza. 'This is a respectable house.'

The briefest glimpse of the premises had told Eliza this was hardly the case. She gave a scornful laugh. 'I am a nurse,' she lied.

'A nurse of what?'

Eliza turned her back. She sniffed the medicine. The smell was of bitter aloes and rhubarb. The door slammed.

'Help me,' she ordered Devil. Between them they lifted Carlo and put the spoon between his teeth. He retched and brown liquid trickled down his chin but most of it was swallowed.

Now that they were alone again Eliza asked him, 'Why do you live like this? You are a performer in a theatre, not a pauper, surely?'

Devil tried a casual shrug. He didn't reckon too much on home comforts because he hadn't known any for so long, but he was ashamed for Eliza Dunlop to see him in this dismal place.

'You think it lacks a woman's touch?'

'Perhaps,' she said.

Her gaze was disconcerting, and Devil was not used to being disconcerted by any woman. He thought that for a good-looker there was something oddly sharp and pointed about her, and she was too young to be so decisive and confident of herself. His instincts warned him to be wary, but still he was glad of her assistance in this present crisis.

Carlo could not be allowed to die, that much he did know.

Eliza said, 'We shall have to take it in turns to sit and watch him. You can take the first rest, if you like.' She cocked a glance towards the shred of a bed where Carlo normally slept.

Devil was surprised and relieved. 'You are staying here? Do you not have a home to go to?'

Eliza paused. 'Not really, until the day after tomorrow.'

Faith and Matthew and her nephews were expecting her to join them for Christmas dinner, and afterwards there would be games, and Faith would play the piano for the carols when their father and stepmother came. Until then no one would be looking for her.

'But why? You don't know Carlo. Or me, come to that.'

'Surely I do, just a little, don't I?' When she smiled, he noticed, her face became lovely as the sharpness dissolved. 'Perhaps I just feel sorry for you both.'

His hand swept the room, a lordly gesture.

'I can't imagine why.'

SIX

The bells of St Giles's church rang out in a hard frost on Christmas Eve. The soot on windowsills and door lintels was briefly overlaid with a sparkling rime like metal filings, and the city's smoke gathered in lavender folds under a vacant sky. Even at the furthermost end of the alley festivity proclaimed itself as Annie Fowler's girls drifted past the tarnished silvery star someone had nailed to the door of her house. The children ran up and down begging for pennies from any passer-by who might be touched by a small degree of goodwill generated by plenty of brandy. Downstairs at Devil's lodgings the Hayes family prepared for their celebration by hanging up a holly branch and carrying in an extra supply of jugs and bottles.

Up in the attic room they heard the bells ring, but there was no thought of Christmas.

Carlo grew worse. The drunken doctor's violent purgative did its work. Time and again Eliza took the tin pail of vomit and flux out to the privy in the back yard and emptied it, only for the dwarf to need it again. His fever still raged. Holding him in her arms as if he were her child, Eliza sponged his face with cool water, spooned bread soaked in warm milk into his mouth, and soon afterwards caught it in the pail. Carlo was delirious, calling out constantly for his mother and sister. His small body shrank and his skin turned to grey paper mottled with dull red blotches. Devil could only watch in despair.

'I won't give him another drop of this poison. It's killing him,' Eliza shouted. She tipped the remainder of the medicine into the bucket. She sent Devil out to buy kindling and coal, food, tea, brandy, lamp oil and soap. When he protested she scolded him. 'Surely you have money put aside. Where is it? In a bag hidden under these floorboards?'

She was almost right, although she certainly overestimated the sum involved. It wasn't easy to save anything out of the money Jacko Grady paid his acts.

'What if I have a different use in mind for my shillings?' Devil grumbled.

'What possible use? Maybe to buy yourself a silk hat? A Turkey carpet for your grand rooms?'

Pricked by her scorn he retorted, 'A theatre.'

'Ah, of course, so you said. But indulge your fantasy next week, not now. Go out and buy what your poor friend needs. Or must I do it myself?'

'No,' Devil sighed. It was easier to spend his money than hold up a bucket to one end or the other of a dying dwarf.

Soon a bright fire was burning and the lamp made a warm glow where Eliza had swept the floor and scrubbed the pots. As darkness came there was nothing left for them to do but sit by the bed and listen to the bells. Carlo slept. Devil estimated from the look of him that the dwarf could hardly survive the night. It was Eliza's turn to doze on the floor, but she showed no inclination to leave her perch at the fireside. Her gaze had been locked into the flames for more than an hour and her absolute stillness seemed unnatural to Devil. He was thoroughly tired of his own company and he wanted to stir the young woman into a response, any response. Talk became imperative.

'What do you think about, all this time?' he demanded. His voice cracked the silence, over-loud.

Eliza slowly turned her head. 'I don't believe I was *thinking* exactly.' She seemed undecided whether to say more. The room was quiet except for the hiss of coals. 'I wait, I look at the fire, and I'm drawn away.'

'I see. Is it a pleasant experience?'

'Yes.'

Her voice softened and this made a difference. Perhaps there were other aspects of Eliza Dunlop that were neither spiny nor scornful.

She added, 'My sister Faith used to hate my doing it when we were children. If we had to sit for a long time in church, or if we were not allowed to play because we were wearing clean aprons, I could be drawn away and she would be left behind. She used to kick my ankles and pull a face like *this*.' Eliza crossed her eyes and stuck out her tongue. 'But I wouldn't even see her. I was submerged. That is the closest word I can come up with, I'm not very good at describing what absence feels like. It doesn't worry me. I have always thought of the ability to take myself elsewhere as a gift.'

'It is a useful gift for an artists' model.'

He had a sly intention to set her off balance with this reference to her occupation but she only nodded, and he regretted the impulse.

'There is a picture on the wall of the life room, where I pose for the students. As a matter of fact they are the same young gentlemen who have been coming to see you and Carlo at the Palmyra.'

Eliza looked for his reaction. Devil said nothing, deliberately absorbing this new information and storing it to be considered at a more opportune moment.

Disappointed, she went on, 'It's a picture of the sea. When I'm holding the pose it's as if I am under the water, but with no sensation of cold or choking or fear. When the hours are over and I come back I feel rested. Clean.'

He waited for more, chin propped in his hand.

Carlo shifted and muttered in his fevered sleep but then he sank again.

'You are thinking it sounds strange.'

'Yes, I am.' Because it *was* strange. Did she expect him to think otherwise? All his own instincts led him to deny reverie, because the images of Stanmore village and a burning barn might rise up. Gabe always seemed close enough. He saw the boy's flailing dark shape in a penumbra of flame all too readily, in his nightmares and in the shadowed corners of his waking hours. He wasn't going to allow him or the past to colonise his thoughts, and so offer him better opportunity for his haunting.

Eliza went to Carlo's side. She stroked his forehead as she listened to his painful breaths. They were irregular, with slow seconds of silence intervening.

'How long, do you think?' Devil asked. He expected to hear the rattle at any moment.

'He will not die,' Eliza answered, as if she could stop death's approach. She poured water from a cracked ewer into a basin, soaped and rinsed her hands and poured the slops into the bucket.

I am alive at least, Devil thought. *We are alive.*

'Will you make me some more of that lemon brew?' he asked.

'If you would like it, yes.'

He had scowled at the long list of purchases she handed him but when Eliza heated milk and mixed it with lemon and honey and a scrape of nutmeg, he resented the expenditure a little less. The sight of a woman stirring a pan over the heat with little flicks of a slim wrist was soothing. When the thick sweet-sourness of the posset on his tongue reminded him of his mother, and little Hector Crumhall sitting at her side, he didn't immediately crush the memory into the darkness of his skull.

When he put the cup aside Eliza rinsed it and replaced it on the shelf. She said, 'One of the professors, Mr Raleigh Coope, showed me a pencil sketch one of the students made of you as the evil philosopher.'

'Of me? I gave no permission.'

She laughed at him. 'I believe this is a free country, and Mr

Coope and his student had paid for their seats. It's a very good drawing, a handsome likeness.'

Devil liked the sound of this. 'Ah. That makes all the difference.'

'The artist, a Mr Gardiner, would like to know if you would care to sit for him in your stage costume?'

'To sit?'

'Yes.' Patiently. 'For your portrait.'

'I don't think so.'

He had nothing to do with portraits. They were for the solid citizens, the possessors of mahogany tables and antimacassars. Devil looked round him. He experienced a sense of dislocation from the room with its faint appearance of order lent by Eliza's presence, the fading dwarf, the echo of Christmas bells and the kiss of frost against the windowpanes. He felt like an interloper in his own existence and he wondered for a moment where he really belonged, and where he would finish up when all the furious activity of his days was finally over. What did Carlo Boldoni have to show for his passage through the world, now that he was about to make his exit from it? Black wings spread over Devil's head, dimming the lamplight, and he shivered. To ward them off he stood abruptly and leaned over the bedside. If – when – Carlo died, there would be no more Philosophers trick, nor would any of the ambitious new illusions they had discussed ever be devised or performed. He would never find another partner with Carlo's skill. The waste of mutual possibilities felt like two jets of pure water swirling away into the gutter.

He leaned down and hissed, 'Come back. Do you hear me?'

It was the opposite of a benediction. Carlo gave no sign. Eliza stooped to sponge the dwarf's burning face.

Neither of them slept. Towards daybreak, as grey light slid into the room and fingered dust and pools of spilled wax, Carlo opened his eyes. The skin of the sockets was purple. He looked for a long moment at Eliza, then his gaze moved to Devil. He tried for some words, his tongue thickened by thirst, and Eliza trickled a few drops of water between his lips.

'Help me,' Carlo begged.

'Yes,' Devil promised.

What did the dwarf mean? That he and Eliza should help him to go more easily? Were they to place the pillow over his face?

Eliza said into Carlo's ear, 'As soon as it's light we'll get a proper doctor. You are not dying, you are not going to die, so don't fear that.'

Her insistence was admirable but misplaced, Devil was certain of that. He went back to his chair and huddled there, waiting for the inevitable.

Full daylight was hardly worth the name, but at eight o'clock on Christmas morning Eliza turned from peering down into the alleyway and took up her coat and hat.

'Are you going home?' Naturally she had her family and friends who would be looking for her at some cheery fireside, but Devil wished she wouldn't leave. He didn't relish the prospect of being alone to witness this death.

She was as tired as he was, but she moved decisively and her voice was crisp.

'As I said, I am going for help.'

'To whom, may I ask?'

'To Heinrich Bayer.' She pulled on her gloves. 'Give Carlo water with a spoonful of sugar, if you can. Don't leave him. Wait for me.'

'Whatever you say.' Where did she imagine he might go? He stirred the dead fire and laid some kindling amongst the ashes.

Eliza marched through the rookery without looking right or left. A seasonal stillness reigned and even the ill-clad children seemed to have found some temporary shelter. There was no one to challenge her or try to beg from her, and by concentrating hard on reversing the route by which they had arrived the night before last she soon emerged into better streets. A carriage briskly rolled by, and rosy-faced people walking to church wished each other a very merry Christmas. Overlapping

122

peals of joyful bells rose from the belfries of Holborn, Fleet Street and the City as she hurried eastwards.

She took a wrong turning in the streets beyond the meat market, but at last she recognised the door that gave on to the internal alley with Heinrich's strange domain lying at the end of it. She hesitated, unwilling to re-encounter the shadows and whatever they concealed within. But she could think of nowhere else to turn for help.

The door was locked, but there was a bell pull. For long minutes there was no response to her ringing although she could hear a muffled jangle somewhere in the depths behind the door. She muttered an impatient word and rang again. At last there was the sound of footsteps and finally a bolt being drawn. The door was opened by Heinrich's servant. The woman was startled to see a visitor, but to Eliza's relief she was admitted to the house rather than the mews housing the automata. She was invited to wait in a hallway, an airless place stuffed with furniture and kept gloomy behind heavy curtains. In a moment the servant appeared again.

'Please come this way, miss.'

In a small dining room a sideboard was backed with mirrors that seemed to swallow rather than reflect the light. Heinrich and Lucie were facing each other across their breakfast table. Lucie was bareheaded, dressed in a silk wrap. She sat with a straight back, smiling into the middle distance. Heinrich stood up, setting the table rocking so that the china faintly clinked. Eliza seized his hands and held them. She was heated from her walk and she could see that it cost him an effort not to pull back from contact with her living skin. A quiver of alarm crawled over her. This was an unlikely place to be seeking help, but she had no choice in the matter.

'How is poor Carlo?' Heinrich enquired as he led her to a seat. Eliza told him and explained why she had come.

'A doctor? I see. Of course, everything must be done. I know a good physician, a fellow Swiss, but today? . . . I don't know. Perhaps not.'

123

'Can we try? Please, Herr Bayer.'

Heinrich eventually nodded. He wrote a note and gave it to the servant to be taken to his friend.

'There. Now we must wait. Perhaps you would like to join us for breakfast?'

With Lucie seated on one side and Heinrich on the other, Eliza drank a cup of coffee and ate a piece of toast with cherry jam. Lucie was so close to her that she could have touched her arm. She couldn't stop herself staring at the poreless stalks of the doll's rubber wrists, and the fingers lacking any of the intricate whorls that marked her own. For all the ingenuity of it, at these close quarters the mechanical construction was grotesquely obvious. The brightness of the glass eyes and the fixed smile were repellent.

Did the inventor kiss those parted lips, she wondered? In removing the silk garment did he stroke the exposed shoulders?

The house seemed unnaturally silent. She wished very much to be elsewhere. She let herself imagine a different breakfast table, at which she and Devil might be seated with a coffee pot between them, amidst the cheerful chaos of a family house something like Faith and Matthew's. She justified the improbable domesticity of this vision by assuring herself that unlike her sister she would be no mere housewife. She and Devil would certainly have some important business of the theatre to discuss together, and he would tilt his black head to listen to her opinion before laughing and agreeing with her. Then perhaps he would put his hand over hers, and their kiss would be a matter of warm breath and moving lips . . .

What was she thinking? Of kissing Devil Wix? Of *marrying* him?

Yes, and not for the first time.

'I am sorry to disturb you on Christmas morning,' Eliza said, as much to distract herself as to break the silence.

Heinrich nodded. 'There is no disturbance. We live very quietly.'

The servant reappeared at last with an envelope on a salver. Heinrich adjusted his spectacles and read the note.

'He will come,' he said.

'Thank God,' Eliza responded, with extra fervour.

Devil threw open the attic door before they reached the top of the stairs.

'I was afraid you would be too late,' he cried as Eliza, Heinrich and the doctor filed into the room. Heinrich had insisted on accompanying them, declaring that Lucie would not mind if he left her for an hour. Carlo lay on his back, his mouth open. The room stank of sickness.

'We came as quickly as we could,' Eliza gasped.

The doctor was already at the bedside, opening his leather bag. He was a neat little man with a black coat and hat and a pointed beard. He could not have been more unlike the individual who had preceded him. In his precise English he asked about the fever and its progression before he turned down the covers to examine the dwarf's body. He raised Carlo's head off the mattress as if to weigh it in his hands.

'Was he in good health before this? Did he walk and speak well?'

'He was a contortionist. An escapologist, a stilt-walker, a juggler. The best stage performer I have ever seen.' Devil offered this tribute sincerely, and wished he had thought of making it while Carlo could still hear and speak. 'I never saw him ill before now. He seemed as strong as an ox.'

The doctor covered Carlo up. He washed his hands and took a notebook out of his bag.

'Will he live?' Eliza and Heinrich Bayer were patiently waiting but there was too much in the balance for Devil to delay the question any longer.

The doctor finished what he was writing before he looked up.

'The condition he has predisposes your friend to certain diseases of the bone and liver, among others. I do not think the present illness is related to this, however. I believe he has a chance of recovery, if he is well nursed, once he has taken the tincture I will prescribe.'

Devil turned to Eliza. She said, 'We will do everything possible.'

Devil took the written prescription.

'Two doses, eight hours apart.' The doctor closed his bag.

'The last medicine we gave him . . .' Eliza began.

The doctor bowed. 'This is different.'

Heinrich murmured to Devil, 'I will deal with the matter of remuneration.'

'Thank you. I am in your debt,' Devil assured him.

Five minutes later Eliza and Devil were alone at the bedside again.

'You did well,' he said.

'You should go now and have the medicine made up. I will stay with Carlo until you come back, but be as quick as you can because Faith expects me.'

Devil did as he was told. It was not easy to find an apothecary but at last he knocked up a fellow obliging enough to unlock his dispensary on Christmas Day. Between them, Devil and Eliza spooned the new dose between Carlo's lips. He swallowed most of it.

'I have to go,' she said once this was done.

Devil nodded. They remembered to wish each other a happy Christmas.

Matthew opened the door.

'My dearest Lizzie, here you are at last.'

Her nephews stumbled from the parlour, each carrying a new toy. One was a jack-in-the-box, the other a brown plush lion. They shouted and jostled at her knees until she stooped to their level.

'Aunt Eliza, see, my gift.'

'And me, lion.'

'You are lucky boys. Please give me a kiss.' Their bright

hot faces pressed against hers and little arms coiled round her neck.

Matthew said, 'Come on in, we are all waiting for you.'

The parlour was crowded. Under paper chains and thickets of garlands made from holly and pine cones her father and stepmother were seated in the best armchairs. Mrs Dunlop had a new cherry-red dress, and a new cap to set it off. Eliza's tiny half-brother stood nervously behind her chair. He tolerated Faith but he had never been at ease with Eliza and lately tended to hide his face against his mother's skirts whenever she appeared. Faith was pink-cheeked and tousle-haired from leading the singing and games. She jumped up from the piano stool to greet her sister.

'Sweet, we began to worry. Matthew even mentioned a search party.'

'Forgive me. A friend of mine is ill with a fever and I sat with him for a while.'

Mrs Dunlop looked horrified. 'A fever? I hope it is nothing infectious. The children . . .'

'No. And I am sure he is already on the mend,' Eliza said smoothly.

Faith took her sister's arm and steered her away to take off her coat and hat.

'Let me look at you. Tell me what has been going on, please?'

'The dwarf from the Palmyra theatre is very ill. Devil – Mr Wix, that is – and I have been nursing him.'

Her sister regarded her. 'I see.'

'No, you don't.' Eliza was almost tottering with exhaustion, but she still laughed at Faith's leap to a conclusion.

'But you like him, don't you?'

'The dwarf?'

They were both laughing as Matthew came up behind them.

'There is a fine piece of beef ready to carve.' He threw open the doors that separated the parlour from the dining room and revealed the festive table. Faith had brought out her best table linen. The children scrambled to take their places and Faith chased after them to stop them bringing down the cloth or cutting themselves with the knives.

Matthew beamed. He loved being the father of the household. 'You know, I have asked Jasper Button in to join us after we've eaten our dinner.'

'You are very hospitable,' Eliza remarked. She sat down beside her father, who kissed her and told her she was looking pretty enough although she could do with eating a few more hearty dinners.

'Look at Bertha,' he said, nodding his approval at the cherry-red vision opposite.

'I will. I do,' his daughter told him.

On the morning after Christmas Carlo woke with the early light, and recognised Devil.

'Are you still here?' he muttered.

'I live here,' Devil said, his impatience blunted by relief.

Sweat soon pearled the dwarf's skin and ran off him in streams. The bedclothes were quickly soaked, and as he was too weak to look after himself and there was no one else available to perform the service Devil sponged his body and wrapped him in dry clothing. Carlo asked for water, and he drank half a cupful without having to call for the bucket. By the time Eliza came in the early evening he was propped up and feeding himself scraps of sugared bread dipped in warm milk. At the sight of her Carlo's face stretched into a smile, although it turned to a wince as his cracked lips split.

'Hush,' she warned and dabbed away a pinhead of blood for him. She took her accustomed place beside the bed and folded his hand in hers. Devil stoked the fire even though the room was warm enough. It would have been a long vigil for him since yesterday afternoon, she thought, and he had clearly nursed Carlo well. Although the dwarf was pitifully gaunt, his eyes and teeth yellowed and much too large for his face, he knew who and where he was. He didn't call out to Sallie any longer.

She advised Devil, 'If you would like to go out to eat something, or to take a drink, I will sit here for an hour or two.'

Devil was pleased that the dwarf looked likely to recover, and therefore get back to work. The Palmyra was always in his mind. He was also hungry and bored. He put on his bowler hat and sloped away. Carlo held tightly to Eliza's hand and his eyes clung to her.

'You didn't leave me to croak,' he murmured.

'No. But it was not me alone. Devil and Heinrich Bayer did all they could.'

'Bayer?'

'He brought the doctor to you. He paid him, as well.'

'The doctor? With the stink of booze on him and a great red face like your worst dreams?'

'That was the first one. Another came after that, a Swiss.'

Carlo shook his head. 'I don't remember.'

'No. You were very bad.'

'My sister Sal was here.'

Eliza didn't try to tell him otherwise. For all she knew Sallie might well have come for her brother. He hadn't followed her, though, which meant the dwarf still had business in this world.

Carlo was quiet and she thought he had fallen asleep, but when he spoke again his voice was stronger.

'For a fellow like me it's not so easy to find a girl. But I'm a man, same as any other. I told the fool Wix that much. You've been tender to me, as affectionate as any woman has been or could be. Could you ever think of me in that way, Eliza, do you suppose?'

She held her face in the same lines so that no surprise or any tremor would show itself. Their hands were still linked. She slowly shook her head, just once. A silence followed but it seemed to Eliza that it was not a painful one.

Carlo's chin rose a little higher. 'No. I see.' He added, 'It wasn't just Sallie who was talking to me, you know. My ma was here as well, dishing out advice like when I was a little lad. And Wix, hanging his black bonce over me, telling me, *Come back, come back.*'

'That did happen. I heard him. Begging you, he was.'

Carlo laughed, a sound like a fingernail scraping on slate. 'Seems to me like we're a fellowship now.'

'A fellowship?'

'You and me, Wix and Bayer. Forged in the flames.'

She nodded. 'Yes.'

He was right, the past days had created a bond. Who knew what such a fellowship might achieve?

She remembered her decision to enlist Carlo's help in devising a playlet to catch Devil's attention. To take her on to the stage at the Palmyra, would that be? Or was the catching of Devil's attention now an end in itself? Colour rose from her throat to her hairline and she stared at her hand linked with Carlo's. Embarrassment caused her to mumble. 'Maybe we can work together, you and me? With your help I should like to devise an illusion with a role for a woman. It should be something light and playful, perhaps for a pair of lovers.'

The dwarf was watching her. 'Aye,' was all he said, exhaling a long breath like a sigh, but she knew that he drew his own conclusions. Her inability to conceal her motives was disconcerting.

She swept on. 'Devil says the old taverns and vulgar halls belong to the past. Audiences nowadays want a show with style and humour. They want to be entertained, with their wives and sisters, and taken out of themselves. An illusion of the sort I have in mind would appeal to a better class. Like the art students, for example. The ones who dress up as philosophers, and their commercial cousins who whitewash palms across London.'

The dwarf was watching her.

'That was your doing, was it?'

'Only in the beginning. I told them about the Execution of the Philosopher and they came to see you.'

'Did you tell Wix so?'

'I mentioned it. He was thinking of other things. He was thinking of *you*.'

130

Carlo was deadly tired. He lay back against the pillow, his face waxy. 'We owe you, then.'

'Not really, it was just a word. The excellence of the illusion was what kept them coming.'

'We owe you,' he repeated. 'And Grady owes us. Thanks to you, it seems, we finally had a good house the last night we did a proper show. Wix has a piece of paper signed by Grady, you know. We get ten per cent of the take above two hundred seats sold. But Grady won't pay it, and now I'm sick and there'll be no show at all and even one hundred per cent of nowt is still nowt.'

There was such despair in his voice. Eliza chafed his hands and tried to speak with conviction.

'You will be better in no time, Carlo. See how much you have recovered already? Try to eat and sleep, and Devil and Heinrich and I will look after you. The fellowship, remember? You'll be back on the stage and Grady will pay up in the end. He is a villain and a cheat, but Devil will get the better of him.'

'It takes one to outwit one,' Carlo said. He fell silent. Eliza bent her head over their joined hands and waited.

Devil was out for more than two hours. When he clattered back he was red-faced and clumsy in his movements. He fished inside his coat and brought out a fistful of bottles, which he set about opening with a device he kept tucked in his waistcoat pocket alongside the watch chain that was missing its timepiece.

'Have you had a lively time?' he winked at Eliza.

'I can see you have,' she retorted. Carlo's eyes followed Devil from table to shelf. Devil wiped a glass with a shirt tail and poured black stout so briskly that the froth rose in a thick collar. He handed the glass to Carlo.

'He can't drink that,' Eliza spluttered.

'Why ever not? Do him all the good in the world. Drink up, my friend.'

Carlo raised an eyebrow. He put his tongue to the cream-coloured froth, tasted, then licked his cracked lips.

131

Devil grinned. 'See? It will put the steel back into him, that will.' Eliza sat at the table to let him come to the fire. He flopped down, spreading his long legs, thumbs hitched in his pockets. He was drunk enough for thoughtless energy to beam out of him. It passed like a current through the air of the stuffy room and pricked the nape of Eliza's neck, and her wrists and throat and other parts of her, so that she had to shift in her seat and stare hard at the boards of the table.

'Don't you want to hear where I've been?'

'I expect you will tell us.'

Devil sucked away the rim of beer that coated his top lip. 'You can be quite the dampener, you know, Miss Dunlop. Does Jasper Button ever object to that?'

'My demeanour has nothing to do with Jasper,' she said between her teeth. Just the evening before he had been making himself at home in Matthew and Faith's parlour, singing and eating nuts and playing forfeits with her father and stepmother, just as if he were her fiancé, or even her husband, before she had even had the chance to look about her. When the party ended he had insisted on seeing her home to Bayswater, as if she were a milky girl who couldn't take care of herself. He would have kissed her too, if she had given him the chance.

Devil laughed. 'I doubt that Jasper would agree.'

Eliza was furious. How had she been manoeuvred into a position that was quite the opposite of what she wanted?

'I am an independent woman. I answer to no one but myself. Jasper is nothing to me but a friend, and I don't look for anything beyond that from him or any other man.'

He didn't laugh now, but studied her instead. Her anger was interesting, and so was the way its seizure made her gasp and catch her breath. He understood for the first time why Jas was in pursuit of this sharp girl, and as soon as he grasped the matter the old competitive spirit stirred in him. He took a long pull at his drink while he thought about it. Carlo's nose and chin, sharpened by illness, poked at him from the pillow.

'I am going to tell you anyway. I have been to the Palmyra.'

With that he gained their full attention.

'There was a crowd of people at the ticket booth. Not at all an orderly queue, more of a mob. And the angry cry was all for the Execution of the Philosopher. No execution, no Boldoni and Wix, and they were disappointed even though they had seen the acrobats and heard the soprano. I am afraid the beautiful Lucie was not enough to satisfy them. Their money back was what they shouted for.'

Devil described how almost every seat in the house had been taken. It was Christmas, and the public wanted entertainment. When he slipped in backstage he heard the booing, and after the curtain fell for the last time there had been a stampede of complaint. Jacko Grady had stood his ground, to be fair to him. Not a penny had been refunded. After the last complainer had trudged away with the assurance that Boldoni and Wix would soon return, Devil confronted the manager in his cubbyhole. He made as if he had already taken some drink.

'Where is the fucking dwarf?' Grady snarled. His fingers were splayed on the desk like bunches of pork sausages.

'Indisposed,' Devil slurred. He made sure that Grady knew that he knew it was their act the people wanted. To have such a bargaining point was almost as good as planting his boot on Grady's face.

'Fine and good. But did he *pay*?' Carlo now put in.

'He did not. I have a better idea.'

The other two waited. Devil stretched his legs in the firelight, acting as demonic as if he was putting on the Infernal Flames for a tavern crowd. He was pleased with himself and he wanted to tell the tale in his own way. Eliza tried not to stare at him as if she were starving in front of a banquet table, but she couldn't help herself.

Brandishing the signed contract, Devil had again demanded the money due from the first eighty-per-cent house they had played to. Grady had flatly refused. He shouted that he was losing money this night and every night that the Execution of the Philosopher was not performed. One broken contract rendered the other void. Devil had nodded at this, as if reluctantly obliged to agree. But like a drunk who couldn't quite tailor his words, he crowed that it was Boldoni and Wix who brought in the crowds and another theatre manager had already taken notice of them. He winked heavily. Maybe it would suit Mr Grady better if they shook hands like gentlemen and agreed to go their separate ways? He swayed closer to the desk and held out his hand.

Grady's eyes bulged as he slapped Devil's hand aside. He had given Wix and the dwarf their chance. He had even paid good money to have trapdoors and ladders built to their design into the Palmyra stage. There would be no taking the Philosophers to another house.

Devil had staggered a little from the impact of Grady's slap. He had given a hollow sigh, as if reaching the tipping point between bravado and sentimentality before plunging down on the other side.

Wagging his finger, he had blurted, 'I'll tell you the truth. I like you, Grady. You're a hard man, but you know the business. You're an example. I don't want to work for another manager, not if I can still appear at the Palmyra.'

Devil drummed his heels on the attic floorboards and rocked in appreciation of his own performance. 'Did I over-egg it, do you think?'

'Go on,' Carlo ordered.

'I told him, "Gentlemen, that's what we are. I know one when I see one. Paper contracts don't matter between *gentlemen*."'

Grady had sat forward, interlinking the sausages as if about to wrap them in greased paper for a prudent housewife. Devil teetered to his side and dropped a weighty arm over his shoulder.

'You know what gentlemen would do? Call for a hand of cards, that's what. I'll play you for the contract. What do you say? You win, I'll rip the paper into shreds.'

Grady's eyes had been like skewer holes in mutton fat.

'And if I lose?'

'You pay us.' Devil smiled, all bonhomie.

A long pause had followed. Grady blew out his cheeks until they rippled in a puff of mocking laughter. 'Bugger off,' he said. 'You and your bloody contract.'

Eliza and Carlo remained silent at the end of this recounting, waiting for the pay-off. Devil leaned even further back, tipped his chin and emptied his glass.

'When do I get to sleep in my own bed?' he enquired as he put it aside.

'Not until Carlo's well again. What *happened*?' Eliza insisted.

'What? Nothing else. I left Grady before I was obliged to punch him. I called in at one or two establishments on the way back here and enjoyed a drink or two in cheerful company. And now you see me.'

'I don't understand what you are so pleased about.'

He pushed himself upright, one eyebrow lifting. 'You don't?'

Carlo indicated that he was no wiser either.

'Then let me explain. I have done no more than plant an idea in Grady's head. A toper's idea, spilled out in his cups and seemingly forgotten as soon as mentioned. But the notion is in there now, taking root in his skull. Once it begins to flourish it will be his own, and when the time comes – naturally, a gentlemen's card game played for important stakes will seem the perfect solution.'

Eliza saw that he was not drunk at all.

He was cunning, and he would outsmart her if he could be bothered to do so. The recognition of their equivalence made him more appealing to her than his long legs and lazy stare, which were only distractions for silly girls. There were certainly plenty such in Devil's orbit, including the little acrobat with the tinkling bells.

But there was nobody like herself, and that was her advantage.

'A clever idea,' she acknowledged. Carlo rested in silence. 'But Grady will have to be brought to the point. And once that is done, you will have to beat him at cards.'

Devil inclined his head. 'I think I can undertake to do that, on both counts. However, I will need help from Heinrich Bayer and from Carlo. Perhaps even from you, Eliza, once I have prepared the illusion and hinged the traps.'

'I shall be pleased to do whatever I can. Carlo believes that we are already a fellowship of four.'

The dwarf lifted his fingers. He was too weary now to offer his thoughts.

'Rest,' Eliza ordered.

She put on her gloves and Devil recalled the other pair, ruined with Carlo's blood. She slotted the webs of her fingers together and stroked the thin leather over her wrists, fully aware of his scrutiny. Eliza Dunlop was a feminine woman, not a coarse bundle of female flesh and blood like Bascia or Maria Hayes, yet she was hardly a fragile creature inclined to faint or wilt. She had held the bucket to Carlo's arse, and wiped him afterwards. She was the one who had gone for Heinrich Bayer's help while he had sat waiting for Carlo to die. He admired her strength, almost as much as he admired Jasper Button's ambition in aiming to catch her.

Eliza kissed Carlo lightly on the forehead and promised that she would come again tomorrow. The dwarf's longing eyes followed her to the door.

'I will walk with you to Holborn,' Devil said as the latch clinked.

'I can make my own way.'

'I know that.'

They made their way down the stairs and out into the bitter night. The alley was silent, although lights shone in Annie Fowler's house and there was a thin trill of fiddle music creeping from an upper floor. Merriment lingered even in the most unlikely corners. Devil hummed the tune.

'I owe you thanks on several counts,' he said once they reached the first dogleg and passed out of sight of Maria Hayes's window. Eliza tilted her head at him. 'For preserving the dwarf, first of all. It's your doing that he's sitting up tonight and tasting a glass of stout.'

'I'm happy to see him recovering.'

'He's sweet on you,' Devil observed.

'He did ask me if I could ever think of him in that way.'

'That is admirably direct. And could you?'

Her sudden smile glinted. 'I am afraid not. As I told him.'

'Jasper will be relieved to hear it. And so am I.'

'Jasper and I are no more than friends, as you already know.' She hesitated, but she could not resist pursuing the other implication. 'And why should *you* be relieved?'

Aha, Miss Eliza Dunlop, Devil thought. *That's where we are, is it?*

As well as the pleasurable stroke to his vanity he felt a distinct quiver of apprehension.

He looked down at her. They had stopped walking, and she faced him in the angle of a house wall. There was silence now except for a rustle that might have been a cat or a rat in the gutter.

'Because I wouldn't care to have to intervene in a fight over you between my two good friends.'

Eliza did not flinch. Instead she came an inch closer, her lips parted and her eyes brilliant with amusement. He felt her warm breath on his face.

'Is that all?' She was teasing him.

Devil murmured, 'I should also thank you for putting in a good word for Boldoni and Wix with the gentlemen from your art school. Did you tell them about the Philosophers illusion while you were posing?'

Their mouths were almost touching. 'I don't speak while I am holding a pose.'

'I see. Or rather, I very much wish I did.'

That was true. He hadn't troubled to imagine the details of Eliza Dunlop without her clothes before this moment, but now the flood of images threatened to overcome him.

Her smile widened and she came another inch closer. The sliver of space between them vanished. His hands cupped her chin as they kissed and a small gasp of eager acquiescence escaped from her. Her arms slid round his body and held him.

To his surprise Devil found this innocent response more thrilling than anything he had done with Bascia, who could roll herself into a hoop with her ankles behind her ears. It was a long moment before he could make himself draw away. Eliza released him and patted her hat into place as tranquilly as if she had just emerged from church, which made him want even more urgently to drag her into the nearest bed and see where he could make her ankles end up.

He offered her his arm instead. 'I think we should walk on,' he said. Eliza nodded and they made their way towards Holborn. There was still some traffic in the wide streets, mostly closed carriages bringing comfortable people back from their dinners and family entertainments, but coming up in the distance she could just make out the lamps of an Oxford Street omnibus.

'I wish I were a rich man,' Devil said awkwardly. Her arm was still tucked under his, just as if they had been out together as an established couple and were now going home to their own fireside. He found this banal picture unexpectedly appealing, and he knew that he had been right to feel apprehensive about associating with Eliza Dunlop.

'Some day you will be,' Eliza assured him. She added, 'We are a fellowship, remember? There is plenty to do, but we shall do it between us.'

The omnibus clattered to a halt, the horses jingling and blowing steam into the chill. Devil handed her up to the step and she made her way inside through the stink of tobacco and crowded bodies. She didn't look back over her shoulder to where he stood on the kerb. A drunken fellow sprawled on the wooden bench looked up into her dazzling face and hoisted himself upright to allow her to sit down. She took his place with a murmur of thanks, and peered through the smeared glass into the magical night.

138

SEVEN

Carlo recovered, as Eliza had predicted. He did everything he could to regain his strength, spooning up soup and potatoes as if it were a task he had set himself and lying down to sleep with similar grim determination.

'I will mend,' he said in answer to Devil's questioning.

The only time Carlo seemed fully his old self was in Eliza's company. She brought her box of Rawlinson paper and they sat with their heads together, murmuring as they worked on the magical playlet for the Palmyra. Carlo wanted to please her, and he gave her efforts his closest attention even though they showed little enough promise to begin with. He muttered, 'That will take too long,' or 'No, no, don't you see? The girl must be in the box *before* he comes in.' Eliza swallowed her pride and accepted his criticism. She was a humble pupil, chewing her pencil as she alternately scribbled and crossed out.

During Carlo's recuperation the fire was kept stoked, and even when Eliza was not present the attic room retained its glimmer of warmth and homeliness. Devil began to enjoy coming home. Eliza did not refer to the kiss in the alleyway, not even with a knowing glance, and he wondered what long move this might be in the game she was evidently playing with him. He decided in the end that she could hardly be a better player of any game than he was himself. He left the two of them to their diversions and concentrated on filling the stage void left by Boldoni and Wix. The jewelled cabinet gathered dust in the wings while Devil performed the Flames and some illusions from his own repertoire of small card tricks and silk handkerchief sleights. The audiences were mostly unimpressed and Devil took it badly when he was rewarded with jeers instead of applause. He begged Carlo to teach him the Orange in the Crystal Ball illusion, but the dwarf only said, 'You don't have the speed, Wix.' He flexed his hands. 'And your fingers are like a bunch of bananas.'

The houses thinned and Grady ranted that if he did not see more effort and ingenuity from all his performers he would clear them out and hire new acts. Heinrich Bayer responded by bringing in his Chinaman. The manikin blinked and showed its porcelain teeth to the manager as the pistons in its innards gave their faint serpentine hiss. Heinrich turned a handle and the ribbon of paper spilled from its slot.

'What's this? A mechanical midget?'

Heinrich was stiff. 'In a sense, but if you will examine it you will see that it is a miracle of construction.' He turned the manikin and opened up the back to reveal the tight-packed cylinders and metal rods. Nothing happened when Grady prodded the mechanism with a fat finger, but when Heinrich stroked the control drum the creature's right arm rose and the four fingers separately curled as if to beckon them closer. Bascia and her brother were watching from a doorway, still wearing their stage make-up. The girl's black-rimmed eyes widened in her painted mask. She shuddered and murmured, 'Horrible.'

Grady said, 'I've already got a real midget. Why in Christ's name would I want to book a tin one? What does the thing do?'

Heinrich held up a garland of the paper. 'Mr Wu answers questions. Or tells ladies' fortunes, perhaps.'

'This will be a surprise to you, Bayer, but the ladies who come to this theatre don't want their fortunes told. They don't want parlour games. I don't notice them going wild for any dancing doll either. They want a sing-song and some smut, and a scaring that lets 'em hide their faces in their fellow's neck. And the fellows want magic preferably with blood and a bang like Wix's Philosophers, so they can put their arm round their girl when she screams. They like to see a bit of leg, and all.'

Bascia pouted and smoothed her flesh-pink stockings over her calves. The bunched darns at knee and heel didn't show under the lights. Devil was leaning against the wall with his arms folded. It had been his suggestion that Heinrich should bring in the Chinaman, but he did not seem in the least surprised when Grady scoffed. He only winked at the offended Heinrich. When they were dressed for the street again and Lucie was folded into her trunk, he told the engineer that he should leave Mr Wu at the theatre. The office where Grady sat to count out payments and thumb through bills was no more than a smoky slot, the only space in the cramped backstage area that could conceivably serve the purpose. Devil placed the automaton on a sturdy shelf in an alcove at the back of the room.

Heinrich protested, 'Why? Some person will certainly steal him.'

'Eggin keeps the place locked up tight.' This was the bruiser paid by Jacko Grady to guard the stage door and to secure the theatre for the night. 'Inside the Palmyra what value would Mr Wu have to anyone but you, since you are the only one who understands how to operate him?'

Heinrich hesitated. He ran a finger over the controls and the Chinaman's head fractionally nodded, setting the round black hat and the drooping moustache quivering.

Devil crossed to the alcove. He adjusted the manikin's position and then stood back to consider it. 'Grady will change his mind, I'm ready to bet. He doesn't know what he wants because he doesn't understand what sells a show. And Mr Wu looks as if he belongs here. Do you not think so? Maybe he will bring us luck. We could do with some, eh?'

Heinrich reluctantly agreed. Devil patted his shoulder.

'Good man. We're about to be lucky. I feel it in my bones.'

*   *   *

141

Within two weeks, Carlo was back in his Philosophers robes. With its demands of timing and physical contortions the effort of playing the role exhausted him to the point that even Devil was anxious on his behalf, but the dwarf never missed a cue. The wax head fell into the basket, the black torso collapsed in a tangle of occult signs, and when Devil threw open the cabinet the disembodied head was always floating there. At the flash of the lights, the huddled body rose to its feet again. It was a mere three nights before the word spread and the audiences began to grow. The nightly stage entrance of the Philosophers was greeted now with a wild burst of cheering. Even Jacko Grady could not deny that the illusion was fast becoming a popular success for the Palmyra.

After a string of good houses, once again a night came when two hundred seats were sold. Devil came offstage and went straight to Grady's office. The Chinaman rested on its shelf, glass eyes fixed ahead. Grady kept Devil waiting while he dealt with the other performers but at last he leaned back in his chair, the fat of his neck compressed by his collar into crimson rolls. He looked at Devil and his lips rolled the wet stub of his cigar. With a sigh Devil took from his inner pocket the paper that Grady had signed. These confrontations were becoming tedious, but he knew what must be done.

Grady stuck out his hand. 'Let me look at that again, Wix.'

'What do you need to see? I believe you have a copy of your own. Unless you have mislaid it, perhaps?'

'Won't do you any good to be clever. Hand it over.'

Devil only sighed again and folded the sheet of paper into its proper creases before tucking it away.

'I believe it would be easier just to pay us what you owe.'

'How d'you propose to make me do that? Chancery, is it, you and your contract?' Grady chuckled at this notion and Devil obligingly joined in.

'No, no. The dwarf and I are paupers. The law's beyond our means. But I don't favour a broken contract any more than the richest lawyer in the Inns. And if you won't honour ours,

142

Mr Grady, one broken contract renders another void. You said so yourself. I can take the Philosophers to another theatre. There has been some interest. The students, the palm trees, the general word of it. The Palmyra's reputation is on the up because of the dwarf and me.' His voice dropped: 'But there is no reason why another house should not benefit in the same way from our popularity. I am being frank with you.'

Grady's face turned a darker shade of puce. Devil's expression was blank, but inwardly he could have danced with delight at the sight of it.

The manager swung aside. Wedged beside his seat was a small square-cornered steel safe with an oval brass plaque and lock-plate. Grady selected a key from the bunch in his pocket and opened up the safe. From a leather pouch he counted out a little pile of sovereigns and some silver florins. He pushed the money at Devil, whose hand closed over it as quickly as if he were performing a sleight. The coins were counted again before they slid into Devil's waistcoat pocket where the watch chain dangled. A single sovereign was kept back and this one Devil caused to slip over and under his fingers and in and out of his fist, as lively as an eel. 'It is a pleasure to do business,' Devil smiled.

Grady locked up his safe. He let the cigar stub drop and he ground the remains into the floorboards under the heel of his boot. Over the man's shoulder Devil looked into the empty eyes of the little Chinaman, and then he wished the manager a polite good evening.

The show was over and the audience had jostled out into the Strand. In his street clothes Devil strolled on to the stage. He stooped to examine the trapdoors and tested the oiled hinges and then he straightened up and looked over the orchestra pit into the auditorium. He examined the box fronts, roughly over-painted by Grady's workmen, and the pillars surmounted by their exuberant billows of palm leaves. He looked up at the rows of cheaper seats in the gallery and the double line of *fauteuils* at the front of the stalls, and as he did so he became aware of a movement at the back of the aisle.

'Evening to you, Mr Wix, sir,' a voice said. 'Good house tonight, I'm told.'

'Evening, Jakey,' Devil said.

Jake was the theatre sweeper. He slipped in every night like a shadow. He cleaned up the crumpled paper and the orange peelings and the remaining debris from between the old seats, he brushed the floors and laid out the mislaid gloves in the ticket office for collection. Sometimes he ran a damp rag over the pillars, thoughtfully digging a black thumbnail into the grooves that mimicked tree markings. No one knew where he lived, if he lived anywhere. No one knew his second name or his age – or anything about him, except that he was young, too thin for his height, and fierce in his determination to go on sweeping the Palmyra theatre for as long as he could keep the work. Devil sometimes spoke to him on his way out if he chose to take the front-of-house exit, as he often did.

'Mr Grady pleased, was he?' Jakey asked.

'In a way.'

Jakey leaned his broom against a pillar. He stuck out his narrow chest and put his hands on his hips. He rolled his mouth around an imaginary cigar and puffed out his cheeks, glaring at Devil like a cornered boar. He could not have been more physically unlike and he had not uttered a word, yet still the manager materialised. Devil laughed and dug in his pocket. The boy slyly smiled, for a moment the same as any child who was pleased with his own cleverness. Devil gave Jakey a shilling and the boy became the sweeper again. He rubbed his knuckles to his forehead and kept his eyes turned down to his feet.

'Thank you, sir. Thank *you*.'

'You're a fine mimic, Jakey. You should go on the stage. Can you act?'

The boy's smile widened. 'Yes, sir.'

'Ever thought of it, have you?'

'Not much, sir.'

'Perhaps you should.'

Devil vaulted down from the stage and walked between the

144

seats, hearing the applause trapped in the musty curtains and stained plush. He tilted his head to catch it, to hear the murmur of the theatre itself, the boy already forgotten.

'Goodnight, sir.'

Devil raised his hand in acknowledgement and went on his way, whistling a tune.

Carlo was waiting in the attic room, one candle lit and the fire gone out. Devil took out all Grady's sovereigns and florins and laid them in a single row. Then with one fingertip he rearranged them in two equal files. Carlo watched closely. The candlelight exaggerated the hollows of his emaciated face.

Devil slid one file aside and scooped it up.

Carlo said, 'Good. That's very good, Wix. I thought you might want more than half, and then I'd have had to take you on.'

Devil gave a cough of laughter. 'How terrifying. No, it's fair shares. We're partners, aren't we?'

Devil took off his bowler and hung it on a peg. He untied his neckcloth, removed his coat and waistcoat and stripped down to his undershirt. Then he flopped down on his bed and lay there with his hands laced behind his head and his gaze apparently fixed on the cracked ceiling. The dwarf blew out the candle and crept away to his mattress.

The old house groaned and creaked as if the timbers were in pain. Feet clattered on the lower stairs, voices were raised and the privy door banged in the yard. Devil sometimes thought that if there were just one more person crammed under this roof the walls would surely split and spill them all into the alley.

He said into the darkness, 'Now that we're launched, do you think, Carlo, you might use some of your new wealth to pay for your own lodging?'

'I could do,' the dwarf said. He sounded reluctant, or offended, Devil couldn't tell which.

'You'll be able to have Eliza Dunlop all to yourself, without me hanging here like a gooseberry on a bush.'

'It's not that way between me and Eliza.'

Carlo could not hide his regret, and Devil was ashamed of his jibe. He turned towards the dwarf but all he could see was the square of less dense blackness that marked out the window.

'You are a fine illusionist,' he offered. 'The best I have ever seen.' Silence was all that met his words.

The great night came when the Palmyra theatre was sold out.

Grady rubbed his hands after the show and attempted some banter with his performers in the line-up for pay. The soprano and the jugglers, the tenor and the acrobats and the coarse comic were uncomfortable in the divide between the manager and the philosophers, knowing that it was Grady who paid their wages and Boldoni and Wix who generated the money that began to gush through the box office. Thus there were now two forces, neatly opposed, for them to mistrust in equal measure. Heinrich Bayer was ranked automatically with Devil and Carlo because everyone knew that they were in alliance, although quite how it had come about remained uncertain. In any event Heinrich was taken up with his own concerns and he did not care or even notice when the other playbill makeweights shunned him.

When Devil's turn came to claim his money, Grady's forced humour dried up like a pump in a drought. He silently handed over the correct percentage of the take, and the eyes of the company followed the transfer from hand to hand.

'Unfair,' a voice muttered.

Devil did not even trouble to identify the objector. 'On the contrary, it is perfectly fair. Mr Grady and I have a gentlemen's agreement.'

Grady's eyes slid to the safe, where his copy of the inconvenient paper was locked up. A gentlemen's agreement. Devil thought the phrase lingered usefully in the air as Grady waved him aside and Bascia sidled by, customarily allowing her hip to brush his. Her red lips sketched a kiss as her brother collected their money, and Devil responded with the equally customary wink. But it was more than a month since he had last bundled

146

her into what passed for a secluded corner of the theatre. From the day when he had speculated about positioning Eliza Dunlop's ankles to his own advantage, Bascia's contortionist abilities had taken on a somewhat obvious quality in his mind. What was there to discover, Devil mused, when everything was on display?

Following the enforced Christmas hours they had spent together over Carlo's sickbed, he had seen Eliza infrequently and then only with her attention apparently all for the dwarf and the little play they were devising. Yet the notion that he and she were engaged in move and counter-move remained with him. It was a strange game, he acknowledged, that opened with a damned dwarf shitting and puking into a bucket.

He laughed, and Bascia saw that he was laughing. She raised her eyebrows at him, but he ignored the invitation.

Carlo found lodgings for himself. The room had previously been occupied by a family but the father had fallen out of work and they had had to move. On the upper floor of a somewhat better house than Maria Hayes's, it was a tiny slice of bare boards and plaster falling away in chalky patches to reveal the laths, furnished with not much more than an iron bedstead and a couple of planks nailed across a corner to form a rudimentary cupboard. The busy street was halfway between the alley and the Old Cinque Ports, and it was noisy at all hours with the clatter of wheels. There was a slaughterhouse in the premises at the back and in the rare intervals of quiet Carlo could sometimes hear the squealing of terrified beasts and smell the spilled blood.

The landlord was a grim fellow who had insisted when Carlo first presented himself that he did not want his sort coming in and out. Carlo opened his fist and showed his money. The landlord stared over the top of the dwarf's head, at the non-existent file of other prospective tenants for the room.

'There will be a full month's rent to pay in advance, if I take you,' he grunted.

Carlo held up the required half-crowns and when he saw that some remained in his hand the man demanded a surety against drunkenness.

'Do I have the look of a drunkard?'

The man spat again. 'A drunkard, a freak, it's all the same to me.'

Carlo pinched his mouth shut. Over the following days he paid a carter to trundle over his boxes and cloth bags of stage accessories, his straw mattress and the few other possessions he had recently accumulated. Eliza came to see his new home. She picked her way up the filthy stairs, drawing her skirts up by a discreet inch in just the way she did at Devil's. She looked around her with less disbelief, however, than she had shown at the other house.

'You'll be comfortable, will you?' she asked him.

Carlo rubbed his jaw. It was not a question he had considered.

In the chinks of time between Carlo's performances and Eliza's classes, they put the finishing touches to their comic playlet. Carlo was finally satisfied that the mounting confusion of box appearances and disappearances could be worked satisfactorily. Eliza believed the story they had devised to be comical as well as touching.

'Charlotte and the Chaperone,' she announced. Charlotte would be her role, naturally. It was an elegant name, one she had always liked.

'Sounds spoony to me. Better something like In, Out and All About.'

'No,' Eliza protested, pulling a horrified face.

'We'll show it to Wix, then. Ask him what he reckons.'

'Of course,' Eliza agreed.

The landlord spied on her as she left the house, then waylaid Carlo.

'That your girl, is it? She's a looker, all right. Likes 'em small, does she?'

Carlo swore and the man laughed at him.

In sole possession of his attic room once more, Devil discovered that he missed the dwarf. Without the clutter of Carlo's boxes and bulging cloth bags there was more room to step about, but also a distinct hollowness that was nothing to do with floor space. He listened to the clamour in the rest of the house with something like envy. Now that Carlo was out of her house and the rent was fully paid up Maria Hayes was all smiles and enticements, but he did not desire her in the least. Loneliness, he realised with a knock against his ribs, was in him as much as it was in the dwarf. What was the value of company, if all it did was make you sore where you hadn't been before?

He scowled at the ashes in the grate, the dirty clothes and wadded paper on the floor, and the remains of too many scraped meals fouling the table. What was the point of a homely glow, if it faded so fast?

Would a married man feel differently? Perhaps, he thought, but the disadvantages of the state certainly outweighed the advantages.

After the show each night Carlo hurried away without waiting to see what Devil might do. One evening, partly out of disinclination to return alone to the squalid attic, Devil asked Heinrich Bayer to come with him to an alehouse. This involved persuading the engineer that he could leave Lucie in her trunk under the care of Eggin at the stage door, so that they would not have to trundle her into the saloon bar with them.

'Don't you worry, gents, the pretty miss will be safe with me,' Eggin leered when they took the trunk into his lair. Heinrich made a show of checking and rechecking the locks and fastening the key on a chain worn inside his shirt.

The two men went across the Strand to the Swan, not as much favoured by Devil as the Ports but still in his estimation a decent house. There was a lightness in the air, a scent of earth and sap even here in the heart of the city that meant spring was on its way. Inside the Swan they encountered a wall of light and noise. Above the heads of the crowd etched mirrors and dark red glazed tiles multiplied the yellow flare of gaslight.

A pianist was thumping the keys and a singer's red face throbbed at the centre of a cheery choir. Heinrich's ascetic pallor looked deathly in this brewer's palace. He consented to a glass of whisky and Devil ordered himself a pint. They had arrived at the happy crest of the night, when drink had already dulled the memories of the past day and delayed thoughts of the one to come, and before bubbles of aggression began to break the surface of the human stew. Devil's spirits rose accordingly. He took a deep gulp of his beer and realised that he was hungry. He could look in to a supper house for a chop on his way home, or he could stop at a stall he knew and buy a mutton pie and a tin cup of hot gravy. This was luxury.

He spread himself against the solid bulwark of the bar and automatically surveyed the room. There were plenty of women. He remembered the autumn afternoon when he had called in to the Ports, the day of the slattern in the red dress and Carlo's expert dipping.

Heinrich Bayer sipped his whisky. He was already glancing into the street, as if he feared the sight of Eggin pushing a porter's trolley.

'You wanted to speak about something?'

'I do,' Devil agreed. The beer was good at the Swan. A second pint was an inviting prospect. 'Mr Wu,' he said.

Heinrich fiddled with his glass, pushing it through the chestnut pools of spilled drink on the bar. He was more preoccupied even than usual, but he gave Devil a meagre slice of his attention.

'Why would I do that?' he asked, when Devil finished talking.

'I will explain why when we have worked out how.'

'We?'

Devil gravely nodded.

Heinrich's eyes returned to the window. It was too dark outside for him to see any passers-by. 'It could be done. The carcass is robustly engineered. I can see no possible point in the exercise, however. Do you intend to make it part of one of your illusions?'

150

'In a sense. And I will cut you in on the proceeds, naturally.' Heinrich made no response to this so Devil added, superfluously, 'But I see your thoughts are elsewhere.'

'I am sorry. I do not mean to appear impolite.'

'Not at all. Won't you tell me what preoccupies you?' Devil gestured for their drinks to be replenished.

Heinrich circled a forefinger to encompass the din inside the Swan. 'I am thinking about voices. In particular the unique timbre of each human voice and the possibility of its capture and reproduction. You have heard of the phonograph?'

'No. What is that?'

'It is a device of American invention, by which – to simplify – sound is captured in the form of grooves scratched on to a wax cylinder. When the cylinder rotates, a needle traces the grooves and the voice is reproduced.'

Devil considered this. Two feet away a woman screeched and then hooted with laughter and her man made a ripe suggestion which made her laugh even harder.

'And what progress has been made in the opposite direction? Is there an anti-phonograph which absorbs voices, perhaps, and puts a stop to their future noise?'

'Just think, Wix. Consider the implications, the possibilities.'

'Let me see. Perhaps a speech to the House of Commons by Mr Gladstone, once pressed into wax, might be reproduced at will, for ever? Until the grooves were worn smooth from repeated demand, that is.'

Heinrich allowed himself a narrow smile. 'Conceivably. I have been working on an adaptation of the phonograph. It is an interesting undertaking for me, you know, to make a voice sound out where there is – ah – no human agency. This might have value in our current line of work.'

Devil had a way of emerging from a state of apparent amused disengagement into concentrated attention within the span of a single second. He made this transition now. Heinrich was almost thrown backwards by the intensity of his gaze.

'It would be useful to the table-rappers and the unseen-hands

151

performers, certainly. Disembodied voices floating in a darkened room, ringing bells, messages from beyond the grave, that sort of nonsense work. Is that what you mean?'

Devil would have nothing to do with seances or spirit voices, even though they were popular with audiences. If the subject were introduced he would insist, 'This is not magic. It is common trickery that plays on absence and grief. We make no pretence that ours are not illusions. The wonder is all in how we manipulate the known world to magical effect, not in falsely claiming some intervention from beyond. Do I insist that I am a real devil, because I go by such a name? Because I dress up in a scarlet suit and a pair of horns and play the part, do I become him? I say, there are no spirits and they possess no hands or voices. It is a crime to counterfeit such things, for money or for mere sensation, and it demeans the craft of the magician.'

His insistence went far beyond the mild demands of whatever debate was current. Carlo had learned not to raise the subject, and Heinrich retreated from it now.

'I am an engineer, Wix. I am interested solely in the mechanical possibilities as they apply to my own inventions.' He glanced round to dismiss eavesdroppers, of whom there were none, and leaned forward to replicate Devil's attentive posture so that their foreheads almost touched across the table. 'I have reached the point where my adaptation of the phonograph is almost ready. You understand what this means?'

Devil shook his head.

'It means that Lucie will *speak*.'

Heinrich's paper-pale face radiated joy. Devil took a moment to marshal his response.

'But Heinrich, how will you capture her voice when – forgive me – she does not have one in the first place? At least, I have never heard her speak. Perhaps I haven't listened?'

Beyond Heinrich and through the throng, Devil saw the coarse curtain enveloping the door pushed aside. The Palmyra manager's bulk pressed into the crowded bar. His eye fell on them at once. If he had been looking for them he was in luck.

Heinrich rushed on. 'Of course, I will have to choose a voice for her. An angel's voice if that were possible, but in reality one that is low and musical, with the right note of sweetness and clarity. A voice like Miss Dunlop's, perhaps.'

Jacko Grady was pushing towards them through the crowd. His mass impeded him, as a barrel sloughing through mud.

Heinrich declared, his face still transfigured with delight at the prospect ahead, 'I shall prepare a series of statements and responses to put into her mouth. I will devise and control her every utterance, but she will speak. Would she consent, do you think?'

'Lucie? Why not?'

'*Miss Dunlop*. To read for me, so that I may record the words for Lucie's voice box?'

Devil found the notion unpleasant to contemplate, and that before he had time to imagine what words he might wish to put into the doll's mouth.

'I have no idea,' he said.

Grady loomed over them. He planted his fists on the table to prop himself after his exertions.

'What are you drinking, gentlemen?'

Devil flicked a finger towards his pint glass, Heinrich covered his with the flat of his hand and shook his head. Grady sat down, causing the table to rock on its clawed feet.

'Where's the dwarf?' he asked.

'I'm not his keeper, am I?' Devil took the drink that Grady gave him and swallowed some of it before the manager could change his mind.

'Two of you will have to do, then. You'll tell the dwarf what I have to say.'

'What is this, Grady? Herr Bayer and I have no connection – beyond our pleasure in working for you, of course.'

'D'you take me for a fool? You are in it together, the three of you.'

There was no reply. Jacko Grady said, 'I will buy you out, Wix. A one-off payment, in cash, with no more twaddle about

153

seats and percentages. Money in exchange for your cockeyed contract, with your undertaking to play the Palmyra exclusively for the next two years. What is your figure? Let's make a deal and shake hands on it, eh?'

Without a blink Devil said, 'Ten thousand pounds.'

'Very amusing. The theatre itself is hardly worth that. Come, name your figure'.

'I have done.'

Grady's expectant smile faded as he understood that Devil did not intend to be bought out. 'I will give you five hundred pounds. That is handsome, I think you will agree.'

'It's a colourless sort of deal, Grady. It doesn't call out to my adventurous spirit. What d'you think, Heinrich? We shouldn't go so quietly, should we? Carlo won't thank me for selling our little share of the profits for five hundred pounds.'

Grady glowered. 'You may regret turning down such an offer. The Palmyra might shut up next week.'

Devil's glance travelled from the man's whiskers to the point where the edge of the table dug a groove in his belly fat.

'It may do, of course. But then you would not have a theatre, while Boldoni and Wix would still have the Philosophers and the other marvellous illusions we are preparing. Is that truly your intention? Well, we shall have to wait and see.' He took another draught of beer and produced a wide, uncalculated, half-intoxicated smile. 'On the other hand, we could have some fun over it. Go on, why not?'

'Why would I choose to spread the cards with a broadsman like you? Sharping's your living. I've seen you fly the pack, palming and bottom dealing and all the other tricks.'

Devil managed an expression that was both hurt and wry. He put his two hands on the table, innocent palms upwards, as if to offer allegiance to the manager.

'For a performance, of course. But not in a gentlemen's game, never that. And we would play by your rules, naturally. Any restrictions you choose to put in place, anything to establish a fair table.'

154

Grady hesitated. 'You're quite the man of honour, Wix. Well then, I'm sorry you've refused my offer. Tell the dwarf what I took the trouble to come here to discuss. Five hundred pounds, remember. It's a tidy sum of money.' He slapped down a coin to pay for the drinks, hoisted himself to his feet and rolled on his way.

'Does he think I can't add and multiply?' Devil exclaimed. 'Five hundred pounds, indeed.'

Heinrich also stood. 'I can do what you asked, Wix. It's a simple enough matter. But do you think Miss Dunlop would consent to be the voice of Lucie?'

'You will have to ask her that yourself.'

'Yes,' Heinrich agreed. 'I shall do so at the earliest opportunity.'

Eliza and Carlo brought their playlet to Devil. She invited him to read the lines but he said that he would much rather she told him the story.

'If you can make your idea sing to me, the chances are that a theatre manager will also hear the tune.'

Eliza stood in the centre of the attic room. She felt peculiarly diffident with the two men watching her – but to be a performer was what she wanted, and now she had better do the best she could.

She began. 'We have a pair of young lovers.'

'A good start,' Devil remarked.

'Let her say her piece, can't you?' Carlo snapped.

'They are trying to escape Charlotte's chaperone by hiding in a garden overlooked by a statue of Cupid. A door in the statue's base, secured by a heavy padlock, leads to a little space inside that is just big enough to shelter two people.'

'A good continuation.'

'Can you not *ever* keep quiet? Eliza, go on.'

'An iron cage wrapped in chains stands nearby. The chaperone's pursuit is interrupted by a mysterious woodman who releases a terrifying wolf from the cage.' Eliza pressed her hands together and sprang backwards, as if the wolf were already at her throat. She spoke faster. 'The young man bundles the two women into the statue niche for safety, and secures the padlock. The woodman seizes him and locks him into the wolf's cage, and the iron chains mean that he will never escape. There will be incorruptible members of the audience on stage of course, to inspect the locks and the chains. Then the woodman throws open the door of the niche but he finds that the two women are gone.'

Devil began to laugh, partly at her happy enthusiasm. Encouraged by this Eliza jumped again, twirling and talking as she mimed the various appearances and disappearances from niche and cage. She waved an invisible sword.

'The lover escapes from the cage and cuts the wolf in half. He overpowers the woodman and locks *him* in the statue niche.'

'Bravo.'

'The two halves of the wolf dance across the stage.' On all fours, Carlo skittered across the floor.

'Oh yes, excellent.'

'The woodman dances out of the trees and reunites the halves to make a whole wolf again. He conjures Charlotte and the chaperone out of the locked cage. He tears off his mask and reveals himself as Charlotte's father.'

'I am quite astonished.'

Eliza was pink in the face now, her dark hair escaping in thick hanks from its restraining combs.

'Father gives his blessing to the lovers and rewards the chaperone for her diligence. The wolf curls up at their feet. The end.'

Carlo lay couchant with his head on what would be his claws. Devil applauded, without having to feign nearly as much of the required enthusiasm as he had anticipated.

Eliza caught her breath, then took out a small handkerchief and patted her throat. Devil watched the pulse in her neck and the escaped lock of damp hair that lay there, and he remembered the response of her kiss in the alley. The play in their game had subtly turned. He did not know how it had happened, but somehow he had lost his advantage. Furthermore he couldn't even calculate the odds against himself because he had no idea what result he favoured.

'The pacing of the effects would need some attention,' he said in a voice that sounded dilute even in his own ears. 'And the sequence needs one more twist but it's a happy little piece. Well done. Had I a theatre at my disposal, I would certainly book you.'

Eliza's gaze dropped. 'Thank you.' She was disappointed, he saw. He felt dull, and dissatisfied with the compromises that circumstances forced on him. A kick of visceral longing to command the Palmyra – *for her sake* – made him straighten up.

'When I do, I will. That is a promise.'

The dwarf yawned. He folded his legs and drew down his shoulders, shrinking himself to the dimensions of the Philosophers cabinet. He turned his head from side to side as if it floated.

'When the day comes,' he said in the good philosopher's decapitated tones.

'It will.' The metal edge in Devil's voice drew Eliza's gaze. Her stare made him aware of how rarely their eyes met.

She turned aside. 'On another subject, do you remember Mr Gardiner's invitation?'

'No.' Devil spoke the truth.

'Mr Gardiner is the promising young artist I mentioned to you. He would like you to sit for him as the evil philosopher. I told him that you will consent to meet him, at least.'

'Did you? In that case what choice do I have?'

Two days later they met by arrangement at the foot of the Albert Memorial and made their way together to the Rawlinson School. As they walked past the grand stucco houses Eliza told Devil about the class she would be attending.

'You don't pose today?'

'No, I paint today. I pay for my tuition and earn a little money by posing for the life class. It's not enough, and I am short of funds. I shall have to find some other work soon.'

'I am sure you will be able to do that. You strike me as a most inventive person. There's no great hardship in living by one's wits, providing one has a good supply of them.'

In fact on a silvery-green spring afternoon with blossom on the cherry trees it seemed an agreeable situation to both of them. The world was full of possibilities, all of them theirs to explore. They mounted the steps of the school and passed through the tall double doors. Devil stopped at the expanse of black-and-white floor and the graceful curve of the stone staircase. Young gentlemen thronged the hallway, moving with the unhurried pace of privilege. Two or three of them wished Miss Dunlop a good afternoon. This was all more imposing than Devil had envisaged. He took off his bowler hat and indicated the portraits that lined the stairs.

'Will I look like one of these?'

'I imagine that Mr Gardiner has something more modern in mind.'

Eliza directed him to the place where he was to meet the painter and went away. George Gardiner was an elegant young man with flowing hair and a loose collar. He shook Devil's hand and told him how much he admired his performance of the Philosophers illusion, treating him with such polite respect that Devil's instinctive antipathy and impulse to mockery soon faded. Mr Gardiner described the intended portrait, in which he planned to capture the moment of the evil philosopher's realisation that he could never escape the power of good. He wanted Devil in his stage robes, the snapped halves of the executioner's sword raised in either hand.

'The essence of it is the tension between illusion, theatricality, the transience of performance, and the eternal moral conflict between good and evil that is the fundament of life. In effect, the portrait is of truth within a lie.'

'I see.' Devil kept his face straight.

The painter showed him the sketch he had made during the Palmyra performance. Devil was quite impressed by its energy, although the staring eyes and flared nostrils made him look

158

histrionic. He should mute his performance a little, he decided. But at Gardiner's suggestion he adopted the required pose and thought himself into the relevant moment of the show. Gardiner made two or three sketches and they agreed that at their next meeting Devil should wear his robes, and then the painter brought up the question of payment for the sittings. Devil held up his hand. The Rawlinson School's atmosphere of high culture and natural superiority made him momentarily eager to belong to such a refined world on its own terms. He declared that he would take no money. Mr Gardiner accepted his refusal with alacrity.

Devil sat on a bench in the hallway to wait for Eliza's class to finish. After a while she came down the stairs, sweeping past the sombre portraits like a debutante on her way to a ball, and he found himself wondering how she had achieved such a level of self-possession. Inside the Rawlinson School, he had to admit, he felt newly second-rate in a way that had never overcome him at the Palmyra or in the Ports. The urgent desire to better himself churned beneath his diaphragm.

He stood up and offered his arm to Eliza.

'How did you do with Mr Gardiner?'

'Mr Gardiner is the greatest molly in Kensington.'

Eliza didn't pretend to be shocked or demand to know what he meant. Her mouth twitched slightly and they strolled out into the afternoon sunshine.

A man had been waiting beside the painted railings that protected the basement area. When he lifted his head they saw that it was Jasper Button.

'Jasper,' she said in surprise. 'Why are you here?'

'I came to see you home after your class, Eliza. What is *he* doing here?'

The two men stood a yard apart. Eliza sighed.

'Mr Wix is to have his portrait painted as the evil philosopher by one of Professor Coope's students.'

'And what else?'

'Nothing else, Jasper. What are you thinking?' Devil protested.

Jasper ignored him. 'Why are you walking with him, Eliza?'

Her face was dark. 'Who are you to demand a reason? I walk with whom I please. I ask you both to remember that. Now I shall go home alone, and I require no assistance from either of you.'

She marched away and Jasper and Devil were left facing each other in silent hostility. In an awkward attempt at mollification Devil thrust out a hand.

'Walk up to the park with me, Jas. Let's not put a woman between us.'

The other swiped him aside.

'Eliza is not just a woman. Why must you always despoil everything, Hector Crumhall? When we were boys you were the one who broke into the dairy, or stole the jug of ale in such a way that the rest of us got the stick. You were the one who set the fire in the barn. Wherever you go there is trouble and pain and it falls upon all around you while you bounce away. My poor mother did well to name you as she did. Have you made a pact with your namesake? Is that your secret?'

Devil was enraged by this nonsense. 'You talk like a superstitious girl. I have no secrets, Jas. None from you, anyway, since you know who I am and where I came from. And you also saw that the fire was an accident. I have lived with the result of it every waking hour since that night, and many sleeping hours as well. You know nothing. How do you dare to accuse me?'

The passers-by in the sunny street stared at them. To escape attention they began to walk towards the park but suddenly Devil swung round. Jasper Button had no right to judge him. He was ready to fight, but the misery in his friend's face stopped him short.

'Come,' he said quietly. Jasper's head drooped and they walked in silence to the gates of the park. The wide avenue in front of the Memorial was crowded with pretty children out with their nursemaids, and with ladies and gentlemen strolling past the tulip beds. A young girl was selling spice-cakes from a basket.

Devil paid her a penny and took two warm cakes in a twist of paper. The two men sat down on the steps below the Prince's throne and looked down at the people going by. Pigeons with blackened plumage dipped and toed for their crumbs.

'I'm sorry,' Jasper said. 'I want to marry Eliza, and she won't have me.'

'Have you asked her?'

'Not in so many words. I am friendly with her sister and her brother-in-law and they are kind, and I have met her father. He is not a reflective person but I think he would accept me. It is Eliza herself who does not incline. I thought if I were patient and did not push matters, she might change her mind. But when she noticed me this afternoon I read impatience in her, not affection. I don't think she would be impatient at the sight of *you*, Devil.'

'I have no intentions in that direction.' But guilt prickled inside his collar like a sweat breaking out. In an attempt to convince himself, as much as Jasper, Devil rushed on. 'How could I take on the trouble of a wife? There is too much else to be done. There is magic, the Palmyra, the dwarf and the work he can help me with. All I want is health and opportunity, Jas.' He was going to say, *You have my word on that*, but he looked and saw to his dismay that Jasper was weeping. His friend's head was bowed and his hands hung between his knees.

'Damn,' Jasper said in a muffled voice.

In place of the grown man sat poor studious talented little Jasper, with his ruined parents and the raw-bones poverty that had stunted his progress as much as his physical growth. Devil knew that his friend could have been a better artist than any of the young fops who postured at the Rawlinson.

He said roughly, 'Listen. I have got business at the Palmyra. I don't know when it will happen, but I am going to need your help in the future. Will you be with me?'

'I don't know.'

'*Will* you?'

'Yes.'

161

Jasper sniffed and raised his head. He looked away from Devil to the branches lacing the sky and the dome of the Albert Hall like a huge leaden blister beyond.

'Good luck,' he said at length.

They did not try to define in which enterprise.

In the next weeks the Execution of the Philosopher made the Palmyra theatre a fashionable destination. *The Times's* theatre correspondent wrote, '*Flamboyant, gory and thoroughly mystifying. See it.*' *In Town's* critic declared that the illusion was '*an utterly magnificent plum set in an otherwise doughy mix of old-fashioned music hall vulgarities*'. Devil did not hesitate to point out the latter to Grady. 'We have some new effects to show you,' he declared.

This was true. He and Carlo had returned to the coffin maker's workshop to design and build the necessary devices.

He continued. 'You could get rid of the comedian and the tenor, at the very least. Give me and Carlo the close of the first half and the finale. We can discuss the terms.'

'Bring in what you've got. But you're getting paid more than enough already,' Grady retorted.

Ten per cent of a steady succession of sell-out houses meant that Boldoni and Wix had some money behind them, but for once they were in full agreement. They spent as little as possible on living, used what they needed to buy materials to develop new works, and saved the remainder.

Devil was exasperated. He shouted at Grady, 'We have to develop, man. People will soon tire of this show, and we must tease their appetites. But we don't give our ingenuity away. No more "magnificent plums" without cash on the table for Boldoni and Wix.'

Grady slammed his hands on the table.

'Get out.'

One evening not long after this, a group of gentlemen in opera clothes sat in the box to the right of the stage. Amongst them was the solid figure of the Prince of Wales.

On the next night, there was a fight outside the doors because tickets that had been sold to one party were claimed by another.

On the third, signs were put up at the foyer entrance. '*The Palmyra Theatre regrets the cancellation of tonight's performance of the Execution of the Philosopher due to the indisposition of one of the artists*'. Devil had brought in the news that Carlo was ill again.

The disappointed crowd were promised tickets for future performances, but when the same sign was displayed on the next night the mob poured into the theatre and howled and stamped with such fury that the show had to be stopped. Grady went out on to the stage and tried to placate the audience, but he was forced to run from a fusillade of hurled abuse and solid detritus.

Backstage as the rest of the performers silently disrobed he hauled Devil into his office. Behind him Mr Wu was gathering dust in the same manner as the cabinet had done during Carlo's last lengthy illness. Devil dropped into a chair, stuck out his long legs and folded his arms, the picture of insolence.

'You think you hold my bollocks in your fist, Wix?'

'I would prefer not.'

'How long will this *illness* continue?'

'I can't say.'

There was a long silence during which both men performed their calculations. A fist thudded on the door jamb and Eggin stuck his head into the room.

'There be a whole crowd on 'em in the street. Had to lock the doors, sir.'

'Dear me. Held prisoner in your own theatre,' Devil observed.

'Find another fucking dwarf, Wix, or restore this one. Get the box trick on again.'

'It is not quite as simple as that.'

Grady's brittle patience finally snapped. His bullying manner gave way to a silky calm that was infinitely more threatening. 'Very well. Here is what I propose. We'll play a little game of cards, just you and me. I will choose the game, and set the rules.'

Devil inclined his head.

'If I win, you will destroy the contract under which you claim a tenth of my earnings from this theatre. And you will play the Philosophers as and when I choose.'

'And if I win?'

Grady found his cigar case. He stripped off the band and struck a match.

'Twenty per cent, all houses. And you can try out any of your material on my stage, no restrictions.'

Devil underwent one of his transformations. He was on his feet, at the door.

'Tomorrow night,' he said. 'Here.'

EIGHT

The next evening Devil presented himself at the theatre much earlier than was customary, while the building was as yet empty. He was accompanied by Heinrich who was wheeling Lucie's trunk. Devil insisted that Eggin stay with him while he carried out some checks of the stage machinery before the night's diminished show.

'If I'm not under observation while I do my work, no doubt Jacko Grady will claim that I'm up to no good. Eh, Eggin? Isn't that so?'

'Most like,' Eggin sourly conceded. He followed Devil out on to the stage and stood there like a person roughly carved from teak by means of a blunt chisel. Devil whistled as he performed a series of minute adjustments to the springs of doors and other stage properties.

He called from the depths below the stage, 'Hand me down that smallest screwdriver, Eggin, would you? And the pot of black paint. I'm obliged. Vanishing acts are really more to do with varnishing, eh? Ha ha.'

After a little while, Heinrich also appeared from the wings. He twisted his hands with anxiety.

'There will be no dance tonight. Lucie is also indisposed.'

'How so?' Devil politely asked as Heinrich sat down and placed his head in his hands.

'I find there is a leakage of air within her compression system. I must disassemble the main piston.'

'I see. That is unfortunate.'

Devil resumed work. Eggin was able to keep one eye on him and the other on Heinrich, thanks to the tendency of his eyes to move independently. Nothing of the smallest interest occurred. Devil declared at last that he was satisfied and wandered away to change into his costume before performing the Flames. Eggin returned to his place at the stage door.

After the show a fresh green baize cloth was laid over Jacko Grady's battered card table. The manager seated himself facing the door and gestured to Devil to take his place opposite.

With the news that Carlo's illness made it unlikely he would return to the Palmyra for some time, notice of the card game had spread through the company. The generally held opinion was that as Boldoni and Wix could not presently perform there was less to play for than there might have been, but just the same as many of the performers as could squeeze into the little room gathered to watch. Eggin was prominent amongst them, having secured the front of house and the stage doors against the night's dissatisfied customers. He frowned in the doorway, his lower lip thrust out. He kept his eyes on Devil, as if he expected him to disappear at any moment through a concealed trapdoor.

Devil sat down where Jacko Grady indicated. He took off his coat and smilingly rolled up his shirtsleeves to show that nothing was concealed. Grady gave an abrupt nod and mouthed over his cigar.

'The cards. You will not object to these items, Wix?'

It was a brand new box of two decks, manufactured by the London Playing Card Company, red-backed with an all-over design of flower tendrils, as ordinary to look at as a dish of bread and milk. There were twenty shops within a mile's radius where an identical box might have been purchased. Devil peered at the unbroken seal and indicated his assent. Grady broke the box open and gave one of the decks a lazy overhand shuffle, passed it to Devil to make the cut, and took it back again ready to deal.

Grady began, 'Let's have a low-stakes hand or two, what d'you say?'

'All right.'

'Five-card?'

'If that's what you favour.'

The audience pressed a little closer. Grady peered through the coiling smoke of his cigar.

'How's the dwarf?'

'Sick.'

Grady clicked his tongue. 'Let's start up with – let's see – your night's money, Wix.'

'Low stakes indeed.'

Devil dropped the ante coins on to the green baize and Grady matched them. He dealt two cards each, one of these face up. Devil's was a nine, the manager's a four. With the lower up card, it was Grady's bet. He put down another half-crown, obliging Devil to do likewise if he did not call the bet or fold his hand. The third cards were a queen for Devil and a three for Grady.

'Again,' Grady said. The coins clinked.

The next cards were a ten for Devil and a king for Grady. The audience watched in silence. Devil placed another coin and Grady dealt the last two cards, an ace for Devil and a three for himself.

'You are a bold player,' Devil remarked as he laid out his hand to reveal a pair of tens.

Grady responded with a pair of kings. He swept up the money.

'Another hand, same stakes?' the manager enquired.

'Certainly.'

This time, Grady folded after the third card when he dealt Devil the ace of clubs.

The third hand Grady won with a queen and a knave to Devil's jumble of low cards.

Devil shifted in his seat. His yawn might have been real. 'I don't know about you, Grady. I am ready for some serious play.'

'Very good,' the manager agreed. 'If that's the way you want it, we shall raise the game.'

From a drawer in the table Grady took out the weighty pouch he had earlier removed from the safe. On the green baize field he counted out an ante of ten sovereigns. At the sight of this much starting money there was a gasp from the spectators and Grady removed his cigar from his mouth for long enough to order silence.

'If you can't shut up you can all get out of here.'

The room was airless. Grady's forehead was glimmering but Devil's face was as expressionless as a royal card. He laid out his sovereigns, allowing no one to see what reserves he had. Devil took the pack and table shuffled it, cut and repeated the shuffle before passing to Grady to cut again. Devil dealt the two cards apiece. Devil slid his hole card to the edge of the table, and lifted one corner to glimpse the index so that Grady could not possibly catch sight of it. There was a long pause. In the corner of the room with his back to the door Heinrich Bayer unfolded a silk handkerchief and touched it to the corners of his mouth. Grady's fist slid over the cloth and opened on another ten sovereigns. Another silent moment passed before Devil did the same. He dealt a third card each, a queen for Grady and a ten for himself. Grady was enough of a player to keep his face composed, but he couldn't staunch the beads of sweat. The room was quiet enough for the ticking of Heinrich Bayer's family pocket watch to become audible.

'Raise,' Grady said softly. 'Twenty.'

He counted out the twenty sovereigns as if it were a stake of twenty halfpence. The gleam of the heaped coins drew the eyes of the acrobats and the singers, and the hungry comedian who had attracted nothing but catcalls from that night's audience.

Devil put down five pounds. 'I shall have to ask you to accept my paper for the remainder.' He scribbled the promise and put the note beside the money. Grady coldly looked on.

Devil dealt two more cards, a deuce for the manager and a knave for himself. The men's eyes met. It was Devil's bet. Betraying himself for the first time in the game he caught the inside of his lower lip between his teeth. His throat seemed to contract as he swallowed, dry-mouthed.

'Here is my bet,' he said.

He placed the folded contract on the table. It was creased and stained from always being kept with him.

'And so we come to it,' Grady murmured. He opened the drawer once again and laid the second copy of the document on top of the first.

Devil dealt the last two cards. The queen of clubs for Grady and the ace of diamonds for himself. He rocked back in his chair.

Grady revealed his hole card. It was a third queen. 'Trips.'

Devil turned over his nine and Grady laughed at the sight. Devil lacked one card for a straight.

'Eight is a lucky number for the Chinese, I believe. I'm sorry it is not so for you, Wix.'

He folded both copies of the contract and put them away. Devil sat in unhappy silence. The performers stared at him, curious and pitying except for Heinrich who looked nowhere at all. The tension in the room leaked away, leaving nothing but smoke and the sharp reek of sweat. Devil stood up slowly, rubbed his hand across the back of his mouth and left the room. Eggin made to block his way, but the manager jerked his chin to signal that he could go. The onlookers began to chatter amongst themselves until Grady flicked his hand at them.

'Clear out. The show's over, and so is Devil Wix and his percentage of my profits. No money, no dwarf, no future. It's a cruel business.'

Bascia giggled. 'Perhaps not so much over, sir.'

Devil reappeared. He was pale but composed, and he looked as if he had undergone a change of heart.

'I want to win my money and the contract back. For the dwarf's sake as well as my own. You'll give me that chance?'

'Aw,' somebody crooned.

Devil pushed through the spectators and took his place at the table again.

'Come on. Play,' he implored.

'What are you going to play with, Wix? Got some more ready money hidden away, have you?'

'I have no money left, ready or otherwise. But I've got what you lack, Grady. Talent.'

'And so?'

In a low voice Devil said, 'I'll secure a loan with the performance rights to the Philosophers illusion.'

Grady considered, for an interval finely calculated to be insulting.

'Very well,' he said. He made a flourish to show that Devil should put his promise in writing. Devil scribbled again and thrust the signed paper across the table. A spot of colour touched his cheekbones and faded as quickly as it had come. Grady counted out the money that Devil had already lost and Devil piled it precisely in two short columns. He kept his eyes lowered but his hands were steady. The performers edged closer to the table. No one spoke. Grady sniffed and dealt another hand.

The cards did not fall in Devil's favour. He seemed to bet with care, smaller sums and on likely hands, but still he lost the next three games and with them all the money that Grady had loaned him. With a spit of laughter the manager tapped the note before pocketing it.

'Thank you kindly. The Palmyra theatre now owns in perpetuity all the performance rights in the Execution of the Philosopher. Gentlemen, ladies, that concludes the evening's entertainment. Bad luck on you, Wix.'

Dismay froze the room. This reversal seemed to have come about with all the speed of a game played for pennies between stage turns. Devil was not greatly popular except with Bayer and Bascia, but none of the performers relished the sight of one of their company losing all to a man like Jacko Grady. Heinrich Bayer buttoned his overcoat and settled his muffler around his thin neck. He murmured some word about Lucie, and touched Devil's shoulder as he made ready to leave.

Devil only shook his head and continued to stare at the mussed cards, evidently trying to collect his thoughts. Absently he collected them and tapped them to square the edges before putting the deck to one side.

Grady stood up and turned his back, busy with a ledger and his bunch of keys, blithe as if his opponent no longer existed.

Another second ticked by.

'Wait,' Devil said, in a low voice.

Grady half turned. 'Wait for what? For you to earn a few more shillings to lose at cards, is it?'

'I will play you one more hand.'

Bascia broke away from her brother's side. 'Fool, fool,' she hissed in Devil's ear. Hooking an acrobat's muscled arm around his neck she tried to pull him from the table but the only result was to make him angry.

'Don't touch me,' he said.

'Late in the day to be telling her that, isn't it?' Grady sneered.

'I will play you one more hand,' Devil repeated.

'Your stake will be?'

With a movement that clearly hurt him Devil put a shabby black notebook on the table and slid it one inch towards Grady. Grady shrugged his indifference but still he picked it up and flicked through pages of cramped handwriting and innumerable drawings and diagrams.

'What's this?'

'My work.'

Grady blew a fart between his thick lips.

Devil patiently said again, 'My work. You have there the designs and methods for dozens of new illusions. Had I the money and a workshop of my own, I would build the apparatus

171

you see drawn here and devise the effects to go with them. In comparison with these, the Philosophers will seem like a school-boy's first attempt to impress his father and mother. Once onstage, they will make the Palmyra home to the finest magic show the world has ever seen.'

'Don't undersell yourself, Wix.'

'Why stop at merely owning the Philosophers? The rights to these unperformed illusions is my surety against one more loan. You could put the notions and the drawings in the hands of another performer and still make your money. Give me the chance, won't you?'

This time Grady did not pretend to hesitate. He sat down again, the chair protesting under his weight. While the fat man settled himself Devil took the opportunity to glance around him, at the brass-bound safe, the cigar boxes, the account ledgers, Heinrich's forgotten chinaman, and the shelves that all lay under a thick layer of dust. He tapped the nearest ledger and a cloud arose. No one took the trouble to perform house-keeping tasks backstage at the Palmyra. The performers were all caught between dismay and fascination as the heap of money was roughly reapportioned. Two piles of ten sovereigns apiece was the ante.

'My deal, I believe,' Devil said. He reached for the cards in a fluid movement, performed an elegant and thorough riffle, cut the pack and repeated the move, then passed it across to Grady. The manager waved the company to the margin of the room, so all of them stood behind Devil and none of them could catch a glimpse of his own hand. Then he stroked the pack, checking the edges for crimps or forcing positions. Satisfied, he slid it back. As Devil picked up the cards ready to deal, the dust made his throat convulse in a dry cough.

Unable to control himself any longer, Heinrich broke violently through the ring of performers.

'For God's sake, man. Stop it. Don't ruin yourself.'

Devil ducked away from him, stooping low beneath the table edge to avoid the engineer's flailing arms.

172

'Eggin!' Grady yelled. The doorman lurched forward and pinned Heinrich's arms at his sides. The engineer was hustled to the edge of the semicircle.

Devil recovered from the interruption and dealt two and two. Grady had a ten up, his own was a king. Instead of sliding his hole card across the baize and lifting one corner, Devil picked it up to study it and then laid it face down next to his king. For the first time since they had begun to play he raised his eyes to meet Grady's. The manager's pupils had dilated.

Devil cupped his fist over the coins that remained to him and gently pushed them into the pot.

In slow motion Grady's tongue passed over his lips. He fought the impulse, but he could not stop himself glancing to one side. The broken-open box that had contained the two new decks of cards lay discarded, with one placed beside it. He knew that it must be the second, thus far unused, that was now in Devil's hands.

The creak of his chair as the fat man shifted his weight sounded as loud as a rifle shot. Devil had Eggin at his back, and Heinrich Bayer, Bascia and her brother and the other witnesses. He raised his eyebrows a fraction of an inch. The silence extended.

'Very well,' Jacko Grady said at last in a low voice. He counted out his bet. Devil dealt two more cards. A fresh bead of sweat broke on the manager's forehead. He looked at his hand. Then he nodded.

'Play,' he commanded.

Now it was Devil who could not quite suppress a tremor. Perhaps not even Grady saw it; the onlookers certainly did not, but they drew one combined inwards breath as they sensed yet another change of balance between the players. Devil must surely have been anticipating that the manager would fold his cards?

'In addition to signing over to you my designs, I will undertake to work on them for you and the Palmyra for five years.' Devil's voice was quite steady. Lifting his chins out of his damp collar, Grady made the same scribbling movement and Devil obediently wrote out his latest promise. Eggin squinted at the writing. But Devil held up his hand as Grady reached out for the paper.

'So I am staking my future,' Devil said softly. 'Money, even your money, Grady, doesn't match that. I require something bigger.'

'What might that be?'

'Let's see. What I have already lost tonight, and the deeds of the Palmyra.'

Grady's features seemed to contract into a scarlet knob of damp flesh. But it was only for an instant. Eggin and all the rest of the company were watching his movements. The manager threw the book and papers on to the table. He was greedy, and he had his hand of cards. He heaved himself to his feet and once more took up the bunch of keys that Devil hated with such passion. He unlocked the safe, took out a parchment envelope and tossed it down. With the tips of his fingers lightly resting on the deck of cards, Devil tipped his chin at Heinrich Bayer. The engineer pressed his steel spectacles against the bridge of his nose as he scanned the document.

'Yes.' He placed it on the table.

Devil dealt again, one card apiece.

Grady snatched at his. The sweat had evaporated on his forehead and his face was a motionless slab. Devil allowed his eyes to drift downwards, to the heaps of sovereigns, to his scribbled promises, the black notebook, and the folded deeds. He picked up the fourth card and studied it.

Grady leaned back, waiting. His eyes returned to dark spots as he sensed victory. The onlookers were forgotten.

Devil gave the smallest of shrugs. In a flat voice with winter in it he said, 'I have nothing more to stake.'

'Play it out,' Grady snapped.

There was no snap or flourish left in Devil as he set out two more cards, face up this time. The three of clubs for himself, the ten of diamonds for Grady.

There was a scrape of feet and the rustle of clothing as the company closed in to witness the kill.

Grady's sausage fingers spread his cards for all to see. Ten, nine, eight, seven, and another ten.

Devil's lips made a white line in his whiter face.

On the green cloth he ranged the three with a two of diamonds and the ace of spades. And then he laid down the one-eyed king of diamonds and the black king of spades.

Bascia gave a cry in her impenetrable language and ran to coil her arms round his neck.

Grady's hands dropped to his sides, heavy as bags of sand. Devil brushed Bascia aside and gathered the deeds, the notebook and the promises. The sovereigns he casually raked away. Then he held out his hand under the manager's nose.

'The keys.'

Grady made no move but there was a ripple as his stage company gathered shoulder to shoulder at Devil's back. Eggin stood apart, his jaws silently working.

Devil's fingers beckoned the air.

'Give me the keys.'

Only now did Grady properly comprehend what had happened. The man seemed to deflate. He wagged his head in an attempt at refusal. Bascia's brother and the hungry comedian were like dogs scenting the change in the wind. The comedian attached himself to Devil's side, and the acrobat curved his lean frame over the fat man's.

'Give him,' he hissed.

'Give him,' Bascia echoed, her voice rising to a shriek.

The company, like a chorus, repeated the words. Their anger at Grady's treatment of them suddenly broke through their submission. They rushed at the manager, pulling him out of his chair and dragging at his coat.

'Eggin!' the fat man wailed but the doorman only stood like a block of wood.

'Give him,' the players howled.

Grady raised one arm to protect his face from the breath

175

and the flying spittle. The fingers of the other hand groped in his pocket and brought out the keys. The metal jangled as he let them fall in Devil's hand.

'Out,' Devil coldly ordered.

There was a drumming and stamping, a clamour of voices and a whirl of elbows and heels and thrusting shoulders. For the first time in its existence the Palmyra company became a united organism. Its hands held Grady upright and its feet marched him out of his office. It bore him through the narrow backstage corridors, bundling him round tight corners and dragging him down uneven steps. Eggin could do nothing but follow in their wake until they came to his stage door.

'Open,' the voices shouted. Eggin unlocked and unbolted, and the organism's boots kicked Grady out into the gusty breath of wind off the river. The fat man staggered on the cobbles and Eggin stumbled after him. There was a ragged cheer and Bascia's brother yelled, 'You finish.'

'Finished!' the hungry comedian and the tenor and the violinist shouted, and they all laughed.

A woman in a hooded cape was concealed between the stage door and the river wall. She had not been aware that this was the place where the poorest of the street women led their customers to couple briefly in the darkness between the mud-slimed piers and the black water, but she could not help seeing and hearing some of their business tonight. The depths to which these abject creatures had fallen had never seemed closer or more real, and she had shivered while she waited. At last she saw Grady and Eggin ejected into the alley by the jeering crew and she gathered her cloak and ran. She slipped through the ecstatic company, briefly flattened herself against the cobwebs of Eggin's one-time sanctuary, then as the shouts pursued Grady and Eggin up the alley she sped on through the empty backstage passages to the office where Devil sat weighing the keys in his hand. Heinrich Bayer quietly stood against the wall.

Eliza put her hood back. Her hair clung to her throat with river damp and her eyes shone.

'You did it.'

Devil nodded and she laughed in wild triumph.

'You did it! I knew you would.'

Heinrich came forward and grasped her wrist.

'Lucie?' he cried.

'Lucie is quite safe in Carlo's room, exactly as you left her. The door is secure.'

The engineer groaned. 'You promised to stay with her.'

'I had to come,' Eliza cried. 'We are four, remember?'

'Wait,' Devil snapped.

The running feet were returning, with the swish of sleeves and skirts against bare brick walls. The company poured back into the room and gathered there, panting and elated, every eye fixed on the new owner-manager.

Devil stared back at them, and as he did so the organism's elation slowly evaporated.

The players shifted and seemed to shrink, separating into individuals and apparently calling to mind the stage performances they had given that night and on other evenings. The comedian sadly lowered his gaze to the heap of sovereigns on the green baize cloth.

To Heinrich Devil said, 'Divide this equally between them, would you?'

The engineer counted the coins into piles. Devil picked up a box of lucifers and struck a light. He held it to the corner of his ten-per-cent agreement and watched as the flame licked and the paper curled. He dropped the last smouldering fragment to the floor and stamped it into ash. He did the exactly same thing with Grady's copy, and his own promissory notes. The black notebook and the deeds disappeared into the inner pocket of his coat.

When there were as many small piles of coins as there were company members Devil gave a curt nod.

'Take them,' he ordered, and hands were instantly thrust

out. There was a chink of metal followed by the hasty fastening of purses and pockets.

Devil said, 'Now. Go home. You may come back tomorrow morning, if you so wish, and audition for me. But I make no promises.'

Watching this, Eliza was surprised by his chill expression and the hard line of his mouth.

Heinrich went with the players to the stage door and watched them leave in a silent file. He slid the bolts to secure the theatre and returned to the office. Devil was sitting in silence, apparently studying his own fists. Eliza was looking across at the Chinaman. Beneath his fingers, there were tiny smudges in the layer of dust that dimmed the oriental fabric of his robe. They were no more noticeable than if a mouse had curled its tail there. Eliza knew the texture of the dust. She had gathered it herself, using a fine paintbrush, from an unused storeroom of the Rawlinson School and had brought it to Devil and Heinrich in a glass vial.

Devil raised his head. 'All safe?'

'Yes,' Heinrich answered.

They went to the Chinaman in his niche. Gently they lifted him and placed him on the floor. The engineer stooped to the rivets that fastened the back of the manikin's torso. When they were removed he took off its curved metal back plate and tipped its round head forwards. The black straw hat fell off and rolled under the card table. In the body cavity another head appeared, followed by a pair of small shoulders.

'Jesus and Mary,' said the dwarf. And then, 'Mind your bloody great self, Wix.'

As soon as he was extricated from the shell of the automaton Carlo hopped in agony from one cramped leg to the other. 'I need a piss.' Devil began a mocking word but Carlo wouldn't hear it. 'You haven't spent five hours being jolted around in a trunk and then looking down the nostrils of a Chinaman,' he yelled, and bolted from the room. They heard him noisily relieving himself in the pot that was kept in the performers' dressing area.

Devil glanced around the sordid space that had been Grady's lair.

'I dislike this room,' he murmured.

When Carlo came back, Devil found a bottle in one of Grady's cupboards. There were no glasses, so they took it in turns to swig at it in response to his toast.

'The Palmyra.'

'The Palmyra,' they repeated.

'It's yours now,' Eliza smiled at Devil. 'Just as you said.'

'Ours,' the dwarf sourly amended.

Devil made a flourish with the bottle. 'It belongs in name to the company of four. Or five, because I would like Jasper Button to join us. But I am the manager, and I hold the keys to the safe. Tonight would not have happened if I had not made it do so.'

'All on your ownsome, was that?'

'Of course not. And I thank you, Carlo, and Heinrich, and Eliza, for your help.'

Eliza waited. She wanted this moment of victory to feel like more of a celebration, but Devil's mood was too dark for that. It was as if it were not a victory at all, but the first precarious step on a long journey.

She asked humbly, 'How *did* you make it happen?' wanting to give them a chance to relive their victory at least a little.

Carlo scrambled into the Chinaman's pose. His fingers lifted barely perceptibly in his lap as if he were playing an invisible keyboard. 'I signalled every damned card in Grady's hand to him.'

'I dismantled Mr Wu. And I left Lucie in your care, so I could bring Carlo in unseen,' Heinrich said severely.

'Lucie is quite safe, I promise.' Eliza turned to Devil, and found that he was watching her. She met his stare as coolly as she could.

His mouth twisted. 'It was too easy. I needed to know precisely what was in his hand so I could lose convincingly enough, that's all. The fat fool was using a marked deck.'

The cards still lay next to the opened box. He picked up the first deck and fanned it into a river on the baize cloth. His forefinger flicked at tiny variations in the tendril pattern on the reverse. As soon as he pointed them out they sprang into clear sight. 'It must have been quite a feat for him, memorising the differences. The second pack was unmarked. It was child's play to switch them. It was a double switch, though.' He did smile now, a quick grin that was like a door cracking open in a dark cellar. 'I'd prepared a score of different decks, all the common patterns and some uncommon ones too. And which one does he pick to cheat with? The most ordinary of the ordinary, Red Tendril.' He added, 'I was almost disappointed. All I had to do was collect my stacked deck from the dressing room and play out the last hand.'

Eliza thought about it.

'There was never a moment after that when you didn't know what would happen?'

'No,' Devil agreed. 'There was not. Never bet on the random turn of a card, my girl.'

Heinrich edged towards the door. The empty trunk and its wheeled frame stood in the dressing room amongst the discarded feathers and spangles and empty porter bottles. 'Lucie . . .' he began.

'I will come with you,' Eliza smiled at him.

Carlo had been stretching his limbs and scowling at the painful cramps in them. 'And me. So, Wix. That'll be that, then.'

Devil stood up too. 'Not at all. Not a bit. It's only the beginning. I'll see you here tomorrow morning, first thing.'

'Aye. First thing, then.' *Foost.*

Yes, Eliza thought. I was right. Only the beginning. The urgent glamour of her naive theatre dreams was already taking on a new, harder aspect. Charlotte and the Chaperone needed to be better if it was ever going to work on Devil's stage.

She felt an appetite that had nothing to do with food begin to gnaw at her.

Better. Better . . .

Devil let them out into the alley, but he didn't follow on. After the rattle of Lucie's trunk on the cobbles had faded he took a lamp from Eggin's cubbyhole and walked through the silent warren of the theatre. In the auditorium he lifted it up and scanned the box fronts, the dim reaches of the gallery. The glow was too weak to illuminate the cupola over his head.

Placing the lamp down he noticed that the boards had been swept. He looked quickly about him.

'Jakey?' he called. 'You here?'

There was no answer except the hint of an echo in the empty hall.

Devil crossed to the nearest pillar. He spanned it with his hands as if it was the most slender and supple of waists, and caressed the smooth wood. His fingers ran over the carved ripples that mimicked a palm trunk. He regretted having let Eliza Dunlop go off with Carlo. He would have liked to have her, here and now, to celebrate this success.

Instead he allowed himself a private moment of triumph. It came as a harsh bark of laughter. Then he leaned forward until his forehead rested against the pillar.

'Here I am,' he said aloud to the silent theatre.

From the shelter of one of the boxes a pair of eyes longingly watched him.

Jakey's eyes very often rested on Devil, without anyone ever noticing it.

NINE

The Palmyra steps provided a good vantage point. Devil scanned the faces of the morning throng in the Strand until at last he caught sight of her. Eliza approached with characteristic briskness, the feather in the brim of her hat tipping the air in her wake. He put his hand to his coat, where the keys that had once been Jacko Grady's gloriously weighted the pocket.

Eliza skipped up the two steps to his side.

'Good morning,' she smiled.

'A *very* good morning, Eliza. Now you are here, I can think of no respect in which it could possibly be improved.'

He unlocked the tall doors with a flourish and they stepped into the foyer. Light streamed through coloured glass, laying bright flecks on the counter of the ticket office and the wall posters extolling acrobats and fire-eaters.

Devil grinned as he looked about him.

'Mine,' he sighed. He took unabashed pleasure in his own pleasure. Then he indicated the way. 'Shall we?'

They parted the musty curtains of moth-eaten velvet and passed into the auditorium. It was dim in here, with only the cupola to admit thin shafts of sunshine. Dust motes swirled as Devil and Eliza advanced towards the stage.

Devil scanned the stalls. It was still early. There would be no one else here for hours to come. The double tier of boxes offered seclusion, and backstage there were plenty of secure niches – as he knew quite well – although he shrank from escorting Eliza into that squalid warren. In fact, it was quite difficult to determine what amorous setting might be appropriate in connection with Eliza Dunlop. This was part of her appeal to him. She was no Bascia, and she could not have been less like Maria Hayes or any other of the women he knew. His lodgings were out of the question, and so was her ladies-only house in Bayswater. Of course there were numerous taverns and houses nearby, where private rooms were to be had, but he would not even suggest that she accompany him to one of those. No, his theatre was the best meeting place, where they had at least the pretext of her playlet to discuss. She had lost no time in reminding him of a promise he had apparently made to her. Now he owned the theatre, Miss Charlotte and her capers must grace the stage.

In the end they sat down in a double *fauteuil* in the front row. Eliza took out the folded papers on which her script was neatly written out. She was wearing pretty earrings with red glass droplets pendent from a neat gilt setting, and he noticed how the beads swung against the translucent skin of her neck.

'Should not Carlo and the others be here?' Smiling, she glanced at him from beneath her eyelashes.

'No,' he said. The very last person he wanted to see at this moment was the dwarf.

'Then how shall we rehearse my play?'

The tip of her tongue emerged to moisten her lower lip. Eliza was being deliberately provocative, and he liked it very much. He moved closer in the double seat until they were separated by barely an inch of plush. He knew that she recalled the kiss in the alleyway as vividly as he did. Her response to him then had been innocent but instinctive, and thrillingly wholehearted.

'First of all I should like to see you up on my stage.'

'Of course,' she murmured.

Devil locked his hands behind his head and lazily stretched his legs. The good morning was steadily improving.

Eliza walked up the steps on to the boards. She continued into the wings and waited in the shadows there for a few seconds.

Now, she thought.

The space yawning in front of her was alarmingly huge. Empty seats mounted to the rear of the gallery and it was all too easy to imagine rows of expectant faces, hundreds of pairs of eyes all fastened upon her. She lowered her gaze to one amused face, the man waiting to see what she would do next.

I am supposed to be Charlotte, so Charlotte I shall be.

Eliza lifted her head. She spoke the opening lines, now somewhat familiar to them both, before breaking off.

'It would be a good deal easier, you know, if I had a leading man to play to.'

'Very well, Eliza. But you look fine up there. I am already convinced.'

A moment later he stood beside her. He took her arm and they walked through the opening scene of the comedy. Under their feet were the concealed trapdoors, waiting to hide or to yield. Like the sea murmuring in a shell she could hear the invisible audience applauding them.

They soon stopped their pretence of a performance, but they didn't move apart. Eliza turned up her face to his. Their lips were separated by a slice of quiet air. She felt heat travel through her. Devil leaned a little closer, twining his finger in one dark curl of her hair.

'And so?' he enquired.

'Will Charlotte play?'

'Ah, to hell with Charlotte and her blasted chaperone.'

They were laughing as they kissed.

Devil drew out the hatpins one by one, took off her hat and bowled it into the wings. He unpinned her hair and knotted his hands in the dark coils, tilting her head back so he could devour her mouth. His lips moved over her throat, all the way down to her prim buttoned collar. His arm tightened about her waist, and his other hand moved to her breast. She became sharply aware of the cotton and worsted that separated her naked flesh from his fingers. He was undoing the buttons of her coat, without hurry and with considerable deftness. She could not stop him. She had no wish for him to stop. Through her mind ran the half-familiar nooks and recesses of the Palymra: the seats from which she had watched the performances, the backstage office that stank of Grady's pungent cigars, the splintered boards beneath their feet. A fold of white lawn emerged between the fastenings of Eliza's outer clothes.

Devil groaned, 'Dear God, how many layers do we have here?'

She remembered the sequinned brevity of Bascia's stage costume, and the landlady's slovenly undress. Eliza considered herself a modern woman, but compared with these two she was encased in armour. And after that the question: Were all these garments of hers to be stripped off *here*? As a prelude to – she knew what, in outline at least, but she had not anticipated that her feelings would be as imperative as they had now become – in her imagination, in accepting Devil's invitation to meet him here, she had been teasing, irresistibly worldly but quite in control of him and herself – and always in the end somehow able to extricate them both from a delicious interlude – but *now* she was breathless, and it seemed that she was in control of nothing and no one. His large hands grew urgent and more insistent.

Soon Devil hoisted her in his arms and they stumbled to the place at the side of the stage where Grady had habitually stood to oversee and disparage his players. Devil peeled off her light coat and pressed his face between her breasts. Then he sank lower, lifting the hem of her skirt, running his hand from her ankle to her calf.

The acrobat and the landlady were not the only intruders in her mind. There were others, faceless to her but real to him. All of them must have shed their clothes for him, in obedience to – but how could she know what had brought them to this point? She knew only her own story thus far, and the variety of possible endings.

185

Eliza was a life model; she was used to nakedness and scrutiny. But she was suddenly certain, *not here*.

This was not the place, not the time. An instinct for self-preservation, an inkling that her worth was greater than this, took hold of her.

And at the same time she recalled the poor creatures she had glimpsed and heard going about their business down at the river margin on the night of the card game. Each of them had her story too; a story with the harshest of endings. There were so many of these women. They were visible and yet unseen. It was fanciful – lurid, even – but she was afraid she might be about to write an introductory sentence this morning. These words and pages could lead on to concluding lines of her own, spelt out down by the reeking tideline.

Devil sensed her hesitation. He looked up and she saw that his eyes had turned black and heavy-lidded. His hands had reached her thighs, the fingertips resting on the tiny rolls of bare flesh above the tops of her serviceable stockings.

I have been naive. The realisation was like icy water dashed in her face.

She stuttered, 'What . . . do you want from me, Devil?'

She sounded in her own ears like a silly girl.

He blinked, and then he laughed, unamused. 'I would like to discuss the weather. What else?'

'I'm so sorry.' She was hot, angry with herself, caught between disappointed hunger and relief at the prospect of salvation.

Devil withdrew his hands. He rocked back on his heels, crouching as if he were about to spring at her throat.

'You know, I could have you anyway. Right now,' he whispered. He was angry too.

Eliza turned her head. Emptiness and silence surrounded them. She had volunteered herself, she understood that perfectly well.

Humbly she answered, 'I know.' She would not *cry*. She owed herself that much.

'So I might return your question. What do you want from me?' His voice had turned cold.

186

A series of wildly un-Devil-like words ran through her mind: they included constancy, devotion, admiration, equivalence, perhaps even a *future,* but she could not utter a single one of them.

'I don't know,' she said miserably. She was not a woman of the world, she realised, nor was her behaviour clever or estimable. She was a tease; she had wanted to play Devil Wix at his own game, but when it came to it she had had to fold her cards at the first hand.

Devil stood up. He brushed his palms together as if to dispense with her. Then something caught his eye, and he reached down to retrieve her hat. The feather was broken and it stuck out at a ludicrous angle, but he removed the pins from his lapel where he had placed them for safety and secured the hat for her. He tweaked the feather into something resembling its proper condition.

At length their eyes met.

'Well, then. It seems a shame to waste the morning altogether, Eliza. Would you like to adjourn to a coffee shop? Or perhaps you would like to take something stronger?'

Annoyingly, he was in full command of himself. He gave her a mocking grin.

'No, thank you. I will go home.'

He insisted on accompanying her down the Strand to the omnibus, and waited to hand her on board. As the vehicle jerked away, he tipped his bowler to her.

'Damn,' Eliza muttered. 'Damn, and damn *you*, Devil Wix.'

The press of carriages and cabs in Piccadilly was such that the packed omnibus soon came to a standstill again. She glanced backwards between the standing passengers, but Devil had long disappeared from view.

There would be further hands to play, she told herself. She would simply have to wait for a fresh deal.

Mr George Gardiner's portrait of the *Evil Philosopher* hung in prime position, on the wall of the gallery opposite the double doors through which patrons and friends and staff and students of the Rawlinson School entered to view the end-of-year exhibition. A small card to the right of the frame announced that the portrait had been awarded the Founder's Prize Medal for the year 1886.

The artist stood beneath his picture, accepting congratulations. Mr Raleigh Coope, with the artist's mother on his arm, made a tour of the rest of the exhibition and pointed out to her the works that were of particular merit. The plumes crowning the lady's hat stirred as more people circulated through the room. Miss Frazier's drawings had been awarded a distinction in the life section. Charles Egan wondered sotto voce to his friends if the achievement would make it easier for her to find a position as a teacher of art in a girls' school, which was her intention now that she had received her diploma. Some of the young gentlemen from the life class would be returning in September for another year's study, but the main group was breaking up. Mr Vine and Mr Egan were to share a studio in Paris.

'We intend to *immerse* ourselves in painting,' Ralph Vine announced.

A dishevelled red-haired boy leaned against a pillar and mimicked Mr Vine's gestures for the benefit of a circle of his own cronies. As Professor Rawlinson passed by in conversation with Mr Burne-Jones the boy shouldered himself upright and briefly removed his hands from his pockets.

Jasper Button had been studying Miss Frazier's drawings of Eliza. Setting aside as firmly as he could the matter of the model's absent clothing, he judged the studies to be technically adept and with a strong line – yet the artist had entirely failed to capture the energy that characterised their subject. There was none of the glitter in the eyes, or the smiling play of tiny muscles around the full mouth that he still loved. With a touch of irritation he stood back to survey the throng. The presence of so many young people who were so sure of their own worth made him resentful of his different material circumstances, even though Jasper had long ago learned that resentment of human privilege was nothing but destructive.

If I had only had a mere *one tenth* of all your opportunities, he could not help thinking. Even the young men from the commercial school, who were visiting the fine art halls only because Professor Rawlinson had notions about availability for all, seemed blithely confident of the world's kindness compared with Jasper's present and even future uncertainty.

His critical eye travelled over the nearest exhibits. Which of them displayed a higher level of talent than he possessed?

None, was the answer.

Naturally he was grateful for his steady employment as a modeller at the Baker Street Bazaar, and Matthew Shaw was a good manager and friend, but the prospects for real advancement were limited. Matters were complicated too by Devil's demands on his time. All through the spring and early summer, ever since he had promised Devil in front of the Albert Memorial that he would be with him, Jasper had found himself increasingly drawn into the work at the Palmyra. Following the ejection of Mr Grady a show of sorts had continued to run, but the restoration of the theatre was what concerned the new owner.

Devil wanted to consult Jasper about the possible renewal of the fronts of the boxes. Could the gilding be embellished with lozenges of bright colour, and if this were done would the effect be of an Arabian palace? If the lovely carved pillars supporting the gallery were stripped and polished, could Jasper model more sumptuous fronds for the capitals? Devil also wanted scenery painted – not a few brush strokes slapped on to coarse canvas, but a woodland glade for a backdrop to Charlotte and the Chaperone.

'I want it so real I can smell the leaf-mould, Jas,' he insisted. 'I know you can do it like no one else.'

Devil also made calls on his friend for costume designs, for illustrations for the programme head and for handbills and posters. He wanted Jasper to be present for discussions about

189

lighting and perspectives and mirrors, and a thousand other matters.

It was not that Jasper didn't enjoy their collaboration, or the new challenges of theatre work, but he had so little time to spare from building his waxworks. The public appetite for new figures was insatiable. Each lately convicted murderer, the actress in the fashionable stage play, the players in this week's society scandal – the Bazaar's patrons expected to see them represented in the gallery almost before the print was dry on the day's newspapers.

'We have to give 'em what they want, Jasper, or they'll go elsewhere,' Matthew said.

'I'm too busy,' Jasper had told Devil.

Devil drew himself up. 'Jas, let the damned Bazaar go hang. Such work doesn't reward your talents. Come to join me and Carlo. I'll cut you in on the profits, don't worry about that.'

'What profits would these be?'

Devil only laughed. 'Carlo's forever grumbling that thirty per cent of nowt is nowt, and I know nowt's all we've got right now, but I guarantee that will change. Once the new show goes on the Palmyra is certain to be a great success. Come on, man. Take a risk for once in your life. Join the fellowship.'

Jasper knew quite well that the original fellowship had comprised Devil, Carlo, Heinrich and Eliza. He longed to spend more time in Eliza's company, although he was already almost certain that nothing would persuade her to favour him over Devil. He contented himself with answering drily, 'You risk enough for both of us.'

At the Rawlinson exhibition he studied the crowd of ladies in silk dresses and young art students in soft collars and velveteen coats, the distinguished professors and painters and the sprinkling of sombre professional men who peered through their steel spectacles at the less conventional works. These last were the patrons, and investors, and relatives of pampered would-be artists. Some of these men must surely have taken risks at some stage of their lives? Clearly they had survived

– even prospered. Perhaps one or two of them owned just such a white stucco house with wide steps and tall windows as he desired for his own family. If he were ever to have a family.

Jasper sighed.

'There you are,' a voice said. 'Why do you look so downcast? Do you not approve of the art?'

It was Eliza, hatless and wearing a dress the colour of new leaves on a thorn bush that he had never seen on her before. Her hair was drawn up from her white neck and her hand rested lightly on the arm of Heinrich Bayer.

'I like some of it a very little,' he said.

She laughed. 'My poor pictures were not even selected for the show. I dare not think what your opinion of those might have been.'

'I'd like to have seen them, Eliza. Good evening, Bayer.'

Jasper and the engineer shook hands. They had met only recently at the Palmyra, where Heinrich had been helping Devil and Carlo with the proposed mechanics for an ambitious new illusion.

'I want the most powerful electromagnet ever devised,' Devil had announced.

'You may want such a thing, but it will not be easy or cheap,' said Heinrich.

Carlo had thumped the desk that had once been Jacko Grady's. 'Why d'you always make everything so difficult, Wix?'

'Because nothing good enough is ever easy,' was the answer.

Now Heinrich peered past Jasper's shoulder at the crowded exhibition room.

'So many people,' he muttered.

Eliza explained to Jasper, 'Lucie is resting at my lodgings. Herr Bayer has been kind to escort me.' She held up a hand before Jasper could protest that he would have been pleased to do so himself. 'Have you seen the prize portrait?'

Jasper had so far only glanced at it.

'Let us take a look together,' Eliza said. She linked her other arm in his and the three of them progressed down the room.

Several of the young men greeted Eliza, and others recognised Heinrich from the Palmyra show and bowed to him. One smirking youth asked for his good wishes to be conveyed to Miss Lucie. Heinrich responded with a distant nod.

They halted in front of the picture.

Devil was portrayed in the black costume of the evil philosopher. He stood with his arms raised, the halves of the broken sword clasped in his hands. The bright steel was smeared with blood. His head was thrown back to reveal the straining cords of his neck, his nostrils flared and his lips were open in what was neither a smile nor – quite – a sneer. The horsehair wig was perched on his head but it was pushed a little awry to reveal a single lock of black hair. The artist had made much play with light and shade, splashing the purples and greens of stage illumination over the folds of the gown and exaggerating the hollows in the philosopher's cheeks and eye sockets. Behind his shoulder were the fantastic pinnacles of the decorated cabinet. At his feet lay the basket, in which another horsehair wig was just visible.

Jasper studied the work. Despite the drama of the treatment, the physical likeness was so good that the portrait seemed not a caricature but a heightened reality. It suggested that the Devil of everyday concealed within himself this more vivid incarnation. Eliza used the excuse of adjusting the sleeve of her dress to withdraw her hand from beneath Jasper's arm. There was some laughter and exclaiming in the group of people that stood behind them.

'Well?' she asked Jasper at length.

'It's good,' he had to say. Of course it was florid, but it was the portrait of a performer in a popular entertainment and not an intimate study. Instead of diminishing Devil with its histrionics it captured his tense and overarching drive to attract attention, of which the theatrical costume was a mere hint.

'I thought so. I wanted to hear your opinion, Jasper, because you comprehend art better than anyone in this room. And of course you also know the man better than anyone else.'

192

Jasper turned his head, but for once he could detect no gleam of mockery in Eliza's eyes. She meant what she said.

'Yes, it's good,' he repeated. 'It deserves the prize.' He was going to tell her about the picture's merits, but her gaze had already slid past him.

Devil stood at the centre of the laughing group. He was wearing his old coat with a rose in the buttonhole. He fell into a pose that aped the stance and expression of his portrait, exaggerating so comically that even George Gardiner was amused.

'Not so, Mr Wix. You are unkind,' the painter protested.

Devil saw Eliza and Jasper looking on. He tipped them a warning nod before adroitly cornering a man in well-cut evening clothes. He spoke urgently in the gentleman's ear, and the rest of the group who had surrounded them strolled away.

'I hear the song of money,' Eliza murmured.

The weeks that had passed since Devil won the Palmyra had been all about money. There had been great bursts and gales of frenzied activity around the stage, but it was the getting of money that underlay everything.

The company of Jacko Grady's days had been re-auditioned. Devil warned them to use only their best material if they hoped to be retained. Others had been dismissed outright. Bascia and her brother had fallen into the second category. Eliza only heard this at second hand from Carlo, a few days after the painful encounter with Devil at the theatre. She had been pleased with the news but she did not speak about it to Devil. They continued to be cordial, even to tease each other, to the extent that none of their companions knew that anything significant had happened, but there was a secret prickle of discomfort between them now that felt like a burr trapped between sheet and skin.

She and Carlo worked on their playlet. They honed the dialogue and speeded up the action, and they added one more twist to the hectic sequence. At Devil's apparently casual sugges-tion they also recruited the strange, lanky boy who swept the theatre floors. Eliza had been sceptical until she saw the eerie way that Jakey could change his very being once he was under the lights. With a twist of his mouth or shoulders he became one person, then with a lift of his head he became another. When he was not physically present she could never recall what he looked like, and when he did sidle into the room he was unremarkable except for his extreme thinness and shabbiness. Yet when he took on a role it was as if he had never been anyone else. Jakey was to play Charlotte's youthful lover, although Eliza had envisaged Devil opposite her. Another player from the general company was to be Charlotte's father disguised as the woodman, and Devil himself took the role of the chaperone – although he insisted that he would engage another actor before the theatre reopened.

While Eliza and Carlo rehearsed, Devil toured the supper clubs and variety halls in search of new acts. Only the best attracted his interest, and these artists dismissed his invitations to appear at his theatre.

The Palmyra's brief flare of popularity was over. Rain had long ago washed the white palms from walls and pavements, and the art students had taken up new interests. The theatre's new proprietor had nothing but promises to offer the owners of magic acts. Devil returned from these unsuccessful missions and he and Carlo threw themselves into devising better and more elaborate illusions of their own. Heinrich and Jasper were daily summoned to work, to advise, to apply their expertise. Jakey worked up a series of parts in addition to his role as the lover in Charlotte and the Chaperone, and sometimes Eliza was called upon to hold up a glass ball or perhaps to lie supine in a box as Carlo and Devil argued the mechanics of a trick. She was so much occupied at the theatre that she missed her final classes at the Rawlinson, and only found time to pose for the life class because she could not live without the shillings the work paid her.

In addition to all this there came the stream of workmen who brought their bundles of tools and their yawning apprentices to the theatre and haggled with Devil about the restoration work. Days when the racket of sawing and hammering drowned out Eliza's rehearsals were followed by longer days of silence after the workmen walked off the job because there was no money to pay them. In the evenings the regular performers clambered over stacked timbers and negotiated gaping holes in the old boards as they made their way on- and offstage. In the end, Devil had been forced to acknowledge that the work could not be done satisfactorily while even a limited show was in performance, and he had declared the theatre closed for the last week of July and the whole of the month of August.

'There will be no one of importance left in London in any case,' he had shrugged, and Eliza and Jasper had laughed at him for talking like the mother of a debutante.

The grand opening night of the new Palmyra was to be on the first of September. It was too short an interval for all the work that must be done in advance, and it was an age to live through without even the small takings from the box office.

'We shall manage,' Devil told his uneasy company.

Eliza watched him now as he murmured and smiled and visibly flattered the well-dressed man.

Money was the constant necessity, and regulating the flow of the little he had into the maw of his theatre had become Devil's first and last thought. Heinrich had loaned him a modest sum, and possession of the Palmyra deeds enabled him to borrow a little more against that security. Devil's obsession left no air in which unconnected thoughts might flourish, but Eliza felt admiration that went deeper than any of her more equivocal feelings for him. She could not imagine when he even rested, let alone slept. The sheer force of his energy, its flow and heat, almost frightened her.

He was concluding his conversation with the stranger. The man nodded his smooth grey head, and the two of them shook hands. At last Devil came to where she stood beneath the portrait.

'That colour suits you,' he said, and she shook out the

leaf-green folds with a flicker of pleasure. Devil rarely noticed appearances unless related in some way to the theatre.

'Thank you. Who was that?'

'Edward Mathieson, of Mathieson and Company. A private bank,' he added, when her face remained blank. 'He is the godfather of one of the young gentlemen.' Devil's tone was dry. He was no more of an admirer of inherited standing than Jasper was.

'Will he give you some money?'

'No one gives money, Eliza. What kind of world do you imagine we live in?'

'Loan, then.'

'Probably not. But he saw the Philosophers, because his godson obligingly brought him along. I gather he enjoyed the illusion.'

'Well. That's good.'

'Where is Jasper? And Heinrich? I saw you with them a moment ago.'

Eliza indicated the two men, now conferring beside a head of a woman sculpted in wax over plaster. From a distance the piece looked like an under-baked loaf of bread.

'They don't seem to be quite lost in admiration,' Devil observed.

'If I were a mere student of art, I would feel nervous at having my sculpture scrutinised by the creators of Lucie and the philosopher's head.'

'If? Are you *not* a student of art as well as an artists' model, Miss Dunlop?'

Nowadays he only called her Miss Dunlop when he intended to tease or provoke her.

Eliza said, 'I did not attend the final painting classes. I am afraid that I can't any longer call myself a student, and I am obliged to acknowledge that I am not an artist. Mr Gardiner is an artist.'

'Yes. I like his picture, even though it took up too much of my time and I omitted to charge for the sittings. I thought I wouldn't care for the finished item, but I do. Someone has bought it, did you know that?'

'Who?'

'An anonymous purchaser. I have no idea. Truthfully, I do not.'

The rose in his buttonhole was scented. She studied the curved petals and tried to work out whether the redness was closer to scarlet than crimson.

'How odd, to think of such a . . . close likeness, in the possession of someone you don't even know.'

'Is it?' Devil shrugged. 'It doesn't interest me greatly. I have other matters to think about. Tell me, Eliza, if you are no longer an artist, or a student, what are you? Are you perhaps going to marry Jasper and settle down after all?'

'No, I shall not do that.' Eliza raised her eyes to meet his. 'You must surely have noticed that in the last weeks I have worked for many hours on Charlotte, and in much of the remaining time I have been an unpaid stage assistant at the Palmyra theatre.'

He was scrutinising her. His side-whiskers were of a faintly lighter shade than his black hair. Eliza remembered precisely how his mouth had tasted, and how her very bones had seemed to melt against him. The green fabric of her new dress stuck to the dip between her shoulder blades.

'Are you asking me to pay you, Eliza?'

'If you were to do so, I could make myself useful without having to worry constantly about how to eat and shelter myself.'

To her surprise he laughed. 'Ah, Eliza. You don't stand apart, you know. We all share those same concerns.'

'I don't believe Mr Mathieson does.'

'No, not him. Not directly, at least. When I say we I mean you and me and Carlo. Heinrich too, although not so much.'

'We,' Eliza repeated. She was pleased.

'Your Charlotte illusion is good. Carlo tells me the act should definitely appear on the programme when the theatre reopens. Would you like to be a stage performer, Eliza?'

'Yes, very much.'

Devil took the rose out of his buttonhole and tucked it in the facing of her dress.

'I am honoured formally to welcome you to the new Palmyra company. I believe that Jasper will also agree to join us. Unfortunately I can't afford to pay either of you, as yet, but we shall somehow find a way to buy a dinner and to keep the roofs over our heads.'

Eliza did mental arithmetic. The answers all came up with minus signs. But perhaps her father might help her, if he could be persuaded that the stage was a better choice than the studio.

'Thank you. I shall hope for an improvement in the terms of my employment in due course.'

'You won't be disappointed, I promise. Under my ownership the Palmyra will soon be the finest theatre of varieties in London.' Smiling, he held out his arm. 'Let us tell Jasper and Heinrich the good news.'

They sailed through the remnants of the gathering. Two or three people wanted to speak to Devil but he sidestepped them. He murmured in Eliza's ear, 'I have heard enough of Mr Gardiner's famous picture, and I believe the money has climbed into its carriages and driven away.'

Jasper finished his study of the sculpture exhibits as they approached.

'Jas,' Devil nodded.

Jasper indicated the sculpted head. 'You see, there are benefits attached to a rough apprenticeship. I may have learned my humble trade at the wrong end of a waxmaker's cane, but I know the rules of proportion and the basics of anatomy.'

'So you did, and do,' Devil agreed. 'We have had a hard life, eh?'

Eliza looked from one to the other, and noticed how they always avoided further mention of their shared history.

Devil clapped his hands. 'Jasper, Heinrich, we have reason to celebrate. I insist that we all make our way to a chop house to eat a good dinner and drink a toast to the future. Miss

Dunlop has this moment agreed to join the Palmyra company.'

Jasper had been prepared for this news, but he still had to swallow his jealousy at the thought of her spending every day and evening with Devil. He told her quite convincingly that he was pleased to hear it.

He added, 'I am thinking of making the same commitment. God will have to help us both.'

If there was anything he could do to shield – or perhaps to extricate – Eliza in the future, he would at least be close at hand. He turned to Heinrich. 'Did you hear that? Devil is inviting us to eat and drink.'

The engineer began to say that he would not come, but Devil nudged him.

'Lucie will wait for you. Why not play hard to get for once? Ladies love that, Jas, don't they?'

The evening air of South Kensington was moist, and the smell of summer grass in the park sweetly mingled with the common city reek of drains and horse manure. Over the area railings of one of the big houses, a rose bush spilled its red blooms.

'Where is Carlo tonight? Should he not be here?' Eliza asked.

Devil waved a hand. 'I think it is generally better not to advertise Carlo's useful size. Not to the inquisitive public at places like the Rawlinson School, at least.'

Carlo was sitting on the Palmyra stage. His back rested against the skeleton of a half-constructed cabinet and his small legs were splayed in front of him. The lights were all extinguished save for a single burner suspended overhead which turned his eyes into dark holes in his face. He looked like a discarded puppet.

He stretched out a hand to find the bottle at his side and tipped it to his mouth. After a long gulp he bellowed into the shadows, 'Are you there?'

A darker shadow moved between the seats.

'Why the hell do you skulk out there like a damned ghost?'

The dark shape moved again. It was Jakey. He came forward to the stage and stood at the very edge of the greenish circle of light. Carlo took another noisy pull at the gin.

'C'mon up here. I like to see who's looking at me.'

Jakey vaulted on to the boards and squatted near the dwarf's feet. Carlo wiped his mouth with the back of his hand and held out the bottle. The boy reached for it and took a swallow, his Adam's apple bobbing in his scrawny throat.

'Haven't you got a home? Where do you live?' Carlo demanded.

'Hereabouts.'

The dwarf squinted. He was very drunk.

'*Here* abouts? Under the stage, is that? Or in that mucky box by the door where Eggin used to sit? Eh?'

'I don't stay in the theatre, sir. I comes in here to do my work. I sleep where I can find, depending.'

'What's that like?'

'Summer times, it's all right.'

'Aye.' Carlo thrust the bottle at him again. 'Drink some more of this. Makes the world a better place, it does. You like working here, do you?'

'Yes, sir.' The boy was wary of the dwarf's tongue and temper.

'You don't call me sir, you poor fool.'

'What shall I, then?'

The question produced a black scowl and a silence.

Jakey rocked on his haunches until Carlo collected himself.

'I used to be Charlie Morris. But poor Charlie's gone and forgotten now, might as well be dead like our Sallie.'

Sudden tears sprang out and ran down the dwarf's face, and he wiped them away with the flat of his hand. Jakey stared.

'Car-*lo*. Carlo Boldini, that's who I am these days. You might ask, who the hell? One half of Boldoni and Wix, that is. Half a man, half a variety act. *Hah*. Some people might think I'm the one what makes the bloody illusions that bring the crowd in. Some people might give me the value I'm due. I'm not saying all people, because that would be a damned lie, wouldn't it?

200

Seeing as I'm hidden here, and they're at an exhibition of *art*. Not good enough to show off, am I? Being only a dwarf, even though it's the dwarf who thinks up the pretty tricks and bangs the boxes and squeezes his body into spaces smaller than Wix's fat head. Who the hell? Who the hell cares?'

'Yes . . .' the boy said uncertainly, just managing not to add *sir*.

'That's it. Good lad. Work together, don't we? Me and you? *Colleagues*. Charlotte and her lover and the chaperone and the poor old wolf. Ha ha. You like being an actor, do you? Eh?'

Jakey's face lit up like a row of footlights.

'Yes, I do.'

The dwarf drew up his lip in a smile that showed his vulpine teeth. 'Well, let me tell you something. You're not one. You're a mimic. You can copy, pick up a mannerism. You even do a voice well enough, or you will be able to when you've worked hard enough at it. But acting, that's different. You have to put in the extra. You have to create a character. Invent him from the inside out and make him talk and walk and cry, and somehow make the audience believe he's as real as they are. Not mimicry but invention. *That's* what acting is.'

Jakey studied the boards in front of his broken boots.

'I'll think about that, I will.'

Carlo swore. He swung sideways on to the palms of his hands, drew his shoulders above his ears and crawled across the stage. His hunched body twitched from side to side in vicious paroxysms. The little finger of his right hand moved in the same rhythm.

It was a grotesque spectacle, but Jakey wasn't startled by it. He had seen the routine plenty of times since they had begun to rehearse the rapid sequences of Charlotte and the Chaperone. Once a suitable pelt had been stitched, Carlo's antics would represent the severed body of the wolf, one half jerking and the other half being jerked by a black thread across the stage.

Tonight Carlo misjudged the distance and crashed into the half-built cabinet. The structure teetered and then toppled on him. The dwarf gave a yelp of pain, but he was not much hurt because he quickly sat up with the wooden frame of a door around his shoulders. Jakey ran to his side. The dwarf swore again and kicked himself free. He began a drunken laugh which grew louder until it convulsed his body. The boy respectfully waited until the spasm subsided. Carlo coughed, wiped his eyes and pointed to the bottle.

'Oh, dear. Give me that. Strip-me-naked, they call it. Did you know, young 'un?'

'Yes,' Jakey said.

Carlo drank deeply and settled back against the wreckage of the cabinet. Little hiccoughs of bitter laughter ran through his body.

'Why are you angry?' the boy asked.

'Eh?'

'Is it because all of 'em are gone out and left you behind?'

The dwarf glared. Jakey shifted backwards, anticipating abuse or even a blow. None came. The last tremors of Carlo's acrid merriment died, and silence spread across the stage and into the darkened auditorium.

'You ask why I am angry?' He gave each syllable a sudden bell-like precision, as if he had never taken a drink in his life.

Jakey ducked his head. Carlo's hand swept the air, indicating his foreshortened trunk and his small legs sprawled on the boards.

'Let me enquire, would *you* not be angry? If you were not tall and handsome and well made?'

'I'm not, am I?' the boy muttered.

Carlo snapped, 'We know who fits the description. What if you were not even like yourself, thin as a broom handle, tallow-pale and round in the shoulders, but like *me*? If you were hid in a cupboard, kept from view, pulled out when needed and then bundled away with a wink and a whisper?'

'I dunno,' the boy said at last. 'You are better off than some.'

The silence of the theatre seemed to grow heavier, the light's greenish glimmer barely breaking the bulwark of darkness. The tentative smells of new wood and shellac and fresh paint faded, overwhelmed by the decades of sour dirt gathered in backstage corners. Jakey hunched his shoulders and shivered. Sometimes the theatre seemed an evil place.

'Better off than some,' Carlo repeated. 'You mean I'm not a poor wretch off the spike? I've got a roof over my head, food in my belly and a job of sorts, yes. But I'm still a dwarf. Only in my dreams can I look another man in the eye.'

'You're lucky enough. Miss Dunlop's your friend.'

'Ah, she can be my friend, Jasper's, Heinrich's, yours even. It's only Devil Wix who'll get a different slice of the cake, sooner or later. Mark my words.'

Jakey didn't disagree. He looked forlorn.

Carlo stuck out his jaw. 'You sweet on Miss Dunlop? Eh?'

'No. But I think she's kind, as well as pretty. Is that why you don't like Mr Wix, because of him and her?'

'Eh? You keep your cheeky questions to yourself, boy. I like him well enough, as it happens. I only can't stand the bloody sight of him, with his grin and his yard-long legs and the damned ooze of his pleasure in being himself.' The force of these words seemed to propel Carlo to his feet. He reached an upright position, swayed disastrously, and would have fallen on his face if Jakey had not leapt to catch him in his arms.

'Take care,' the boy warned.

Carlo gave a sigh, such a gusty breath that it might have stirred the stage curtains. 'If I don't, no other living creature will do so for me.'

Jakey lost his patience. He shook the dwarf by the shoulders.

'I think you are a mite too sorry for yourself, as well as wasting good effort on being angry about what you can't change. You're little, but like I said, plenty of people would gladly take your place instead of theirs. See where you are? See all this?'

The boy indicated the proscenium arch and the invisible depth of the theatre with its pillars and gilded box fronts all folded in darkness. The sinister breath in the air had faded and

Jakey's gaunt face shone with simple awe. 'You and Mr Wix have got this theatre and your plays and tricks to perform in it, and you get your bread from what ordinary folk think is all pleasure and romance.'

Through the gin's maudlin fumes Carlo caught the sense of this rebuke.

'Aye,' he said at last. 'Aye, maybe. You're a sharp lad, aren't you?'

Jakey was afraid that he might have spoken out of turn, even though the dwarf was drunk enough for everything to be forgotten by the time morning came.

'I dunno about that,' he mumbled, once more biting back the *sir*.

Carlo swung away from him and stooped for the gin bottle.

'Have another drink. Here's company, all the company a man needs. Strip-me-naked and let me lie, boy. Here on the stage under the spotlights where I belong. Come on, don't you hold back.' He brandished the bottle under Jakey's nose. 'Take a swig, what are you waiting for?'

Jakey shot a glance up into the murk overhead, and sideways into the black wings. From a few feet away a prop mirror reflected the single light onstage like a glimpse of a lost soul.

'To tell you the truth, I'm waiting to make the old place safe. Put out the lights, lock her up, ready for another day.'

The prospect of the Palmyra being placed at risk from the dwarf's drunken neglect of a candle or a lamp's flame, or the slow hiss of gas from a brass tap, was more than Jakey could bear. The new opening, the thunder of potential applause locked in the silent air, made all the deprivations of his life tolerable and nothing was to stop that glorious day coming about. There was a pause while Carlo frowned at his words. Then the dwarf wearily nodded. Jakey took the opportunity to steer the little man off the stage, and to lodge his bottle in a niche for safety as he did so. They passed along the narrow route to the stage door, Jakey's head turning from side to side as he mentally scanned the theatre's nooks and lightless corners. When he was satisfied that all was as secure as he could make it, he helped Carlo down the steps that led into the alley and fastened the Palmyra's final heavy padlock. A gulp of night air made the dwarf reel, and he showed signs of sinking on to the cobbles. Jakey propped him upright.

'Where's your place?'

Carlo waved an arm to the north, across the slate roofs and smoky chimneys of Covent Garden and Holborn.

'Come on then,' Jakey muttered.

The tavern was one of Devil's favourites, a rough meat-and-potatoes establishment with splintery bare tables and serving women with greasy red arms, but the four of them had eaten well. Devil made sure that the food kept coming until his guests waved away the last ladle full of browned beef gravy. The waitress bent low as she offered it, to make sure that all three men at the table could see down the front of her bodice. Eliza might have chosen to be dainty about such a dining room, but she reminded herself that she was a theatrical performer now. She could leave behind considerations of what was proper or seemly, and do whatever she chose. If the freedom of choice happened to suit her, of course. There might be times when it would be useful for an actress to fall back on claims of propriety. This thought made her compress her lips over the beginnings of a wry smile, but then she looked diagonally across the table to Devil who had already seen the smile and its suppression. There was not much he did not notice. She sat back and allowed her glass to be refilled with dark red wine. Heinrich was still talking to her. He had been talking for half an hour, his eyes bright behind the discs of his spectacles and his Swiss pronunciations exaggerated by his unusual animation. Eliza tried to follow the thread of his complicated explanations. All sounds were vibrations, was she aware of that?

She shook her head.

There was a new machine called the phonograph. There was a way to capture the sound of the human voice as a series of vibrations, which could be inscribed in the form of grooves in wax. If the indented wax were affixed to a rotating iron cylinder or a disc, another device might trace those grooves and turn them back into sound at any time. Was that not intriguing?

'Intriguing,' she echoed.

Heinrich's head was cocked. He was waiting for her questions.

'What practical use might this instrument have?' she attempted, and immediately registered his disappointment at her lack of acuity.

'What use? I can think of many, many. But for us, a very special use. To give a voice where there has until now only been silence.'

Eliza noticed how he leaned closer, and that the heat from his forehead had faintly misted his spectacle lenses. He took them off at once, exposing his eyes, and polished them with his handkerchief.

'Silence?' she murmured.

'Lucie has never spoken.'

'No,' she agreed.

'I wonder if you might let us use your voice, Miss Dunlop?'

'My voice? How?'

Heinrich Bayer replaced his glasses. 'If you would let me record your voice, as I have just described, I could capture the sound vibrations in wax and replay them via a small disc mounted within Lucie's chest cavity. Rotation of the disc, perhaps powered by compressed air in the way that is familiar to us all, would enable the recording to be replayed at will, as if the captured sentiments emanated from Lucie's own mouth. As if they came from her own heart.'

The last words were uttered in a voice so low that the clatter of the dining room almost drowned them out.

Eliza could not help staring. But all she saw was Heinrich, familiar in his shyness, with his fingers hooked around the stem of his glass.

'What would I have to say?' she blurted out.

206

She looked to Devil again, but he and Jasper were poring over a set of drawings scribbled in Jasper's notebook. Devil was stabbing at the page.

'Like this. But more. More spectacle, Jas.'

She had never seen Jasper touch drink, but tonight he was in a strange mood. His glass was empty and patches of dark red colour showed on his cheekbones. She turned back to Heinrich. His gaze beseeched her.

'Say? Why, the sorts of remark that Lucie might make. She is a young person of good taste and excellent character, as you are yourself.'

'I . . . am not sure. The truth is that I feel a little uncertain about putting my voice into another . . . person'.

Into a mechanical *doll*.

'It is a matter of scientific advance, Miss Dunlop. An interesting experiment in the technology of sound. Are you apprehensive about the realms of science?'

'No, I'm not. Of course not.'

The engineer's spectacles glinted as he nodded his approval. 'That is good,' he said. 'I am delighted.'

Without Eliza understanding how it had happened, the matter appeared to be settled.

Jasper snatched his notebook out of Devil's grasp and stowed it in a pocket. Devil clicked his fingers to summon the waitress. The plates and glasses were finally empty and the evening had clearly reached its end. While Devil counted out florins and shillings, Jasper offered as he always did to accompany Eliza as far as her lodging. In return she thanked him as she always did, and replied that she had no need of an escort. This evening Jasper did not try to insist otherwise. He merely wished her goodnight and left in a hurry with Heinrich in his wake. It was Devil who helped Eliza to put on her coat and walked with her down the steep wooden stairs into the street. It was ten at night, but the western sky still held the memory of daylight. She thought she could hear above the rattle of wheels the last of the birdsong from the trees in the park. She wanted to catch this moment of standing on a new threshold, and hold on to it.

She put her fingertips on Devil's arm.

'Heinrich Bayer asked me a strange question. He wants me to lend my voice to Lucie.'

'He has mentioned the idea to me.'

They were standing close together, in the narrow space between a closed shop front and the gutter.

'And what do you think?' she whispered.

'What do I think about what, Miss Dunlop?'

There were always two dialogues between them, she thought. The spoken one, and the other silent and insistent.

'About Lucie and the voice device, whatever it is.'

His voice rippled with amusement. 'I had forgotten we were discussing Heinrich and Lucie. Let me see. You will say nothing improper, of course?'

'I would hardly do that.'

'Then if your contribution consists of "Extremely well, thank you," and "Very pleasant indeed for the time of year," and so forth, what harm could come of it?'

'None, I suppose.'

'Poor Heinrich.'

He meant that Heinrich deserved their sympathy because his passion was for the inert Lucie, whose unprinted fingertips felt nothing, whose parted lips were cold rubber, and whose heart did not wildly thump within her ribcage. Unlike their own, however they chose to dissemble it.

Eliza deliberately looked away. The street lamps and the shuttered shops came back into focus.

'Indeed,' she said.

Devil took her hand and lifted it to his mouth. He kissed her knuckles, and the old-fashioned gesture held both a knowing mockery of itself and a grace that touched her.

'Goodnight, dear Eliza. I think you know how pleased I am that you are joining me at the Palmyra.'

She did not trust herself to murmur more than a word before

she began to walk away from him. They had crossed the park earlier, and from here it was less than half a mile to her lodgings. Her feet flew. The ordinary streets had never seemed more open to her, or the scents of privet and cab stands and fried herring more lovely and enticing.

The house was dark, and she had thought her fellow lodgers must be asleep. She undressed and lay in her bed with her thoughts whirling. The mattress rolled slightly with the effect of the wine she had drunk. From tomorrow, she would belong to the Palmyra. There were a hundred tasks to be dealt with. Charlotte and the Chaperone must be rehearsed until it was perfect. Costumes must be devised and stitched. How was the wolf pelt to be made? Breeches for Jakey, yes. Devil as the chaperone in a bonnet and plaid shawl, perhaps. Charlotte herself must have a rustic dress that was not over-fashionable, yet was also charming and pretty. Eliza was no seamstress. She could perhaps ask Faith to help her.

She heard the floorboards creak overhead as Miss Aynscoe trod softly from her washstand to the bed. Eliza imagined her in her nightgown, on her knees on the rag rug. Sympathy spilled through her, for Miss Aynscoe who did not know Devil Wix or the Palmyra, and for the rest of the world that was similarly deprived.

Her thoughts ran round and round. Perhaps the upstairs lodger with her atelier experience might be willing to advise in the matter of stage costuming? Eliza could hardly afford to pay her, unless Devil could be persuaded to make the money available. Perhaps she would like a pair of tickets to the opening night of the new show?

Eliza closed her eyes, then quickly opened them again. Like Jakey, who was at that moment curled up under a table without the benefit of a mattress or even a blanket, she heard the magnificent thunder of potential applause. The first of September. Hardly a month away.

TEN

On a bright August afternoon Heinrich Bayer's workshop seemed even more peculiar than in the darkness of Eliza's first visit. Sunshine slanted through the skylight, but layers of dust over the glass gave the beam a greyish cast. The light faded where it first struck, as if reluctant to challenge the pall of shadow. Heinrich stood half in and half out of the weak glimmer, studying a sheet of paper covered with close handwriting, his face and his coat sliced into dark and less dark.

She had earlier refused his offer of a cup of tea, not wanting to place any obstacle in the way of taking her leave as soon as possible. But now she regretted the decision. It would have been comfortable to know that the quiet servant would soon appear with a tray. She cleared her throat for the reassurance of the sound, only for it to emphasise the room's silence. There was no noise from the streets outside. She could hear her own breathing, nothing else.

The blonde doll, Hilde, now seemed to be complete. Fully clad in a dark blue dress she sat upright with her hands still resting in her lap, her unblinking eyes fixed on the wall. The little Chinaman had been returned to his place. His round black hat sat on his head. Eliza had no way of telling if the innards that had been removed to make way for Carlo had since been replaced. A draped figure – Lucie – lay on the cushioned surface that disturbingly resembled a catafalque.

Eliza looked away. Her eyes passed over the workbench, the tools and the dismembered legs and hands laid out to reveal the rods and pistons within. The microscope that had stood at one end of the bench was gone, replaced by a small cylinder horizontally mounted on a long brass rod. Next to it stood a curved horn like an oversized ear trumpet. The floor beneath the lathe had been swept clean of the tiny coils of metal.

Heinrich said abruptly, 'Very good.' *Gut.*

His voice startled her and she almost cried out. She raised her hand to her mouth and coughed to cover the squeak.

'Does your throat trouble you, Miss Dunlop? If it is not quite comfortable for you to speak, your voice may not sound at its best in our recordings.'

She considered pleading a sore throat and making her escape, but only for a second. She had no reason to be afraid of Heinrich, nor of the strange contents of his workshop. He was a maker of automata, and Lucie was one of his mechanical dolls. How many times had she watched them dance while audiences yawned or booed? Heinrich's shyness made him awkward. He was different from Devil and Jasper and even Carlo, but he was one of their company who had helped Devil to win the theatre. He had paid for the doctor who had saved Carlo's life. What would it cost her to speak a few innocuous sentences for his phonograph?

Her fingers curled against her palms as she counted the points.

If she feigned illness now she would only have to come back some other time.

Heinrich had loaned Devil money.

His continuing goodwill was important to the Palmyra.

She cleared her throat with intentional finality, and smiled.

'It doesn't trouble me in the least. But I would like a cup of tea, after all. May I see Lucie's words?'

She held out her hand. Heinrich passed her the sheet of paper and rang the bell for the servant. Eliza scanned the page. Lucie's lines were innocent, of course. If anything, they were unnerving in their banality.

Lucie was very well, and so was her mama. She had enjoyed a pleasant stay in the country, but she was happy to have returned to London where there so many diversions. She loved the waltz, and she would be honoured by another dance. And so on. Insipid creature.

Putting aside the paper she wondered, 'Is this what you really want her to say?'

Her question seemed to hang in the air. Heinrich did not meet her eyes and a dark flush rose above his stiff collar.

'It is how young ladies speak, is it not?'

'Old-fashioned young ladies on first acquaintance, perhaps.'

Poor Heinrich, who had probably never progressed beyond first acquaintance with a woman who had blood in her veins.

'Wouldn't you like me perhaps to use less formal language?'

There had been a touch of teasing in the words but as soon as she uttered them Eliza was sorry. Heinrich's hands twisted as if he wanted to break something. His back and his thin neck were visibly rigid with tension.

'In public?' he managed to say.

More gently, masking her own rising embarrassment, she asked, 'Is that where your conversations will take place?'

He was helplessly staring at the body on the catafalque.

'Onstage, yes.'

'On*stage*?' She was startled.

'I want the world to admire Lucie. It is why the theatre must succeed.' His tongue flicked the corners of his mouth. 'Lucie is a work of art. And when she can speak, in a voice such as yours that is pleasant to the ear, naturally the public admiration will deepen.'

Now it was Eliza's turn to blush, for shame at the workings of her mind.

She knew their stage performance, every turn and every

212

note of the waltz and the polka, and she had always assumed that Heinrich and Lucie must dance to a different tune when they were alone. But perhaps after all they did not. She was not alone in leaping to such a conclusion; she had heard the coarse shouts of the Palmyra audiences and the sly insinuations of the Rawlinson students. And surely Devil believed the same? She had read the glimmer in his eyes. As soon as the thought of him entered her head, it was too late. She tried her hardest but the picture of the engineer and the doll was inevitably replaced by one of herself and Devil. Her thoughts regularly ran in that direction nowadays, often to the point of distraction.

There was another question. Why did she feel obliged to try to suppress these speculations? She didn't think that the little acrobat with the bells on her costume troubled to do so, nor would Devil's plump slattern of a landlady. On the other hand she was sure that her sister Faith was naturally modest and faced no such problems. It must be females such as she, clinging to the skirts of respectability, who found difficulty in matching their hidden nature to the conventions of polite society.

But she was a member of a theatre company now. She was living on the last of her inheritance and – her father having refused further assistance – quite soon she would have to rely on her wits alone. In such circumstances, surely, she could think and even *do* what she wished? Respectability was not her chief ally.

The silence grew heavier. Despite her internal resolve Eliza dared not look in Heinrich's direction in case his eyes had shifted from Lucie to settle on her. In case he could read her churning thoughts.

There was a knock and to her relief the servant appeared with the tea tray. Eliza hurried to unfold the card table at which she and Devil had eaten ham and potatoes on that first evening. By the time the cups and the silver teapot and cream jug had been laid out she was in command of herself again.

'Perhaps you would like to read the lines aloud for me,

213

before we proceed to the recording?' Heinrich said pleasantly.

She did as he asked. The commonplace remarks did not take on any added lustre.

'Your voice has a most attractive timbre, Miss Dunlop. But you speak a little too quickly, and sometimes you do not sound your final consonants. Here in London many people display the same fault. May I ask you to bear this in mind?'

She tried again, speaking much more slowly, drawing out the vowels and forming the word endings with elaborate care. To her own ear she sounded chill, so she smiled in the hope that warmth would be reflected in her voice.

After three attempts Heinrich seemed satisfied.

'I think we shall go ahead. Let me explain what my instruments will do.'

Eliza was to speak quite loudly into the trumpet. Heinrich pointed to the cylinder on its rod of brass. Her voice would cause a diaphragm to vibrate and the vibrations would be transmitted, via an electromagnet to which an embossing point was attached by means of a moving arm, as etched lines on the warm wax face of the rotating cylinder. He showed her the reservoir of hot water from which rubber tubes ran into the core of the cylinder to keep the wax at the critical temperature, neither too hard nor too soft.

'I see,' she said, and indeed she did catch the principle. When the wax had hardened a different machine would be employed, translating the etched grooves into signals carried through a wire, which could then be amplified via another diaphragm as the sound of her disembodied voice.

They became absorbed in their task and her uneasiness lessened. Heinrich lifted his hand, the cylinder turned and the arm jerked as she began to read. But the machinery distracted her, her throat closed and she stumbled over her words.

'Begin again,' he said, but again she faltered.

She didn't like not giving of her best.

'Let me turn the other way.'

He moved the horn so that she did not face Lucie lying prone under her shawl. She found a voice that seemed to belong to someone – something – other than herself.

'That would be delightful,' she read, reaching the foot of the reverse page. 'Thank you. I shall look forward to it.'

Heinrich stooped over his cylinder, his nose almost touching it. He lifted the embossing arm clear and studied the etched surface.

'Good,' he murmured. *Gut.*

Eliza's tea had gone cold but she drank it anyway. She replaced the cup on the card table.

With the corner of his thumbnail Heinrich tapped the cooling wax. He had forgotten her. She hoped that he had also forgotten the earlier moment, whether the misunderstanding had been hers alone or the result of each of them trying to rein in their awkward thoughts. Her discomfort returned and she wanted nothing more than to escape this shadowed room and walk out into the sunlight.

'Do you need anything further?'

He straightened up, visibly startled to find that she was still there.

'No, no. Thank you so much. I will embark on my work. There is much to do. To engineer a rotating disk that will fit within her chest cavity, to find a way to make the sound emerge from her mouth. But we have made a beginning.'

He moved towards the bell but Eliza had already gathered up her outer clothes. She patted her hat into place and skewered it, then saw that he watched her as if she were a specimen, noting the turn of her wrist and the angle of her head and throat.

'Please don't trouble. I know the way out,' she whispered.

She opened the low door into the interior alleyway and hurried towards the street door. The servant emerged from the house entrance and bobbed to her. Eliza broke out into the daylight and the hubbub of Clerkenwell.

The walls of the Palmyra facing out to the Strand had been stripped of the boards that had concealed them in Jacko Grady's time. The stalks of buddleia were long gone too. Now, thanks to a series of precarious loans, principally from Heinrich Bayer, Devil's builders scampered up ladders with hods on their backs. They were replacing crumbling masonry with expanses of smooth stone and render. The cracked lintels had been made whole again, the steps scraped and filled. The cupola had been repainted to match the facade. Eliza tipped back her head to admire the transformation. The building was emerging like a young bride in her wedding dress. Her own appearance seemed shabby and neglected in comparison.

She proceeded through the foyer, where the renovation work had hardly begun. Laths and buckets and bags of plaster lay everywhere and the floor was coated with a layer of white dust. The cost of all this must be almost beyond counting. No wonder Devil drove himself, and everyone around him.

Within the auditorium the restorations were further advanced. New gilding on the box fronts enclosed faceted plaster tablets that had been painted to resemble precious stones, ruby and sapphire and emerald. The palm columns soared upwards, bursting overhead into fronds of plaster leaves. The inner skin of the cupola was painted cream and gold and decorated with more plaster palm wreaths. Colour was laid on colour against the thicket of modelled tree and leaf. There was more gilding and ornament than in a caliph's palace but the effect contrived to be less florid than exuberant, and it made Eliza feel happy whenever she saw it.

An old man and a boy dressed in leather aprons were working between the rows of old seats. The worn upholstery had been torn off and new horsehair stuffing and green plush covers were being sewn into place. The best seats, the two rows of *fauteuils* at the front of the house, were already finished, their arms padded and polished, the plump seats waiting for an audience to occupy them. The old man straightened up, his lips pinched on a tack, his hammer in his hand. He nodded respectfully at her.

Jakey emerged from behind the curtain of a side exit.

'Afternoon, Miss Dunlop. There's a lady waiting to see you, backstage.'

'Thanks, Jakey. Is Mr Wix here?' Jakey always knew Devil's whereabouts.

'He is, miss, in a manner.'

That meant he was busy and unlikely to be where they needed him. Devil had little time to spare for Charlotte and the Chaperone, but neither would he pay another actor to take over his role. Eliza sighed to think of how much was still to be done and the diminishing number of days left in which to do it all. She picked her way through the cramped passages behind the stage and found her visitor sitting on a packing case outside the artists' dressing room. Miss Aynscoe jumped to her feet as soon as she saw her. She was so thin and pale that the light seemed to shine through her bones.

'Miss Dunlop.'

'Oh, please. I am Eliza.' They ate their dinner most evenings at the same table, but it was clear that her fellow lodger was uncertain of Eliza's status in this theatrical setting. Well, she was not exactly alone in that. It was good of her to have left her atelier for an hour to come to the Palmyra to measure and estimate for stage costumes. She had insisted that she would somehow find time outside her already long hours to make them up. And if she could not do it herself, she had said, she knew plenty who would be pleased to have the work. Eliza winced to remember the tiny budget Devil had allocated for costumes. To be able to pay the seamstress, she would have to buy or otherwise procure most of the materials herself. There was a street market at the other end of Holborn where seconds of cloth were sometimes cheap enough if you were ready to overlook the stains and flaws.

She opened the door of the dressing room and took a precautionary glance inside. There was no semi-naked actor or conjuror, no visible piss bucket, and there was even space on the table and a yard of available floor. Miss Aynscoe obediently followed. She took a tape measure and a notebook with a pencil out of her battered black bag. Eliza gave her the play-script and some sketches she had made and went off in search of the actor who was to play the dual role of Charlotte's father and the woodman. Sammy Hill was also the theatre's carpenter. She found him bare-chested and perspiring beneath a pair of elastic braces, sawing planks in the pit under the stage.

'Come and be measured. It will only take five minutes.'

Sammy pulled out his tobacco tin. 'I'd rather do your bidding than this grind. It can take as long as you please.'

The seamstress glimpsed the man's chest and looked away in horror. Eliza understood how much her own routine accept-ance of bare flesh was shaped not just by the Rawlinson life class, but by the months of exposure to people dressing and undressing in the hubbub of the theatre. She was already much more akin to Bascia and Maria Hayes than to Sylvia Aynscoe and her own sister. There was nothing to mourn in that, partic-ularly. Any more than there was anything to celebrate about excessive modesty.

She put her hand on the other woman's arm.

'Miss Aynscoe, Sylvia that is, we are theatre people here. You must forgive us if you can. Here, Sammy. Let us take your measurements.'

Sylvia gamely stretched her tape about the man's damp chest, his hips and broad shoulders and down the length of his leg, and Eliza wrote the inches in the notebook.

'Will that be all, ladies?' Sammy grinned when the job was done.

'Yes. You can go back to your work now.' She would not let him imagine he could neglect his tasks.

Jakey came in and stood patiently while they repeated the procedure, then slipped away again. There was no need to look for Carlo. He arrived at the precise moment Eliza expected him, with a paper-wrapped roll of something heavy in his arms. It was to Sylvia's credit that this time her expression did not change, even at the sight of a three-foot man. She shook his hand, agreed that it was a pleasure, and picked up her tape once more. Carlo submitted to the measuring, shifting impatiently from foot to foot until Eliza had to order him to keep still. He broke away as soon as he could and tore the wrappings off his bundle. He shook out an animal fur. The matted black pelt stank as if a wolf had died and then lain in it for some months, or years. Carlo went down on all fours and twitched the fur over himself.

'There is more than enough to cover me,' he said in a muffled voice. 'But can you cut and stitch the animal's skin in two parts, with some hooks to hold the halves together? Jasper Button will model the head for me, with a moving jaw and a fine set of large white teeth.' Carlo tossed his head and snapped his own teeth.

The two women looked at each other. Something unusual was happening to Sylvia Aynscoe's face. Her chin trembled and her pale lips curled. She was laughing.

'What is this . . . creature for?'

'It is our wolf, from Charlotte and the Chaperone. Carlo gives a very fine performance,' Eliza explained.

The dwarf stuck his head out to see if they were mocking him, but Eliza gravely continued, 'We have very high hopes for the illusion. So the costumes must be of the highest quality. Whilst not being too dear to make, of course.'

Carlo stood up, flushed in the face. 'Can you stitch it?'

Sylvia lifted the fur with the tips of her fingers. 'This is quite unlike my usual work. But I believe I could do something.'

Eliza had already provided her own measurements, so now only Devil's were missing. At that moment he whirled into the room. Carlo swung himself out of the way.

Devil was heated, in a great hurry, thoroughly preoccupied. He had been auditioning potential acts. He was often auditioning, usually to be disappointed.

'Miss Aynscoe, how do you do? Tell me, do you sing? Dance? Juggle with meat cleavers, perhaps?'

'No.'

'That is a relief.'

'If you would just let us take your measurements? We are making the costumes for Charlotte.'

'I am yours for the next ten minutes, Eliza.'

He offered himself up in the middle of the room, arms raised above his head. He was very large and strong, and with his black stare and red mouth and quick movements he seemed to fill even more of the confined space. Sylvia edged round him, her eyes lowered so she did not have to reckon with more than an arm or a leg at one time. Her tape dabbed in the air to avoid direct contact with such unbridled male energy. She looked as if she might faint if he came any closer.

He stuck out his leg and obligingly held the upper end of the tape as the seamstress stooped to his ankle. 'What am I to wear, Eliza?'

She was scribbling in the notebook. 'A modest dress, dove-grey or perhaps dull lilac. If you were not so large we could buy one from a governess shop, but as it is I think not. I am tempted by a plaid shawl. You shall have a false front of hair and a becoming bonnet.'

'Gentlemen will mob me at the stage door. I'll not have to pay for my own dinners this side of Christmas.'

He laughed heartily and Eliza joined in. Even Carlo was amused. Sylvia scuttled aside with a pink face.

The task was completed. Eliza and the seamstress agreed the next stage of the costume creation and they walked together to the stage door. Sylvia carried Carlo's wolf skin wrapped in a cloth that didn't quite contain the smell.

'Maybe a few hours in the air will help,' she murmured. She looked back over her shoulder into the bowels of the theatre. 'The theatrical world is not at all as I imagined.'

'I know. It is always *more*, somehow, more difficult and more intriguing all at the same time.'

Sylvia Aynscoe nodded, her strained face almost animated.

Eliza found Devil in his poky office scanning a little sheaf of theatre playbills and trade reviews. He flung himself back in his chair.

'"Mr Howard presents the Miracles, a feast of magic and illusion to delight young and old." The *Stage* critic unfortunately declares it to be less a feast than a famine. "Mr Harry Hewitt and the divine Dorelia." Divine? Really? Have you seen her? "An Arabian Night's Fantasy." It's not my fantasy, not in the least. Eliza, we must do so much better than this. We have to be original as well as familiar. People want to be entranced and not threatened. Achieving wonder is a difficult balance.'

'We will achieve it.'

'We have less than two weeks. Have you seen the foyer?'

'Of course.'

Devil put his head in his hands. 'And the bills to go with it,' he groaned.

'We will deal with those when we have to. We shall have a magnificent opening, and the rest will follow.'

The programme for the first night was already settled. It included Charlotte as well as the Philosophers, and some bold new illusions devised jointly by Devil and Carlo in which Jakey, Eliza and Sammy Hill all took various roles. Heinrich and Lucie were to dance, and Mr Wu would also appear as fortune-teller. Contributions from outside the company included a mind-reading act that had taken Devil's fancy because the artist was modest and convincing, some female acrobats who performed to a higher standard than Bascia and her brother and whose costumes were guaranteed to interest a certain segment of the audience, and a comedy juggler. The rest of the evening was taken up by guest magicians with whom Devil maintained a precarious relationship. They would appear for a few nights and then give way to new faces. The constant pressure to introduce novelty weighed on Devil.

'Carlo is the best of the lot,' he told Eliza. Devil still yearned for tricks like the Orange and the Crystal Ball but Carlo would not yield his secrets unless he performed onstage as himself.

Devil continued to insist that they must conceal his size from the public or risk giving away too much.

'He comes and goes from the theatre quite openly. It is only

221

a matter of time before the truth is known and then he will be at liberty to perform as himself or the Queen of Sheba, whichever he prefers. But until that time, not.'

Devil insisted to all of them that they were a company and a fellowship, but he never forgot that he was the owner and the manager of the Palmyra and therefore the last word was always his. The only one of them to whom he did occasionally give ground was Heinrich Bayer, and that was because of the loan.

'I'm grateful for your optimism, Eliza,' Devil sighed. 'Once in a while my own belief does fail me.'

'I know.'

There was a pause. Sometimes it seemed that there was an understanding between them; at others they lived on different continents.

Devil slapped his hand on the desk. 'I forgot. Did you supply the voice for the beautiful Lucie?'

'I did.'

He looked so pleased that she did not have the heart to tell him how the workshop and the phonograph apparatus and Heinrich himself stirred her fears. In any case she could not have given him any rational account of what troubled her.

'Very good. I am obliged to you. Heinrich will be in a good humour now and won't mention terrible things like repayment. I expect you want me to rehearse Charlotte?'

'Yes. Carlo and Jakey and Sammy and I are here in readiness.'

Devil tossed his papers into a heap and sprang to his feet.

'I am yours to command. Let's do better than the Miracles,' he said, and she knew that until the next crisis arose, in an hour's time or even less than that, he would give the play his best attention. They made their way out on to the stage where the rest of the cast waited, and the rehearsal proceeded with the upholsterers still tap-tapping at their work in the stalls.

Sammy Hill had constructed a base upon which the statue of Cupid would eventually stand, and Carlo had devised the system of springs and trapdoors that lay within it. A few feet away from the base stood a cage made of iron bars. In his role as the woodman, as the lovers tried to escape from Charlotte's doddering chaperone, Sammy took a huge key and unlocked the cage. Within it, hitherto unseen, Carlo the wolf stirred and then roared to freedom.

The next sequence of moves had to be acted in character and played for comedy, but they had also to be timed with precision.

The wolf chased the women, the lover was torn between chasing away the wolf and trying to save the women, the woodman chased the lover. Eliza and Devil were bundled into the niche in the statue's base and Jakey bolted them within for safety. The mysterious woodman's power briefly subdued the wolf. The creature cowered at his feet with his head between his paws, at which the woodman whirled about to seize the lover and lock him inside the wolf's cage. All was designed to allow the laughter time to build without being too drawn out.

Devil and Eliza were crammed into the small wooden box. Eliza felt the warmth of his breath as he counted the beats between movements outside. She clung to her concentration.

'Timing. Damn it, *timing*,' he murmured in her ear.

Jakey could act, and thanks to his thin frame he could perform locked-box escapes almost as well as Carlo, but he wasn't a born comedian. Sammy struggled over everything, most of all in the quick changes from woodman to Charlotte's father. As soon as attention was all on the iron cage, Devil slipped the catch of the trapdoor and he and Eliza scurried down a ladder into the space below the stage. Devil grasped her ankles and guided her feet to the rungs. Overhead, invited members of the audience would be examining the locks and chains that were to hold Jakey captive in the cage. As soon as the audience were distracted again by the woodman's discovery of the empty statue niche, Jakey made his exit to hide behind a tree. Devil and Eliza took his place in the cage via another trap and a mirror screen. Jakey was now free to dart out, seize the woodman's axe and chop the wolf in half.

'Faster,' Devil groaned as he peered through the cage bars. And then, 'Slow down, don't throw your laughs away.'

Carlo's body twitched across the boards.

'How'm I to be sure of this without trying out the animal suit?' he grumbled.

Eliza promised, 'You'll have it soon. Miss Aynscoe said she could make it very quickly.'

'Get on with it,' Devil howled. Jakey pinioned the woodman's arms and wrestled him into the statue niche. Doors flew open and banged shut, bodies appeared and vanished again, the woodman made the wolf whole, the woodman revealed himself as Charlotte's father, the lovers were prettily reunited. Through all of this Devil limped and misheard and played up the chaperone's comical disabilities for all he was worth. Sammy Hill snorted with uncontrollable laughter and earned a scowl from Carlo.

Eliza's heart was pounding from the joint demands of physical exertion and mental concentration. At the end of the second run-through she lay down on the boards and pitifully gasped for breath. Carlo looked at her with the brief advantage of height.

'And you wanted a stage career?'

'I do. I can do it.'

Jakey and Sammy helped her to her feet. To mark his improved status Devil had recently started wearing a timepiece on the end of his pocket chain. He was vague about the exact circumstances of its acquisition. He took it out now and studied it. 'It runs for seventeen minutes. It should be faster. Every minute needs work. We'll do it again and better.'

That was how it was for the next two weeks.

Eliza had never worked so hard. She rarely went home to her lodgings, and when she did creep into her bed it was to fall into a sleep so heavy that it came close to unconsciousness. For every hour of each day and through most of the nights as well, the Palmyra buzzed with rehearsals, set building, musical practice, lighting and costume improvisations, shouting, hammering and sawing, cursing and ever-impending catastrophe. As all this took place the building renovations were still changing the front of the house. Devil was there and yet not there, as he struggled to make the last of the borrowed money stretch ever further, to patch the company's straining morale, and to create the public anticipation that would sell tickets in advance. There were new shows opening in other theatres as the summer ended, and there was no reason as yet why any man with a shilling or so in his pocket should prefer the Palmyra to any of the established houses.

'We could do with some more stunts by the young art gentlemen,' he said to Eliza and Jasper.

Jasper had given up his employment at the Baker Street Bazaar to join the Palmyra company. Faith told Eliza that his removal was considered a great loss to the waxworks gallery, but Matthew understood why his friend had made the choice. Faith could not resist adding that from the little she had seen of it, the theatre world was rackety enough and she still could not understand why a man like Jasper would wish to throw in his lot with such a crew, let alone her own sister.

'I know,' Eliza agreed with her.

Of course Faith did not understand. Exhausted and yet thrumming with nerves, bruised from scrambling through trapdoors, aching in her body and anxious in her mind, in the days before the opening Eliza did not always comprehend her own choice. But she had made it, and she was never one for looking back.

Jasper took over the management of all backstage matters, and also acted as Devil's deputy. Their old friendship, although never referred to, reinforced this alignment. Ever combative, Carlo became the spokesman for the rest of the company. He brought forward their various resentments over payment, positioning on the playbill, and countless other complaints and simmering rivalries. Jasper interceded wherever he could, and

225

thus Devil and Carlo mostly avoided directly confronting each other. Heinrich Bayer was absorbed in his engineering and his automata and took no part in running the theatre. For now, Eliza accepted that she was a mere woman.

Her voice would not always be inaudible: she promised herself that much.

The first day of September arrived.

It seemed a long age since the momentous night of the card game, and yet the opening was upon them much too soon. London had sweltered throughout August and sullen heat choked the theatre. The audience languidly drifted in. There were gratifying gasps of admiration for the gilding, the brilliant new colours and lavish cascades of palm fronds. Devil had expected the house to be full but it became evident that the oppressive weather worked against him. Looking through the chink in the heavy green-and-gold stage curtains – not yet paid for, despite the maker's repeated presentation of his account – he could see empty seats, even in the front rows, like gaps in teeth. There was a constant ripple of movement from the ladies' fans.

Eliza was already in her Charlotte costume. Sylvia Aynscoe had sewn a pretty dress from a remnant of cheap muslin, with a tiered full skirt in the style of forty years ago, exactly as Eliza had planned. But she was able to take no pleasure in her fetching appearance because stage fright gripped her like the jaws of a trap. She was half certain that she would be paralysed when the awful moment came for her to skip on to the stage with Jakey and Devil. Her mouth was as dry as a desert and there was a knocking against her ribs that would surely make it impossible for her to speak a line, even if she could remember what the line was.

Every member of the company was fully occupied. A seam in the wolf's fur had ripped apart to reveal Carlo's belly. Sylvia Aynscoe with her mouth full of pins did not have a spare moment to calm her. It had suddenly come to Devil's attention that the best new illusion, a box trick in which Jakey's arms and legs became detached from his body to wave at the audience from apertures five feet apart, was dangerously under-rehearsed. Jasper scratched his head until his hair stood on end – the mind-reading act was unwell and the running order had to be rapidly revised. Eliza crept through the chaos, nauseated by the smell of bodies and greasepaint. Had there really been a time when she found all this enticing, even glamorous?

She left the wings and passed the artists' crowded dressing room, hoping to discover a breath of cooler air in the dark passageways beyond. The stage door would be shut but there was a high window that looked out on to the alley, and she would stand beneath that until the nausea passed. She turned a corner and almost collided with a man who stood with his back to her. His black evening coat melted into the shadows. He held a woman in his arms.

The woman said, 'I would be honoured by another dance.'

Eliza's step faltered. It was her voice in Lucie's mouth.

She had not heard the phonograph recording. Heinrich had rehearsed alone and she had avoided talking to him about the experiment.

She gasped, 'How strange. She sounds unlike me. And yet I know it is me.'

Heinrich turned, still holding Lucie as if they were dancing. The doll's glass eyes caught a pinpoint of light. The rubber lips were slightly parted.

'It is you, unmistakably. You don't know because you have never heard yourself speak.'

Eliza's skin prickled with horror. In her state of heightened awareness it seemed that Heinrich had taken a part of her, no less of herself than her hands or her lips, and through the medium of the doll made it his own.

Lucie's head blindly turned. 'Good evening. Good evening. Good evening.'

The repetition, the unseeing glass eyes, the doll's heavy hair, were all suddenly hideous.

'Excuse me. I . . . I'm sorry.' Eliza tried to move past him but Heinrich caught her wrist instead of the doll's.

'Sorry? For what reason?'

Eliza tried to break away but he held on. His grip was too firm.

'I am quite well, thank you,' Lucie said.

'And your mama?' Heinrich whispered as if he were himself an automaton.

'My mother is dead,' Eliza cried. She managed to pull away. He stood between her and the stage door, staring at her old-fashioned dress and shawl.

Then Heinrich blinked and shook his head as if to clear it. His pale face betrayed his confusion.

'It is I who must apologise, Miss Dunlop. I . . . have been working very hard, rehearsing, listening over and over again to our recordings.'

He let her go and Eliza took one step backwards, then another.

'Good evening,' Lucie repeated.

The engineer slid his arm about the doll's shoulders. In subsiding she bowed her head and emitted a faint sound, like a sigh or a hiccough, but with a mechanical acquiescence that struck Eliza as the most disturbing note of all.

'I must go.'

She turned and ran in the direction she had come.

'Please, wait a moment,' Heinrich called after her but she moved faster. She came to the open door of Devil's office. The empty room was lit by a single lamp, the niche where Mr Wu had sat for weeks was now piled with boxes of printed programmes and handbills. The familiar disorder reassured her. She took refuge by closing the door, knowing that the engineer would not pursue her in here. She sat down in Devil's chair, once Jacko Grady's, and breathed deeply to control her heart's unpleasant thumping.

After a moment the wished-for stillness enfolded her.

There was no sea picture in which to immerse herself. She

fixed her gaze instead on a piece of canvas, painted by Jasper as a set backdrop and subsequently discarded. The brush strokes of blue and green were infinitely soothing. She thought of artist's pigments, the depths of cerulean and cobalt blue, viridian's power. Eliza left behind her anxious self and the night's disturbances. She floated through the filaments of pure colour and submerged herself, as blessedly as she had always been able to do.

The reawakening was abrupt, like emerging from sleep. Someone was shouting at her.

'What are you doing? Are you trying to sabotage everything?'

It was Carlo in his animal-skin costume with the magnificent wolf's head modelled by Jasper grasped under his arm. It had a jaw lined with enormous teeth and a crimson plush tongue. The dwarf hauled at her arm but she needed no further warning. She pitched to her feet and they ran together to the wings.

'We've searched the bloody theatre.'

'I was trying to calm my nerves.'

'By giving everyone else a heart failure?'

She could hear a patter of applause. Through the slips she could see the yellow-white glare of the lights. Heinrich and Lucie had already given their performance and made their exit to the opposite side. There was no time for stage fright. The musicians were already playing the first bars of the pretty gavotte that opened Charlotte and the Chaperone. Jakey was handsome in the suitor's tall collar and cutaway coat. Devil's black eyebrows made a furious line under the brim of the chaperone's bonnet.

At close quarters all their faces were lurid with greasepaint. Jakey tossed over the posy of country flowers that she was supposed to hold.

She caught it by the bunched stems, arranged the ribbons, tugged at her bonnet. 'I am ready.'

'I am delighted to hear it,' Devil snapped.

Their musical cue was playing. Precisely on the beat Jakey and Eliza ran out into the lights with the chaperone stumping in their wake.

229

Her first proper audience was a double bank of faces, cut off from her by the footlights, too much in shadow to be more than so many inanimate dummies. There was nothing material out there. It was the stage and the actors that were real. To her astonishment her first words came out crisp as a bite into a ripe apple. She heard her voice once again as if it emerged from elsewhere. But now all her terrors fell aside. The performance was under way.

Carlo's emergence from the cage was greeted with gasps of alarm and a gratifying ripple of applause. The lover bundled Charlotte and her chaperone to safety. In the niche beneath the Cupid statue Devil and Eliza crouched together, the space filled by the billow of their hooped skirts. Their necks were angled so the brims of their bonnets did not collide. The laughter of the audience allowed them to catch their breath after the escape from the wolf. A strip of light pierced a chink in the planking and lay across Devil's painted face. He was so intent that did not notice her body pressed against his. She was no more than a cog in the illusion's mechanism; they knitted together and the wheels smoothly turned, just as if they were one of Heinrich's automata. Devil's lips moved as he counted the steps outside.

The moment came for their escape beneath the stage. The trap opened and Devil swarmed down the ladder, barely touching the rungs. Eliza followed and dropped into his arms. Their hearts beat together as two members of the audience trod overhead, up from the front seats to examine the padlock and the iron bars of the cage. Jakey was judged to be satisfactorily captive. It was Sammy's heaviest responsibility to make sure that the scrutiny went so far and no further.

The breath caught in Eliza's lungs. Here was the pivotal moment. The substitution, Carlo and Devil called it. Timing, timing, Devil would say.

Overhead Sammy flung open the door of the statue niche. His staggering amazement had been rehearsed a thousand times. The roar that greeted it now was like a giant balloon inflating to lift the Palmyra's extravagance clear of the Strand. Devil and Eliza flew up the ladder and entered the cage at the precise instant that Jakey left it. The mirror angled at the rear allowed them a tiny hiding place.

Jakey burst out into the open and snatched up the axe. He swung it high and then brought it down on the wolf's hairy body.

The shocked silence lasted no more than a single second. Every nerve in Eliza's body was stretched to its utmost. Her eyes were fixed on Devil's face, and he grasped her hand as they waited.

She knew, without even forming the thought, that she had never felt so alive in all her life.

There was a gasp from beyond the lights. She heard the two halves of the wolf's body swish across the stage. Every pair of eyes in the house would be following.

Devil lowered the mirror and a boy perched aloft removed the shutter from a lamp. A bright beam shone down to reveal the chaperone and her charge, locked up in the cage where Jakey had been a moment before.

The illusion played out to its finish.

Charlotte's father linked the lovers' hands over the posy, and they kissed. Two or three whistles sounded from the gallery. The chaperone stumbled over her boots for the last time, and at their feet the wolf reclined with his tongue hanging over his teeth.

They linked hands and came to the footlights to take their bow. The cheering and applause was as loud as it had been in Eliza's and Jakey's dreams. Charlotte and the Chaperone had begun its progress into the Palmyra's repertoire.

When she came offstage as the first half of the show closed, Eliza was limp and trembling. She looked for Devil but he had already whirled away. Her eyes met Carlo's through the holes in the wolf's head. The dwarf gestured and she helped him to ease it off. His hair was soaked with sweat from the heat within.

'Now you are a performer,' Carlo said. 'And so you will

231

have the pleasure of doing the same thing all over again tomorrow, and the next day, and twice the day after that.'

Jasper stood at her shoulder. He was ever present backstage, overseeing all the changes between the acts. His coarse brown overall coat was not unlike the one her father used to wear, before he was able to employ men to unload carrots and cabbages for him from the market carts. He gave her a cup of water and she drank it at a gulp.

'You did well,' he smiled.

'Thank you,' Eliza said. She was pleased to have his praise but she wished he didn't look at her with such feeling. She wished also that Devil had given her the same brief word of assurance.

PART TWO

ELEVEN

Late at night Devil sat over his ledgers in the narrow office. He dipped his pen and scratched out provisional balances, frowning as he reached a new total almost always less favourable than he had hoped. He had never cared for accounting, or bookwork of any kind, but he forced himself to be scrupulous. More than two years had passed since the reopening under his management, but the Palmyra theatre was not yet the great success he had envisaged. He wiped the nib and laid the pen aside, then rested his chin on his fist. He was very tired.

At this hour there was no one to disturb him. The evening's performance had ended two hours ago and even loyal Jakey had finally put on his cap and gone home. The boy had a room now, directly overlooking a yard behind the fruit market. The porters' carts were stored overnight in the yard and the racket when they were wheeled out at two in the morning was more than most people could have borne. But Jakey didn't care in the least. He had a door to close against the world, and a bed of his own to sleep in, and he considered himself fortunate. At his shy invitation Eliza and Sylvia Aynscoe had visited his new accommodation, and noted that the smell of rotting fruit was so deeply ingrained in the walls and floorboards that every step released a waft of it. Jakey didn't care about that either, remarking only that some days the stink was rich enough to be a meal in itself.

Devil wished the boy were still at the theatre. They might have had a drink and some talk; Jakey was always a responsive listener.

He pressed his fingers into his eye sockets, trying to massage away the teeming figures.

The ledgers told their desiccated version of the story. Even by Devil's exacting standards most of the acts were good enough, the houses were respectable, and takings came in steadily enough from the box office. But in the opposite column, artists and stagehands all had to be paid. It was inconvenient but unavoidable. (Was it possible that he was close to sympathising with Jacko Grady? Devil gave a grim little smile at the thought.) The costs of running the theatre were substantial whether houses were good or bad, and in addition there were the debts from the restoration work to be serviced as well as constant investments to be made in devising and building the apparatus for new illusions. Thus money flowed out at the same rate as it came in – or usually a little faster.

The last line showed that not only were they not prospering, they were in fact barely surviving.

He swore in a low voice. And then he collected himself.

He was no longer a mere conjuror. These days he was a substantial theatre manager who could smell the proximity of real success like a good dinner coming to the table. The plate was not yet in front of him, but he must always believe it worth keeping his knife poised. If he did not retain his appetite, he thought it was unlikely that the rest of the company would invest their efforts on behalf of the theatre.

Devil ran through the list of his current concerns.

Charlotte and the Chaperone was fanciful and charming, as well as comical, and it had become a popular success. He had tried once to take it off the bill in order to rest the cast and offer space to other acts, but there had been heated complaints from patrons who claimed they came particularly to see it. The Philosophers were definitely overtired, however. An outstanding replacement act would have to be devised and perfected.

Heinrich Bayer was another problem. The lovely Lucie had never been much admired, even though she now made her eerily dutiful responses in Eliza Dunlop's voice. The recording of voices was not any longer a novelty. Mr Wu had also been tried out, but no one wanted to watch a Chinaman play chess or smoke a cigar on stage or even have him read the cards. Unfortunately Heinrich's automata were the least admired items on the bill. The public appetite was fickle and fashions changed: the engineer would have to be told as much.

Devil took a half-pint of brandy from the drawer of the desk and poured a small tot. He hesitated, and doubled the measure before corking the bottle. He rocked back in his chair and raised the glass to himself. He was drinking a farewell toast to the hand-to-mouth fellow who had once been able to dodge and rampage with the very best in the city. The new man had burdens to carry, but there were compensations. To demonstrate these to himself he hooked his thumb in his watch chain and drew out the timepiece. The gold pocket watch lay in his palm, its steady tick measuring the silence. It was past one in the morning, and he had been at the theatre for seventeen hours. He had dined at five on a cold meat pie and a pint of stout, and since then he had taken nothing. No wonder he felt bone weary and the brandy burned like brimstone in the pit of his empty stomach.

He turned the watch and briefly glanced at the twined initials engraved on the case. He didn't care what name they stood for, and had barely troubled to decipher them. A dipper had approached him in the Cinque Ports, he had handed over a pair of sovereigns in exchange for the watch, and they had both been well pleased with the transaction. Devil yawned as he let the smooth weight slip back into his waistcoat pocket. He was so tired that his head nodded. It was time to go home. He leaned forward and blew out his candle – and at once he became aware of the night sounds of the Palmyra.

There was a scratching behind the wall to his right. The theatre was overrun with mice. Jasper said that a cat could deal with them in a week and Devil was inclined to agree, even though Carlo claimed that the damned animals made him sneeze and he'd rather let the mice run. The scratching stopped, and started again.

The old boards out in the passageway creaked and suddenly the hair at the nape of Devil's neck stood up. There was no drowsiness now.

The room was cold.

'Who's there?' His voice rasped with fear.

He stood up and as he did so he heard the creak again, the sound of a footfall no more than a few feet away. His view was obstructed by the half-open door. All he could see beyond it was a thin slice of the opposite wall. He waited for a shadow to fall across it, but there was nothing.

'Who's there, I said?'

He knew there would be no answer. He couldn't stay put and let whatever it was come to him. He bolted forwards, his thigh catching the corner of the desk with such force that the pain made his eyes water. He stumbled to the doorway and kicked the door wide. The passageway was lit by a single gas jet. Behind him lay the route to the stage door. It was in darkness, but he knew every step that separated him from the alley and the Strand. Ahead were the dim twists and turns leading to the stage. Props and boxes were stacked on top of each other, creating fantastic shadows. He stared at a row of empty coats on pegs, trying to see if anything moved. The silence deepened until it seemed to press into his eardrums.

The creak sounded again.

It was another measured footstep, closer to him now.

'Jas? Jakey?'

Devil registered with distaste that his voice shook like a girl's.

Another creaking step, closer still.

Unable to run, Devil stood rigid as he stared past the limits of the meagre light into what he could not see.

The seconds passed. At the furthest end of the passageway, where the light was no more than a brownish glimmer, his straining eyes made out a darker shape. The gleam of gaslight seemed to waver.

'What do you want?' Devil howled.

Another shape formed within the outline of the first. He thought he saw a face that had black craters for eyes, and a mouth stretched open in a scream of agony. This was the old face from his bad dreams, and he knew it too well.

It was Gabe. For months he had left Devil alone; either that or through his obsession with the Palmyra Devil had been able to extinguish his presence.

Why had poor Gabe come for him now?

Did he want to acquaint himself with the new Devil, the man of property who had just drunk a farewell toast to his old murderous being? Was he here to let Devil know that he might change his name, alter his circumstances, do whatever else he wished, but he could never erase what had happened?

'Leave me alone,' Devil begged.

Silence was all that followed, weighing down on his skull until he thought the bones would crack. The icy darkness was deep enough to fall into and be lost.

Devil took one faltering step, and somehow the movement set him free. He reached up and extinguished the gas. Then he turned his back and dashed through the blackness, blindly thundering down the familiar turns of the passageway, his bruised leg stabbing with pain. At every step he expected the thing at his back to seize and engulf him. He flung himself out into the alley. He banged the door shut and locked it to contain the horror, then doubled up against the wall and coughed as he tried to catch his breath. The brandy swilled within him and he thought that he might vomit.

A voice came at his elbow. 'In trouble, are you?'

He pushed himself upright and saw a whore who must have been making her way up from the reeking shelter beneath the river landing stage. The lowest type of her kind. He had seen her before, he thought, working her dismal territory where the alley ran out into mud and foul water.

Devil rubbed his mouth. The terror slowly drained away as the night air revived him but he did not think he had ever felt more weary, or more in need of human company.

'You could say that.'

She put her head on one side, the brim of her wretched little hat crumpled by her last encounter. There was a stump of a feather mashed into it and this broken decoration unexpectedly brought Eliza to mind. The thought of her was always welcome even though their relations nowadays were professional, and mostly confined to the theatre. He must have smiled because the gap-toothed whore grinned back at him.

'That's better, dear. Why not let Margaret help you forget your worries for half an hour? Got somewhere nice and warm for us to go, have you? I've seen you up and down here and you're a handsome one, I must say.'

Her hand came out and grasped his arm. He was briefly tempted, more in the longing for obliteration than the expectation of pleasure. It was a time since he had had a woman. This one was young and had once been pretty, but she had pox sores around her mouth and a sidling manner that he didn't like. He shook off her cold fingers.

Her smile faded at once. 'Next time, then. It's Margaret. Don't you forget me,' she taunted as he walked away.

Nothing followed him except the drab's resentful stare.

Gabe had gone, back to wherever he waited and watched.

Devil moved towards home as fast as he could. He was exhausted, but he could not be sure of sleeping deeply enough to be safe from the dreams. Perhaps Maria Hayes might still be awake. A bout with her would help him to oblivion, although it had been months since he had last enjoyed his landlady. But even that straightforward business of itch and scratch brought its own complications: the notion of a more demanding liaison still tempted him far more strongly. Eliza Dunlop possessed a mind of her own and impressive strength of will; she had also refused him once. He would have to look elsewhere for a warm and compliant body to block out his terrors.

As he threaded his way up the pungent route to his old lodgings Devil didn't allow himself to reflect further. He fixed his mind on business instead. Sleep first, if that could be achieved. Then tomorrow he would at last do what he had been putting off. He would have a difficult talk with Heinrich Bayer.

The two men made their way to the Swan where Devil ordered two pints, and two glasses of good whisky to chase them down. It was that hour of the afternoon when the outside world was in the midst of its day's work and the empty snug of a public house was a tranquil retreat. It was the first properly cold day of the winter and a bright little coal fire tempted customers.

They sat down. Devil had a new bowler hat with a tight roll to the brim and he brushed invisible dust from the felt crown before placing it aside.

'I want to make some changes to the programme,' he announced without preamble.

Heinrich Bayer had arranged his drinks to stand precisely in line with Devil's and with the edge of the table. It was weeks since Devil had had anything more than a routine exchange with the engineer. They discussed the performance of the machinery Heinrich was building, or skirted the possible repayment of a proportion of the loan, but nothing beyond that. Day after day the man arrived with Lucie in her trunk on the porter's trolley, night after night they went onstage and danced together, and afterwards he left the theatre with no one but the doll for company.

I am not Heinrich's brother or his keeper, or his priest, Devil thought. *I am merely his business associate.*

Heinrich lifted his gaze from the fire but did not quite meet the manager's eye. His pallor was more noticeable than usual.

'Changes?'

'Yes. I am going to put on a different act in Lucie's place.'

Heinrich seemed not to hear. He lifted his glass, and replaced it in exactly the same spot without having touched it to his lips.

Devil forged on. 'We know that audiences are fickle. Fashions come and go, unfortunately. If they did not our lives would be so much simpler, eh?' He waited again for a response but there was none. 'From this Saturday, you and Lucie come off. I may try out Carlo's crystal ball. He has made enough noise this past year about performing in his own right. I have to listen to him, don't I?'

'I am not interested in fashion.' Heinrich was as white as chalk.

'I know. But the box office . . .'

'The box office can go to hell.'

Devil nodded, trying to be as conciliatory as possible. 'It could indeed, but then how should we all eat?'

In his mind's eye the Palymra became a vast alimentary tract, forever consuming.

Heinrich was visibly struggling for control. His mouth pinched on his words.

'It will not be the show without Lucie. What am I to say to her?'

Devil knew that he must tread carefully. 'If you explain matters, she will certainly understand that she must withdraw . . .' He hesitated. '. . . in order to play a more private role, for the time being.'

This was not as straightforward as he had hoped. He didn't want to see Heinrich's imploring expression or read the pain in his eyes, yet he found that he was unable to ignore the man's distress.

'I am very sorry, Bayer.'

We are talking about nothing more than a damned doll, he reminded himself. Lucie was a rubber carcass packed with pistons and rods and magnets, and a cylinder with Eliza's voice scratched in it.

It wasn't as if the man was going to be without work and therefore unable to feed himself or a wife and children. There would be plenty for him to do in and around the Palmyra if that was what he wanted. He had no money worries, unlike

242

the rest of them. In all of this Heinrich was fortunate, but he was not like other people. The question was: How *un* like was he?

The huge bruise on Devil's thigh began to throb with its reminder of the night before. He was the man who only hours ago had fled from his own theatre, terrified by the memory of a boy who had been dead for years. Then he had lain awake for much of the night, longing for sleep and afraid to close his eyes and glimpse what lay behind them.

There was no ghost, there was nothing beyond death, yet over and again the blind machinery of his mind raised the spectre of Gabe.

Who was he therefore to judge who was normal and who was otherwise?

More briskly than he intended he said, 'That's settled.' He knocked back his whisky. He would have liked another, but he was even more eager to get away from the Swan and from Heinrich.

The man murmured, 'What has Lucie done, to cause displeasure? I should like to know, so I can tell her as much. I wish only the best for her, you know.'

For God's sake, Devil thought.

'Of course you do. Lucie has done nothing wrong. How could she, being what she is? It is a matter of what audiences will pay to see, Heinrich.'

This was increasingly awkward. The engineer was deeply upset. Surely he was not going to weep? They were *men*; they owed it to each other to act with dignity and not to rake out their weaknesses like housemaids clearing ashes from a grate. For his own part Devil would rather have faced the terror itself, than let Heinrich Bayer know that last night he had run out of his own theatre in a paroxysm.

Heinrich mumbled, 'What shall we do? There is Hilde, of course. I have been doing more work with the phonograph and soon she will be able to sing. Schubert, quite possibly. *Im Abendrot*, something of that sort. It will be charming, audiences

243

will enjoy the music. I have only to find a suitable vocalist.' He looked at Devil at last, a long stare. 'Does Miss Dunlop sing?'

Devil said in a louder, firmer voice, 'Automata are no longer as popular as they were. This is what we are discussing, Bayer.'

Heinrich winced at the use of the word *automata*, although he had once been easily able to utter it. Devil suspected that the engineer was losing the ability to distinguish between an automaton and a human being.

The man was impossible. Devil picked up his new hat, smoothed the nap with the inside of his wrist and angled the bowler on his head.

It was time to be at the theatre. It was always time to be at the theatre.

To close the conversation he smiled and said, 'I need your ideas. People are hungry for novelty. You must help Carlo and me with our new apparatus. We've got the Floating Lady, the Strongbox, Jack and the Beanstalk.' He named the illusions they were currently developing. 'Come and see me on Monday morning.'

He pumped the engineer's hand and strode away before Heinrich could mention money.

Heinrich remained in his seat beside the fire. When Devil glanced in through the window he was as motionless as one of his dolls left in repose, and his face was hidden from view.

Eliza often visited her sister and her nephews on a Sunday afternoon, which was her only real free time in the busy week. She liked to have Faith to herself, but that was almost never possible. Today they sat in the parlour for half an hour, but Faith's head was bent over her work basket with its pile of shirts and socks waiting to be darned. The two little boys squirmed at their feet, and Matthew read the newspaper in his armchair. Their talk was pleasant but inconsequential.

'Shall we go for a walk?' Eliza suggested.

Faith looked surprised. There had been several days of fog,

during which the city was covered with a yellow-brown pall so dense that people out in the streets had to feel their way along the house railings. When they came to the kerb they hovered and stared into the murk, afraid of the cart or omnibus that might roll out of the depths and knock them into the gutter. Today, however, the miasma had lifted sufficiently to reveal the houses across the street and even the bare branches of the plane tree at the end of the road. But there was no sky to be seen, and the light was dim even for a late November afternoon.

'It is so much more pleasant than it was yesterday. I even walked up here,' Eliza reminded her.

Faith had recently let her sister know that she was in an interesting condition again. She was hoping with all her heart for a girl. Eliza steered her thoughts away from her sister and brother-in-law in their brass bed. In her role as a maiden aunt she was trying to knit an offering for the new arrival, just as she had done for the other two. Sylvia Aynscoe told her that if she dropped so many stitches the little garment would simply unravel as soon as the baby looked at it.

She gently cajoled, 'Do let's, just for half an hour. The fresh air will be good for you.'

She did not point out that the lingering veils of damp and dust probably made the outside atmosphere worse than inside the stuffy little house.

'All right,' Faith said. She levered herself to her feet. She had no ailments other than that she was often tired. She remarked to her sister that even though she had Biddy to help her, being a wife took up all her time. There were the boys to manage, as well as the endless cleaning and cooking and laundry. Matthew liked to see an orderly home.

'All men do. It's natural. And he works so hard.' Faith was quick to defend her husband, even against herself.

Eliza usually tried to make the proper sympathetic responses, but she privately took the view that Faith had made a free choice. Nor was her unencumbered life exactly a matter of reclining on cushions and reading the latest romance. The new fashion for afternoon performances meant that they now played to two houses every Wednesday and Saturday, and all the rest of her time was taken up with rehearsals or costumes or administrative matters. Devil drove his company as hard as he did himself.

She smiled at her sister. 'I'll get your bonnet for you. The blue coat, is it?'

Matthew drowsily stretched his legs and folded his paper. He was on the point of dozing off. It quickly transpired that Faith and Eliza were to take the boys with them rather than leaving them with their father. Eliza wondered why they could not perhaps go out and play for an hour on their own in the yard beyond the scullery, until she remembered that the tiny space was cluttered with a wringer and a tin washtub and piles of clay pots, and the baby perambulator was parked under a shelter of planks.

The boys must be dressed in their caps and mittens and numerous extra layers of clothing in case they took a chill. It was a long time before everyone was ready, but at last they were out in the street. The younger boy, Edwin, was tethered to his mother by a rein but his brother Rowland took the opportunity to scamper ahead. Faith was so concerned that he might run out of her sight or dash into the road that she was unable to talk at the same time. Eliza linked her sister's arm beneath her own and contented herself with inspecting the houses as they passed. There were so many of them, each one brick red with a pointed gable, hemmed in by a tiny garden, finished with a miniature gate and a path leading past a sooty shrub to the front door. Even the privet and laurel seemed to strain for a glimmer of light and clear air. She imagined the streets that ran parallel to this one, then the same again, and the identical ones beyond those, stretching as far she could envisage all the way out to the margins of London, where more bricks and more slates were daily delivered for the construction of more houses and streets. The swelling vastness of the city was difficult to comprehend, but its annexing of distant fields made her think of an unstoppable machine that gobbled up grass and spewed out streets as it churned onwards.

There was so much building. Walls rose within scaffolding, and skeleton structures took shape to become factories and warehouses and terraces and railway stations, in turn filling up with people, all of them needing to eat and work and find a roof to shelter themselves. The din grew louder, the streets more choked, the air ever thicker with dust and smoke.

Usually Eliza was able to consider all this with equanimity, occasionally even affection, but today she felt crushed by it.

Maybe it was because she sympathised with Faith, who seemed unusually dissatisfied with her life, or because she feared the claustrophobia of the Shaws' little house on her own account, or just because it was a raw depressing day with the last of the meagre light already seeping away.

Then she thought of Devil. He would have said of the crowded city – in fact, she had heard him do so – 'All the more and merrier to buy tickets at the Palmyra.'

She laughed, and squeezed Faith's arm under her own.

'You are happy,' Faith absently remarked. 'Rowland! Come back at once.'

A little further on, at the junction of two dark red streets, they came to a triangle of grass bordered by paths and enclosed by tall railings. Faith latched the gate to confine the children and then set Edwin free. Immediately the boys launched into a noisy game and the sisters were able to sit down on a stone bench. Faith gave a small sigh.

'At last, five minutes' peace.'

'Are you very tired?'

Faith looked down at the hem of her skirt and the ruff of fresh dirt clinging to it.

'I am, a little. Some of the work of being a wife and a mother is very boring, I can tell you, although I would not say as much to another soul. Yet even if I could change anything, you know, I would not. Well . . . perhaps I would like to have some more money, but who would say differently? In any event, let's not discuss my affairs. I think you want to talk. How is the theatre?'

Faith had never really understood her sister's decision to enter such a disreputable and precarious world. But she took care not to be too critical of it and the two of them remained close, even as they grew older and their differences became more apparent.

'I have a lot of work to do, also. But at least none of it is boring.'

In the two years since her debut, Eliza hadn't overcome the stage fright that gripped her before every performance. Jasper assured her that apprehension led her to be at her best when she did take the stage; Devil and Carlo shrugged and said that she would have to conquer the fear or learn to live with it. The theatrical cycle of queasy dread before and elation afterwards had become part of her life. There was no point even in discussing it.

She wondered if she should tell Faith instead about Heinrich Bayer, and the unease she increasingly felt in his presence, but in the end she did not because there was nothing precise enough to relate. The engineer's presence had made her uncomfortable ever since the voice recording, but there was no more to it than that. In the end she decided that it was his sadness that disturbed her. Just once, out of sympathy, Eliza had suggested that they might sit companionably together as she completed a mundane task for Devil and Heinrich waited to test a new piece of apparatus. She had looked briefly into his eyes and she had the impression of a stage trapdoor opening and then snapping shut again.

It was a memory that made her shiver.

Heinrich had said that he found himself unable to wait any longer and hurried away.

While Eliza was considering these matters, Faith went unerringly to the most central of her concerns.

'How is Mr Wix?' She gave her sister a teasing smile.

'He seems to be quite well.'

'What does *that* mean?'

'It means that he is not ill. He works exceptionally hard and he appears to enjoy it. He does all he can to make a success of the theatre. It is a way of life that requires a good deal of effort, which I hadn't realised when I entered it with too many romantic notions about glamour. *Those* were soon dispelled. It sounds as though our different experiences are quite similar, doesn't it? Who would have thought to compare being a wife with working as a magician's assistant? Possibly everyone's life reaches a point of disillusionment, don't you think, whatever path they choose to follow?'

'Our stepmother's hasn't,' Faith pointed out. They often privately mocked Bertha Dunlop for her happy laziness. She avoided any activity more strenuous than berating her servants.

Eliza laughed again. 'That's true. She is the exception to every rule.'

Faith grew solemn. 'However, as married women Bertha and I do have the support and love of our husbands. Father is an affectionate and loyal man, and Matthew is as good as he can be.'

That last was ambiguous, but Eliza only agreed. 'Indeed you do. And they are.'

Her eyes followed the children as they dashed around the enclosure. Rowland made a racket by dragging a stick along the iron railings while Edwin's yells at not having a stick of his own added to the din.

'Play gently,' Faith called to them. She asked in a low voice, 'Don't you wish for the same?'

'Perhaps I do sometimes. But whom should I marry?'

'I thought perhaps Mr Wix. You seem . . . affected by him.'

Affected, Eliza thought. Yes, that was true enough. He affected her constantly, whether he was near or not. But their relationship, if it could be described as such, had long ago settled into a professional pattern. It was hard to imagine how it might change, although she *did* imagine it.

'Unfortunately Mr Wix is not interested in me. Or perhaps

it would be more truthful to say that he is not interested in becoming any woman's husband.'

The way they sometimes touched, cramped together in the statue niche and the realms under the stage, forced into intimacy by physical circumstance yet still deliberately wanton, *that* was not husbandly. Or wifely on her part. Outside in the light and air they never discussed what lay between them. Desire felt like a burr snagging the innocent expanse of their working partnership. Eliza sometimes compared her recent existence to a very long and somewhat boring card game, played by tired chaperones on a dull evening without music or conversation.

She had begun to wish that she had taken her chance that giddy morning at the Palmyra.

'Oh, Lizy. Would you like him to be interested?'

She nodded. Faith took her hand and their gloved palms rested together.

'What will you do?'

'Do? Nothing whatsoever. Carry on at the theatre, earn my living, rejoice in my freedom and independence. See how I can come up to visit you on a Sunday afternoon, eat my supper with Sylvia Aynscoe, walk down Regent Street or Bond Street and look into the shops, do whatever I please, and no one questions me?'

'Oh, Lizy,' Faith repeated.

Her sister's concern made Eliza wish she would stop before she made them both feel worse. But Faith was not going to give up.

'You know that Jasper Button cares for you, of course? Jasper would be a good husband. He would protect you and provide for you and your children, even though . . .'

'Even though he works in the hellish, murky, immoral, improper theatre, just like me?'

Faith lifted her chin. 'Yes. At least he understands what your life is.' Some respectable men would not, was the unspoken rider.

'I can't marry a man I don't love.'

'And you do love Mr Wix?'

It was always Eliza's instinct to keep her real feelings to herself. It had been a surprising relief to reveal them this far.

So she said, 'Yes.'

If this turbulent mixture of longing and apprehension and admiration and the physical discomfort that accompanied it was *love*, she did indeed. If listening for his voice and prickling in his presence and fretting in his absence were indications, and so on.

Did Faith feel the same about Matthew? Eliza regretted that she had never bothered to ask when her sister became engaged. But then Faith had always been so composed and proper, and the match had been so very suitable, that passion had perhaps not been the biggest part of the contract. Yet here were two small boys, and now there was the hope of a little girl.

What *did* marriage mean? Why could she not behave like Bascia the acrobat and seize what she wanted, all jingling bells and flashing eyes? Certainly Devil would be glad if she did. Eight times a week they compressed their bodies into the statue niche, eight times she hurled herself down a ladder into his arms. She knew and he knew about the burr and its chafing, but for opposite reasons neither of them was prepared to remove it. That was what their understanding amounted to.

Reviewing her situation under her sister's concerned regard, Eliza had to acknowledge that she must be almost as conventional as Faith herself. So much for the rackety life of a variety actress.

'It's a very uncomfortable feeling,' she said.

'I don't know what to advise,' Faith sighed.

Eliza withdrew her hand. She adjusted her glove before she replied, 'You don't have to advise me. Don't be concerned, either. I expect to be back to normal some day quite soon. That's what happens with love, isn't it?'

'Perhaps.'

Faith might have taken the opportunity to confide further, but Edwin embarked on a sneezing bout. His nose was a moist

251

crimson button. Faith jumped up and cleaned his smeary face with the pocket handkerchief pinned inside his coat.

'I don't want him to catch cold. We had better go home.'

Matthew had drawn the heavy parlour curtains and lit the lamps. The overmantel glass and a pair of wedding-gift silver candlesticks reflected the warm light. He had been on his knees toasting muffins in front of the fire but he jumped up to put his arm round his wife as the boys tried to clamber up his legs.

'Look at your rosy faces. You are the picture of health while I have been frowsting indoors,' he laughed. 'Your suggestion was good, Lizy.'

Faith cheerfully responded, even as she stooped down to clear up scattered crumbs and blobs of butter from the hearthrug. 'Here, Matthew, give the toasting fork to me. Let's all have tea. Can you stay, Eliza?'

She did stay, and told her nephews a story about a magician before they went to sleep. It was late when she finally made her way down the Edgware Road to Bayswater via the Paddington omnibus.

At the beginning of December Carlo at long last took the stage as himself.

Devil's playbills commanded the public to

See the Incredible Inimitable Colossal
Carlo Boldoni
in Person

He had capitulated gracefully enough as soon as giving way to Carlo's constant demands became inevitable. He made over the last quarter of the show to the dwarf and allowed him to include whatever material he chose. Carlo rose to the challenge. His act was a rapid series of bold illusions, made all the more notable because so much speed and artistry was displayed by such a small person.

On the first night he strode on to the stage in immaculate

252

evening dress, swishing the tails of his coat and making a low bow over his ingenious silk hat. The audience responded, sitting forward as soon as he took his place under the spotlight. The applause began even before the climax of the opening illusion.

In one sequence Eliza reclined on a dais and he caused her to float up into the air. He took a golden hoop and passed it from her head to her feet to show that there were no wires suspending her. For the next she sat in an ordinary upright chair placed on a Persian rug to make it evident that there was no trapdoor involved. Carlo draped a paisley shawl over her and as soon as he had finished arranging the folds to cover the tips of her toes he whipped it away again to reveal the empty chair. An astonished gasp sounded before the applause burst out.

The regular stage box apparatus had been suitably adapted. Now it was the versatile Jakey whose wrists and ankles were roped or chained to make escape appear impossible. And then he duly sprang to freedom. Devil conceded that it was almost easier to have Jakey perform the necessary manoeuvres than it was to conceal Carlo's real stature.

As he worked through his act Carlo moved from large effects to more intimate feats of magic with cards and silks. The circle of light that contained him grew tighter and brighter. The audience was drawn in as under a spell. Carlo performed the Orange and the Crystal Ball trick so much admired by Devil, only now he used a ripe peach. There was a suitable-looking lady in the front row of seats, so he commanded her to the stage. He leapt up on to a stool and produced the perfect fruit from the nape of her pretty neck.

For his finale he borrowed a diamond ring from the lady and placed it in an envelope. Then he set a match to the corner of the envelope and burned it to ashes, the ring apparently with it. Carlo searched inside his silk hat, revealing its emptiness, and passed the victim the hat while he hunted inside his shoes. He made an increasingly panicked investigation of his clothes and stage props until the audience and his target were convinced that the trick had gone wrong and the item was lost. Ripples of anxious laughter rose from the auditorium. The jewel's owner covered her mouth in dismay. Crestfallen, Carlo took back the hat and immediately a dove fluttered out of it. The bird circled before settling on his outstretched hand. Tied to a ribbon around its neck was the lost ring.

Devil watched from the wings. He had seen the final rehearsal and he knew the act was good, but the cheering and clapping took him by surprise. It was so loud that it shook the elaborate gasolier in the shape of an inverted palm, and threatened to lift the cupola clear of the roof.

The triumphant dwarf ran off after his last bow. He swept Devil another bow all to himself.

'Told you, didn't I?'

They squared up to each other.

'I believe you did, once or twice.'

The audience's appreciation continued long after the curtain fell.

'Listen to that. Do you want to put your old Flames up against my act?'

'No, thank you.'

Carlo pulled off his white tie and wiped his face with a rag. Smeared make-up made him look grotesque. When he smiled through the streaks of red and black paint he was more wolf-like than the mangy beast in Charlotte and the Chaperone. Devil held out his hand but Carlo did not like to accept an olive branch too readily. He considered for a long moment before shaking Devil's hand.

'Well done,' Devil said. He meant it. He could already hear the money gushing into the spanking new wood-and-brass till register recently installed in the box office. He was delighted with the machine because it prevented any possibility of pilfering.

Carlo preened. 'Thanks very much. By the way, did you see who was out front tonight?'

'Who?'

'Jacko Grady. Larger than life.'

The intricate business of devising illusions and constructing the necessary apparatus had long outgrown the coffin maker's premises. Devil rented a disused bakery behind the wharves and tanneries on the south side of the river, and here they set up a workshop that was part joiner's yard, part blacksmith's shop and part scientific laboratory. The gaunt old building was spacious enough for all their needs though it was always cold except when the sun shone directly overhead, and then it became as hot as a furnace.

Jasper liked it because it resembled his studio up by the railway lines in Camden Town. His black kettle made its appearance and he brewed pots of tea while he worked. Carlo made one corner of the premises his own and he settled to the business of flexing his limbs, scribbling cryptic notes, tinkering with arcane props, and occasionally lying flat with his eyes closed which meant he was dreaming up new illusions. Sylvia Aynscoe's sewing machine occupied the corner of the bench nearest to the fire. She felt the cold more acutely than anyone else, so she measured and stitched wearing her coat and a pair of gloves with the finger ends cut off. In the early days, while she was still employed at her atelier, she had been so conscientious that rather than let Eliza down she would take urgently needed costumes home with her and work on them for the whole night. In the morning she would go directly out to her real job. For months Eliza pleaded with Devil to ease her circumstances and give her a permanent position.

'We'll always need a wardrobe mistress. A theatre calls for costumes as much as performers and a stage. There is nothing Sylvia cannot make, and she does it so quickly. Her work is of the highest standard. We should count ourselves lucky to have her.'

'What? A *wardrobe* mistress? I can't pay another full wage. This isn't the Savoy Theatre, and my name is not D'Oyly Carte.'

There were a dozen of them in the permanent company already, including old William Crabbe and his son Roger who operated the lights, and the two large brothers named Dickinson, tavern acquaintances of Devil's, who dealt between them with front of house and the stage door. These two wore a green livery embellished by Sylvia with important braid and buttons.

There was no slack. Sometimes Devil put on the livery and sat in the glass box office cubicle, sometimes Jasper or Sammy did. Everyone stood in for everyone else when necessary, because that was the way Devil ran matters.

'You must give Miss Aynscoe a proper job,' Carlo insisted. This happened at about the time that Carlo's act became the most popular on the Palmyra bill. The theatre critic of the *Clarion* wrote, '*Mr Boldoni is a small individual but his talent as a magician is massive. Make your way to the Palmyra at once.*'

The audiences obligingly did so and Carlo gained a new bargaining strength. Devil had been wondering when the dwarf would bring this into play, and he was relieved that the first demand was not more outlandish. Miss Aynscoe was at last invited to join the permanent company, at a weekly wage a shade higher than the pittance she was already earning.

'Thank you,' Eliza privately said to Devil.

'You should address your thanks to Carlo,' he replied.

Slowly, by steps that were governed by Sylvia's reticence, the two women were becoming friends. On the day she realised she would be able to leave the atelier, Sylvia shyly grasped Eliza's hand. Eliza pulled her closer and impulsively embraced her. The seamstress's body felt as weightless and brittle as a moth.

'I am so happy,' Sylvia murmured. She lowered her eyes but Eliza saw how they shone.

One day Heinrich appeared at the bakery. Lucie and the other automata were no longer on the theatre bill and the engineer had not been seen for weeks. The first time he did no more than step inside to scribble a note for Devil. Three days later he left a diagram of an ingeniously wired switch mechanism. Each time Jasper looked up from his bench to offer tea, and on the third visit Heinrich accepted his invitation. Eliza was present, standing immobile while Sylvia pinned and tacked the calico toile of an evening gown on her. The ladies in the audience liked to see glamorous creations on stage and this one was being made for the new Strongbox illusion. Jasper was also at work wiring paste gems and coloured feathers to the carnival mask that was to appear in the same illusion. He had recently done some repair work to the battered wax philosopher's head and this lay at his elbow with the gory neck exposed. It was such a familiar sight that no one glanced at it.

Heinrich barely acknowledged Eliza. He kept his eyes turned away but she found this rigid detachment more troubling than his attention. Carlo emerged from behind his screen. The dwarf had been practising manoeuvres in his contortionist's rig of close-fitting black woollen garments. Devil once joked that he looked like Satan, and Carlo tartly replied that the name and the role were already allocated within the Palmyra circle.

Carlo said, 'You could help me for an hour, Bayer. Jasper is always too busy.'

Heinrich drank his cup of tea and did what Carlo asked of him. The bakery's atmosphere of quiet and cheerful industry must have soothed or reassured him because he came back the day after that, and before long he was a regular visitor. He appeared to enjoy listening to theatre gossip and plans, although he spoke very little. If he had a choice, he tended to take his seat near Sylvia's sewing machine.

'Aha,' Devil winked at Eliza.

'No!' she cried and earned herself a surprised stare in return. 'It would not be the thing at all. Not for either of them. Please don't even joke about it.'

She wished he would stay away, but she could have given no reason for her growing aversion and so she suppressed it.

One afternoon in the darkest part of the year Heinrich was at the bakery with Sylvia and Jasper and Sammy Hill. Eliza was leaving for the theatre, a little earlier than usual because Devil required her help in revising a sequence. They would almost certainly be alone together, but in such dangerous circumstances she was used to locking up her feelings like Carlo in the wolf's cage.

As she fastened her coat and pinned her hat she felt a prickle of dread. She looked up to see Heinrich waiting beside her.

'I will walk across the bridge with you,' he said.

These were the first words he had spoken directly to her since he had returned to the company.

The way led beside the river wharves and beneath warehouse gantries to steps up on to Waterloo Bridge. There would be few people about in the twilight and the alleys were not well lit. She glanced across to Jasper but he was busily hammering. Sammy was at the sawhorse. Sylvia nodded at her and smiled – Heinrich was her ally nowadays.

Eliza could only mutter, 'Very well.'

They made their way between high walls towards the black glint of the river. She could hear the slap and suck of the tide-water against wooden pilings and the creaking of an iron chain. All this was familiar, as was the distant clank of a train pulling out of Charing Cross. Only a few hundred yards separated her from the yellow glow of the Palmyra, and Ted Dickinson running his carpet sweeper across the foyer floor. She could not look round, but she knew Heinrich was at her shoulder. It felt unnatural to walk in silence so she asked the first question that came to her.

'How is Lucie?'

She regretted it as soon as uttered.

'She is unwell.'

'I am so sorry to hear it.'

Heinrich's step slowed.

Eliza's breath caught. She had recited these exact words into his recording apparatus. Her voice, even her intonation, these now belonged to Lucie. Or Heinrich believed they did.

'She is very unwell,' he whispered.

'I . . .'

However she tried, out of her blank mind she couldn't summon a conventional phrase that was her own. They had slowed to a halt, and he moved closer, cutting off her escape. Against Eliza's back reared the damp wall of a warehouse. It was almost dark now. She looked left and right but there was no other person in sight.

'I still have Hilde.'

She angled herself away from the wall. How far to the lighted bridge?

When she managed to speak it came out as a gasp.

'The theatre. I must go. Devil expects me . . .'

'Wait. Will you sing for me?'

'*Sing?*'

'You have a lovely voice. You should try a little *Lieder*. So charming.' He lifted his hands, and he hummed as he traced the outline of her windpipe. Then his fingers tightened around her throat.

Eliza gasped. She twisted violently and somehow broke away from him. 'No. No, I can't do that. I'm sorry. Goodnight.'

She ran over slippery cobbles all the way to the steps. She hurled herself up them and gained the safety of the busy thoroughfare.

'All right, miss?'

It was a uniformed policeman, squarely planted between her and the way ahead to Wellington Street. Only then did she look over her shoulder but there was no sign of Heinrich.

'Yes. Yes, thank you.'

'Someone's following you?'

She was panting for breath. 'A friend. I work with him. In the theatre. There's no trouble.'

The officer scrutinised her, and then saluted. 'Very good. This is not Whitechapel, miss, but still there is a man out there. You should take care.'

Like everyone else Eliza had read about the murders, and seen the terrible pictures in the newspapers, although she had looked quickly away. She lingered amidst the safety of the crowd until her breath came more easily and then she hurried on up to the Strand. Avoiding the alley she banged on the closed door of the foyer until Ted Dickinson let her in.

Devil was on stage in his shirtsleeves, smoking and repeatedly probing the mechanism that made a bunch of flowers spring from the bare earth in a brass pot.

'Heinrich frightens me,' she blurted out.

He looked down into her eyes. 'Why is that?'

When she had recited the reasons he nodded. He thought for a moment.

'I understand. Heinrich is a strange creature. His brilliance makes that inevitable. He lives with his inventions and his grasp on reality is less firm than yours or mine. But he would not really hurt anyone, least of all you.'

Instead of reaching for her he held out the stage prop. The flowers miraculously unfurled and he presented her with the bouquet.

The next morning at low water Sammy Hill went down early to the river.

He came running back, his face blanched.

Devil and Carlo and Jasper and Eliza were all at the bakery.

'Stay here,' Devil ordered her when she tried to follow the men.

The body was lying face down in the mud, clothing shredded, her legs lapped by black water. A small crowd had already gathered. Two policemen climbed down the iron ladder and turned her over. Her head flopped backwards because her neck was cut through to the spine.

Devil wished he had not seen it but he recognised the contorted face of the woman from across the river. She had told him her name.

She had called after him. 'Next time, then. It's Margaret. Don't you forget me.'

TWELVE

The murdered woman was a prostitute by the name of Margaret Minchin, whose home was in Granby Street, not far away.

The bakery became a fortress. The street door was kept locked, and any caller had to put his mouth to the iron flap of the letterbox and identify himself before the bolts could be drawn. Devil asked Eliza and Sylvia if they would prefer not to come to the bakery at all, but the two women agreed that they must try to continue with their work. If Jasper could have acted as their bodyguard for the entire twenty-four hours of each day, he would have done so.

Carlo muttered, 'Can't live under siege for ever, murderer or no,' but he would not countenance either of the women walking out alone any more than Jasper or Devil would.

Devil immediately took the Philosophers off the theatre bill. Jasper wrapped the grisly wax head in a square of sacking and stored it in a box in the furthest recess of the bakery. They did not discuss it, but everyone felt more comfortable once the prop was put away, and the coffin lid was masked by some discarded scenery flats. Of Heinrich there was no sign. Eliza could not even speak of him, believing that if she referred to what had happened between them it would be to suggest that he was guilty of something infinitely worse than merely frightening her.

A few days later a police constable called to see Sammy Hill, the discoverer of the body. Sammy had already told the police everything but he repeated what little he knew, after which the constable informed him that although no arrest had yet been made in any of the cases it appeared almost certain that there was no connection between this victim and the deaths in Whitechapel.

'How do you know?' Sammy asked.

'I can't tell you that, sir, it's police information. But there are ways of establishing the differences in these killings. It's in the detective work.'

'Peeler didn't know any more'n the rest of us,' Sammy later reported. 'But likely she was just a poor girl who went with a fellow violent in drink. It's a sad tale.' He shook his head and sighed.

The dark days of January slid by. There came a rattle at the letterbox, and a voice begged for admission.

'It's only Heinrich,' Devil said. 'Let him in, Jas, will you?'

The bolts slid back. Eliza sat in her place, the heel of her hand pressed to her mouth and a cold trickle of fear running down her spine.

Heinrich wheeled in his porter's trolley. In place of Lucie's trunk were some smaller boxes and unwieldy pieces of equipment that he proceeded to unload. He was clearly expected.

'Very good, Heinrich,' Devil chuckled. 'I am looking forward to this.'

Eliza shivered. He had put his hands to her throat. Yet here he was in daylight, the same shabby Heinrich as always, pale and intent, his eyes shielded by his spectacles. His gaze slid towards her and he gave her an innocent nod of greeting. She could not help staring and wondering, had *he* done this thing? What sharp blade or blunt instrument might be hidden within the boxes? And yet it seemed the maddest speculation to connect Heinrich with such violence. She glanced at Sylvia Aynscoe but the other woman's head was tranquilly bowed over her sewing.

262

Devil and the other men helped the engineer to carry his equipment to a corner of the bakery. A handsome rosewood table with polished brass uprights and a waisted coil was unpacked. There was another heavy cylindrical coil mounted on a wooden stand, a series of glass bottles, more instruments and a dozen books.

The corner of the bakery opposite to Sylvia's was to become Heinrich's territory.

The men gathered around the rosewood table, which they referred to as the experiment table, murmuring of circuits and contact arms. Electricity was deeply fascinating to Devil. Jasper and Carlo equally were intrigued by the challenge of harnessing its power to create illusions. They drew closer and Carlo perched on the end of the bench where he could see more clearly. Heinrich became the natural focus of the little group. When he was explaining or demonstrating a principle of science his diffidence left him.

'Please turn that handle,' he ordered, and Devil did as he was told. There was a crackle and a brilliant scarlet thread sprang between two metal posts. Miss Aynscoe gave a little gasp.

'There you have electricity,' Devil exclaimed, as happily as if he had personally generated it.

'Miss Dunlop, would you care to experiment by receiving a small electrical shock?' Heinrich turned to her and held out two smooth wooden handles like those of a child's skipping rope.

'Thank you, no.'

'It would be only the mildest sensation. See, this instrument is a rheostat. It reduces the current from the coil to the lowest level.' With the tip of his index finger he slid a metal knob that ran in a slot along the length of a horizontal bar. 'You know that the procedure has therapeutic value? Medical men use it widely to treat a number of ailments.'

'So I believe,' Eliza said tonelessly. 'But I am quite well, thank you.'

Too late, she remembered she had recorded this very answer.

263

Heinrich gave no sign of having heard her words, but still she could have cursed her own stupidity. Would she never be able to speak to him without inadvertently mouthing Lucie's words, like some half-animated doll?

Sylvia spoke up. 'May I?'

'Certainly.' Heinrich put the wooden paddles into her hand. 'Are you quite ready?'

He moved a lever. Miss Aynscoe gave a small cry, more of surprise than dismay. She put down the handles.

'How strange. That is a most unusual sensation. Am I to feel relaxed or invigorated?'

Devil grinned. Eliza refused to look at him.

Later, as they walked across the bridge towards the theatre to prepare for the evening performance, he asked her, 'Is something wrong?'

She considered her words. It was important to be rational.

'Is Heinrich to spend more time working with us at the bakery? Now he has brought in all that equipment, I mean?'

'Yes, I think we shall see more of him. It is useful to have him close at hand, rather than shut away in that Clerkenwell hideout of his. The more he is involved, the more he will be inclined to commit himself to us. You know what is involved.'

She did know. As always, it was all about money. Devil meant that the more personally involved Heinrich became in the daily struggle to keep the Palmyra afloat, the less likely he would be to ask for the repayment of his loans.

'I follow your reasoning, but . . .'

He broke his stride to look at her. 'It is not like you to take against a person, Eliza.'

She burst out, 'It is not without reason. He wanted to throttle me.'

'He wanted you to sing for Lucie and you refused. You know the doll means everything to him. There was a flash of anger, I imagine. It was wrong of him to frighten you, to lay a finger on you even for a second. If he were a less awkward person, he would surely apologise for his lapse.'

264

She said, 'I am not his doll. I am afraid that he begins to
. . . to confuse me with her. How much further might his
confusion extend?'

Devil sighed. 'Let me reassure you again. But to be fearful
is not at all unnatural, after what has happened on our doorstep.'

The river ran below them, oily in the twilight. A steam launch
was making its way upstream against the tide, lead-grey clouds
billowing from its tall iron funnel. Eliza never crossed this way
without thinking of the wretches who jumped from the central
arch to drown themselves. She supposed they were desperate
in all the different ways that the city was able to provide, but
traditionally they were women crossed in love. The bridge was
even sometimes called the Bridge of Sighs.

She felt as cold as if she had just been hauled out of the icy
water. Devil was watching the river too. He had not listened
to what she was trying to say and she was disappointed in
him.

He said suddenly, 'I saw her, you know. Before she was
murdered.'

She tried to take this in. 'You saw her on that day? You
knew her?'

'No, no. I encountered her one night near the stage door.
She was coming up from the river. She was trying for some
more business, poor creature.'

Devil still felt ashamed of his terror that night, but he had
not forgotten the intensity of it. He would not betray any of
this to Eliza.

She said, 'I suppose we may never learn the truth about her.
I think of her, though.'

Eliza pitied poor Margaret Minchin, and she felt a strange
kinship with her. Whatever misfortunes had led her to her sad
end in the river mud they were unlikely to have been of her
own making. The harsh world unjustly reserved its most severe
punishments for women.

Devil nodded. 'Possibly she tried to dip the wrong pocket.

Or maybe her mark thought the price too high. The world did not serve her well, whatever sad route led her to the end. Tell me, what would you like me to do about Heinrich?'

Speculation about the murdered woman's plight had cast Eliza's concern for herself in a fresh light. What real cause for anxiety did she have? A man's eyes had unnervingly widened. His hands had moved to her throat and she had evaded his grasp. That was all. She supposed it was self-indulgent to think of herself as threatened by a man she knew well, a *friend*, when another far less sheltered and privileged woman had been brutally murdered.

There was nothing to be done, she decided, short of asking for Heinrich to be removed altogether, and that Devil would not and could not do. She could remove herself, perhaps. But the Palmyra was in her blood. She was wedded to it now, not to any man.

When she did not answer Devil remarked, 'You know, Eliza, you acknowledge stage fright, yet you walk out night after night into the lights without betraying a tremor to the audience. You feel sympathy for Heinrich and so you are more alert to his oddness. You read more into him than the rest of us because you trouble to look more deeply. But fear? I don't believe it. I think the truth is that you do not fear anything.'

He was wrong, but she could not make him understand how.

In silence, they reached the north side of the bridge and walked up towards the crowded dazzle of the Strand. It was the hour when clerks left their desks and flooded towards the railway stations, so they were battling against a tide in the same way as the launch ploughing on towards Battersea. The shouts of news vendors and street merchants filled the air between them. Eliza bowed her head in frustration. Their little history, the forced intimacy of their nightly incarceration, was after all a flimsy basis for believing they knew one another. In fact they knew each other hardly better than the strangers streaming over the bridge. Their only true links were the ravenous demands of the theatre, the friendships they shared, and the industry of the bakery. She had been right not to let him make love to her.

In the midst of the crowd, caught up as she was in her work and with family and friends to call upon, Eliza had never in her life felt as lonely and rudderless as she did at that moment.

Devil stopped walking. He put out his hand and tilted her chin, forcing her to look at him. They studied each other's features as if they were trying to read an unfamiliar language, and deciphering nothing. The crowd parted around them and flowed onwards. Eliza abruptly stepped away.

She manufactured a smile.

'We should be at the theatre.'

'We are in good time,' he said pleasantly.

The evening's performance went off without a hitch.

This time, Carlo and Devil both saw Jacko Grady positioned in the centre of the stalls.

Each time he came to the bakery Heinrich stayed a little longer. He brought in more of his apparatus, and gradually embedded himself in his corner behind ramparts of machinery. Eliza recognised the voice-recording device. None of the automata appeared. She took care not to make any enquiries, least of all about Lucie.

The men became increasingly involved in planning new effects – Devil's strategy for drawing in the engineer was clearly working. Heinrich had little direct involvement with the two women, however. He was formal in his manner, always hemmed in by his diffidence, but Eliza was aware that there was now an added layer of difficulty in his dealings with her. He watched her covertly, as if trying to choose the right moment to speak, yet as soon as she looked in his direction he pretended to be engaged elsewhere.

As the days passed the threat of the outside slowly diminished and to her relief the bakery doors were sometimes left unlocked.

She felt easier in her mind when the world was not shut out, because for her the danger was already within.

She spent as little time at the workshop as she could manage without neglecting her work there.

Then one day Heinrich shifted the recording cylinder to the front of his bench. Light glinted on his spectacles.

'Will you not sing for poor Hilde after all, Miss Dunlop? You know that a recording will not take up too much of your time.'

This very abruptness of the question told her it had long been turning in his mind while he waited for the opportunity.

'I am sorry. No.'

'Why not?' He drew nearer. 'Why so adamant? What possible harm could come from singing a song?'

Carlo was tinkering nearby. He raised one eyebrow and laughed.

'Heinrich, have you ever heard Eliza sing?'

'I have not had that pleasure.'

'Then don't press her too hard, or she may oblige you.'

Heinrich's expression did not flicker. But he was angry. He stood so close to her that Eliza could feel it, powerful waves within him that he contained with difficulty.

'Thank you for your advice,' he said. He strode past Carlo, took his coat from its customary peg and left the bakery.

Carlo was startled.

'Our friend prefers a submissive attitude in his women. I am surprised he is extending his interests to include you, Eliza. Your outspoken ways would not suit him in the least. Unless it is in the attraction of opposites, like a pair of his magnets?'

The dwarf made a suggestive gesture but Eliza did not even bother to frown at him. He added, 'Where is Lucie these days, anyway?'

'I have no idea. Lying on her altar in Clerkenwell, I imagine. Heinrich wants to steal my voice. In his mind he confuses me with his dolls. Lucie speaks in my voice, he believes I am in some way his. I wish I hadn't done it. I will never, ever sing for him.'

'Of course not, if you don't want to.'

Carlo climbed on a chair and when their faces were level he put his hands on Eliza's shoulders.

'You are sad these days.'

She began a sturdy denial but she could not find the words. Tears welled up and she had to search for her handkerchief. Carlo's natural gentleness was usually kept well hidden, and to see him looking so troubled on her account brought all her defences down.

'Don't cry,' he whispered. Immediately she began to sob like a child and he took out his own red handkerchief and dabbed at her eyes.

'I am here. Don't discount me, Eliza. Remember the fellowship?'

Herself, Carlo, Devil and Heinrich. Jasper the final initiate. All of them like flies in a thick grey web of wanting and denying and wishing for what they couldn't have. Why was desire so painful and why was love more denied than granted? Why could men and women never be equal? With all this roiling in her head it was a relief to cry. She lowered her forehead on to Carlo's shoulder and he held her there, patting her heaving back.

'I'm sorry,' she sniffed at last.

'Tell me your troubles.'

That was impossible. She could not bewail the lack of one man and the unwanted attentions of other men when one of those involved was Carlo himself. She improvised some explanation about having looked for glamour in the theatrical world whilst discovering only hard work and long hours, but the dwarf was not deceived. He scowled, reverting to his more familiar face.

'Damnation to Devil Wix. There are times when I could happily slaughter him. Throwing his remains in the river would be altogether too kind.'

269

Eliza would not be the object of anyone's well-meaning pity, even Carlo's.

She protested, 'I don't know what you mean.'

'You don't, and I'm the Pope in Rome.'

Devil and Jasper made their way back from the metal foundry at Southwark. They carried between them a bar of metal the size of a small coffin, cast in the shape of an ingot. On the floor of the foundry it had looked too heavy for ten men to lift, but the two of them hoisted it easily. The ingot was hollow, its metal skin no thicker than a baby's finger. Devil was delighted. As they pushed their muddy way between carts and pedestrians he crowed, 'Six stout men down from the cheap seats and they won't be able to budge it. Then I shall step up and almost throw it into the air. An excellent spectacle.'

Jasper's next task was to paint the item to resemble real gold. Devil was working up some comic business about an attempted theft. Eliza was to provide stage assistance, dressed in a shimmering gold costume sewn by Sylvia Aynscoe. The secret of the illusion was the strong electromagnet constructed by Heinrich Bayer, to be switched on and off beneath the stage by Sammy Hill.

Jasper had been pleased by the fact that each of them would contribute to devising and engineering and staging this particular trick. It had seemed a useful emblem of their working harmony, and a thoroughly good sign for the future of the Palmyra. He believed passionately in equality and democracy, both in the wider world and in the small realm of their theatre. He protested, 'I thought Carlo was to do the lifting.'

Devil at least had the grace to look faintly embarrassed. 'No, I intend to perform the illusion myself.'

'Eh? Surely it will be all the better as a spectacle if the strong arm is the dwarf's?'

'The dwarf already has a good share of the stage. We should not put him in everything. Audiences crave variety, Jas.'

'Particularly if the variation is yourself.'

270

Devil laughed, easy and handsome with his hat tipped to the back of his head. He believed in democracy as sincerely as Jasper did, but with himself at the head of the theatre just as the Queen headed the nation. Except that she chose to keep herself hidden at Windsor, and he liked to be on stage in full view.

'Are you vexed for Carlo?'

'No,' Jasper said shortly. He was irritated by the rivalry between Devil and the dwarf, and the clash of vanities that was at the root of it. Most of the time it lay submerged but sometimes it broke out in furious arguments, and threatened worse. Devil could hardly use his fists on the dwarf, although once or twice Jasper had had to haul on Carlo's coat to stop him launching himself at Devil. He feared what might happen if he were not always there to keep the uneasy peace.

Devil stopped short and Jasper rammed the metal bar into his rear, not entirely by accident.

'Hey. Mind what you're doing, can't you? Jas, I'm parched. What do you say to stopping in here?' They were passing a public house. 'I'll even stand you a refreshing lemonade.'

Jasper looked into the sawdust interior. It was a filthy, dismal place, not one of Devil's gaudy gin palaces.

'No, thanks. But you may come to a coffee house with me.' It would be a good idea, he thought, to try to persuade Devil to change his mind about taking Carlo's role.

Jasper's preferred establishment stood on a corner half a mile from the bakery. There were clean-swept wooden floors and a row of little wooden booths along the wall opposite the counter. The shop's owners, a respectable woman and her daughter, took pride in its pleasant homeliness. Amidst the city stinks it offered appetising smells of coffee and fresh pastry. The two men rocked their ingot on its end and stood it behind the door where they could keep an eye on it. They found seats in a snug panelled slot and Devil peered around him with a sceptical expression. The daughter in her white apron and cap came to take their order. She smiled at Jasper and blushed when he greeted her.

'Who's sweet on you, Jas Button?' Devil teased as she went away.

Not the one who matters, Jasper could have replied.

Instead of slopped-over pots the girl brought coffee in a pewter jug, clean china and a plate of fresh apple turnovers wrapped in a cloth to keep them hot. She had loosened her cap just enough to uncover a thick lock of yellow hair. Jasper thanked her warmly and slid the plate to Devil.

'Try these. They're as good as your mother used to make.'

'Did she? I can't say I remember.'

It was not their habit to recall their boyhood days, bad times or better. But Devil bit into a turnover and nodded with his mouth full.

'Excellent.' Sugar powdered his chin and flakes of pastry stuck in his side whiskers. Jasper drank his coffee and thought about how he might persuade Devil to step aside from the Ingot trick. The window opposite them was steamy from the warm interior and at first all he could make out was a loss of light as a large shape interposed itself. Then a reddish pumpkin face loomed through the glass. There was no mistaking Jacko Grady.

Devil saw him too and immediately swore. 'What does this fat arse want from us?'

'Revenge?'

'Ha. Let him try.'

Grady pushed into the coffee shop and made his way to their booth.

'Morning, gents,' he said. 'Mind if I join you?'

'Yes,' Devil snapped. The man only laughed.

'Time to let bygones do what they are supposed to do, Wix. We are fellow managers. Men of the theatre.'

To fit himself into the tight space of the booth he had to compress his flesh with a corset of two hands as his knees folded. When he was seated a roll of fat clothed in greasy waistcoat overflowed the board. Devil ostentatiously moved his cup and plate to one side.

Grady produced a theatre bill, smoothing it with sausage fingers before sliding it across the table.

Devil and Jasper studied it.

HAGGERSTON HALL was the heading, in a typeface identical to the Palmyra's current bills.

Home of the Spirits

Devil yawned.

'Of course, my new hall is not the Palmyra,' Grady sighed. He held up one hand. 'But you won that from me. It was neither fair nor square I might say, although we won't drag all that out again, eh? I have my new theatre, in the East End, not quite the first location I admit, but a very promising beginning. And my new presentation will be the finest in London. None of your cheap conjuring of bunches of paper flowers and moulting birds and such tat, no Gipsy fire-eaters, no flummery with locked boxes and dwarves. Haggerston Hall presents only the genuinely supernatural. We harness the power of the mind, and we respectfully open worlds that lie beyond our own.'

Devil was the picture of boredom. With the tip of one finger he pushed the programme back to Grady.

'"The Remarkable Miss Angela de Launay" is a tired old witch.'

'She is gifted with second sight.'

'Of course. And what else do you offer? Table rapping, I'll bet. Ardent messages from the other side? Noisy spirits with their bells and trumpets? Swathes of ectoplasm, I am sure. All done in subdued light. Half-darkness is a cheap effect to lay on, fortunately.'

'I have the Harding brothers, direct from New York. They conduct a remarkable seance. The quality love these things.'

'Do they, indeed? I would wish you luck, if I cared enough. Why not tell me what you really want, Grady? Why do you keep popping up at the theatre, and following me and Jasper through the streets as we go about our business?'

The fat man shrugged, setting up a ripple of flesh.

'What? *Following* you? I happened to see the two of you

walking along proud as peacocks with your new tin box, and I came in to offer my compliments. As for the Palmyra, I like to know what's going on at the old place. You have painted it up very bright, I must say. It looks like a Mayfair house of accommodation. I still think of it as my own, you know.'

'Then you should stop doing so, because it is mine.'

Grady chuckled. 'Well, well. To show that there is no ill will I am inviting you to Haggerston Hall. As my guests. Bring the dwarf, if you like, and the handsome girl with the temper. You will enjoy the show.'

'No,' Devil said. His face turned black, and the sight seemed oddly satisfying to Grady.

'Thank you for the invitation,' Jasper put in politely.

Grady leaned forward. 'Why not come, Wix? Surely you want to see what we are doing? I guarantee you will be interested in the performance.'

'Charlatan,' Devil spat.

Grady only laughed. 'What troubles you, man? The show is innocent enough. And many people are inspired by the presence of the spirits. Give us the benefit of the doubt, eh?'

'I would not give you the benefit of a bucketful of turds.'

The fat man shook with laughter. He compressed his belly with his two hands and began the process of standing up. Once he had broken free of the booth he winked at them, and as he passed the ingot he gave it a hearty kick.

'Disgusting person,' Devil pronounced.

'I think we should take up his kind invitation. Why not? It pays to know the competition.'

'Grady is no competition for us. And I will not go to any seance.'

Jasper smiled faintly. 'If you don't believe in the home of the spirits, and I think you do not, what do you have to fear?'

'I don't fear. I am a man now, Jasper.'

'Indeed,' Jasper agreed. He let the past slip away again. 'By the way, I am still of the opinion that Carlo should perform the ingot lifting. It will make a much better spectacle.'

274

'Should I care about your damned opinion? Look, here comes your girl to offer you fresh coffee.'

'She's not my girl. She is sixteen years old.'

'That is a fine age. However, let us get back to the bakery. There's work to be done.'

For days afterwards Devil continued to insist that he would not visit Jacko Grady's entertainment, even though Carlo agreed with Jasper that they should see what the fat man put on his new stage. Sylvia Aynscoe ventured the information that one of the sewing girls she used to work with had been to Haggerston Hall, and her dead mother had actually spoken to her through the medium.

'And what did the young person's late ma have to say?'

Sylvia lowered her eyes. 'She told her to be a good girl and to work hard. Her reward would come.'

'Ha. I could have given her the same advice myself and saved her mother's eloquence. Not to mention the shilling for her seat.'

'Don't,' Eliza reproved him. 'If the girl found it a comfort to believe her mother spoke to her, is there anything so very wrong in it?'

Devil laughed, without humour. 'Who would be comforted by yards of billowing muslin, a cold draught and some shrieked nonsense that could be taken to heart by any credulous fool in the hall?'

She looked at him, wondering. There was a black glare in his eyes that she had never noticed before. Intending no more than to provoke him because he had dismissed her own fears, she said lightly, 'You protest so strongly against a mere entertainment. What are you afraid of?'

Jasper made a warning sign, but she did not see it.

Devil hesitated. Then he sneered, 'Nothing at all. If you are determined to waste time we'll make an excursion to Haggerston and you shall see for yourself.'

'Good. I am quite interested in Grady's Home of the Spirits,' Carlo said.

On the following Saturday evening, after the Palmyra show, Devil and Eliza made their way east with Carlo and Jasper. Devil was unusually silent on the omnibus, but in the din and clatter of the journey none of them noticed it.

The Hall offered to the street a plain frontage and heavy double doors, the upper storey surmounted by a classical pediment. It had more the appearance of a sombre Nonconformist chapel than a place of popular entertainment. By the time the Palmyra group arrived there was a stream of customers for the late performance. A noisy crowd of street sellers worked the steps outside, variously hawking pies and potatoes heated by glowing charcoal in tin boxes, hot soup, ham sandwiches, and porter from tall cans. Everyone was taking care to fortify his physical incarnation with plenty of food and drink before entering the Home of the Spirits. Wafted by steamy air and well provided with meat pies wrapped in newspaper, the audience surged into the foyer.

Devil paid for four of the best seats in the house.

'I thought we were to be guests of the management,' Carlo said.

'I won't take a gift from Grady,' Devil retorted.

The auditorium was a plain room furnished downstairs with rows of hard chairs and upstairs in the gallery with wooden benches. Devil and the others took their places in the centre of one of the front rows and Devil turned to survey the crowd.

'I see that Haggerston Hall does not draw the quality, whatever Grady imagines,' he remarked. This was true. Instead of the well-behaved family groups and members of the discerning middle classes there was a large contingent of the raucous type he tried to keep out of the Palmyra. The worst elements were already putting up some unrestrained stamping and catcalling from the cheapest seats.

Carlo sniffed. 'What's the difference between a quality shilling and a common one? He has very nearly a full house of paying customers here. Including ourselves, of course.'

The stage apron was bare, there were no musicians, and the

curtains were plain dark red plush, not very clean. Jacko Grady was evidently no more eager to spend his money than before. Jasper noted that the high windows at the sides were equipped with heavy blinds, not yet drawn. Not a finger of street lighting or even moonlight would be allowed to brighten the activities of the spirits. He folded his arms and sat back to wait for the show to begin.

Eliza was also looking about her. Dotted here and there, in the rows of sniggering clerks and better-off working men with their girls who would turn up for any novelty, she saw a scattering of pale, intent faces. These people gazed hungrily at the drawn curtains. They were the believers in their sceptical midst, waiting and hoping for a message from the other side. She felt sorry for them, but she also felt a small anticipatory shiver on her own account.

Devil's knees were pressed into the chair in front. To one side of him Carlo knelt on his seat, which was his preferred way to see over the heads and shoulders that otherwise blocked his view. On the other he was aware of the folds of Eliza's skirt and her hands resting in her lap. Beyond Eliza was Jasper's impassive profile.

Let us see what fakery Grady is up to, Devil thought grimly. He wanted very much to witness fakery.

Three loud piano chords sounded from behind the curtains. The red plush swept aside and Jacko Grady smiled centre stage in his straining evening coat, with his stiff collar and white tie digging into the cascades of his neck. The only article behind him on the stage, apart from the upright piano and a lady pianist in a plain dress, was a chaise longue upholstered in red plush.

Grady held up his hand, even though the applause was not so loud as to require much subduing, and in a few words welcomed them to Haggerston Hall. If he saw the Palmyra party seated directly in front of him he did not make any acknowledgement.

'Ladies and gentlemen, this is not a variety show. You will see no conjuring or escapology tonight.'

'*Cheapskate*,' Carlo muttered.

'We are just the channel through which the spirits come to you. I ask of you no more than to open your ears and – if you so wish – to allow your belief. We will begin with a demonstration of the power of second sight. I am proud to present to you the eerily gifted, the outstanding, the only *Miss Angela de Launay.*'

At her cue Miss de Launay came onstage and after her bow seated herself on the chaise longue with her back to the audience. She was of middle age, and stout. Her assistant came forward and blindfolded her, and there was some extended business around calling up a committee from the audience to make sure that she could see nothing. The hall was well lit and the window blinds remained open.

The assistant moved along the rows of seats, collecting trinkets belonging to the audience. Grinning, Devil slid his gold watch from his waistcoat pocket and handed it over.

'Are you ready, Miss de Launay?' the assistant enquired.

The audience stopped eating and gossiping and came slowly to a state of attention.

'I am ready,' she said in a clear voice.

Facing the audience, the assistant silently held up Devil's watch. It swung a little on its chain, catching the light as it did so.

'The article is a watch,' Miss de Launay said.

There was an appreciative murmur. The assistant nodded his head and held up a finger for silence.

'A gentleman's watch with a double case.'

There was a pause. Miss de Launay tilted her head a fraction and Devil leaned forward, frowning in concentration that matched the performer's.

'The material is gold.'

The assistant put his finger to his lips.

'The maker is . . . Longines.'

The murmur became a buzz as the assistant invited a front-row matron to examine the watch.

'Quite *right*,' the woman called out. There was real applause now, but again the assistant gestured. He asked the performer, 'Shall I return the item now?'

She replied, 'Not yet. I believe you have forgotten something.'

'Have I? What is that?'

'There are engraved initials on the reverse of the case.'

The man turned the watch in his hand.

'Yes, I see you are correct. Say what they are. Let's hear it. Ready?'

The exuberant crowd waited for the response.

Miss de Launay lifted her head. 'I can see the letters clearly. The initials are C . . . J . . . W.'

Another front-row occupant confirmed that this was so. Loud clapping and admiring cheers followed as the watch was passed back to Devil, but a boy leaned over the gallery rail and hollered down to him, "Oo are you, ven? 'Er bruvver, is it?'

Devil stood up. To his surprise, he found that he was enjoying himself at Grady's show. 'Not at all. I don't know the lady, but I doubt she has second sight. This is a stage trick, and a very nice one.'

Eliza pulled at the tail of his coat. 'Sit *down*.'

Devil noted that the feet of the chaise longue were sheathed in brass, and then did as he was told.

Carlo glowered at him. 'Why can you never, ever keep your blasted mouth shut?'

'What? I might well have been her accomplice. There's one seated hereabouts, that's certain.'

A large man seated behind them dropped his hand on Devil's shoulder.

'That's enough from you,' he warned.

Devil contented himself with watching and listening carefully as Miss de Launay correctly identified a series of items ranging from silk handkerchiefs to ladies' fans. With some extra thought she could even give the date on a coin. The audience was impressed. Little tremors of awe at the demonstration of supernatural power shivered along the packed rows.

Devil leaned across Eliza to catch Jasper's attention. He held up one hand and closed the thumb and forefinger to make a circle, then separated them again.

Jasper nodded.

Miss de Launay stood up and faced the audience to take her bow. Her grey face was flushed from her efforts.

Devil loudly applauded. 'Bravo,' he called out. 'Clever fakery,' he added in a whisper. He felt much more comfortable. Inside Haggerston Hall at least, the supernatural was evidently only a matter of electrical circuits, signal codes and a disciplined memory.

In the interval they went outside to eat oysters from a vendor's tray.

'How was that all done, precisely?' Eliza asked.

The three men were pleased to explain.

The trick was nothing new. The assistant gave the correct reply each time as a code in the precise formulation of his question. The only special feature was the feat of learning and memory involved. They were all agreed that it would probably be easier actually to acquire second sight than to undergo this.

'But no one uttered a word about Devil's watch. How could she have known he held a gentleman's gold watch, and that there were initials engraved on the case?'

Devil patted his waistcoat pocket. Carlo almost skipped with pleasure as he nudged Devil's hip with a sharp elbow. 'I told you it would be worth coming, didn't I?'

'It's done with the aid of an electrical circuit,' Jasper explained.

'Electricity? Is electricity the answer to every question these days?'

Devil nodded. 'Yes. We believe it is.'

He closed his thumb and forefinger to form a circle.

Jasper described how one of the brass feet of Miss de Launay's chaise longue rested on a small brass plate screwed to the boards of the stage. From there, electrical wiring ran to a seat somewhere in the theatre. In response to the first accomplice's set of gestures the second man could close the circuit by pressing a plate underfoot or perhaps a button concealed beneath his seat. This action, he hazarded, would cause a hammer to tap somewhere inside the upholstery of the chaise. The taps would follow an intricate code to indicate the details of every object that was held up behind Miss de Launay's ample back.

'Very clever,' Eliza said admiringly.

'Not nearly as clever as we are,' Devil said. He offered her his arm to climb the shallow steps. 'Boldoni and Wix and the company of the magnificent Palmyra Theatre are second to none.'

Eliza wondered, briefly, why he must be so insistent. Who was he reassuring, if not himself?

They took their seats for the second half of the programme.

The thick blinds had now been drawn over the windows and the lights were lowered. As Eliza sat down she drew her coat over her shoulders. The hall seemed to have grown cold. It was no longer a place of entertainment, much more a waiting room or even a chapel. The audience became subdued and the interval talk subsided into whispers. Even eating and drinking were forgotten.

Without as much as a piano chord Jacko Grady appeared before them.

'Ladies and gentlemen, direct from their famous tour of the great cities of the United States of America, Haggerston Hall is proud to introduce the Harding Brothers.'

The curtains opened. In the dim glow two pale, spruce young men stood at centre stage. In their dark coats and high collars they looked like bank clerks. There were no sniggers, or merry remarks from the back of the hall. The audience simply waited, rows of faces turned up to the stage. With no fanfare, without uttering a word, the brothers took their seats across from one another at a plain deal table. They placed their hands palms down on the surface.

There was a sigh, like wind in winter trees.

Then the rapping began.

It was a wild, undisciplined noise that seemed to come from many hands, from all parts of the hall. Under the assault of it Devil wanted to crouch and cover his ears. He had to force himself to sit still. Eliza was a shadow beside him, and Carlo's profile seemed carved from stone. The rapping grew louder and harder and all the time the brothers sat expressionless, their hands never moving.

At last the elder one looked into the crowd.

He said calmly, 'The spirits are among us.'

The rapping slowed and steadied, growing quieter until it became one insistent steady knock, like bare knuckles on an inner door.

It seemed to say, *Let me in.*

'Who is there?'

Slower knocking now, at the same speed as a heart's pulse.

'Who do you wish to speak to?'

'Do you have a name?'

Mark and Luke Harding spoke in turn, in quiet Yankee voices that carried to every corner of the silent hall.

'One knock for yes, whoever you are. Two knocks for nay.'

One firm knock. Several people near Devil moved forward in their seats. They wanted this, he had no doubt. They wanted to hear what the spirits had to tell them. He pressed the flat of his hands against his thighs to still their trembling.

'Will you use the lights?'

Another knock.

Luke Harding lifted his forefinger and at this signal a black wheel was carried on to the stage. The assistant rotated it, and passed his hands through the centre to show that there were no attachments. He stood it upright and left the stage.

There was just enough illumination to see that the flat rim of the wheel was painted with the letters of the alphabet.

'Please tell us your name,' Matthew said.

Under the letter M a tiny red light glowed, like the eye of an animal at night.

282

Electricity, Devil told himself. He made to close the scientific circle of finger and thumb, but his hands now seemed fixed to his thighs.

The light moved around the circumference of the wheel, A, R, G, A, R, E, T.

'Margaret,' said Luke.

His brother stared into the hall. 'Margaret is with us. Who does she wish to speak to?'

There was a kind of groan, terrible to hear.

'My child,' a woman's voice cried out, and at the same time a man said, 'My mother.'

The light winked again. M.

The silence in the hall was heavy. U, R, D, E, R.

'Who knows this poor creature?'

Now no one spoke. Margaret Minchin. Devil realised that the only sound was the pulse inside his skull.

'Next time, then. It's Margaret. Don't you forget me,' she had said to him in the alley that led down to the river. His pulse drove a slow, sickening surge in his ears.

'What do you want?' one of the brothers asked.

The light made its rapid circuit of the wheel. R, E, V, E, N, G, E.

It was not me. I did nothing, not to you.

There was a sudden cacophony of rapping and in the silence that followed Devil shivered convulsively.

'The spirit is gone,' Mark Harding said.

Another steady knock came. This time there were more obliging answers from a different spirit, but still a woman in the gallery was left sobbing and wailing. Voices began to call out from all over the hall, begging for a word from a dead relative or a beloved friend. The answers came, cruel or kind, as the brothers sat impassive on the stage. Devil knew that all of this seance must be just another illusion, no less of a trick than Angela de Launay's memory game, but he could not escape the dread that it stirred in him.

'Who are you?'

It seemed that yet another spirit had come.

The light moved much more slowly. It spelled out, B, O, Y. 'What boy is this?'

A long interval followed. Devil waited for the tremulous call from the bereaved mother in the front seats or the lost sister in the gallery. The brothers did not move.

The red eye picked out another letter. B.

And then it flickered so quickly that he could barely follow. U, R, N, E, D.

Luke Harding lifted his head. 'Burned boy? How is this? To whom do you wish to speak?'

Flickering at speed again, H, E, C, T, O, R.

'Is there any Hector here?'

The audience shifted, peering through the chill darkness at the faces of its nearest neighbours. Devil was aware that Jasper did not move a muscle. Beside him Eliza was warm, her lips slightly parted in her intense concentration, her hands still folded in her lap. Out of the terror clamping Devil's skull came a longing to throw himself against her, to crawl within her. In a parallel place where he was not afraid, he could still lose himself in a woman. He could not reach that place now, and his present abject fear made him crave its comfort even more – not any woman's comfort, but Eliza's. He tried to reach for her hand and clasp it, to draw its warmth into himself, but he found that he could not move.

The two mediums now turned to face the audience. They beckoned, and everyone could see that they spoke to him.

'Hector? Will you answer?'

Carlo and Eliza turned and stared at Devil in astonishment. Only Jasper sat motionless and Devil tried to do the same, but now he was shuddering uncontrollably. The convulsions rocked his chair and made his teeth rattle.

He saw the red eye make an inexorable circuit of the wheel, spelling out I, A, M, C, O, M, I, N, G.

'The spirit is here. Do you wish to speak to the spirit, Hector?'

He had no voice. All he could see was the malevolent eye,

flanked by the two brothers with their pale faces and stiff black coats.

'You must take notice, Hector.'

Then the knocking began again. It swelled in volume, filling the hall, unmistakably angry and threatening. Bells rang and a terrible shrill whistling made them all crouch in their seats. From behind the Harding brothers rose sheets of pale quivering mist that hung in the riven air.

The dwarf sprang on to his seat and shook his fist at the stage.

'Trickery,' he bawled over the din. 'Grady? You're nowt more'n a blooming trickster.'

Voices from all over the hall shouted him down.

Devil could not look away from the stage. Within the veils of ectoplasm a dark figure took shape. It was the same as the apparition he had glimpsed at the Palmyra. It was Gabe.

'You should be ashamed of yoursen',' Carlo was yelling. The emotion of the moment brought back his northern cadences.

The black Gabe did not move. The mist seemed to swirl about him and then subside. There came a blast of icy air, a last clamour of the bells and whistles and a loud bang. Gabe was suddenly surrounded by a live penumbra of flame.

Devil watched in abject horror. The fire licked around the boy's body, just as it had done outside the blazing barn. The shape swayed and seemed to fly towards him but the flames were too greedy with their fuel. The spectre convulsed, on the very point of consumption by the fire, before collapsing in a shower of sparks. A pathetic charred bundle lay on the stage as the curtains came down.

Run, run. The same instinct that had gripped him in Stanmore.

He found a way to lurch to his feet. Pushing the dwarf aside he stumbled to the end of the row, his eyes and throat stinging from the smoke. Jasper and Eliza came after him, and Carlo who countered the hisses from those who were trampled in their passing. They burst out into the foyer of the Hall, and from there escaped into the gaslit street.

'Lovely oysters, gen'lemen. Fresh as the tide,' a woman's voice sang out.

'What's the matter with you?' Carlo shouted. 'It's only the Flames, man. Your own bloody trick, such as it is.'

A cold sweat soaked Devil's shirt. He was gasping for breath and staring over his shoulder.

'The Flames?'

Carlo stood with his hands on his hips. 'What else? Are you mad?'

'Shh,' Eliza warned. 'Devil? Tell us what is wrong?' She grasped his wrists and tried to look into his face.

'I . . . I fear the dead.'

'*What?*'

They stood in a huddle at the foot of the steps leading up to Haggerston Hall. Perplexed, Eliza tried to take in Devil's muttered words.

A smiling man emerged from the double doors of the Hall, as if to breathe the night air. He rummaged in his coat, that garment being stretched over his immense belly, and brought out a cigar. He lit it and sucked in a long, satisfied breath.

'Faker,' Carlo bawled. 'Bloody charlatan.'

Devil broke away. He half ran, half stumbled into the thick of the crowds.

'Catch him,' Eliza cried but Jasper held on to her arm. He was pale and his mouth was set in a line.

'Let him go.'

'What? Why? We must make sure he comes to no harm.'

'Devil has his terrors, as we all do. He will recover once he is away from here.'

She wanted to run after him, but the darkness had swallowed him up.

THIRTEEN

Eliza passed the whole of the following day in a visit to her sister. There was little opportunity to reflect on the night before; to Faith's great delight the longed-for girl had arrived the previous week, a pretty and placid little creature who was to be named Elizabeth in honour of her maternal aunt, and who was already known to her doting family as Lizzie.

At the bakery Carlo and Jasper were at work on new apparatus. It was unusual for Devil not to put in a Sunday appearance, but they assured each other that he would be sleeping off the drink he had no doubt taken after the Haggerston Hall seance.

When Monday came and the full company reassembled, there was still no sign of Devil. It had become his practice at the beginning of each week to gather everyone together and encourage or exhort them, using a rough mixture of praise and asperity, but today they waited in vain. There was only a slack silence where the busy motor of the theatre usually throbbed. As the time for the evening performance approached and still no message came from the manager, they all understood that something was amiss. Ted Dickinson was urgently dispatched to Devil's lodgings to search him out. He came back alone.

'No one there,' he reported. 'Room's empty. Landlady thinks he's been back since Saturday night, but she can't remember for sure. She ain't that reliable, I'd say.'

Jasper and Carlo made hasty plans. Jasper would go on in Devil's place in Charlotte and the Chaperone, Devil's own segment of the show would have to be cut and the other acts extended to fill the time, and an expanded repertoire of Carlo's illusions would take up the entire second half. The audiences loved Carlo's act, and he was always eager to indulge them. The immediate crisis, at least, was capable of solution.

'It's lucky some of us are ready to work.' The dwarf tried for a disparaging sneer, but his anxiety drained the comment of the necessary venom.

Eliza sat in her Charlotte dress, waiting to go onstage. Sylvia was helping Jasper into the chaperone's skirts. Once he was trussed up Jasper laid a gloved hand on Eliza's arm.

'Try not to worry,' he advised.

'What can have happened to him?' She couldn't conceal the extent of her concern. Every muscle in her body was taut, every unexpected sound made her spin in the hope of seeing Devil.

Jasper sighed. 'I don't know. There will be an explanation, there always is with him.'

'What did he mean, *I fear the dead*? Why did Jacko Grady's seance disturb him so much?'

Within the hairy mat of his wolf costume Carlo stretched and flexed, methodically preparing himself for the stage. He never let external affairs interrupt his concentration before a performance. The red plush tongue lolled out of the animal's wide mouth. Sylvia fussed over him, checking that the two portions of the pelt were correctly fastened. Jakey stood to one side in the lover's costume. On his regular Palmyra wages and with a roof to shelter him, he had filled out and his limbs had lengthened. He was a handsome presence now.

Jasper only said in a low voice, 'Perhaps you should ask Devil himself.'

Will Dickinson stuck his head round the dressing-room door and gave them their call. On their way to the wings they squeezed past the guest act coming offstage, a troupe of painted contortionists sweating in their sequins. Eliza remembered her first visit backstage, and how the seedy glamour of it had thrilled her. She took her place at Jakey's side and listened to the greedy murmur of the waiting audience. As the musicians struck up Charlotte's overture she gathered herself for the breaking wave of fear. At this moment it invariably flooded her throat and swamped her guts with nausea, but this evening she could only think of Devil. For the first time in her brief theatrical life she found herself indifferent to the audience.

I would rather suffer stage fright, she dismally reflected.

Jakey tucked her hand under his arm, Jasper gathered his skirts and they sprang into the lights.

Minutes later she slipped through the trapdoor and dropped into Jasper's arms. Their bodies were confined in the tiny space under the boards but she could feel how he held himself apart, acutely aware of their bodies and at the same time trying not to press himself against her. He was not Devil.

But then, no one was anything like Devil. The Palmyra was a dismal shell without him in it.

I *will*, she resolved, thinking of Jasper's advice. If he is safe, if no tragedy has taken place, I will ask him at the first opportunity what troubles him.

The laughter and applause overhead sounded less enthusiastic than usual. Charlotte was not receiving the response they were all used to. Carlo exercised the two halves of the wolf as violently as he could, but Devil's absence seemed to leach the energy out of him. As they counted the seconds to the next cue Eliza grasped Jasper's hand. He squeezed hers in return before they flung themselves up the ladder and crouched behind the mirror in the locked cage.

The last act before the interval was the Golden Ingot. Time for their costume change was limited. In the dressing room Eliza scurried behind the screen where Sylvia helped her into the golden gown and fixed the mask. Devil had continued to insist on performing in the Ingot himself, but tonight Jakey would have to go on in his place because for all Sylvia's ingenuity the strongman's costume couldn't immediately be adjusted to fit Carlo's small body. Jakey insisted that he knew all the lines.

'Don't you worry, miss. I can do it for you, easy as pie.'

Sylvia Aynscoe had been helping him with his reading and writing. She had often told Eliza how quickly he grasped and retained whatever scraps of information came his way. Eliza caught sight of him through the leaves of the dressing screen as the boy applied the necessary new make-up – but he was no longer a boy. He was tall and straight. He had abruptly grown up.

Their new illusion was already a favourite. An eager cohort of men charged up on to the stage to attempt the lifting of the ingot and Jakey directed their efforts with authority. Devil had written a supporting rigmarole about a poor man trying to win the love of the golden girl by strength alone. It was a humdrum showcase for the trick, but Jakey managed to invest the strongman with pathos. An attentive silence deepened as he moved through the build-up. He did not have Devil's willingness to play for laughs but he was a far better actor, speaking the banal lines as if they came straight from his heart. No one fidgeted or sniggered and not one pair of eyes looked anywhere but at Jakey. All Eliza's anxiety briefly disappeared and she felt a moment of pure delight in being on the stage with him. Her role consisted in not much more than standing still and trying to look beautiful, so she drew herself to her full height and tilted her head to stir the feathers. She was so absorbed in watching Jakey that she missed her cue, not once but twice. Coolly he prompted her.

When the reveal came and he finally thrust the golden bar into the air, his face under the greasepaint vivid with triumph, a great cheer burst out. Jakey and the Ingot had lifted the audience from apathy into wild enthusiasm.

The curtain fell and Eliza turned to him. He was good as the lover in Charlotte, but in a principal role he had been magnificent. Even in her preoccupied state she recognised there was a talent here. Everyone backstage knew it; the Crabbes stared down from their lighting perches in clear surprise.

'Bravo,' she said.

'Thank you, Miss Dunlop. Obliged to you.' Already Jakey had reverted to his offstage manner. He seemed to diminish in stature as he slid into the wings.

The second half of the show was Carlo's. Either in an attempt to match Jakey or to demonstrate that Devil was superfluous, he gave the best performance of his life. The final curtain fell only after a series of curtain calls that brought the whole company onstage to take a bow.

There had been a crisis and they had demonstrated that they were more than equal to it.

Afterwards the dressing room seethed with rebellious elation. From the outset Devil had presented himself as their energising force, but now they suspected he was not so central. If his absence were to be prolonged, the mood seemed to suggest, they might do better than merely survive. There might even be opportunities for advancement, for territorial extension.

Eliza saw the Dickinson brothers muttering with the senior Crabbe as they prepared to close up for the night. Carlo's face was bisected by a knowing grin, and even loyal Jasper murmured to her, 'We did well, you know. We worked together as a company, the way I've always known we could.'

'Tonight was just one show, Jasper. For next week, next year, we'll need Devil.'

Jasper said, with a touch of grimness, 'He'll be back.'

Heinrich had been beneath the stage with Sammy for the performance of the Ingot. He drew closer now, clearly listening to what they were saying. His spectacles shielded his eyes. He had grown thinner lately, and dark scoops of shadow lay beneath his cheekbones. Eliza tried not to shrink from him.

Jasper said, 'I'm right, Heinrich, eh?'

'I could not determine,' was the only response.

Jasper took the engineer off with him, saying they might walk up the Strand and drink a glass together. Eliza was grateful for this protection. She told Sylvia Aynscoe to go on home without her, claiming that she had some theatre business to attend to, but in reality wanting to be alone for an hour. She wandered into Devil's office and sat in his chair, her hands spread flat on the desk. There were piles of papers and account books stacked here, and more in the niche once occupied by Mr Wu. She flicked through the books with their columns of figures, frowning a little at the illegible loops and scratches of Devil's handwriting. The papers were mostly programmes from rival houses and letters from the managers of other magic acts. She tried the drawers of the desk but they were locked as securely as the safe. She was sure that Devil kept the keys about him. If an accident – or worse – had befallen him, it would be next to impossible for the rest of them to take over the theatre. This was intentional on his part, of course. Devil did not share his financial or management decisions with anyone in the company for good reason – for all his claims of cooperation and collaboration, the Palmyra was really his fiefdom.

A cold chink of logic opened in the wall of her anxiety. If he returned – when, *when* he returned – this state of affairs would have to be changed.

She was the last to leave the theatre, apart from Ted Dickinson who waited with his bunch of keys at the stage door.

'Goodnight, miss. We'll be seein' what tomorrer brings.'

He winked as he locked the door behind them.

Eliza did not sleep.

Early in the morning, resolving that she must do something rather than nothing, she took the omnibus along Oxford Street and stepped off near St Giles's church. There were new roads and numerous buildings under construction here and the difficulty of negotiating wheeled traffic and crowded pavements and mud underfoot was made worse by the great pits excavated in the streets and the scaffolding that blocked the routes. It was almost a relief to turn off the main thoroughfare and pass through the grim warren of alleys to Devil's lodgings. The tenement houses closed in on her, walls and small windows webbed with filth looming as if ready to topple on to the cobbles and bury her. She remembered the way precisely, even though it was so long since she had helped Devil to nurse Carlo over the bitterly cold Christmas. Here was the angle between two walls where he had kissed her. She passed the place without turning her head.

She arrived at Maria Hayes's door and knocked. Some time elapsed before the landlady emerged, fatter and blowsier than before but with the same knowing smirk.

'I am here to see Mr Wix.'

Mrs Hayes shrugged. 'Best of luck to you.' She opened the door just wide enough to let Eliza pass.

The stairs appeared narrower and darker than she remembered. A man and a woman stumbled past her; the house seemed to rumble and shiver from the pressure of so many people housed within its walls. She had no idea what she would find when she hammered on Devil's door. There being no response to her knock, she pushed the door open.

He was in his bed. He lay huddled with his back to the room, his black head motionless on the pillow ticking. On the floor beside the leg of the bed was an empty glass phial with a smear of brown residue in the bottom.

Eliza took two steps to the bedside and stretched out her hand. She dreaded the feel of lifeless flesh. But breathing warmth greeted her fingers. Almost gasping with relief she shook his shoulder, receiving only a snore in response. She stooped for the bottle and sniffed before throwing it aside. She shook him harder before leaning over to shout in his ear.

Devil rolled on to his back. His mouth hung open, the corners glued with a string of mucus. Another thick snore came out of him. Eliza scanned the room. It was as bleak as always, but there were some scraps of kindling in a bucket and a few lumps of coal in a sack next to the grate. She made a fire, poured the remains of the water from the ewer into a pan and set it to boil. Then she pulled the blanket off the bed. He was half-dressed in a soiled undershirt. Another snore escaped. Eliza went briskly to the window and threw it open. Cold fresh air poured into the attic.

She went out again, made her way to a dingy little grocer's shop in the shadow of the church and returned with purchases wrapped in paper. She refilled the ewer from the communal tap on a lower floor, noting that the dismal house had gained piped water. Once she had made tea and laid out some bread and cheese, she filled a skillet with cold water and poured it over Devil's head.

He jerked and thrashed his legs, which caused the undershirt to rise up and expose the lower half of his body.

She did not stare, but neither did she look away.

She had studied art, and so was acquainted with the naked male form as represented in marble or stone. In tending to Carlo during his illness she had been confronted by his male body, and for more than two years she had been sharing a dressing space with a succession of fire-eaters and jugglers and acrobats. None of these glimpses, however, had prepared her for this – in the matter of rigidity and sheer prominence.

With a shock, she realised that Devil's black eyes were open and he was watching her.

She snapped, 'Are you not ashamed of yourself?'

He lifted his head off the pillow, wincing a little.

'Ashamed? Let me see. Yes, my lodging, I believe. I am at home in my own bed. I might ask you the same question, therefore. Are *you* not ashamed, to be spying on a man in this way?'

He lay back, not attempting to cover himself. Eliza snatched up the blanket and threw it over him before turning away.

Devil yawned and audibly scratched himself. 'I'm obliged.'

She had to bite the inner corners of her mouth to stop herself laughing.

The bed creaked as he stuck out his legs again and hauled himself to his feet. He groaned, filled the basin from the ewer and submerged his head. Droplets of water flew everywhere as he shook himself like a dog. He rubbed himself down with a discarded shirt, strolled back to the bed and propped himself against the pillow.

Eliza poured out a cup of tea, glancing to make sure that he was still decently covered before she handed it to him. He drank deeply and sighed.

'My belly thinks I'm long dead. Is that bread and cheese for me?'

She passed it to him. He ate like a starving man.

There was nothing significantly wrong with him, she realised. Relief passed through her, followed by a healthy wash of irritation.

'What are you doing here?' he asked with his mouth full. 'Not that it isn't a delightful surprise to wake up and find you at my bedside.'

'I came to look for you. I was concerned, naturally. All of us were.'

His black eyebrows rose.

'Concerned? About what?'

'The theatre. Last night's show. Filling the programme at short notice because of your unexplained absence. Small things, but still likely to generate anxiety, do you not think?' There was ice in her words.

Devil looked to the window. He put aside the last of the bread.

'Last night's show? Eliza, what day is it?'

She said, 'It is Tuesday.'

'*Tuesday* . . . ?'

There was a long silence. She held up the empty bottle for his inspection.

His face darkened. In a low voice he said, 'Yes, since you ask. I am ashamed, Eliza.'

He took the bottle from her hand and threw it into the corner of the room. It shattered against the wall and shards of glass spread over the floor.

'Why?' she asked him.

'Sleep,' he said. 'I needed to sleep, so I took a dose of laudanum. I suppose you think that was cowardly and contemptible?'

She found the empty teacup lying in the blanket folds and refilled it for him. Then she carried a chair from the corner of the room, placed it beside the bed and sat down.

'Perhaps if I knew why you did so, I might not make any such judgement.'

'Please don't judge. It doesn't suit you.'

That was more like him. She persisted.

'Won't you tell me why you were so disturbed by the seance? These effects are trickery, you told me so yourself. Jacko Grady was only trying to retaliate. He found out about your history and used what he discovered. Your real name is Hector, even I know that much. And as for the message about the boy, and the burning—'

'Stop.' The teacup went flying. He snatched at her wrist. 'Stop, please,' he begged.

She waited. If she allowed him silence and space, without prompt or interruption, in the end he would surely tell her what troubled him.

Devil was shaking his head in disbelief. 'I have lost two days. Sleeping, dreaming. Sleepwalking, I think. What happened yesterday at the theatre?'

'There was no Monday gathering. No manager to direct us regarding what must be done and what amended. When you didn't arrive for the show itself, we sent Ted Dickinson up here. He came back with the news that the room was empty and your landlady had no information to give us.'

Devil dug thumb and forefinger into the sockets of his eyes, as if he wished to gouge out the eyeballs. 'I remember. Was it last night? I woke up in a state of wretched confusion. I went out for an hour, maybe a few hours. I wanted drink, company, and the means to yet more sleep.'

'And did you find them?' The coldness of her voice cut him.

'Drink, yes, of course. The available company didn't appeal. No . . . wait. In the condition I was in, I didn't appeal to the company. That's nearer the truth. And I obtained the soporific, evidently.' He gestured at the shattered phial. 'I'm sorry. Go on.' He laced his fingers in hers, keeping her close.

His touch was familiar enough, from working the box tricks and taking their bow every night. But this was both insistent and imploring. Eliza was finding it more difficult to breathe. She noted a constriction in her chest, a pressure gathering around her ribs as if her laces were pulled too tight.

Enough. She was no swooning girl.

She regained control before continuing in the same cool tone. 'Doing the best we could, therefore, we rearranged the programme. Jasper went on as Charlotte, Jakey took your place in the Ingot. The entire second half was Carlo's.'

'Carlo agreed to perform some extra turns? I'm astonished.'

Eliza frowned. 'He was very good. It was an appreciative house. There was plenty of applause, and I think more curtain calls than we would have received on an ordinary night. Everyone was pleased afterwards, even though there was concern about your whereabouts. But Jakey was the hero of the evening. He shone more brightly than the lights. He was so true and real, I can tell you there was not a single person in the theatre who wasn't willing him to pick up that ingot and win the lady.'

Thinking of the tawdry, pantomime premise of the illusion and the way he had brought it to life made her flush with pleasure.

Devil studied her with precise attention.

'I see. I must thank the boy when I see him tonight.'

'You must let him go on again. I insist you do. Jasper, Carlo – everyone will tell you the same.'

'I see,' he repeated. There was a thoughtful pause. 'So – I am away from my theatre for a mere twenty-four hours and changes have taken place?'

Their eyes met.

'Yes.'

What had happened was a shift in the balance of power. It

was invisible but it changed everything. Like electricity, she thought.

'That is fascinating news. I must find out more.'

Devil was smiling, showing his teeth in a manner that suddenly reminded her of Carlo. Carnivorous, that was the way they looked.

'But now,' he murmured. 'We have *now* to deal with, Eliza, do you not agree?'

He was naked but for the undershirt and a blanket, making her conscious of the stuffy folds of her clothes. He pulled their linked hands closer and lifted hers to his mouth, touching his lips to it and circling his tongue over the thin skin until she shivered. He found the inside of her wrist and kissed it.

'To deal with?' she echoed, to her own ears sounding stupidly like Lucie again.

Don't pretend you don't know what is at stake, she warned herself. *Don't dissemble to him. Now or ever.*

'Yes, Miss Dunlop.'

The Palmyra was nothing. The balance between the two of them constantly changed, she thought. One or other of them chose to break the circuit and then to close it again, sending the charge rushing through them. She had been as much a part of this game as Devil. She had her own power to command or deny, as she had demonstrated on that morning at the theatre. She was not an inanimate doll, nor was she condemned to poor Margaret's spiral towards the riverbank.

'Won't you come and lie here beside me?'

Eliza saw black eyes, a red mouth, and the blanket sliding away. She made a decision, for herself and freely, even though in that moment it was only a hair's breadth short of an imperative.

'Very well.'

With a movement as sudden and violent as the crack of a whip, Devil jerked her off the chair so she landed on top of him in a flurry of clothes and blanket. He gripped her shoulders to steady her and they paused.

Here we are, Eliza thought. *Here and now, finally*.

In her spinsterly bed, and in other moments of solitude amidst the clamour of the theatre and the industry of the bakery, most particularly in the confines of the statue niche where the images had been so difficult to dispel, she had imagined this moment.

Now that the reality had arrived she was ready and willing.

Devil wound his hands in her hair and pulled her mouth down to his. She closed her eyes and she could taste his smile as they kissed. His knees parted to accommodate her hips before he locked her body against his. There was an alignment of breastbone, thigh, ankle. With his hand cupping the back of her head they rocked together, an exploratory movement.

She began to understand. Only a murmur as yet, but these were the first faltering syllables of a new language.

With a magician's deft fingers, Devil leaned away and set about undressing her. He undid the buttons at her throat and wrists, uncovering the blue crooks of her elbows, the scoop of her clavicles. He stroked her goose-pimpled skin and laid his mouth to each new hollow as he exposed it. There were impediments of buckles and laces, but they helped each other. Her clothes fell away in a tangle of serge and linen.

When she was naked she instinctively drew back. Pushing away his hands she sat upright on the rumpled blanket, straightening her spine and letting her limbs fall into a pose, consciously inviting his gaze as if he were a painter in the life studio. Devil paused in his explorations and leaned back on his elbows to study her.

It was midday and a thin shaft of light struck her shoulder. The fire had burned down to a knot of red cinders.

'Look at you,' he breathed.

She was new and surprising. None of his varied experience had prepared him for this moment. His defences came down and they were equals.

Eliza abandoned her pose. Shyly she reached out her hand to capture him.

'You will have to instruct me.'

299

He laughed at that, closing his hand over hers. 'I don't know any woman like you, Eliza. You make me feel the novice. So we'll have to go forwards together.'

The going forwards felt strange, and awkward enough until some of the strangeness dissipated and curiosity took its place. Knowing as much (or as little) of the theoretical procedure as she did, and with no practical experience, Eliza had imagined an act of impalement. She had conjured it for herself with words like spearing or piercing, but the discovery was quite different. There was a sharp pain to begin with – a *stab*, admittedly – but it was soon over.

After that came eagerness. You used your hands and mouth, Eliza learned. Words were part of it too, such innocent but true words. You were not classical sculptures or twin clockwork devices, and most certainly not Heinrich Bayer's automata, but seeing and breathing people. You were supple creations of joined flesh and appetite, and using this new language it was possible to be frank in a way she had never conceived in all her imaginings.

At the end, too soon, his spasm alarmed her.

'Are you hurt?'

Their hair was sweat-damp, their skin glued with it.

He gasped, 'No, Eliza, I am not hurt.'

'I don't understand.'

'You will. I promise you.' He lifted her hand and closed the circle of her thumb and forefinger. 'Be a little patient.'

They lay in each other's arms and briefly dozed. Eliza woke and listened to his heart beating beneath her ear. He was awake now too – she heard him sigh, as if the return to consciousness was unwelcome. The sun had moved and the light was subsiding into the mundane afternoon.

'I would still like you to talk to me about the seance.'

'Would you? I have apologised for my behaviour, and I will have amends to make when I get to the theatre tonight. Will that not do?'

She thought about it. There was tonight's show, and after

300

that next week's shows, and all the months of shows to come. There was a theatre to be funded and managed. There were the locked desk drawers in Devil's office, mysterious accounts to be deciphered as well as loans repaid. All their livelihoods were invested here, not just the owner-manager's. If Devil had some secret, some impediment that affected them all, she must do what she could to fathom it. She stretched her body along the length of his. Devil lazily stirred and rounded his hand over her breast. She was not so innocent that she didn't know that now, this afternoon, was her best opportunity to disarm him. She gently removed his hand before putting her lips to his ear.

'I want you to tell me what troubles you. I am not idly curious. It's for the sake of the theatre, so that I can assist you.'

He sighed again and fell back against the mattress.

'Very well. But if I must talk, I'll need a drink.'

Eliza smiled. 'Why not?'

They splashed in the last of the water and assembled their scattered clothes. Devil knew how to fasten a woman's buttons and hooks as well as how to undo them. Outside in the alley two sad young women loitered. Eliza looked away, wondering what had brought them here and where her own route would now lead. Her mouth was sore from kissing and her skin felt raw. Her belly knotted in an unaccustomed low ache, but these differences were invisible. Did she *look* any different from the girl who had stepped off the omnibus this morning? Almost certainly not. Far from disadvantaging herself – although the decent world would insist she had now set foot on the path that led to the women across the street, even to the river mud – she believed she was stronger. Self-knowledge was strength, she reasoned. And so was shared intimacy. Devil and she would do better together than either of them could have managed alone.

She smiled at the crooked doors and overhanging eaves of the squalid rookery. Their presence here was temporary. Devil Wix should – would – have a better place than this to live.

He escorted her through the roar of traffic to the glittering beacon of the Old Cinque Ports. Inside it was the quiet time of the afternoon when the unfortunate working world was occupied elsewhere. They established themselves on tall wooden stools at the curve of the brass and mahogany bar. The barman who nodded at Devil but did not claim familiarity pulled him a pint and set up a small glass of shrub for Eliza. They raised their glasses to each other in a knowing toast.

'First time I ever saw Carlo was just over there. A fight kicked off and he was dipping pockets in the thick of it. I thought he was a child, but I could see he was good and I followed him outside. I was surprised to discover a dwarf, I can tell you. I was interested enough to pay for his dinner and a talk. One thing led to another, from Jacko Grady all the way to this lovely day. Are you hungry, Eliza?'

They shared a plate of cold pork with bread and apple sauce, and talked about Carlo and the Palmyra. Devil was expansive, enjoying his conquest and the mellow afternoon as if no shadow had ever fallen on him.

Eliza accepted another small rum and lemon.

'I think you have known Jasper for a long time?' she said. 'Jasper said I should ask you why the seance was so disturbing.'

'You won't give up, my girl, will you?'

'No.'

'What is it you want to know?'

Their hands rested a few inches apart on the bar. She had taken off her gloves and folded them into her bag. He knew how neat and decisive she was in everything she did.

'You said to me, "I fear the dead." Then you turned and ran, and it seems you wanted to get so far away that you dosed yourself with laudanum and lost two days of your life. What does that mean?'

Devil reflected. A healthy bout between the sheets had eased his mind as well as his body. With Eliza Dunlop, indeed, the outcome had been even better. He felt buoyant, and more optimistic than he had done for many weeks. The task was to return to the theatre and re-establish control over his company.

That would be easily done. In the meantime he was ensconced in the Ports with an hour or so of leisure ahead, and with Eliza's distractingly lovely eyes fixed on him. He had not decided, as yet, what direction their future relations might take, but he didn't imagine they would be free from complications. For this reason, he had steered away after she had provocatively rejected him that morning in the theatre. Now he discovered that after all he didn't mind the prospect of complication – having explored her remarkable body and discovered her ardour, he was even looking forward to it. The challenge she offered was part of her attraction. This was a distinct novelty for him.

The prospect of confiding in her, who had just given herself to him, was no longer unthinkable.

He searched for the words and then he began.

'Jasper Button and I were country boys together. We had few advantages in life, either one of us, but I was a little luckier than poor Jas. And less able, I might say. My pa was the schoolmaster, and he always said that Jasper was a clever boy.'

He liked the way Eliza listened. Her head was bent and she had turned her eyes down so he could speak more freely, but he knew she took in every word.

He told her about Jasper's wretched parents. He described the village and the schoolhouse and the churchyard, and the view over London from Stanmore Hill. He told her about the visit of the travelling magician, the man's shabby repertoire of tricks, and the effect the show had had on him. Devil's notion of how to bestow *wonder* had expanded since then, but he believed in it just as fervently.

'I knew from that day that I would be a magician.'

Eliza smiled. He covered her hand with his.

'Wait. That was the beginning of everything good and everything bad, together.'

'Go on.'

He told her about his mother's death, and the altercations with his father. Then he came to the dreadful last day. And the days following it, until the moment when he looked up and saw the advertising sign that read 'Wix's Elixir. It does the trick'.

She listened attentively.

'That night I took Ma Button's name for me and put it together with Wix, and there was no more Hector Crumhall. I felt the loss of myself, but it was necessary. Gabe was even more lost, wasn't he? That's what I thought, anyway. But it turned out that he wasn't gone altogether. I see him. On fire, in blackness, coming for me. I fear his appearances, Eliza, when I am awake and in my sleep. I long for sleep and I dread it, because the dreams are bad. And he was there on Saturday, in Jacko Grady's hall.'

His buoyancy deserted him. He waited to hear what she would make of him, and for her shock at the thing he had done. But she was subtler than to come straight at it.

'You never went back to Stanmore?'

'Never once.'

'You never saw your father again?'

'No.'

'Are you sorry for that?'

'Yes. I'd have liked him to see me as the owner of a theatre. Maybe he would have thought better of me. But he's long dead.'

Her thumb moved gently over his hand.

'So is Gabe,' she said.

'I see him.'

'Yes. I don't doubt that. There are many matters that we can't understand, and more places that our eyes don't see. What I don't believe is that such otherness is under the command of Jacko Grady, or his American fakers.'

'Nor do I. But it is easy for me to say as much, sitting here in the brightness with your hand in mine. When I am alone in the darkness and Gabe appears . . . Eliza, you will think I am hardly a man, now you have heard all this, but I am glad we have spoken of it. You told me, long ago when Carlo was sick, about your own other place.'

304

Her face shone at him. 'You remember that? Mine is a benign dislocation, unlike yours. I was a rebellious child who was obliged to be good, so perhaps I developed it as a retreat from unwelcome authority. Only nowadays, I find that I can't summon the reverie as easily as I used to. Perhaps I am getting too old, or perhaps I care less for authority.'

'Maybe. But your experience makes you forgiving of mine. Whatever the case, I'm grateful that you don't condemn me outright for taking a child's life. And I thank you for not dismissing my fears. I sound a feeble creature, but they are real.'

She moved closer to him. Their heads almost touched, closing out the bar and the afternoon drinkers.

'Listen, Devil. You took no one's life. It was a terrible accident. You were no more than a child yourself.' She paused. 'Would it be presumptuous to offer you a theory?'

'Quite possibly. But please go ahead.'

'I think your apparition may be your own guilt dressed in Gabe's shape. I think the shock of that night, arising from what you saw and your losses afterwards, was driven deep inside you. You have kept the guilt and grief locked there, never speaking of it, but your mind works and works on the unbearable and it has found its own way to vent itself. You see the apparition, or you dream a hideous dream, and the terror bursts out of you. It is a way to release pressure.'

Alternatively I have a woman, or I drink myself insensible, he thought.

He said, 'It is a theory, but you make me sound like a railway engine. Puffing through the tunnel from Paddington and bursting out at King's Cross in a cloud of steam.'

This made them both laugh. Eliza was newly aware of the suggestiveness of such an image, and she had to blot tears of shy mirth at the corners of her eyes. 'But am I right?'

'I haven't the faintest idea.' He was grinning now, the familiar Devil.

She was ready to persist, but she said no more. They had

305

come far enough for one day. He slid the gold watch from his waistcoat pocket.

She forestalled him. 'I know. The Palmyra beckons.'

As she smoothed her gloves over her fingers, Devil said lightly, 'I was right in my reading of you, too. You fear nothing, Miss Dunlop.'

You are wrong, she almost retorted. *I fear Heinrich Bayer, for example.*

But she did not say so.

News of Devil's reappearance spread in seconds from Ted Dickinson at the stage door to every member of the company. Carlo heard it and came directly to confront Devil in his office. The dwarf gave Eliza a hard look as he passed her outside the dressing room.

'You've brought him in, then?' he said.

'I didn't have to bring him. It would have been impossible to keep him away.'

'Tell everyone that yesterday's company meeting is today, now,' Devil said to Carlo.

The dwarf grumbled that he was not a messenger boy but he made the rounds. Everyone assembled as usual in the front rows of the theatre, settling with entitlement in the *fauteuil* seats, legs outstretched and elbows firmly planted on the green plush armrests. They were united by their triumph of the previous night and by suspicion about what Devil might be up to. Even Jasper seemed a part of the movement. They glanced at Eliza as she waited quietly in a side seat. She sensed the ambivalence of her position. She could only hope not to be called on to display loyalty in either direction. The house lights blazed, highlighting the gilding and the jewel colours of the decorative lozenges. She gazed upwards, past the inverted palm with its glittering cascade of gas jets, into the lofty cupola. Someone slid into the seat next to her.

'I am relieved that you have not also disappeared.'

'Why might I disappear, Heinrich?'

'In pursuit of Devil Wix, perhaps.'

The engineer looked unwell. His pale skin was sheened with sweat.

She tried to smile. 'No, I am here, as usual.'

Heinrich's arm insinuated itself next to hers on the green plush. The cuff of his coat was worn threadbare.

'And also here is Wix, of course.'

It was Devil's usual habit to address them from the stage, darting about as he demonstrated how to improve their acts. This afternoon he came down the centre aisle and humbly stood at their level.

'I must apologise to you all,' he said. Eliza slid her arm away from Heinrich's.

Devil explained quickly, fluently, that he had been unable to come to the theatre the day before.

'Unable also to send us any word?' Carlo growled.

Devil did not flinch. 'I dosed myself into oblivion. I had some pain, and I tried to treat myself. I was insensible for two days. As I told Miss Dunlop when she came to my rescue, I am ashamed of myself. All I can do is promise that it will never happen again. You have my word. I will not let the company down, in this or any other event.'

He could be convincingly contrite and sincere when he wished.

Ted Dickinson was nodding his grizzled head.

Devil continued, 'I want to thank you all for what you did last night. Miss Dunlop tells me you gave a magnificent performance.' Eliza was looking straight ahead, her neck rigid with the effort, but she felt Heinrich Bayer's gaze drilling into her. 'In particular, I am obliged to Jasper for understudying the chaperone, to Carlo for the entire second half, and to Jakey for understudying the strongman. Jakey, where are you?'

There was a moment's silence before the young man spoke up from the shadows beneath the gallery.

'I am here.'

'Jakey, I would like you to take over the role. You will be the strongman, from tonight onwards.'

There was a ripple of surprise. Eliza was startled. Devil was well known to love himself in the Ingot illusion, so to be generous as well as apologetic was a clever touch. Carlo bounced up on his seat, pounding his hands together.

'Aye, good call,' he shouted. 'Well done, Jakey lad. You deserve it. You're far better in the part than Wix will ever be.'

The rest of them laughed and clapped, pleased for the boy's sake, and aware that Carlo had wanted the role for himself.

'Thank you,' Jakey muttered, red to the ears. He stared at the floor an inch from the toes of Devil's boots.

'So let's get to work,' Devil called. He was buoyant, having successfully brought the mood round.

Jasper caught up with Eliza as they hurried backstage.

'It seems you have saved the day,' he said.

The openness of his homely face made Eliza feel miserably duplicitous. Even though she didn't feel the smallest regret for what had happened, she would not like Jasper to guess how she had actually spent her morning. She hoped he would not detect the wild pulse that hammered inside her.

'I did nothing much. The meek speech, then renouncing the Ingot role, were all his doing. He knows how to handle his company.'

'Indeed. And we live to put on another show. You did talk to him, though?'

'I did. He told me the story in the end. Yours and his, and Gabe's.'

Jasper paused. Now that she knew the history, might she think differently about him? More kindly, or less so?

'And so?'

'Oh, Jas. He has made the best possible life out of the most difficult beginnings. Gabe's death was tragic, but no one could lay the blame on Devil. I admire his resolution and his courage.' She saw Jasper's face and added, too late, 'And yours too.'

Jasper tried for lightness as he responded with a laugh, 'I

would wish for much more than admiration from you. I should give up hope, shouldn't I?'

Sadness was too visible through his cheerful mask. Eliza was sorry to have caused him pain.

'We are friends, Jas,' she murmured. He broke away and hurried to escape from her company.

Sylvia Aynscoe was waiting for her in the dressing room. Charlotte's bonnet and gloves and the nosegay and the hooped cage were laid out, and the seamstress defended their small changing space against the wriggling and strutting contortionists. These performers talcum-powdered their limbs to make it easier to pull on their tight costumes. The air was clouded with it, and dense with the reek of sweat. The musicians in rusty evening clothes would soon take their places in the small pit and play the first note. Outside in the Strand was all the din of London's evening entertainments. She was in the place where she belonged, Eliza thought. For all the difficulties, and the short-lived enchantments.

'Eliza?'

Sylvia was ready to fasten the cage around her waist.

'I'm ready.'

She stripped off her outer clothes, stepped into the hoops and Sylvia tied the tapes. The quaint dress slipped over her head. Eliza jumped at the lightest touch; her body seemed oversensitive, her skin and the muscles and bones beneath were all quivering. Her back was turned but she sensed the instant Devil came in. Gathering up the chaperone's dress from its place on the wardrobe rail, he called out a joke to Sylvia and went away to his office where he would squeeze into his dress, eat a ham sandwich and read the theatre press all at the same time.

Sylvia put her hands on Eliza's shoulders and turned her about. The seamstress had a meek demeanour but she missed nothing.

'Eliza?'

The other woman could see plainly enough.

Eliza would have liked to confess, *Yes, and I am happy*, but the contortionists were already thrusting their way to the stage. Charlotte and the Chaperone was the next act. Jakey was pulling on the lover's boots, the wolf's tongue lolled a yard from their waists. Instead Eliza looked wordlessly into her eyes.

'Oh, my dear,' Sylvia said.

Eliza waited in the wings for her entrance. She was calm and her breathing was steady. She had found her stage confidence at last.

Inside the statue niche Devil's mouth searched for hers. They had to suppress their laughter.

'No.'

'Yes.'

'Stop.'

'What if I can't?'

The trapdoor flew open and they dropped beneath the stage. Down here with the electrical apparatus for the Ingot and other new illusions was another of Heinrich's realms. He wasn't here tonight and in any case she felt safe because Devil was beside her.

'Next Sunday?' she whispered.

'Of course.' The flash of his smile under the absurd bonnet brim.

'Next Sunday, we should go together to Stanmore.'

FOURTEEN

On the following Sunday morning Eliza and Devil met beneath
the columns of the Euston Arch. He tucked her arm beneath his
and they crossed the courtyard to the railway ticket hall. The
first whisper of spring's warmth was carried on the gritty breeze.
Devil was wearing his best bowler, Eliza had a new hat in
blonde straw with a wisp of veiling, and their Sunday outfits
combined with the sunlight and the pealing bells of St Pancras
Church to lend the outing a holiday atmosphere. But once they
had bought second-class tickets for Harrow and taken seats on
the train, the mood changed. A fat woman in the opposite
corner smiled at them as if they were a young couple on their
way to pay a family Sunday visit, which made them more
conscious that their mission was a darker one. They studied
the passing scenery rather than engaging the woman or each
other in conversation. Devil leaned forwards until the curled
brim of his hat touched the window and their knees awkwardly
knocked in the confined space.

They passed through tunnels leading to black cuttings and
brickfields. Factories and warehouses crowding close to the
tracks gradually gave way to ranks of grey and red terraced
houses, not unlike the street where Faith and Matthew lived.
Eliza eventually remarked on this.

'How is Mrs Shaw?' Devil politely asked.

'Very well, thank you. She is occupied with the new baby.'

Another echo of Lucie. Why must she sound like the wretched doll?

Eliza wished passionately that she had never lent her voice to Heinrich Bayer. The discomfort it caused had deeper roots than mere dislike of the engineer – although that affected her seriously enough. It was the submissive role itself she feared, as if she might in the end stop trying to be independent and turn into a doll-woman out of sheer weariness. In the same way she dreaded the suburban confinement of her sister's life, for its very proximity to hers.

She stole a covert glance at Devil's profile. By welcoming her into the Palmyra he had offered her choices she might never otherwise have had. Devil didn't try to confine her, nor did he expect her to be decorous. She took to the stage, she was an equal participant in matters of business, and she knew that her contributions were valued. As for the encounter in his attic bedroom – heat prickled under her Sunday dress at the thought of what they had done and said – those acts and endearments had been her choice as much as his. Her decision to take him as her lover had been freely made and she had not regretted it for a second.

She really was an emancipated woman now, Eliza proudly thought.

She resembled neither Lucie nor Faith – and she would never be like poor Margaret Minchin. And yet, in the heart of herself, she wanted to be married to Devil. She longed to mother his children. It was perplexing to discover that her grasp of independence was quite so superficial. Perhaps, she reasoned, together they might redefine the institution and achieve a marriage of equivalence. That was why she could never marry Jasper, because what Jasper required was a wifely woman like Faith.

Eliza watched the backs of the little houses through the veils of rushing steam. In a tone as unlike Lucie's as possible she remarked, 'My father, being in the greengrocery trade, told me that not long ago this ground was covered by market gardens.

There were cabbage fields and bean rows as far as you could see. The smallholders sent their vegetables down to the market every day by horse and cart. Now all the land yields is brick and soot, and we fly through it in minutes.'

Devil smiled. 'Don't tell me that you resent growth and progress, Eliza?'

'Not in the least. It's tiring to hold the extent of London in mind, because it is so vast, but I would be nowhere else. I want to be in the thick of it, what's more. Don't condemn me to a little house in a small street and a blameless life.'

'No, that would not suit you,' he said equably.

The open country, when they emerged into it, was tinged with the palest green of budding copses and waterside willows. Harrow station was an imposing building resembling a church. Out here the bells were also ringing, and the people of Harrow were making their way to Sunday worship with prayer books in gloved hands. Devil and Eliza felt their metropolitan distance.

'Can you walk a small way?' Devil asked. 'Stanmore is up in that direction.'

They took a lane leading northwards through open fields. On a sheltered bank was a clump of primroses, with crystal beads of rainwater held in the crinkled leaves. Devil picked two of the innocent flowers, one to slip behind the brooch on Eliza's lapel and one for his own buttonhole. In the nearest field were new lambs, and Eliza insisted that they stop to watch as the little creatures chased between hummocks and nudged at their mother's hindquarters. A plume of blue woodsmoke rose above the hedge, and when they approached they found that a dip in the ground concealed a great gash of earthworks. Here was a temporary camp with shelters made from canvas slung over wooden staves, and a gang of rough-looking men smoking pipes beside their Sunday fire.

Devil nodded to the men.

'Good morning. What's under way here?' he asked.

A bear of a fellow with a dark face half hidden by shaggy whiskers took his pipe out of his mouth.

''Ear 'im. Don't ee knaw?' he snorted to his companions.

'I don't know, that's why I'm asking. I was a boy not far from here.'

The workman jabbed with the gnawed stem of his briar towards the diggings. 'It be the cuttin's fer the new railway.'

'Eh? More railway?'

'Up from 'Arrow to Stanmore now. Come next Christmas yer miss 'ere and you'll be able to ride instead o' takin' Shanks's pony.'

'Such progress. I'm obliged for the information. Take a drink, won't you?'

Devil gave the navvy a small coin and the man flipped it in the air before pocketing it.

'You kin come agin, maister.'

'An' the lady too,' someone else guffawed.

Devil and Eliza walked on.

'The railways,' he murmured. 'Reaching all the way out to Stanmore, in the heart of what was once nowhere.'

'How long is it since you left?'

'Close to twenty years.' He walked more slowly, his eyes fixed on a ridge of land ahead of them.

Devil's face was set, and there was no more holiday banter. Eliza kept her questions to herself as they walked under tall elms past the lodge of some great house, and finally came into Stanmore village. The long street was lined with mean-looking cottages with low doorways. There was a row of almshouses with miniature porches and tiny front gardens. Devil walked as if every step hurt him.

They stopped in front of a grim building, closed up and beginning to crumble from disuse. He pointed an accusing finger, as if he would shoot at it and blow apart the injustice it represented.

'That's the workhouse, as was. Jasper's ma and pa ended up on the parish, inside there. That's where they died.'

'And she gave you the name Devil.'

'I deserved it. I choose to go by it to this day, don't I?'

A few yards further on, enclosed by an L-shaped yard and a stone wall, stood the free school. Its stone belfry framed a bell, and Eliza found she could easily conjure up its weekday clanging and the yells of a gaggle of children pelting down the adjacent lane. Devil and Jasper Button raced at the head whilst poor Gabe struggled at the back.

The schoolmaster's house was a somewhat larger cottage, with four windows set in a plain wall and a door in the centre. A brick path was laid from the road to the front step, and evergreen shrubs were planted on either side. It was the most ordinary-looking dwelling.

'This is where you grew up?' she said.

'Under that roof I waited for the time to pass. I did my growing up elsewhere.' Devil looked up and down, as if he expected the past to spring out from behind a hedge and hobble him. 'Come on. Let's get to the Vine and have a drink.'

Eliza knew the work they had come to do, and she wouldn't let distractions intervene. 'Not yet. Which way is the barn?'

'I don't want to go there.' His impatience and irritation masked fear.

'I know.' She put her hand to his shoulder, letting it rest there. 'We'll just go quickly.'

There was a stand of trees, a group of farm buildings, and a footpath leading away from the village along the margin of a ploughed field. Near the trees stood a new wooden barn, roofed in tin, with one of the big doors standing open. Devil walked still more slowly and painfully, but Eliza let him draw ahead. He came to the barn door and looked inside. There were the few remaining bales of winter hay, a soft drift of grey shadow, and the bright spokes of spring sunshine.

'It was over there, the old barn,' he pointed. Clumps of lush nettles marked the place a dozen yards away.

One night there had been flames, and screaming children.

Devil put his hands to his ears. His face twisted and she thought he might weep. She walked a little distance away from him and studied the twisted shadows of the trees. A flock of

315

crows rose from the topmost branches, their black silhouettes scattering against the impassive sky.

She became aware of Devil at her side once more. He retraced their steps in silence along the path and she followed him. A pair of crows pecked down the ploughed furrows and Eliza found herself wishing for the clamour of the Strand.

Stanmore's solid new church stood a little to the north of the village. A square tower overlooked the graveyard and the congregation emerging from morning service. Eliza and Devil stood under a yew tree to watch. The rector presided in his fluttering surplice as his parishioners were borne past him on a swell of organ music. There were good coats and fashionable hats worn by substantial families, and a following of less spruce village people who were properly deferential to their betters.

Devil kept his head down, although it was hardly likely that anyone who might have known him as a boy would search for Hector Crumhall under the tight curl of his bowler brim.

'I hate to see so much bloody goodness,' he muttered.

'It's just a form. It doesn't mean good, necessarily, any more than it means bad.' This was Eliza's opinion of formal religion.

'It means smug. I hate this damned place. Why have we come here? Let's go, Eliza. I need a drink.'

'Soon,' she said gently. 'Give yourself a little time.'

Before long the congregation had dispersed to their Sunday dinners, and the graveyard was deserted. They emerged from the shadow of the yew tree and began a circuit of the church walls. As they came to the west door Devil diverged along a path between headstones, then abruptly stopped at a grass mound surmounted by a simple stone cross.

'This is my mother's grave,' he said.

'And your father?'

'Interred with her, I imagine. I was not present.'

Stiffly Devil took off his hat. Eliza stood back and let him make his silent peace.

From somewhere not far off, at last and to her relief, came the clamour of real children playing. After so much imposed

316

decorum it pleased her that they were temporarily released from Sunday restrictions. The voices rose to wild shrieks and she found herself thinking of her nephews and newborn Lizzie Shaw. The ache she had experienced lately was the physical longing for a child. She had begun to imagine a family of her own, and the way she would anchor it with love and devotion. Indulging herself, she pictured rosy firesides and toys and scampering feet. But with a man like Devil Wix and given her own principles, could that ever happen? She reflected that modern progress did not merely relate to railway lines and brick buildings, but to enlightened behaviour. The future was theirs to make. There had been grief and suffering in Devil's family, and in Jasper's and Carlo's, but with the changes in the world that they could bend to their own advantage, there was no reason to transmit further damage to the new generation. She could think of herself as a pioneering wife.

Devil covered his head. He was startled to see the brightness dancing in Eliza's face.

'What are you so pleased with, beside my parents' grave?'

'I'm sorry. I meant no disrespect. I was thinking about the future.'

'I hope your imaginings include a lively public house that also offers a good plate? Damn the Vine. I want to be within sight of Oxford Street.'

'I was looking a little further ahead than this afternoon.'

'Is that wise, in the precarious world of the theatre?'

He enjoyed a tease, she thought, even here. The moment for proper seriousness would come. They walked arm in arm towards the further gate in a hawthorn hedge.

'What do you feel, seeing the old place again?'

He said somewhat absently, 'I'm sorry for my ma, and even for my father, but I feel much as I always felt about Stanmore, which is that I would rather be somewhere else.'

He stopped short. His attention was drawn by a boulder that stood against the darker hedge. The stone bore a metal plaque.

'What is it?'

Devil said, 'Gabe.'

The iron tablet read simply: '*Gabriel Grigg 1870*'.

Devil froze.

'Gabriel Grigg. I don't think I ever even heard his full name. He was always just poor Gabe. He lived with a Mrs Evans, who was either his grandmother or an old aunt. His ma and pa had left him here with her because he was simple. That's all I know.'

He reached out to brush the rough stone with his fingertips. 'It's not very much, for a life, is it? A life that I took away?'

There were clumps of celandines growing in the shelter of the hedge. The flowers and the mats of leaf surrounding them were coarser and more exuberant than the delicate primroses.

'I would like to sit for a moment, Eliza.'

'Shall I leave you?'

'No. Please stay.'

They sat down in the bed of celandines, leaning against each other for support. Devil laid his arms on his knees and rested his head. If he wept, he did not want Eliza to see it. She also knew that he did not want her words, or her arm across his shoulders.

After a long time he lifted his head again. She saw that he was dry-eyed. He took the primrose from his buttonhole and laid it at the foot of the boulder, and Eliza followed suit.

'Jasper told me that they got up a subscription for a memorial.'

She looked across the lines of headstones to the handsome church. She said, 'You know, there is nothing threatening or fearful here. It is a place of rest.'

'You still think I haunt myself.' It was not a question.

She hesitated, 'In a way, yes, I do.'

He took her hand. An inch of skin was bared between her glove and cuff.

'I still fear him. I fear death. But thank you for making me come out here. The reality is less dark than the dreams.'

318

'We are alive,' Eliza said.

'Indeed we are. Come, let's get back to the dirt and the din.'

The Old Cinque Ports was full of Sunday drinkers. A gathering less resembling the sober congregation at Stanmore church would have been hard to find. The bar was crowded three men deep, so Devil and Eliza retreated to a booth against the wall. The din of shouting and singing made their conversation as private as if they had been standing in the middle of a field. Devil was pursuing his favourite topic, the imminent success of the Palmyra and himself. He waved his arms expansively.

'Up in Stanmore today we saw the future, as well as my bad past. This is the new suburban splendour, my dear Eliza. The old life of rural poverty is over, at least for any place within reach of a railway station. The middling people have money now, from manufacturing and banking and shop owning, and money buys them leisure as well as secluded gardens, fine houses and clean air. And given leisure, what do people look for?'

This was not a very new question. 'Entertainment,' she obediently replied.

She was wondering how to introduce her own topic.

Devil was in his stride now. 'Entertainment not in the disreputable old halls and saloons, but elegant theatres, clean and comfortable, suitable for ladies, for the good people to come and enjoy magic, to experience *wonder*, before they catch the last train home. The Prince of Wales came to the Palmyra one night, you recall, but we need not look to the great and their condescending nods to the vulgar world. *Stanmore* is our proper audience. We need to find a way to let 'em know as much . . .' He pointed towards the door, in the general direction of South Kensington. 'We need those young men who admired our Philosophers, do you remember? We need some clever ideas. Not just on the stage, but in all our business. We must learn to peddle ourselves more effectively, against the Savoy Theatre and the Palace of Varieties and a dozen-and-a-half more of our competitors. This is the way to develop.'

319

'I have an idea,' Eliza offered.

'Yes?'

'Last Monday night I sat for a few moments in your office, after the rest of the company had gone home.'

Temporarily he was relieved of the past and was therefore full of humour and high spirits, but he still gave her a sharp look over the rim of his glass.

'I see.'

'It occurred to me that if the worst had happened, if you were permanently gone . . .'

'But I was not gone, as you discovered. A pleasant discovery, I hope?'

There was the carnivorous smile again, which Eliza ignored.

'*If* you were not to come back, it would be close to impossible for the rest of us to take over the proper management of the theatre. We do not have access to the accounts, to any of the funds, or to the details of the outstanding borrowing. Who would own the Palmyra? Heinrich Bayer? Have you even drawn up a will, for example?'

Devil murmured, 'Less an idea than an inquisition, it seems.'

She raised her chin. 'Hear me out. You should make me the Palmyra's joint manager. I will take the administrative burden from your shoulders, you will be free to devise new illusions and pursue the best outside acts, and to make us better known to the world.'

There was no response, unless a fractional lift of the black eyebrows counted as a reply.

She met his gaze.

'This would come about once we are married, of course.'

Devil spluttered into his drink. He wiped his mouth with the back of his hand before giving way to uproarious laughter. 'Jesus Christ, Eliza. No one has spoken of marriage. I am not a marrying man.'

This was no less than she had expected. She held steady, countering his laughter with a smile.

'Is any man? But consider the normal course of events. You

need an ally, Devil. An equal partner whom you can trust in all matters.'

'I already have Carlo and Jasper Button and I don't have to walk either of them to the altar.'

She shrugged, her good humour undimmed. 'You have just set out your grand intentions to offer the middling people decent entertainments in exchange for their new money. But in reality you are not thinking beyond next year.'

'These are *my* plans. If I am let down by Jasper or Carlo, or if Heinrich calls in his loan, I shall make other arrangements. This is not a wife's business, even if I were to take a wife. I am sorry to sound brutal, Eliza.'

Eliza's eyes sparkled with enjoyment of their debate. 'So you prove me right. Where is the future in this? To whom will you pass on your famous, thriving business, built up with such effort and ingenuity, if you do not have an *heir*?'

He paused on the point of another riposte. The crowd of topers swirled in front of them, each man apparently intent on spending the old week's money before the start of the new one. Crimson faces and open mouths and disordered clothing were the outward signs of lives lived for the moment, and to hell with the future.

Eliza's voice was a calm murmur. 'Wix and son. The Wix family theatre. The third generation of the Palmyra company.'

He couldn't help but see how her composed expression and neat appearance stood out to advantage against the massed crew of the Old Cinque Ports.

He protested, 'I *shall* marry, in due course, with handing on the business in mind. But I don't intend it yet.'

'Who will the lady be, Devil, if not me? Your landlady is already taken, I believe. The little acrobat? Miss Aynscoe, perhaps?'

'Not Mrs Hayes, thank you. Miss Aynscoe would make a more tractable wife than you. And the acrobat has certain abilities.'

Her smile faded. 'You are not a fool, I know that much. Why do you pretend to be one?'

Devil sat up. For perhaps the first time in their acquaintance-ship he gave her a full appraisal. He looked her up and down as if she were not a woman at all.

'Well, Miss Dunlop, *you* most certainly are no fool.' To remain true to himself, he added, 'And you are also very pretty.'

She set about gathering up her bag and her gloves, touching one finger to the brooch where he had earlier fixed the primrose flower. Devil remembered the bank of celandines and the boulder with its iron plaque. There was a tug of relief in him at having shared the day's experience with Eliza, as if her neat person might somehow, from now on, stand between him and the figure in the fire.

Uncertainly he asked, 'Where are you going?'

She looked surprised. 'Home, of course. Tomorrow is Monday, and there is work to do.'

This was always the right note to strike with Devil. He followed her as they pushed their way through the crowd and emerged into the darkness. Out here, with astringent air in his lungs and the stimulus of her company still heating his blood, Devil realised how very much he wanted her in his bed.

It was only a short walk home through the alleys.

'Goodnight,' Eliza said sweetly.

'*Wait*.' He took her face between his hands and kissed her, hard. 'Come with me.'

'I couldn't possibly. We are not betrothed.'

'Fuck *betrothed*. Eliza, we have already fucked each other, remember?'

'Your language is very coarse. Of course I remember. That was then. *Now* I have made a business proposal, and you should consider it.'

He could not help laughing at her defiance, even in the inconvenient but lovely rush of his desire for her.

'Ah, don't break my heart.'

'Goodnight,' she repeated. She walked away, as brisk and proper as a governess, to the refuge of a waiting hansom cab.

Only when she was safely inside did she fall back against

the musty cushions and let out a gasp of relief. Dragging herself away from Devil Wix, wanting him quite as much as he wanted her, had been one of the hardest things she had ever done. The cab had travelled halfway to Bayswater before she could apply proper logic again.

But their day had been a success, she thought.

The advance and retreat of their conversation in the Ports had been the opening skirmish of a mock battle that she was quite likely to win in the end. Women desired marriage, men were less inclined; the ensuing gavotte was hardly more than a formality, she believed.

No – the real achievement had been the excursion to Stanmore.

Eliza was taken aback by the rush of desire and sympathy and admiration and greedy longing she felt for Devil Wix, body and soul. The feeling deepened every day. If this was love – and what else could it be? – she could not bear the man she loved to be assailed by terrors, whether they were tricked out by Jacko Grady or whether they came from deep within him. Devil Wix was a complicated man who liked to appear simple. There was much to be unravelled, and they would have time for that. For now, she hoped that the sight of the vanished barn and their walk through the peaceful graveyard – and above all the prosperity of his old and feared world – had gone some way to soothing his spirit.

She paid the fare and looked up at the lodging house, noticing a light in Sylvia's window. A moment later she tapped on the seamstress's door. Sylvia was in her nightgown and her hair lay in a plait over her shoulder.

'Eliza! I have been waiting to hear you come home, and you have been out so many hours I was beginning to be afraid.'

'May I come in? Is it too late?' She was too excited and too full of the day to think of sleep yet.

Sylvia's room was ordered in every detail. Her few possessions were folded or their corners were placed square to the room. There was a candle on the night table and a plain wooden crucifix on the wall over the bed. The contrast with Eliza's room was marked. Eliza was energetic, but she was not naturally tidy. Her chair tended to be a nest of discarded stockings and stays and her bed was heaped with clothes and books that must be pushed aside before she could sleep.

'Your hands are cold,' Sylvia scolded. 'What have you been doing? Come in under this cover.'

Eliza kicked off her boots and scrambled under the eiderdown at the foot end of her friend's bed. Sylvia sat up against the bolster. She had been reading her Bible and had put it aside at Eliza's knock.

'Your feet are even colder than your hands. You should take better care of yourself.'

'We have had an interesting day, Sylvia. We have been on an outing to the country, where Mr Wix grew up, with the intention of laying some ghosts from his childhood.'

'The two of you, alone together?'

The iron bedstead creaked. The seamstress's sallow face was creased with dismay, but Eliza also noted a glint of vicarious fascination. Sylvia was not in the least averse to hearing about her closer involvement with Devil. The past week, whenever he had come by at the bakery or in the Palmyra dressing room she had coloured and stared harder at her stitching.

'What do you fear?'

'I fear your ruin, my girl.'

'Don't worry about me.'

'After what you have already confessed, Eliza, I have everything to worry about.'

'Shhh.'

'What if there should be a *child*?'

The eiderdown was drawn up beneath Eliza's chin.

'That might not be quite the worst outcome . . .'

Now Sylvia looked truly shocked.

'But it's not in my plan. What happened between us on Tuesday is not to be repeated, but to remain in the memory. Tantalising, don't you think? Until we are married, of course.'

'Why should he marry you now? Forgive me, but I speak sense.'

'It's an old-fashioned version of sense, Sylvia. We live in a modern world.' Eliza waved her hand. 'I asked him to marry me this evening.'

There was a squawk, the night table rocked and the candle flame flickered in the draught from the flapping eiderdown. Eliza could not help laughing.

'He was almost as shocked as you, I might say, and he insists he is not the marrying kind. But he will change his mind, because he will see that marriage is a sensible course for both of us. We are colleagues, and we have a shared business interest. I can help him, and I will do so with all my ability for the rest of our lives together. In the meantime . . . What I have bestowed I can also withhold, of course. That is my intention from now on.'

Sylvia could hardly speak. 'I have never *heard* such unfeminine calculation. Where are your modesty, and your natural emotion? Are you a woman at all, I wonder? You talk and act much more like a man.'

'I have made a series of calculations, I admit, but they are not all for my own benefit. I truly believe that what I want is also the best for the Palmyra and for the whole company.'

Sylvia unbent a fraction. 'You are such a determined creature, I am quite afraid of you. Or I would be, if you weren't here under my bedcovers like a wicked little girl, with feet like two blocks of fishmonger's ice.'

'Since when has determination been a sin? Not that I care about sin, in any case.'

'I know that.' Sylvia glanced at her Bible. 'Tell me one more thing, at least, after all this godless talk. Do you love him?'

They looked at each other in the candle's umber light.

In a rush, Eliza said, 'Oh, I love him, yes. Sylvia, I love him so much that I can think of nothing else, so much that the room falls dark as midnight whenever he walks out of it. I can't imagine how I would live my life without him. You may think I am a calculating woman, but in fact I have taken a great gamble with my own happiness. But then, Devil is a gambling man himself. I think he will understand and appreciate the game I am playing.'

Sylvia understood that it was her love Eliza had come to declare. Eliza had been unable to keep her happiness to herself. The rest of her confession – and her calculation – was only the packaging around the truth.

'I love him,' she repeated. 'I do, with all my heart.'

The older woman was mollified. She took Eliza's supple hand and rubbed it between her brittle fingers. Sylvia Aynscoe would never utter the words *I love him*, and flush with delight at having done so. But it was better to hear the declaration at one remove than to be excluded altogether, she thought.

'Now I am happier,' she said. Eliza Dunlop was the first real friend she had ever had and her concern for her was genuine. Sylvia was shrewd enough to recognise that the girl was headstrong, and possessed a calculating streak that could make her appear unfeminine and quite unlike her graceful sister. But even so she was not in the least surprised that Mr Button and the poor dwarf were both in love with her. Even Heinrich Bayer, that strange man, admired her. It was only natural. Eliza overflowed with humour and affection, and her vitality infected everyone around her. The Palmyra would have been a muted place without her joy. Sylvia could only hope that Mr Wix would treat the girl as she deserved. She would put the two of them in her prayers. Surely the Almighty would forgive the circumstances?

The days that followed, stretching to weeks and then to a full month, represented a strange lull. The company was busy, but at the same time everyone knew they were waiting for something to happen. What that something might be was not yet apparent.

A revised programme gave Carlo the solo prominence he had enjoyed on the night of Devil's absence. The dwarf continued to expand his repertoire of small-scale sleights and conjuring tricks, including some ingenious electrical circuit effects engineered by Heinrich. The intimate scale of the little man's performance in a tight spotlight suited the Palmyra auditorium. Always the perfectionist, Carlo practised and improved his routines. Charlotte and the Chaperone and the Golden Ingot were also popular, especially with Jakey appearing as the strongman. Devil was amused to note that the boy was separately gaining his own cult of female admirers. A handful of them even came to the stage door to waylay him after performances, but Devil did not anticipate Jakey's interested response. The boy's inclinations tended elsewhere.

Eliza appeared in the latest mirror illusion, named Ayesha. Wearing a Grecian robe she posed elegantly on a small four-legged table, with four candles burning in a sconce beneath it to show that there was nothing else occupying the space. The table was enclosed on three sides by a folding screen, and another cylindrical screen was lowered over her from above. Devil ran on from the wings and fired a pistol at point-blank range into the cylinder of fabric. There was a flash of light followed by smoke and then fierce flames licking out from the top and bottom of the cylinder. The candles were still burning as the fabric rose seconds later to reveal only burning embers, a pile of bones and a grinning skull.

'Vulgar but effective,' said Carlo.

A Russian conjuror, billed as the finest in Europe and enjoying a high reputation, demanded a bigger fee than Devil had ever paid to a guest act. He complained and tried to haggle, but finally agreed to the man's terms. The performer turned out to be fonder of the bottle than anyone could have guessed and one or two of his shows shivered close to disaster.

Devil groaned, 'What am I supposed to do?'

'Try booking a Spaniard? Or an Eskimo?' Eliza said.

Every night, after days at the bakery and evenings onstage or in the wings, Devil retreated to his office and his columns of figures. His current obsession was with finding the money to electrify the theatre. Electric light was desirably clean and safe, but there was no approaching Heinrich for further funds. The engineer grew ever more silent and obsessive. He arrived at the bakery at exactly the same minute each day, and left according to the same clockwork timing. He attended to his responsibilities before and during performances with grim precision, laying out his tools and props always in the same order, placing his coat on the same hook and rolling up his cuffs to the same height, first the right and then the left. He spoke only when it was necessary, and if he was interrupted or delayed in any way he became disturbed.

'Where is my measuring rod?'

'Ah, it's over here, Mr Bayer,' Roger Crabbe called out. 'Borrowed it for a moment, I did.'

Heinrich's head appeared through the trap in the stage. He leapt on to the boards and advanced on Crabbe, seizing the young man by his collar and dragging him close.

'Never take my tools.'

'No, sir. Very sorry.'

Heinrich stared him down, and then slowly released his grip. The young man backed away.

'He's turned into one of his own queer machines, he has,' Crabbe said later to his father and the Dickinsons. 'He's got cogs and pistons whirring inside him, not messy old guts like the rest on us.'

Carlo was Heinrich's principal ally nowadays. They worked together in silence, broken by terse mutterings related entirely to their task. Both of them seemed to turn their attention inwards, denying the uncertainty that stalked the theatre.

Spring advanced and the days lengthened. There were no more murders in the East End and public memory of them began to fade. The newspapers turned to newer topics, less lurid and disturbing than accounts of how and why the Whitechapel victims had died. Eliza and Sylvia travelled through the city with easier minds, although they usually left the theatre together

at night. It was Eliza's custom to look into Devil's office immediately after she had changed into her street clothes and before
leaving for Bayswater. He would jump up from his papers,
pleased at the sight of her, and ask hopefully if she would like
to accompany him to a supper house. She always declined, and
wished him good progress with his work before going away
with Sylvia. These polite exchanges were heightened by their
mutual recollection of an hour earlier, when they had been
pressed up against each other under the stage or in the wolf's
cage. Wickedly he would put his mouth to the nape of her
neck, or his hand to her breast. Eliza invariably arched away,
as far as was feasible in the cramped spaces.

'Torturer,' he whispered.

Eliza only smiled, a tiny glint of amusement in the dim light.

No one spoke about the electric current between the manager
and his principal lady. Sylvia was the only member of the
company who knew the truth, but not one of the others was
unaffected by the charged atmosphere. The hot days of the
summer season lay ahead, during which they needed to fill
every house until the dead days of August finally arrived, but
collective enthusiasm sank to a low point. They presented a
series of lacklustre shows, and audiences began to show their
disapprobation by staying away.

In the end it was Jasper who confronted Devil. They were
on their way back from the metal foundry again and had called
in for refreshments at Jasper's favoured coffee house. The pretty
daughter of the owner served them in their usual booth. Jasper
called her Hannah and asked after the week's business. Devil
raised a lazy eyebrow.

'What are your intentions towards Miss Hannah?' he teased
Jasper when she had gone away.

'I could tell you to mind your own damned business, or I
could turn the question on you,' Jasper retorted. 'Are you
planning to let matters simmer with Eliza until we are playing
to entirely empty houses?'

Devil might have protested innocence, or counter-attacked,

329

but instead he let out a sigh. His shoulders slumped and he drummed a tattoo on the scrubbed table.

'I don't know, Jas. She is a formidable creature, that I do know.'

'What has happened?'

'The truth is that I took a liberty with her.' Devil shrugged, aiming for nonchalance. 'Now she expects me to marry her.'

Jasper threw himself across the table and his hands closed round Devil's neck, dragging him almost out of his seat.

'You did *what*?'

Devil choked. 'Christ. Wouldn't you, if she turned up in your bedroom? I didn't force myself on her. What kind of man do you think I am? Let go, Jas. If you want to fight me it'd be better done out in the street.'

Hannah and her mother eyed them in dismay. Jasper flung Devil back into his chair.

'You'll marry her now, Hector Crumhall, or I will kill you.'

Devil looked up into his friend's face, and it became clear that it was not a figure of speech. Jasper meant what he said.

Jasper hissed, 'If she'll really have you, that is. If she does, you'll be the luckiest man in London and I only wish you were not so vain, selfish and generally loathsome as not to know that already. Don't you feel a shadow of fear that you might lose her? To a better man?'

There was no trace of amusement or indulgence in him, only bitterness.

Devil said humbly, 'I'm sorry, Jasper. I know how you still feel about her.'

The serving girl came with their pot of coffee. She laid out the crockery and silverware before returning with a plate of the hot apple turnovers.

'These are from my ma and me, gentlemen. Compliments.' She put the dish down and hurried away.

'Well?' Jasper said. The word stabbed like an icicle.

Devil nodded. He looked away into the street, scanning the faces in the crowd as if he hoped to read their lives and learn from their decisions. He had become aware that Eliza Dunlop exerted power over him. When she was present he felt happy, and when she was absent even the Palmyra seemed a less enticing place.

'Yes,' he said in a low voice. 'I'll marry her. Anything will be better than the present battle of wills.'

'Speak to her father first. He is a decent man and he may well have objections about giving away his daughter to a creature like you.'

Jasper slammed on his hat and walked out. Devil sat where he was, making his calculations whilst the coffee and turnovers went cold in front of him.

That afternoon he wrote a letter, to which he received an immediate reply. As soon as he had read this he took the underground train to Paddington and walked from there up into Maida Vale.

The next day Eliza paid her usual Sunday visit to Faith and Matthew and the children. She seized the baby Lizzie and bounced her on her lap, admiring her sturdy limbs and her Sunday ribbons, and pressing her nose into the soft groove at the nape of her neck. The infant smelled sweetly of soap and new skin and Eliza found herself breathing in this precious perfume as if it were a medicine. The low ache of longing gathered in her body had become almost constant.

'She is not always so sweet,' Faith laughed. She was sitting comfortably on her sofa. Following the safe delivery of a healthy infant her tiredness and discontent with her lot had faded together. She was very much the wife and mother again, at the centre of her home, restraining her boisterous sons and laughing at her husband for his doting attentions to their tiny daughter.

'It's as if I no longer exist. Miss Lizzie Shaw is the only female in the world for him these days.'

'What rubbish, Faith.' Matthew kissed the top of his wife's head before taking Rowland and Edwin out for their walk.

'He is very good,' Faith said fondly when she and Eliza were finally alone. 'He helps me a good deal now Lizzie is here, and he loves her dementedly. Will you bring her to me?'

Eliza passed over the shawled bundle.

'What is your news, Eliza?'

'There's not much. We have had a rather poor week. It's not so hard to put together a good show and keep it running for a few nights. The real difficulty is to keep it good, and then to make it even better than that. Variety is what audiences crave and these days there is more and more to tempt them.'

Faith gave her an appraising look. 'You sound very business-like.'

'We have to be so, if we are to make money.'

'And you are very loyal, to speak of *we*. How is Mr Wix?'

She always asked the question because she couldn't help doing so.

'He is well . . .'

Faith waited. She knew her sister and it was evident that there were changes afoot. There was a bright glow in Eliza's face that might have been caused by a fever, and a quick anxiety in her movements, yet she was slow to respond to questions because her mind was busy elsewhere.

Eliza said no more. She did not want to worry Faith with what could not be altered. As the weeks passed and Devil did not change his tack, despite her rejections of all his physical advances, her confidence was beginning to waver. Perhaps Devil Wix was not the right man to gamble against. She remembered his meticulous preparation of the decks of cards to defeat Jacko Grady. What had he said, with the deeds of the Palmyra newly in his possession?

Never bet on the random turn of a card, my girl.

How – and why – had she been certain that to play the card of *herself* was so far from being random as to represent no risk at all?

It seemed that she might have made a miscalculation.

'I'm glad he is in good health,' Faith said drily, when it became clear that she was to be told nothing more. 'Shall we have a peaceful cup of tea before Matty and the boys come back?'

The company meeting took place as usual on Monday afternoon. Heinrich sat alone near the back of the theatre and the others lounged in the best seats at the front. Ted Dickinson wrung out a rag in an enamel bucket of soapsuds and scrubbed at the painted lozenges. The layer of oily soot came off, but so did the bright colour underneath.

'Nothing for it but to wash and repaint the whole lot on it,' he muttered. 'And Lord knows when that might happen.'

Sylvia and Eliza occupied a pair of *fauteuils*. They were laughing at Carlo who was playing the piano in the musicians' pit and improvising saucy words to a sentimental ballad. The dwarf was in an unusually good mood. Jasper sat with his hands laced behind his head and his legs sticking out into the aisle. He had tried to suggest to Ted that they might clean and paint when the theatre closed in August, but the handyman was determined to be gloomy. This was only an echo of the prevailing mood.

Everyone was waiting for Devil.

He appeared at last, parting the drapes that covered the foyer doors and dashing down the aisle. But instead of jumping straight up on to the stage he stopped to thank Ted for his efforts, offered a quick word to Jakey and a whisper and a wink to Sammy Hill. He tapped Jasper on the shoulder as he passed by. Within seconds he was trailing a ripple of approval and optimism. Sylvia Aynscoe clasped her hands as if she only just stopped herself from applauding. When he set out to charm, Devil had no equal.

Eliza studied the green-and-gold folds of the curtain.

When he did take the stage, Carlo crashed out a rising chord. Devil made a bow and was awarded a cheer that was not entirely ironic.

There was nothing unusual in the meeting. The Russian conjuror had come to the end of his contract, which would not be renewed.

'Not now, not ever,' Devil asserted.

There were some small adjustments to the week's programme. The result was to give some more prominence to other performers, thus reducing Devil's appearances even further. By the time he came to the end of the list of business, almost everyone was in a happy humour.

The move to the dressing room was beginning and the junior Crabbe dimmed the house lights. Devil came forward to the footlights and held up his hand.

'There is one more important matter.'

Everyone turned to him. The palm chandelier bore up its dozens of flaring jets.

The silence lengthened. Jasper lifted his head in alarm.

'Get on with it, whatever it is,' Carlo muttered.

'I am asking this question here in the Palmyra, in front of you all. It's the biggest question I have ever asked. Maybe it is the biggest question I ever will ask.'

Now they were all staring.

Heinrich Bayer shifted to the edge of his seat. His spectacles reflected a triangle of light.

'I want to ask Miss Eliza Dunlop if she will do me the very great honour of becoming my wife.'

Somebody whistled. Devil's eyes met Eliza's.

He said softly, 'Eliza?'

Then he held out his hand.

There was nothing to do but join him on the stage. A pulse beat in her throat as he took both her hands and kissed her. Sylvia began to applaud, the clapping spread and loud cheers followed. Jasper nodded and blinked, but he gamely added his voice to the din. Carlo did not look at Devil, but he stabbed out the first notes of the 'Wedding March'.

'Eliza?' Devil repeated.

'I will,' she said.

A seat loudly banged at the back of the theatre. The foyer doors closed behind Heinrich Bayer.

*   *   *

It was a full week before any of them saw the engineer again. Caught up in the whirlwind of being a newly engaged woman, Eliza barely noted his absence. But his reappearance when it came was disconcerting enough.

She was hurrying down the Strand towards the theatre, alone and late for the matinee because her stepmother had made a surprise call on her at her lodgings. Bertha Dunlop had precise views on how a wedding must be celebrated and she wanted to convey these to Eliza in person, in detail. Eliza had been patient with her although she had barely had time herself to get used to the change in her circumstances, and as a result when Mrs Dunlop belatedly made her departure she was obliged to scurry all the way from Bayswater. She was already breathless when a man stepped out of a shop doorway and blocked her way. Panting a little, she excused herself unnecessarily and tried to step past him. The man matched his step to hers so she could not evade him. Only then, emerging from her state of preoccupation, did she see that it was Heinrich.

'Eliza.'

His eyes slid over her, seeming to linger at her throat. She put up her hand to shield it.

'Heinrich? You are on your way to the theatre? I am late, I must . . .'

The scene was unpleasantly reminiscent of the time he had accosted her beside the river, on the night of Margaret Minchin's murder.

'Please.' He spoke in a low urgent voice. She very much disliked the idea that he had been waiting and watching for her. *I must stay out here*, she thought wildly, *in full view of all these people and the swirl of traffic.* She would enter the theatre by the foyer entrance instead of by the stage door in the quiet alley.

'I want to talk to you.' She saw his hands flutter and then clench in to his sides, as if he fought to control himself.

'At the theatre, Heinrich. After the, after the matineee.' She tried to laugh but only a strangled bleat sounded. She was frightened now, even though a hundred people held her in plain view.

'Not at the theatre. In private, I beg you.' The lenses of his spectacles were clouded, his Adam's apple painfully bobbed. Eliza's dislike mingled with pity and a confusion of sympathy.

'Why? Is something wrong?'

He lifted his fist and pressed it to his mouth. The skin around his lips turned white before flooding crimson.

'Don't marry him.'

She stared. Then she gathered herself. In a rush of words she cried, 'Of course I am going to marry Devil. I love him, Heinrich. Body and soul. With all my heart. I want to be his wife more than I have ever wanted anything in my life.' It was too much, spoken too insistently, but she needed to tell him and to leave no room for misunderstanding.

He took a step backwards, shrinking as if she had struck him. Eliza pressed the advantage.

'It's the truth, Heinrich. I'm sorry.'

He did not speak or move. She turned on her heel and walked, unhurriedly, to the steps of the Palmyra. He did not try to follow and she thought, *There, that's said and done. I'm glad of it.*

The dressing room was in a turmoil. Sylvia gasped with relief at the sight of Eliza.

'Thank goodness you are here. I was worried. Give me your hat.'

Devil raised a questioning eyebrow and Eliza managed a smile.

'Bertha called. And then I bumped into Heinrich.'

'Yes? Where is he?'

'I don't know. He was a little . . . agitated, but I think he will be easier now.'

She spoke calmly, turning as she did so to allow Sylvia to unhook her bodice. She must costume herself, and Devil and her friends were all busy in the rush that preceded every performance. She slid behind the screen and Sylvia handed her the dress of gold tissue.

'Ten minutes,' Ted Dickinson called from the doorway.

Heinrich was forgotten by all of them.

FIFTEEN

One morning not long after this Eliza went to South Kensington to pay a call at the school of commercial art in the mews buildings behind the Rawlinson.

As she crossed the hall beneath the portraits she thought briefly of the blue sea painting, and Raleigh Coope's life class where a different model now took up the pose for a new generation of young gentlemen. She could no longer conjure up her trance state, and her time as an artists' model seemed to belong to another life.

In the secretary's office she obtained the information she needed. She folded away a slip of paper with a name and address written on it and strolled back to the underground station. Her intention was to take the Metropolitan Railway from South Kensington to Bayswater. Once home she would write a letter to the person whose name was written on her piece of paper, and after that she would proceed to the Palmyra for the evening's performance.

The day had a luminosity that was nothing to do with the weather. In the station hall the white moon-face of the clock, the polished brasswork and the wooden arched window of the ticket office – even the whiskered cheeks of the ticket clerk who peered from this aperture – seemed to glow. Eliza understood that these furnishings of the humdrum world shone only because she viewed them through the prism of her own happiness. There were so many plans waiting to be put into place, at the Palmyra and in her future life with Devil. It was a significant component of her happiness, in fact, that these two were so closely associated. She was marrying the theatre and its affairs as much as the man.

Her head was full of pleasant thoughts as she paid for her ticket, passed through an iron turnstile and hurried down the steps that led to the trains.

The sloping subterranean passageways were lined in brick and dark red tiles. Somewhere close at hand she could hear footsteps, heavier and moving faster than her own. She looked over her shoulder but there was no one in sight. A rush of steamy air swept over her as a train rattled through a tunnel.

A small handful of passengers was gathered on the northbound platform. She took her place halfway along and studied the lettering of the station name as she waited. She was musing about designs for theatre posters and handbills when an uncomfortable sense of being watched made her turn her head.

Her heart lurched. At the other end of the platform stood Heinrich Bayer. His old coat and hat, the flat planes of his spectacles, all were so familiar that even now her instinctive reaction was to greet him with a smile. But the threat he emanated was a stronger force. She froze, apprehension pinning her where she stood. She gazed straight ahead, although he must have known that she had seen him.

Two minutes dragged past before she felt vibrations underfoot and then heard the whistle of the approaching train. The engine rushed out of the darkness and clanged to a halt in a great billow of steam. There was a small surge of people stepping off and on. Eliza waited, holding herself ready either to jump into the carriage or to race back up to the ticket hall. She could not make herself even glance to see what Heinrich did. The guard's flag was raised.

''Urry up, please-*ah*. Are you hintendin' to travel, madam?'

In a single movement she sprang up the steps into the carriage

339

and the guard slammed the door. She folded herself on to the wooden seat, breathing against her heart's wild thumping. As the train slid out of the station she stared through smoke and steam, hoping against all reason to see Heinrich left on the platform, but there was no one there.

They raced towards Gloucester Road. At this station and at Notting Hill she tried to work out whether it would be better to jump off and run up to the street where she might lose herself in the crowds, or to stay where she was with the two occupants of her carriage as a small measure of protection. They were a thin little man who might have been a clerk or a shop assistant, and an old woman who appeared to be wearing two hats. But they were already pulling into Bayswater. The familiar streets leading towards her lodgings, and the sturdy front door past which no man ever penetrated, promised safety that was too close at hand to resist. As soon as the train stopped she threw open the door and hung on the step, using the door's weight of wood and glass as a kind of shield. She waited until the guard gave a warning blast on his whistle, at which she bounded down to the platform, slammed the door and hurried towards the exit.

She did not look for Heinrich. She persuaded herself that naturally he would be travelling on to Farringdon before walking home through Clerkenwell. Seeing him at South Kensington had been a simple coincidence. She began to rehearse what she would say when they met at the theatre, and how she would lightly apologise for seeming to ignore him.

It was a quiet time of the afternoon. She was walking briskly through the dark red tunnel when she heard the footsteps following her.

The tunnel angled to the right. As she whisked round the corner she glanced back over her shoulder and saw to her horror that he was close behind. She hitched her skirts and tried to run but it was too late. He caught her up and his arm came round her throat. She tried to call for help but his grip savagely tightened, cutting off her breath. There was a recess in the tiled wall just ahead of them. Heinrich was very strong. He pulled her off balance and dragged her with one arm into the niche. The horrible little slot housed a soot-caked grating. It stank of urine.

Then Eliza saw what she had failed properly to register before this moment. With his free hand, Heinrich was towing Lucie's trunk on its porter's trolley wheels. The sight of it was so familiar it was as if it were a physical part of him. Releasing the handle of the trolley, Heinrich put his hand inside his coat and brought out a rag. That was her last second of consciousness. He pressed the rag over Eliza's mouth and nose and she sagged in his arms.

The pain was briefly more real than anything she had ever known.

Before she opened her eyes she even saw the vivid colour of it – it was dark red and shiny, with a surface that pulsed as if it had stolen the heart out of her.

She cracked open her eyelids, winced at the stab of light and closed them again.

She realised that her legs and arms hurt only because they were cramped, not because they were broken as she had at first feared. Flexing her fingers, she found they performed in the usual way. Her toes did the same, and her ankles articulated with her feet even though the movement sent drills of pain running up her shins to her knees. She rolled her head an inch or two in either direction and discovered how badly it ached. It was the pounding within her skull that lent the red wall its pulse. She ran her dry tongue over lips and discovered that her mouth and throat were agonisingly parched. She swallowed on nothing and then weakly coughed.

Her first glimpse of the world beyond the redness had triggered a wave of terror far worse than any physical pain. All her instincts told her to keep her eyes closed and deny consciousness, but still they snapped open.

Full cognisance flooded over her.

Her terror was justified.

She was in Heinrich's workshop, all the way down the covered alleyway at the back of his silent house. The shadowy space was more disordered than it had been, with tools and papers and wires and boxes muddled together.

She was lying – wasn't she? – on Lucie's catafalque bed.

Eliza struggled to sit up.

Heinrich was at his bench, a magnifying eyepiece screwed into his eye, intently working at some small core of metal and wires. She discovered that straps encircled her wrists and cords ran from the straps to a secure point that she could not see. The illusionists had practised so many tricks with bindings just like these. They had trussed one body or another, locked it into a box or a cage, invited members of the audience to come up and inspect knots and padlocks. Then would come the contortion, the sprung trap or the flipped mirror, and the escape would be revealed to delighted applause. All this was familiar, but now it was wrong. Already she knew that no bodily twisting or sleight of hand or trick of the eye could release her from this place.

'Heinrich,' she called. It came out as a whisper when she intended a shout. 'Why am I here? Please untie me.'

The engineer put down his work, removed the eyepiece and came to her. He placed his hand on her forehead as if she were a child with a fever.

In a sad voice he said, 'Dear Eliza, I am so sorry. Are you uncomfortable? I am afraid Lucie's box was a little too small for you. But I had no choice, you see.'

'Untie me. I want to go home.'

'You shall,' he promised. 'Not just yet.'

She was gazing around her, trying to escape his touch. There was more to see. More, and worse.

Here was Lucie, whose place she had taken on the catafalque. Heinrich's doll had not been seen for many weeks, and now Eliza understood why. She lay on the floor at the end of the workshop, blue eyes wide open and gazing at Eliza, her lips

342

parted as if she were about to say that her mama was very well, thank you. She was no longer dressed in her fashionable clothes. The pale rubber of her naked limbs was exposed and her naked torso had been brutally chopped open. The place that would have been a human abdomen was a mess of curled shreds of rubber skin pierced by shards of metal. Lucie would not waltz again, nor utter her stilted remarks in Eliza's voice.

Looking beyond her, Eliza saw another tumbled body. This one was naked too, and it was headless. Broken shafts protruded from the neck. The severed head lay a yard away. The facial features had been smashed beyond recognition but from the flaxen hair Eliza knew it was the doll Heinrich had named Hilde. The little chinaman, Mr Wu, was here too – or what was left of him. This intricate automaton looked as if it had been attacked with a heavy hammer. Elsewhere, the half-constructed hands and body parts that Heinrich had once been working on were thrown in broken piles.

The workshop was a mechanical charnel house.

The sight recalled the newspaper photographs of murdered women that Eliza had struggled to wipe from her memory. These broken bodies lying in Heinrich's workshop were not and never had been human, but the depths of anger and hatred the destruction suggested struck terror into her. The position of Hilde's sprawled limbs seemed to mimic Margaret Minchin's in the mud at the river's edge. Heinrich's hands had been at Eliza's throat on the very same night. What had he really done?

Eliza writhed against her bonds. Her strength returned as the cramps from being locked in Lucie's trunk and the chloroform headache gradually subsided, but she could not free herself.

'Why have you destroyed your dolls?'

Heinrich said, 'Why? Because disobedience must be punished.'

She struggled for a rational response to this.

'But . . . they are, they were, automata. They can't obey or disobey you. All they can do is what you have engineered for them. You are their creator.'

'Yes, I am. And their destroyer. You cannot escape, you know. Lie still and rest, dear Eliza.'

He was apparently gentle and full of regret and she knew that he was mad. She marshalled her thoughts. Keeping her voice as soft and level as his, she asked, 'Why have you brought me here? What do you want?'

'I require your help. Lucie and the others would not obey me. I thought they would, but I was wrong. They were mute, you see. They would not talk or sing. *You* spoke for me, though. You will sing for me too, won't you?'

'Heinrich, you must listen to me. You are an engineer of automata, I am a . . . magician's assistant. We are not machines. You, me, our friends – Jasper, Sylvia, Carlo – are living, breathing people.' She had stopped herself in time from mentioning Devil's name. 'We are strong but we are also frail, each in our own way. We can't always be perfect, or behave as everyone around us might wish. We can help one another, work together, we may like or even love each other, according to our different principles and affections, but we don't have to obey. Not as colleagues and friends. Obedience is only for master and slave.'

Or perhaps for man and wife. Love, honour and obey. Even as she came to the end of her little homily the words of the marriage vow sounded in her head.

Heinrich's mind worked faster still. Savagely he jerked the cord around her wrists until she almost cried out.

He hissed, 'You must not marry Devil Wix.'

Eliza did not know what to say. She kept her eyes averted from the bodies of Lucie and Hilde. What time was it? How long had the chloroform kept her insensible?

Think, she exhorted herself.

With the tip of one finger Heinrich began to stroke her cheek. The caress was infinitely slow, and somehow gloating. He murmured in her ear, bringing his mouth so close that she felt the moist warmth of his breath.

'You must promise me you will not marry him.'

344

She clenched her jaw and tried not to let him see that she was shivering.

Think.

The quiet servant, who had brought the meal to them when she and Devil came here the first time. The same woman had served her breakfast on Christmas morning at the height of Carlo's illness. Lucie had been seated with them at the table dressed in her pretty wrap. If I scream loudly enough, Eliza thought, even if I am able to do it only once before he gags me, will the servant hear me?

Heinrich leaned closer still. His breath was tainted. Playfully he twisted a lock of her hair.

'Mrs McKay does not come down here. I have recently forbidden her even to enter the alley. This is our place, Eliza dear, yours and mine. No one will interrupt us.'

The dusty skylight framed a square of blue-grey sky. It was very early evening, she judged. The Palmyra evening performance was due to begin soon and once her absence was noted Devil would naturally start the search. And as Heinrich was missing too, surely Devil would make the connection and come straight here?

She must humour the engineer until rescue arrived.

'Please, Heinrich, may I have something to drink? I am so thirsty,' she said.

'We mustn't let your pretty throat dry up.'

He poured water from a jug and supported her as he held a glass to her lips. The rim of it rattled against her teeth.

'There. Is that better? Are you hungry?'

Her stomach lurched. 'No.'

'Very well.' He made her lie down again and turned away to his bench. He clicked heavy switches and an amplified noise of scratching and hissing filled the workshop. Heinrich smiled.

'Listen,' he said.

Her recorded words boomed out. 'I should be honoured. Mama is very well, thank you. Another dance. That will be delightful. Good morning. Good evening. How do you do? It will be a pleasure. Good morning. Goodnight.'

Growing louder and louder, the banal phrases became sinister through repetition. The engineer stood behind Eliza where she could not see him. He must have clicked more switches because now there were two voices partially overlaid, both of them hers, repeating the same hateful meaningless words to each other. Then there were three voices, and four, until the mechanical antiphony turned into a mosaic of babble. The volume was deafening. She couldn't cover her ears to block it out.

'Make it stop. Please,' she shouted.

There was a click, and superficial silence. She knew he was close behind her. The phonograph recording with its metallic timbre rang mercilessly in her head.

'You were right, Eliza.' She jumped, fearing him all the more because he was out of sight. 'You told me that Lucie should speak less formally.'

'Did I?'

'Poor Lucie.' He sighed. Eliza kept her neck rigid so as not to look at the disembowelled doll. 'She did not please the audiences, did she? So in the end she did not please me either. Perhaps one might say that the attachment did not hold. But let us not be too melancholy, now you are here with me. You will dance and sing, Eliza, won't you?'

Her head throbbed. She must act with extreme care. The door to the alley would surely be locked. There were no windows except for the skylight, twelve feet over her head. There was no way of escape, even if she could free herself from the bonds. The only hope was somehow to humour him, and to play for time.

She tried a little laugh. 'I am no singer, Heinrich. You know that.'

He jerked savagely on the cords and the straps cut into her wrists.

'But you will try. To please me, Eliza. I have a great fondness for Schubert.'

'I don't know any Schubert.'

'What songs do you know?'

She racked her brains but could not think of a single one. The only tune in her head was a lavender seller's ditty that they had both heard a hundred times, bawled out into the din of the Strand. She began to hum it but Heinrich leaned over and wrenched her arm. A flare of terror ignited deep inside her. He was certainly deranged, perhaps even a murderer, and he was going to hurt her.

'A proper song, if you please.'

'I can't sing lying down.'

If she could stand, there might be some way to hit out at him. Was there a hammer, or any heavy implement within her reach?

He came to the foot of the bed with a length of rope in his hands, and hesitated. His face had been blank but now it flooded with uncertainty tinged with shame. She realised that his intention was to bind her ankles, but he was not sure how to handle her legs while she was awake. He did not know how to approach a living, conscious woman.

He saw the dawn of pity in her eyes, and anger scorched away his shame.

'Don't move.'

He roughly grasped her ankles, forcing them together. The leather cuffs of her boots bit into her skin. He wound the rope and knotted it securely. Next he freed her hands from the straps and helped her to sit upright, her bound legs dangling over the edge of the catafalque. She looked round for a weapon but he was too quick for her. He twisted a rope about her wrists and secured it with the same deft knots.

'You have spirit, Eliza. You are no doll.' He was almost shy in his admiration.

He helped her to stand. Blood rushed from her head to her legs, she swayed and nearly collapsed. He supported her in his arms and his lips brushed her temple.

'Ahhhh,' he breathed.

'I have remembered a song,' she gabbled. She must keep him at bay as long as she could.

'Good.' *Gut.* He released her, and she held herself upright. 'Begin when you are ready.'

Her mother used to sing it, when she and Faith were little girls. It was a pretty tune, with sad words. Eliza took a breath.

'Down yonder green valley . . .'

In her ears her voice was thin and on the verge of cracking. But there was none of the reedy hiss of the phonograph's sound. She was here in the present tense. She was alive.

She reached the end of the first verse.

'Ah! Then little thought I how soon we should part . . .'

Heinrich nodded. He appeared calmer. Listening intently, he drifted across the shadowy workshop. Following him with her eyes she saw a piece of outlandish machinery that was new to her. Fully four feet high, taller than Carlo, it resembled a fairground wheel made from two metal plates. A thick square of rubber matting was laid on the floor. The apparatus seemed doubly sinister because she could not guess at its purpose. She looked away and began the next verse of 'The Ash Grove'.

Devil tore through the theatre. The company scattered before him.

'Where is she? God damn, hasn't any one of you seen her today?'

Sylvia Aynscoe quailed. 'She was not at the lodgings when I left. I thought she must already be here.'

The curtain was due to rise in less than half an hour. The audience was gathering in the foyer and soon the seats would fill up with people eager for entertainment. The musicians had been ready to file into the pit, but now they were caught in the backstage confusion. The violinist distractedly plucked a single note, again and again.

'Improvise,' Devil shouted at the performers and stagehands eddying around him. 'Who can play her parts?'

It was a measure of Eliza's loyalty that they had never had

to call an understudy, nor even considered the need for one. Devil paused at Sylvia. She was the only other full-time female member of the company.

'Not me,' the seamstress whispered. 'I cannot go onstage.'

'Come. Not Charlotte perhaps, or Ayesha even. But surely you can do the Ingot at least? All you have to do is to dress up and stand there for Jakey.'

'No, Mr Wix. I beg you.'

Jasper was in the master of ceremonies' tailcoat and white tie for the show's opening. He said now, 'It seems that the electromagnet does not work. And Heinrich isn't here either.'

Devil whirled round as the significance of this dawned on him. He was costumed for Charlotte, and the chaperone's dress caught about his ankles. He savagely kicked out the hem.

'Why wasn't I told? Is Eliza with Heinrich? Christ alive, one of you must know. Speak to me. Have you all been struck dumb?'

Sylvia didn't move, but her bony face revealed her fears.

Jasper was white to the lips.

'I think she must be with him,' he muttered. 'Don't you?'

Ted Dickinson hovered in the crowd of performers, clearly wondering whether to give the fifteen-minute signal. If he did it was likely that the irate manager would turn on him, and likewise if he did not.

Carlo removed the wolf headpiece and put it aside. Grim-faced, he peeled off the upper half of the animal skin to reveal his muscled arms.

'If Eliza is missing, we go in search of her.'

'I'm coming,' Jasper said. He undid his white tie and wrenched off the stiff collar.

Devil rounded on the two of them. 'What the hell are you doing? Eh?'

Carlo's chest glistened with sweat. It was always hot in the dressing room; tonight it was like a furnace. He said, 'If Eliza is with Heinrich, we know where to find her.'

'If Eliza is with Heinrich, she will be safe enough until after

349

the show,' Devil answered. She had told him of her fears, but Devil could not concede that she had any grounds for them. Poor Heinrich. Heinrich who had lent his money to the Palmyra.

'After the show, we'll hunt for them both.'

Jasper gaped in disbelief. 'Why not this minute, you bastard?'

'Because we have sold tickets to two hundred people who will be entertained whatever comes.'

Carlo ran at him. Slick with sweat and with his lower body still furred he looked like a malevolent satyr.

'Eliza is to be your *wife*. You go out there, tell the audience someone is indisposed, give 'em their money back.'

Devil tried to soothe him. 'The night I let you down, you and Jasper and Eliza performed in my place. You did well.'

'That's because I don't give a tinker's arsehole for you, Wix. It isn't you tonight, it's *her*. I'm going, and I'm going right now.'

Devil stooped, thrust his face into the dwarf's. He hissed, 'We do the show first. You and me and Jasper. So switch the acts round to fill it. Get those bloody acrobats to double.'

Carlo swung his two fists and punched Devil in the jaw, left and then right. The dwarf was strong and Devil tottered, spitting expletives. As soon as he regained his balance he lunged forward and grabbed the dwarf by the throat. The wolf's clawed feet kicked as Devil hoisted him off the ground.

Jasper and Ted leapt to pull them apart. Devil surrendered the dwarf to them. He massaged his jaw and spat a trickle of blood as Carlo was set on his feet, panting and cursing. The violinist helplessly spread his vulnerable hands.

Jasper placed himself between the two of them.

'All right. Stop this. Carlo, we'll go up and the minute the show's over we go to Heinrich's. She may not even be there; this may be nothing to do with him.'

Devil wiped his face with a cloth nervously offered by Sylvia. The dressing room was packed with gaping faces and drooping costumes.

'I'm glad one of you can see sense, Jas. Eliza's not some

350

wilting girl. She can take care of herself for two hours. Now get moving, the lot of you.'

Carlo's mouth twisted.

'You are a stinking piece of ordure, Wix, but you are the one she's agreed to marry. Which is quite beyond my understanding.' He shrugged an arm into the hairy sleeve of the wolf.

Devil only snapped, 'How many extra minutes can you fill?'

The dwarf said, 'The bills outside this theatre should read *The Carlo Boldoni Show*, because that is what it is.'

Devil didn't bother to retort. He tore off the chaperone's dress and began to costume himself for the Flames. He shouted to the musicians, 'Get out and start playing. You can keep on until we're ready to go up.'

'Ten minutes,' Ted Dickinson called.

Eliza came to the end of her song.

'Ye echoes, oh, tell me, where is the sweet maiden?

'"She sleeps, 'neath the green turf down by the ash grove."'

Heinrich nodded. He stood beside his threatening contraption, apparently considering the circular plates. 'Thank you. A little sentimental, but pretty enough. Let us have another.'

Nothing came to her mind, not a single note. To fill the silence she asked, 'What is that machine?'

There was a handle at the base. Heinrich turned it and the discs counter-rotated. A low hum was followed by a sharp crackle and a strange smell reminiscent of a cool breeze over running water.

'It is an influence machine.'

This meant nothing to Eliza. 'Influence?'

'An electrostatic generator. See this.'

He touched a metal knob and a miniature lightning bolt leapt from the index finger of the other hand. For a split second one side of his face was illuminated, as if he had the power to command the elements. Heinrich winced as the electric shock ran through him.

The flash also revealed something else to Eliza, something

351

buried in the shadows, which she had not seen before. It was hidden again as soon as she had glimpsed it but she had to swallow down the acrid fear that rose in her throat.

'Electrostatic induction multiplies the charge, and plate separation increases the voltage. But I think I speak above your head, Eliza.'

'You do. I am interested, nevertheless. It makes a fine illusion, but what is its real purpose?'

He stepped off the rubber mat and rolled it up before putting it aside. It looked heavy. She wondered if she could reach it, and if so whether she could manage to strike him with it.

He said softly, 'It is no illusion. There are many, many possible uses for a stored electrical charge of this magnitude. But we are not here to explore science, Eliza. Let us have another song, please.'

She shifted on her feet. The rope around her ankles was tied so tightly it impeded her circulation. She raised her head and began to sing 'Greensleeves'.

The final curtain came down to tepid applause. Devil was off the stage in a second and stripping off his costume as he ran.

'Who is coming with me?'

Jasper and Carlo were ready without a word.

'I need a couple more strong men. Ted?'

'Aye. For Miss Eliza, of course. And my brother. The two of us'll find 'er for you.'

'Five of us will do. Quick as you can.'

Beyond the West End the streets were quiet. Silently they skirted the glare of the meat market with its attendant stink of blood and fat, and hurried deep into Clerkenwell.

They reached Heinrich's secluded house. With two fists Devil pounded on the door.

When the servant opened up she stepped back, alarmed at the sight of four men looming on the step and the dwarf bobbing at their backs. Devil knew how they must appear, so he mustered all his charm.

'Good evening, ma'am. Please forgive this late intrusion. I hope you can help us with a matter that concerns us?'

He said that one of their company was missing, perhaps the doorkeeper would remember her, the young lady who had visited Herr Bayer? Once accompanied by himself, and once or twice more after that occasion?

The woman pulled the door almost closed until she frowned through the crack.

Devil was concerned but courteous, the picture of plausibility. They were here to enlist Herr Bayer's help, of course. Was he at home, and could they speak to him as a matter of urgency?

'Herr Bayer is not at home.'

She tried to shut the door but Devil's foot was wedged in it.

'Are you certain? Is he in his workshop, perhaps?'

'He is not.'

It was clear the woman was lying. She was too simple to practise deception.

'Where is he, then?'

'He is my employer, sir. I don't know his whereabouts. Perhaps he is at his place of work.'

Devil's charm was evaporating. He growled, 'We *are* his place of work.'

The woman struggled to close the door. Devil would have broken past her but Jasper and the Dickinsons restrained him. The door banged shut and they heard the bolts slam.

'That was not the way to do it,' Jasper sighed.

Devil shook off their clutches and ran to the side door that led into the alley and thence to the hidden workshop. He rattled it but it was securely padlocked and bolted. The old hinges held.

Carlo looked upwards. 'What's behind here?'

Devil described the layout and the workshop beyond. 'Quick. The servant will be warning him.'

Carlo listened intently. His eyes were turned up to the roof-line as his fingers flexed and released. At end he said, 'Right. Help me, Ted.'

The handyman knelt as Carlo indicated, and the dwarf sprang

on his shoulders. Climbing like a squirrel he went hand over hand up a drainpipe, gained a ledge and then an upper sill, pressed his hands to the parapet and finally vaulted on to the alley roof. Devil watched him go.

Eliza had sung every song she could think of, although this amounted to a meagre recital. She seemed to have been in the workshop for a long time. The square of sky above the skylight was pitch black.

'Perhaps you would like to perform one for me?' she suggested in rising desperation. Heinrich declined with a sour shrug. He was becoming agitated again, pacing backwards and forwards and fidgeting with the tools on his bench.

'I am sorry, Heinrich. I am afraid I cannot sing any more.'

Why did nobody come? Where was Devil, for all these hours? Perhaps he was not looking for her at all. She could not think how she might extricate herself if he did not come.

Heinrich picked up a small cylinder and pointed to his phonograph.

'Then we shall dance instead.'

She shivered at the first amplified hiss, but it was music that spilled from the machine and not her voice. Heinrich opened his arms.

'May I have the pleasure?'

She lifted her bound wrists in response. 'I cannot dance. I am tied up.'

Lucie had never said that, at least. Eliza fought back an alarming urge to laugh.

Heinrich bowed. 'My most profound apologies.'

He came at her brandishing a sharp-bladed knife and the laughter died in her throat.

If Heinrich had ever appeared normal, he was far from it now. Behind the lenses of his spectacles his pupils were enlarged. There were sweat beads on his forehead and his lips were drawn back from his teeth.

'May I, Eliza?'

He gestured with the knife. She nodded without words and the blade sliced through the cords at her wrists and ankles. Prickling spasms from the restored circulation shot through her wrists and ankles, but with his eyes fixed on her there was nothing she could do but step into his arms. They began to waltz. He held her so close that she could feel his heart thumping.

As soon as the music ended he started it up again, twice, three times, then over and over again until she lost count. His lips brushed her forehead before tracing her hairline. Sweat from his palms glued their hands.

Eliza imagined that somehow she had turned into Lucie. It was to be her fate to dance with Heinrich Bayer for the rest of time, her aching limbs trapped in repetitive motion and the hideous music spiralling in her head.

A possible escape route was via the blade of his knife. It lay on the catafalque, where he had set it down after untying her. Could she somehow, by the smallest steps, direct their movements to within reach of it? By exerting infinitesimal pressure through her hips and hands she tried to do this, but immediately their feet tangled and she almost stumbled.

'Oh, my dear, was that my clumsiness?' Heinrich murmured. He knew what she intended, and to show her it was a hopeless plan he steered her across the studio, nearer to the influence machine and what lay in the shadows behind it. They were close to the giant plates, her skirt almost touching the winding handle, when the music halted yet again.

Heinrich stopped dancing. His hand held her wrists in a crushing grip.

She had no choice but to look over his shoulder, directly at what had once been Mr George Gardiner's prize-winning portrait of Devil in the costume of the evil philosopher.

The face had been neatly sliced out of it, leaving a black rectangle. Lower down another slice of canvas had also been chopped out, more savagely and without precision, leaving the canvas hanging in shreds and tatters.

She moved her stiff lips. 'It . . . seems a wicked shame, to have destroyed the portrait. Mr Gardiner is already becoming a well-known artist. Opinion has it that some day he will be one of the greatest.'

'So I understand.'

'Why, Heinrich?'

He angled his head to look down at her.

He said in a voice so low that she could hardly hear it, 'Because I could.'

There was, by implication, so much that he could not do.

Such depths of bitterness and of despair meant that she could not but pity him. He was certainly mad, but madness was striated with loneliness and strangeness and longing to be what he was not.

'Heinrich, we are all your friends. You are a brilliant man. Why do you need to hurt and destroy? In the end it is only yourself you are damaging.'

He threw his head back and howled, 'I have no friends.'

Even Lucie had been destroyed. He was going to destroy Eliza Dunlop too, and he would have done the same to Devil Wix, not just his portrait, if he had dared.

She closed her eyes.

'I am faint,' she whispered.

He hoisted her and half-carried her to the catafalque. Before he laid her down he threw the knife aside, and she heard it clatter and slide into the shadows. He pressed her down against the cushions, one hand at her throat and the other on her breast. His breath came very fast as he planted his mouth on hers. Eliza tried to twist away.

In that second, staring upwards in the grip of stark fear, she saw Carlo's face pressed to the black square of the skylight.

She widened her eyes, blinked and the face was gone.

Had she seen it, or imagined it?

The dwarf slid back over the roof's edge. His short legs briefly pedalled in the air. At the same moment Ted Dickinson ran round the corner accompanied by a police constable.

'Catch me.' Carlo leapt, and Devil and Jasper bore him up in their arms.

The dwarf gasped, 'She's there. At the back. He's on top of her.'

Devil hurled him aside and began kicking like a maniac at the alley door. The dread that he had suppressed all evening swelled up and burst out of him. The doors creaked and shivered under the battering, but they held.

He bellowed, 'Let me in. Heinrich, in the name of God, can you hear me? If you hurt her I'll kill you.'

'Stop that,' shouted the policeman. He stared in disbelief as the dwarf bounded in front of him.

Carlo shouted back, 'There's assault taking place in there. Worse, likely.'

'All together,' Devil ordered.

Four strong men threw themselves at the door. The iron hinges began to splinter away from the jamb.

Heinrich held still, tilting his head on one side as if he were listening to muffled music.

After the waltz there had been silence, but now there came a sound that brought Eliza's heart into her mouth. It was the noise of distant banging and hammering, briefly stopping and then breaking out again.

'Eliza, my dearest Eliza,' he whispered. 'What's this?'

She thought he was scanning the floor for the knife. He would kill her before Carlo and Devil – surely Devil was here at last? – could break down the doors.

'Wait,' she begged.

He smiled, mirthless, unseeing in the lamplight.

'For what?'

He walked away and knelt in front of the influence machine. He bowed his head and then began to turn the handle.

As the din of people trying to force an entrance grew louder, he wound faster and faster. The plates counter-spun until they melted into a blur. She could hear the effort in the engineer's gasping breaths.

The loudest crash was immediately followed by a splintering slam.

Please, Eliza silently prayed.

Voices clamoured in the alley. Someone was shouting out her name. Devil was calling her.

She remembered that she was free to move and instantly hurled herself off the catafalque. On all fours she scanned the floor for the glint of the knife blade. She saw it lying under the engineer's bench and crawled towards it. Heinrich was intent on his machine. The same eerie smell of wind over water filled the close air.

Footsteps pelted down the alley and then the men were at the door of the workshop itself. The crashes became coordinated rushes at this inner door and she could see the thin panels shivering and bowing under the assault.

Heinrich stared at her over his shoulder. His teeth were bared in a snarl and his face poured with sweat from his exertions. She reared up on to her knees, grasping the handle of the knife and preparing to wield it when he ran at her.

One of the door panels smashed open. Through the splintered wood a burly shoulder appeared. A second panel broke. Her eyes were dragged back to Heinrich. She heard the door give way and the men fell into the workshop.

Heinrich let go of the winding handle. His hands flew briefly in the air like Carlo's doves. He grasped the two metal knobs that protruded from the influence machine.

There was a crack that seemed to cleave the world and Heinrich's body was thrown backwards. A terrible stink of burning flooded the workshop.

Devil saw Eliza kneeling, her head thrown back and a knife held aloft.

'Don't touch him.'

The order came from the policeman. His tunic buttons and his belt buckle glimmered as he crouched over the engineer.

'Is he dead?' Eliza whispered. No one answered her and she cried out, 'Is he *dead*?'

'Yes,' Devil said.

He had to prise her fingers, one by one, from the knife handle. He put it aside and gently helped her to her feet. She was convulsively shuddering and he folded her in his arms.

'Did he hurt you?'

'No'. She tried to hold back tears but they scalded her eyes and ran down her face. 'Poor Heinrich.'

The policeman spread hands on his thick thighs and levered himself upright.

'Death by electrocution,' he said. 'I have never seen it before, but that is what it is.'

He took a blanket from the catafalque and let it fall over the sad huddle that had been Heinrich Bayer.

Devil held Eliza tightly as she sobbed. He murmured to her, 'You're safe now. It's all right. We're here.'

He saw the cut ropes, and the deep red marks where they had bitten into her wrists. He might easily have arrived too late to save her from more serious injury. The body under the blanket might have been hers, not Heinrich's. Fear crawled over him as he contemplated the unthinkable. How would he go on, what meaning would tomorrow and the next days have, if he were forced to live them without Eliza?

Jasper cried out, shock robbing him of his habitual calm. 'We should have been here hours ago.'

'Please be quiet for now, Jas,' Devil begged.

Carlo wore a face of stone. The Dickinsons stood awkwardly aside, their heads bowed in the presence of violent death. They had all seen the dolls, the influence machine, and the ruined portrait.

The servant woman appeared in the broken doorway. Her hands were at her mouth. The policeman began writing in a notebook.

'This lady is my fiancée,' Devil said. 'She has suffered an ordeal. I want to take her home.'

The policeman placed his pencil in the fold of his book.

'I'm sorry, but I must ask some questions first.' And then to the weeping servant he said, 'You too. What is this place? What is the victim's name?'

Eliza detached herself from Devil's side. The policeman brought forward a chair.

'You may sit, miss.'

'Thank you,' Eliza said.

Somehow, she regained sufficient composure to answer the questions. Keeping her eyes averted from Heinrich's body she described how she had been drugged, and brought here insensible inside the trunk used to house a mechanical automaton. She had been tied up and the man had forced her to sing songs and then to dance with him. The constable's face was impassive as he noted down these details. Devil sat with his head in his hands, remorse beating in his head. He had not listened to Eliza's fears when she had confided them, and he had failed her this evening. He knew that Jasper and Carlo looked on him with disbelief, if not outright disgust. They had every reason, he acknowledged. If only he could put matters right, he would wish for nothing more.

'The deceased approached the electrical machine and turned the handle of his own accord?'

Eliza nodded. 'He did.'

'He took hold of those knobs there, quite of his own accord?'

'He did.'

'You saw that much for yourself,' Devil put in.

'I will thank you to remain silent. You will have your turn to speak.'

The servant woman submitted to the interrogation next. Two more policemen arrived. After gaping at the dismembered dolls and the apparatus they began to take notes and measurements.

The questions for the rescue party did not take long because they all vouched for one another. After considering matters with his colleagues, tapping his teeth with a thumbnail as he did so, the constable was at last satisfied that in spite of the baroque details this was a case of suicide. Arrangements were made for the engineer's remains to be removed overnight to

360

the police morgue and for the workshop and its contents to be secured. The servant retreated to the main house and the rest of them emerged into the street. It was long past midnight. The Dickinsons mumbled a subdued goodnight and melted away.

Devil was one side of Eliza with Carlo and Jasper on the other. She sensed the powerful currents of discord between the men and that her place was always to be in the midst of them. She felt unspeakably weary.

'Why did you take so long?' she asked.

Devil said, 'We came the moment the show was over.'

She stared at him. 'You knew Heinrich had taken me, yet you waited until after the performance?'

Jasper held out imploring hands. 'It's as much my fault, Eliza. I should have made him cancel the show. Carlo and I both wanted to come at once.'

'It's true, they did,' Devil humbly said. He must acknowledge the extent of his culpability, at least. 'It was a mistake. I am very sorry for it.'

'You see the man you have promised to marry?' Carlo snarled.

'Enough, Carlo. This is not the place. We have lost poor Heinrich and it's very late,' Jasper told him. 'Let me see you back to your lodgings, Eliza. Matters will look different tomorrow.'

Eliza stood still. It was Jasper's way always to temporise.

'Come with us,' Carlo echoed. 'You will be safe.'

She kept her eyes fixed on Devil.

He said softly to her, 'I will look after you from now on, Eliza. I swear it. I will never let you out of my sight.' And then he added, 'If that is really what you want.'

Her gaze held. Devil had allowed her freedom and opportunity, and to embrace freedom was to acknowledge that there were dangers in doing so. In a steady voice she answered, 'To be over-protected is not what I want or need. I am a woman, not a doll. I distracted Heinrich, didn't I, until you were quite ready to come to my rescue?'

Devil was not surprised, but he was impressed. Eliza's courage

361

was notable. He would have a formidable wife, when the day came. If she would forgive him.

Carlo came forward. He bowed his forehead against Eliza's waist.

'Won't you come with me instead of Wix? It's not too late.'

Painfully Eliza lifted her hand and brought it down to rest on the dwarf's head. She stroked his thick hair.

'I'm sorry,' she whispered.

Immediately the dwarf sprang away from her caress. His jaw stuck out like a bowsprit.

'Of course. Come on, Button. We are surplus to requirements and we'll have to trust against the odds that Wix will behave like a decent man.' He almost spat, 'For once.'

Eliza watched her friends walk away into the darkness and she was left alone with Devil Wix. She began to tremble again.

'I have hurt them both. And Heinrich is gone.' A sob broke out of her.

'Hush, my darling. You have done nothing wrong. There is nothing to fear now.'

If Heinrich had hurt her . . . he thought. If he had really failed her, after all she had done for him, even after she had marched him to Stanmore and shown him that his ghosts had no real power. To acknowledge what might have happened tonight chilled him to the core. At the same time, he experienced a contradictory kick of physical desire.

'Come with me now.'

This depth of longing was quite new to him. It meshed with a need to protect her and a troubling uncertainty about his ability to do so.

Eliza's body ached with shock and exhaustion. She tried to summon a smile but managed only a wry twist of her lips.

'We are not yet married,' she said.

'Then marry me tomorrow. As soon as it can be done. I don't care about bouquets and breakfasts. Marry me now, won't you?' He was begging her.

They were planning a summer wedding on a scale calculated

by Bertha to reflect her husband's means. It was to take place during the theatre's annual closure, followed by a journey by the newlyweds to see the Eiffel Tower.

With hindsight, Eliza was a little disappointed that Devil had made his original proposal of marriage a public matter for all at the Palmyra. But in this stark moment she saw the man, stripped of all his bravado and his considerable guile, and she knew he was truly hers.

Heinrich had captured and bound her, his mouth had slithered over her face and his hands over her body. She could still feel and taste the dead man. And here was Devil, warm and urgent, offering her passion that would defer some of the horrors of the night. Afterwards she could lie in his arms and let sleep carry her away.

'Yes,' Eliza said. Both to the marriage and to his bed.

After the necessary investigations and formalities Heinrich Bayer was laid to rest in the cemetery of St John's Clerkenwell. Eliza insisted that the engineer must have a respectful committal and Devil agreed to pay for everything. News of the sad demise had been hastily sent to Switzerland, but there was no response save a formal acknowledgement from a lawyer. It appeared that Heinrich did not have close family. Apart from his housekeeper the only mourners were the friends from the Palmyra. Every member of the wider company came, even including the yellow-haired girl and her mother from the coffee shop favoured by Jasper, because Heinrich had also been a favoured customer of theirs. The front pews of the old church were quite full.

Carlo stood up beside the coffin and spoke of the dead man's genius.

Eliza and Sylvia Aynscoe clasped hands and wept for him.

A week after that, early one morning, Eliza Dunlop and Devil Wix were married. The bride was attended by her sister and by Sylvia, and the groom's man was Jasper Button. A simple breakfast was held afterwards for the Dunlop family but there was no other celebration to mark the event and no honeymoon journey.

The couple set up home in a small rented house in Islington. Eliza continued to play her stage roles, and to work with Sylvia at the bakery on making new costumes and set dressings, and she also assumed responsibility for the theatre accounts and wages. She and Devil were one, their work was entwined, and the Palmyra did and would prosper. This was what she had intended.

Devil was Devil, as always.

'Are you happy?' Faith asked her.

'Yes,' she said.

PART THREE

SIXTEEN

August 1892

The little house was in a quiet side street. There were brick-and-stucco walls and arch-framed windows, and the front doors with brass furniture sheltered behind gates and railings. It was an area populated by city clerks and the middling sort of shopkeepers and merchants. Most of the steps were kept decently scrubbed. Clean windows reflected sunlight and cherry trees shaded the pavements, although this suburban impression was somewhat dispelled by a glimpse of the horse buses that trundled past the end of the road. Close at hand too were the construction works for a new electric tramline that would transport Islington residents even more speedily to Holborn and beyond. White dust presently flew up to thicken the summer air, and loud clanging of machinery and the shouts of the labourers echoed down the street.

The ease of transport to the area allowed Faith to visit Eliza regularly. This morning the sisters were sitting out in the tiny rear garden in the hope of a cool breeze. Rowland and Edwin were at school and little Lizzie remained at home with her nurse. Eliza absently pushed the hair from her forehead with the back of her hand before loosening the ribbon at the collar of her wrap. Faith smiled at her.

'I remember I used to feel so tired, as if I could sleep for a hundred years. Then when I did lie down and close my eyes I couldn't find a comfortable place. My legs and arms would ache, or jerk like a puppet's, and I would have to clamber upright all over again.'

'Oh, I feel well enough. But the days go so slowly. What am I supposed to do with myself, when Devil is always at the theatre?'

'Rest and make ready.'

Eliza blew out her cheeks. 'I can't rest all the time, and thanks to you I am quite prepared. If I didn't have you, Faith, I don't know what I would do.'

These days Eliza felt closer to her sister than ever before.

Faith had brought her all the little garments she had knitted or stitched for her own babies and these unfeasibly tiny items now lay folded in an upstairs drawer. There were blankets and shawls too, laid in the crib that had last been occupied by Lizzie. Eliza was grateful for this generosity because she was no needlewoman herself, but she was even more pleased simply to have Faith's company while she waited out the tedious days. She was ashamed to remember how absent she had been while Faith was preparing for her own confinements. She had dismissed her sister's maternal instincts as narrow and her willingness to accept the close horizons of a home and a marriage as dull, and imagined that she would never yield to the same restrictions. And yet, time had caught up with her and here she was in the identical place. She had a house to manage, which turned out to be as tedious as she had expected, and soon there would be an infant.

All of this was the natural and happy consequence of being married to the man she passionately loved, and therefore of being a woman, but the forced inactivity – the waiting, the heaviness of her body, the exclusion from the theatre and the wider world – all of it made her wriggle and seethe.

Faith's smooth forehead creased. 'There is still the perambulator. I can't bring it over myself, I don't think. It is such a heavy thing. Perhaps Matthew will come on Sunday, or maybe Devil . . .'

Eliza flung her head back and thumped her feet on the flag-stones.

'I am so bored,' she groaned. 'Forgive me, Faith. I know I should be composed. But *oh*. How much longer?'

Faith laughed at her. 'Where has your absence gone? You used to be able to sit in church like a statue and fix your eyes on the distance for hours at a time. I'd make faces or pinch you and you'd hardly respond.'

'I can't do that any longer. I don't know how. The trouble is that I miss the theatre. Off Devil goes every morning. There is so much for us both to do there; so much I want to be doing.'

Faith had begun to fear that there was never going to be a child. She thought privately that her sister expended too much energy in diving through stage trapdoors and running up ladders, although she had not confided as much even to Matthew. Now, three years after Eliza's marriage, that anxiety was finally past. She was sure that when Eliza did become a mother she would be as absorbed by it as any woman could be, and until then she could afford to be as generous and consoling about the Palmyra as Eliza wished.

She soothed her, 'You will be able to work your stage wonders again, if that is what you really want. Give yourself a little time. What is the news from the theatre?'

'I'm not sure I have anything interesting to tell you. Sylvia comes to visit me, but she is so good and only ever sees the best in everyone, which is not always as amusing as gossip and innuendo can be. Devil talks about the carpentry work for the new revolve, or the box office receipts, and then he sighs and complains that a man ought to be able to come home and forget his place of business.'

'That is understandable.'

Eliza was seriously concerned about the theatre, but most of her concerns related to money and ownership and the squabbles amongst the company members and she would not share these with Faith.

After Heinrich's death, no note or record of his loans to the theatre was ever discovered. Jasper had tried to insist to Devil that the company must repay the outstanding sum to the engineer's estate, so that it would eventually reach his heirs, but Devil had not favoured this proposal.

'For all we know, Heinrich might have intended to give us the money in the end. What heirs did he ever mention? Did any family member present himself at his funeral?'

Jasper appealed to Eliza for adjudication. The sale of the dead man's house and workshop and the removal of his effects had been impersonally dealt with from Switzerland. They had no idea where and to whom they might return the borrowed money, she declared, so how would they set about it?

But this all happened soon after Devil and she were married, at a time when no one knew whether she spoke for herself or as Devil's wife. It was difficult for them all.

Soon afterwards Devil succeeded in raising another substantial loan. He went to Mathieson and Company, the bank, where his slight acquaintance with Mr Edward Mathieson gained him an introduction and a hearing. The banker and his wife claimed theatrical and artistic interests. Mr Mathieson studied Devil's proposals, revisited the theatre, and agreed to put up the money.

Devil had immediately embarked on a new round of improvements, including the restoration of the cupola and the electrification of the building. There was money left over to invest in expensive stage apparatus and quite soon, for the inventiveness of its magic and the opulent glow of the interior, the Palmyra did become a place of wonder. Audiences flocked. Unfortunately Carlo and Jasper felt pushed to the margins by Devil's need for constant innovation. Disputes regularly broke out between the three of them, in which Eliza became the mediator. Although she never openly opposed her husband she did her best to convince the others that she represented their interests to him.

A solution was eventually reached with the formation of the

Palmyra Theatre Partnership. Devil, Eliza, Carlo and Jasper each had an equal shareholding, with smaller portions allocated to Jakey and Sammy Hill. Sylvia Aynscoe wanted only regular wages and a quiet life and the Dickinsons and the Crabbes and the other permanent company members were retained on a good wage. The Partnership leased the theatre from Devil, and paid him annually a commercial rate for the right to perform in it. This agreement was drawn up by a lawyer – despite Devil's expressed loathing for all members of this profession – and signed by the parties. One copy was kept in the office, locked away in the old safe that had once belonged to Jacko Grady.

Eliza might have taken satisfaction in the formalising of the business arrangements, because this had been one of her earliest intentions, but she soon found that a contract – even one like this with expensive festoons of clauses, signatures and appended wax seals – could not prevent rivalry or outlaw jealousy. The currents of ill feeling could run underground for weeks, before bursting out in raucous arguments.

This was *theatre*, she reminded herself. Under the stage lights and in the airless backstage crannies every word and gesture was exaggerated, every small scene was embellished by costumes and greasepaint and either played for laughs or spun into a tragedy. The charged atmosphere was what had attracted her in the first place. But now the laughter backstage was not always good-humoured, and she feared that they all kept their real tragedies to themselves. She could not even be there in person.

She realised that Faith was watching her, head held on one side and eyes a little narrowed.

Lightly she said, 'What can I tell you? Oh, I know. Mr Cockle is visiting the company today. He has clever ideas.'

Jerry Cockle was her protégé. He was the Rawlinson technical school pupil she had sought out four years ago, on the terrible day of Heinrich's death. Eliza shifted her bulk against the cushions. She tried to remember Heinrich for his genius and

371

his generosity to the Palmyra, and to forget his death and the circumstances that led to it.

'It was Mr Cockle who splashed London with palm trees, in the days of the Philosophers illusion, do you remember? He is in the advertising business now.' Eliza waved her arms in the air. '"Soap, dogma, newspapers, banking, bootlaces, patent medicine, truth, lies, even magic. Lend your burden to Cockle & Co. and we'll give it wings." That's the sort of thing he tends to say.'

Faith raised her eyebrows. 'Does he?' She reached for her basket and took out a tiny bonnet trimmed with satin rosebuds. 'Isn't this pretty?'

Her sister peered at it. 'Do you think perhaps too pretty for a boy?'

This was Faith's favourite topic, at last. She could speculate for hours at a time.

'Oh, Eliza. I can't wait to know. A little girl, it's such a joy to have a daughter. What do you feel?'

'It lies very still.'

'A girl,' Faith said decisively. 'Lizzie was so quiet, and Edwin and Rowland both pummelled me almost to death. But Devil hopes for a boy, I suppose.'

Wix and Son, Eliza thought. An heir for the theatre.

'I think so,' she smiled.

Devil leapt on to the stage, beaming widely, every jig of his legs and sweep of his hands signalling enthusiasm. His colleagues warily regarded him.

'Here is our friend Jerry Cockle,' he cried.

A red-haired young man appeared in front of them. Apart from his hair and the insistent cut and colour of his coat he was entirely unremarkable. Carlo audibly groaned.

Devil only grinned and held up one finger for attention. 'We have a new show, the best in London. We must sell it with all the style and imagination it deserves. Selling, selling, selling is the art and the foundation of theatrical success . . .'

'Is it? And here am I, thinking it was stage skills,' Carlo murmured to Jakey.

'. . . So we must market our wares, ladies and gentlemen. And of that art Jeremiah Cockle is the acknowledged master.'

'What do you and Jerry have in mind this time?' Jasper mildly enquired from the second row of the stalls.

'I am glad you asked us that question, Jasper,' Devil smiled imperturbably. He was spruce in a new summer coat in a fine lavender-and-cream stripe. 'What we plan is to *tease*. We shall tantalise and torment the public with longing to see more of the Palmyra show. No more static posters or shilling inserts in the press for us. We shall be our own living advertisements.'

There was a silence.

Jerry Cockle was a confident person, and in this company his lack of personal popularity did not trouble him at all. He strode forward with his thumbs hitched in the pockets of his loud waistcoat.

'This is my proposal, ladies and gents. You should consider yourselves your own finest advertisements. We will go out into the streets and put on a free illusion for all to enjoy.' He held up his hand. 'There will be style and beauty. There will be magic. And there will be the best elements of comedy and tragedy, as in the Greek drama.'

Jasper frowned and Sammy Hill scratched his head. 'What's the feller on about?' he mouthed.

Carlo's face hardened.

'You propose that we put our work on in the streets, for no charge? Even though the streets are already full to bursting with people hawking fly-papers, or dangling puppets for a penny in the hat?'

Jerry Cockle's confidence did not waver. 'Your special signature – that's what we call it in my business, Mr Boldoni – is being angry. But my advice is not to overdo it. It loses its value.'

The dwarf snarled. 'I don't give a fart in a bottle for your advice. I am not a starving tumbler or a barrel organ Italian with a monkey dressed up in a red coat. I won't work the streets. I don't suppose any of the rest will do it either, not just because you tell 'em to.'

Jerry Cockle shrugged.

Jasper said, 'There might be a notion here, Carlo. Don't dismiss the idea just because of its begetter.'

Amiably Devil put in, 'The difference between the street rabble and ourselves is that we ask for nothing. No passing the hat. It is a privileged free glimpse that we are offering. That alone will catch the attention.'

'What rubbish,' the furious dwarf snapped.

'Do me the courtesy of hearing Jerry out,' Devil replied.

Waving his arms until his red hair stood up in tufts and the bold checks of his coat danced in front of their eyes, Jerry explained how they would take an enticing little illusion out into the waiting world. They would visit the approaches to the grander City institutions, or even the steps of the Pall Mall clubs, and perform there. Just once, and then they would move on to the next location.

Carlo interrupted him. 'Pay attention. I do not work in the streets. I am not a Punch and Judy man.'

Jerry said, 'Wait. We do only a very few performances. There will be stories in the newspapers, and pictures too, and the people who read them will want to catch a glimpse of you in the flesh. And the more they want their glimpses, the harder we shall make it to get them. Unless they make their way here, that is.' Jerry gestured to the window and the brass cash register that stood behind it. 'To the box office.'

Carlo said, 'Flummery.'

The expert in advertising smoothed down his rusty spikes of hair. 'Expertise. Ingenuity. Modernity. The way forward, Mr Boldoni.'

'That's enough,' Devil said. He was losing patience. 'Carlo, you and I and Jasper will work up a suitable illusion. It will be an interesting problem. We should allow ourselves a week, don't you think?' He consulted his gold watch. 'I am going home to see my wife before we go up tonight. Let us meet tomorrow morning, at the bakery. Nine o'clock sharp.'

Carlo uttered a single profanity.

Jerry Cockle winked at them. 'Timing. That's another cornerstone of success in my business.'

Devil and the advertising man made their exit.

There was plenty of muttering and head-shaking amongst those who were left, but the members of the company slowly dispersed to their business until only Carlo and Jakey and Tilly Lacey remained. Miss Lacey had recently joined the company to appear in Eliza's roles. It was no secret that Tilly was gone on Jakey. She twisted a curl of hair round one finger and gazed at him.

'What do you think, Jacob?'

Jakey considered matters of theatre promotion to be outside his concern, but he smiled. 'I am not sure how we are to introduce the Greek drama into an illusion for the streets.'

Jakey had ever been an attentive student of manners and appearances. He only needed to eavesdrop on a languid young gentleman for half an hour, after which he could mimic his social opposite as accurately as if the two of them had shared a nursery. Nowadays the actor was a tall, handsome presence, with hardly a trace of the street urchin he had once been. Yet he kept the same gentle manner he had always shown.

'Cockle is a priceless arse,' Carlo complained. Wearily he rested his large head on one hand as the fingers of the other raked through his hair. This was streaked with grey now. Deep lines from his nose to the corners of his mouth emphasised his scornful expression. 'I would like to shoot him in the head, but he doesn't deserve such a merciful end.'

Somewhere backstage Sammy Hill lowered a switch. Devil's long-planned electrification work was now complete and the palm chandelier instantly blazed with clean and glorious light. A second switch illuminated the gilded box fronts, the painted tablets and the smooth inner curve of the cupola, and a double spot locked on the empty stage. The effect was still new enough, and sufficiently lovely, to take them by surprise.

375

'It's really, really pretty, isn't it?' Tilly chirped. 'The nicest theatre I've ever been in. My ma and pa think the same. They're proud of me working here, but heaven knows what they'll say when they hear of me taking to the streets after all they've taught me.'

'Precisely. We already have a *theatre*.' Carlo waved his hands at the lamps and the sumptuous velvet of the new stage curtains. 'Wix has borrowed and spent a fortune on doing it up grander than a duchess's boudoir. We charge the public to park their arses on *these* cushions and to gape at *that* stage. So tell me where's the logic in hauling out into the dirty streets and giving it to 'em for nowt?'

Jakey remarked, 'It might just work. What he says about teasing is right enough, and to take a little gem of a trick and put it on in the right place is a fair way to catch the attention of people with money in their pockets. I'm not saying it'll do any good, but I don't mind trying it.'

For offstage Jakey this was a long speech. Tilly touched a finger to her lip as if he had echoed her very thoughts.

'Oh, I think you are *so* right. A little gem, you know?'

The lights abruptly snapped off. Sammy would be saying that he didn't want Devil Wix on his back when the account from the electric company came in. Carlo tapped Tilly's shoulder.

'Off you go.'

The girl prettily blushed, flicked a smile at Jakey and tripped away.

Jakey studied the folds of the curtain and the elaborate golden tassels. He was used to Carlo's moods and he knew how to humour him. The two of them were friends even though they made an odd pair, the little magician strutting beside the handsome actor. They were thrown together even more regularly nowadays, since Jasper had begun seriously courting Hannah Dooley from the coffee shop.

'Where's Jas gone?' Jakey asked.

Carlo sniffed, but not too dismissively. 'Do you need to ask?

Off to his sweetheart, lucky bugger. He doesn't get much time off from this place. Let him enjoy himself while he can, eh?'

'Yes.'

'Seems to me, while we're on the subject, that you'd do all right if you were to start looking at Tilly Lacey that way. She comes from a good theatre family.' The dwarf lasciviously chuckled.

'Perhaps. But I don't think I'll try it.'

'Aye. You're probably right. She hasn't got the brains of a feather duster. You want wit in a woman as well as a bonny face and a tidy pair of jugs.'

Jakey only nodded. His life was his work at the Palmyra, his books, and their occasional drinking bouts in which he acted as Carlo's minder. His affections were unalterably fixed elsewhere but he could not hope for any reciprocation.

Carlo produced a coin and moodily set it snaking between his fingers.

'Eliza's behind all this. Cockle is her man. I don't believe Wix himself gives a damn for marketing. He'd just slap up a poster or take half a page in the papers, like always. Eliza is stirring the pot and pretending not to.'

Carlo flipped the coin. Jakey did not expect to see it land and true to form it vanished into the air.

'I'm going to pay a call on madam tomorrow, and we shall discuss her friend Cockle and his fine ideas,' Carlo muttered.

Devil came home in the interval between his work at the bakery and the evening performance. People did not flock to the theatre at the dog-end of summer, but Devil was determined to keep the doors open except for the two-week interval during which they would put in the apparatus for the new show. The afternoon had grown heavy, with a purple haze hanging in the sky. He lifted the hair from the nape of Eliza's neck and kissed her damp skin.

'How do you feel? What have you done today?'

Eliza was hungry for company and diversion.

'I'm well.' Still she heard the echo of Lucie's mechanical voice. 'Faith came for an hour this morning.'

They were looking out into the garden. Devil put his hands on her belly and she rested her head against his shoulder. Beneath her shoulder blade she could feel the gold watch ticking in his waistcoat pocket.

Eliza sighed.

'I wish I could come to the theatre.'

Tilly Lacey was the daughter and granddaughter of music-hall performers and she had made her stage debut as a toddling infant in a touring comedy act with her parents. She thought no more about performing than she did about eating or breathing. Eliza was jealous of her, and was also ashamed of her jealousy.

She felt a twitch of impatience in Devil. He did not want to hear her bewail her circumstances. He cupped his hand over a small protruberance that nudged and shifted under his wife's clothing.

'I feel him moving. There.'

'Or her.'

'It is a boy.'

She let him hold his certainty.

Devil said, 'Jerry and I spoke to the company about the street magic. There was opposition from Carlo, of course. But he will come round in the end.'

'Good.'

Their embrace ended. He took out the pocket watch and looked at the time.

'I'll have a wash before I eat my dinner,' he said.

Eliza followed him up the stairs and ran cold water into the basin. There was soap in the dish, and a thin towel folded on the rail. Before they took the lease the landlord of the property had installed a tiny bathroom in an angle of the landing, but he had stopped short of installing pipes to take hot water to the upper storey of the house. On stifling days such as these this it didn't matter, but in winter it was a task to carry jugs of hot water up to the fixed tub that stood on a sheet of lead with upturned edges to counter the possibility of overflow. Eliza had already decided that when the baby came she would bath it downstairs in front of the fire, as her own mother had bathed her. One of her earliest memories was of the abrasion of a coarse towel against her warmed skin.

Devil stripped off his coat and shirt. Eliza perched on the enamel rim of the bath and watched as he splashed his chest and armpits and lathered himself. The smell of soapy sweat reminded her of the dressing room at the Palmyra and she felt a stab of longing to be back at the theatre.

'We shall have to think about a nursemaid,' she mused.

Devil splashed again, sending droplets flying over the varnished walls. He straightened up, the sparse dark hair on his chest glistening with water. Through the open door they could see along the ribbon of linoleum leading to the bedroom, and the brass knob on the further corner of the bedstead. Once he would have scooped her up and propelled her there, taking her as she was with her skirts pulled up and her legs spread wide for him. Now he stuck his black head under the cold tap and soaked it before vigorously rubbing his hair until it stuck up like a cockscomb. When he emerged he saw her face. He threw the towel aside and pulled her close. He kissed her, cold-lipped from washing and with his tongue hot in her mouth. His teeth mashed her lip and his hand explored her swollen breasts. Eliza groaned. The baby was a solid bulwark wedged between them.

'Minx,' he said before he released her. He briefly pressed the sides of her belly before turning away to his clothes on the back of the chair.

'There is a clean shirt on the chest.'

'Thank you. I'll eat my dinner quickly, I need to see Jasper as soon as I get there. He's never there when I want him.'

'Jasper is in love with Hannah. I'm so happy to see it.'

It was a relief, she had decided. Jasper needed a pliant woman, not someone as awkward as herself.

'Love,' Devil repeated, and laughed as if she had said something comical.

Eliza gripped the banister as she slowly descended the stairs. She felt sticky and cumbersome, even more so when Devil reappeared in the kitchen in his lavender-striped coat with his hair combed down and his handsome face shining from the brisk wash. He sat down at the table which she had laid with cutlery and covered dishes.

'What have we got?'

'The last of the cold mutton. Cucumber, bread and cheese.'

'Faith cooks a hot dinner for Matthew, I believe.'

'If hot dinners are what you require from a wife, you should have married Faith or somebody like her.'

He laughed again, delightedly. 'I prefer the wife I've got, even though she doesn't shine at housework.' He gestured with a buttery knife at the neglected kitchen.

Eliza pushed a jar of pickled onions at him. 'I am pleased to hear it.'

Devil looked at the newspaper while he ate, and Eliza stared dreamily into the garden. Ten minutes later he was ready to go back to work. She levered herself to her feet.

'You'll bring the bills and the books home for me?'

He kissed her again, quite thoroughly, before hurrying away. By the time he came back and climbed into bed with her, hot and tight as a coiled spring from the night's performance, she would already be asleep.

Carlo did not often travel outside his circuit where he was well enough known not to attract too many stares or rude comments. Today he had barely endured the smirks and coarse remarks of some boys sitting on the top of the omnibus. He had surprised them by flying down the steps and darting faster than they could follow through the crowds at the Angel. In Eliza's street two matrons were gossiping over shopping baskets and he tipped his hat to them with elaborate politeness. They stared as he walked up the steps to the front door.

He could not reach the brass knocker, so he banged with his fist instead.

Eliza opened the door.

'Carlo? What a surprise. I'm so pleased. Come inside.' She lowered her voice: 'Leave those old witches to gawp at someone else for a change.'

She led the way through a narrow hallway, somewhat dusty and cluttered, and down a short flight of stairs to a door standing open to the garden.

'Let's sit outside, shall we? It's so hot.'

There was a little tin table out here, in the shade of a robinia tree that drooped its bright leaves in the midday glare. Two chairs were set beside the table. Carlo envied Devil his domestic Sunday evenings, if they were spent sitting opposite Eliza in this pleasant spot.

'Would you like a cup of tea, or some lemonade? I can be quite housewifely, you know, when I want. It will only take a minute. I even have a young girl to help me, nowadays, although she has gone to run some errands this morning. Oh, dear, Carlo. Tell me, am I turning into my sister Faith?'

She was half laughing, but there was a real need for his reassurance.

'No, you are not,' Carlo said. 'Nor will you.'

Eliza went inside, and through an open window he heard the clinking of china and teaspoons. Soon she came back with a tray and a teapot.

'Let me carry that.' He jumped up but she was already setting out china cups patterned with garlands of forget-me-knots.

She held up one for his inspection. 'These were a wedding gift. A tea service! We have come up in the world, haven't we? Remember that first Christmas, in St Giles, when you nearly died?'

'I don't recall much of it. And I would rather forget even that.'

'Yes. It was Heinrich who saved you.'

She stood for a moment with the teacup poised in mid-air.

'How are you, Eliza?'

She was blooming in her floral dress and a wrap with a ribbon bow at her throat. She also looked a little older, with a touch of melancholy in her eyes. This and the lines around her mouth lent her the appearance of riper maturity, which suited her. Maybe that was what happened to women when they bred. Carlo had no expertise in these matters.

She handed him his cup of tea.

'I am very well, thank you.' She went on talking. 'I find this heat a trial, but in a few weeks it will be all fogs so I'm trying not to wish it away. And then, not very many more weeks after *that* I shall be back to my work. I miss the Palmyra a good deal. I am not really cut out to be a housewife, you know, although there are cosy moments.' Her eyes sparkled. 'Tell me some news?'

Carlo laughed, from deep in his chest, as he rarely did. He missed Eliza and he looked forward to her return as eagerly as she did herself.

'Let me think. Tilly Lacey moons about after Jakey. We see Jasper only when he must appear, but to my eye he is as happy as a dog with two tails.'

'Oh, *yes*. Hannah is a good girl. They are coming to eat their supper with us this Sunday.'

'Are they?'

Eliza saw his expression. 'Why don't you join us? Would you like to?'

'No. It will be too sweetly connubial for my taste.'

'Carlo . . .'

He waved his hand. 'This life's not for me, is it, the way I am? I'll never meet anyone small who could compare with our Sallie, anyroad. Enough of that. When do you, ah, expect?'

'In about a month's time. Devil hopes for a boy, of course.'

'Aye.'

'Would you like some more tea?'

She refilled his cup, and they gossiped about the theatre people until Eliza was satisfied that she had all the news.

'Talking to you is as good as to a woman, Carlo.'

'Am I to take that as a compliment?' He sat back, his fingers laced and his legs dangling. 'Now. We have to discuss Jerry Cockle.'

'Do we? Don't tell me he's making a play for Sylvia?'

'No. He has put forward an even less likely scheme.'

Eliza gave him her full attention, although Devil and she had already discussed the idea of street performances and the first notion of it had been hers, not Jerry Cockle's. The dwarf did not hold back.

At the end she asked, 'Is it shaming to do this? Is that your objection?'

He gave her a contemptuous look. 'Do you think I am not used to humiliation? Every day of my life?'

Eliza was the only person to whom he ever spoke honestly about his size. To the rest of the world, except occasionally to Jakey when they were afloat on a tide of drink, he presented his dwarfism as a talent that normal people were not privileged to share.

'No, Carlo. I know what you have to endure.'

'I will hold up my head anywhere. In your house, in the theatre, or on the horse bus to the Angel. I am an honourable man, regardless of my size.'

It was not a rebuke. Carlo was stating his case, as much for his own benefit as for hers.

'You are. And a loyal friend, also.'

Carlo struck his fist into his palm. 'And I am a performer. The best. I don't understand why your husband asks me to work for nothing in the common streets.'

'Doing what Jerry proposes will help us to sell more tickets.'

'How is that?' Carlo held up his hand. 'No, please don't try to explain. It will be all about teasing and suchlike. Why do you put faith in a man like Cockle, Eliza? Do you have to be modern?'

'There is no harm in modernity.'

He glared at her. He was angry, and she knew that his

383

opposition to their street scheme was only a mask for a much deeper and entirely ineradicable fury. Carlo inwardly raged at Devil because he was tall and handsome, and because he was married to her. Carlo loved her and she was no closer to knowing how to deal sympathetically with this than she had ever been.

Most damagingly of all, the dwarf raged against himself.

She reached across the little table and touched her hand to his.

It was pleasant in the garden. There were scented stocks planted in a little tub, and the companionable burring of doves sounded from a nearby loft. As Eliza withdrew her hand her wrap fell back from her wrist. Carlo watched these small movements and in spite of himself he found that he was soothed. Some of his dissatisfaction faded, to be replaced with a tired calm. His head grew heavy and for a moment he could almost have dozed. They sat quietly until Eliza finally stirred and smoothed the printed fabric of her wrap.

'Will you do this for me?' she murmured.

'Eh? For you, is it? You call in rent on a poor dwarf's devotion?'

He joked, but only in part and she answered with the same degree of lightness, 'Or for the Palmyra, if you prefer.'

'I would much rather for you, Eliza.'

'Thank you.'

'I will be the best Punch and Judy man in London.'

'I know that. Whatever you do, you will be the best.'

A little later Carlo took his leave.

'We don't want your husband to come home and find me here. What might he suspect?'

She begged him, 'You will think about what illusion will be suitable to perform, won't you?'

'I will. But Jeremiah Cockle can kiss my cooler.'

She stood in the doorway of her little house and watched him down the street.

*   *   *

384

Mr Edward Mathieson emerged from the banking house and surveyed St James's Square. At fifteen minutes before one o'clock he was on his way to luncheon at his club in Pall Mall. The bank's uniformed page, whose job it was to attend to the front doors, had already handed him his hat and cane.

The slanting angle of the sun held the first premonition of autumn. The leaves of the tall trees in the square were brown at the margins and the shrubs were laced with the webs of fat tortoiseshell spiders. An unexpected movement caused the banker to glance to his right and he became aware of a tableau framed by the arched gate that led into the square's garden.

A young woman in a white dress was posing for her portrait. The artist was intently working at his easel, darting backwards and then swooping in with his palette held at a theatrical angle. The banker could not see the picture in any detail, but a glimpse of the composition made him glance at the model once more. Her modest white dress was contradicted by a red scarf and bright red stockings, and by the way that her head was thrown back to offer up her bare throat. The recollection of one of Mr Whistler's *Arrangements* floated into the banker's mind, and at the same instant he realised that the artist looked passably like that painter himself. There was a self-portrait, he recalled, with a grey smock and a luxuriant moustache topped by a black velvet beret.

In any case it was a pretty spectacle and a knot of passers-by was gathering to look. The Mathieson and Company page peered out between the tall doors of the house.

A shrill whistle blast came as two figures burst out of the garden. One was a masked man carrying a sack over his shoulder and the other a police constable with his whistle clenched between his teeth. Mathieson blinked. This policeman was hardly more than three feet tall.

'Stop, thief!' cried the artist and the woman in white.

The onlookers gaped as the thief swung his sack off his shoulder, brought out a pot and hurled it at the policeman. It seemed that he missed his target, because a plume of thick black paint splashed all over the portrait. The painter responded with a cry of pure anguish. The policeman somersaulted after the thief, seized him by the ankles, and as he did so the sack fell open and a pair of white doves flew out. The artist shook out a black cloth and mournfully draped it over his ruined work as the doves dipped a sad salute overhead. The model held out her arms and the birds came to roost, one on each wrist.

The policeman snapped a pair of handcuffs on his prisoner. He marched him off the way they had come. The birds rose into the air again, flew in a circle, and followed captor and captive out of sight. Left behind, the artist despairingly hung his head and the woman in white took his hand. To watch them seemed an intrusion, and the little crowd awkwardly shifted.

The miniature policeman dashed back out of the garden. He paused in front of the easel and stared up at the portrait, his legs planted apart and his hands on his hips. There was a ripple of surprised laughter. More people were moving in from the four corners of the square.

'The nation is flingin' a pot of paint in the artist's face. That's the charge,' the officer cried. At the same moment he caught one corner of the black cloth and whisked it away.

The canvas was undamaged, just as it had been at the start. But there was one difference.

Edward Mathieson stared harder, before detouring across the road for a closer inspection.

The arms of the painted woman were now outstretched, and a dove was perched on each wrist.

The painter and his model embraced. The policeman marched across to a woman who had been watching the whole scene as it unfolded. She carried a wicker market pannier on her hip, which he now took from her.

He lifted the lid, and the doves flew out. The officer blew a long blast on his whistle.

'You, birds. The pair of you are under arrest.' The birds

386

homed obediently to him and he stowed them away in the front of his little tunic. As he marched away there was laughter and applause.

The artist and his subject held up the black cloth. The words embroidered in white and gold read simply:

THE PALMYRA THEATRE

The banker applauded. The artist swept him a bow and the model dipped into in a full curtsey. Mr Mathieson nodded and thoughtfully strolled away in the direction of Pall Mall.

As soon as he was out of sight Sylvia Aynscoe closed her wicker pannier, Tilly put on a cloak to save her white dress and Jakey folded the legs of his collapsible easel. Devil emerged from the garden from where he had stage-managed the illusion.

He called out to the audience, 'You've had a stroke of luck today, ladies and gentlemen. Tell your friends, won't you? And if you want to be further astounded and delighted, the Palmyra Theatre is ready to welcome you.'

The performers melted away. Their presence had enlivened the morning in St James's Square for no more than five or six minutes. Mr Mathieson's luncheon guest was waiting for him beneath the gloomy pictures in the drawing room of the club.

'My dear fellow. I am so sorry to keep you,' the banker said. 'I have just been watching a magical illusion performed in the street outside the bank. It was put on by a theatre company in which we happen to have a small investment.'

His companion laughed.

'I think that cannot be a coincidence.'

Eliza's pains began at midnight, a little under two weeks before the time she had been advised to expect her confinement. She lay in bed for an hour until it became too uncomfortable to keep still. Not wanting to wake Devil just yet she slipped out from under the covers and made her way slowly down the stairs. The treads creaked underfoot. Halfway down she had to stop and lean on the banister. In the kitchen she wrapped herself in a shawl and took the chair next to the range. Faith had warned her not to send for the midwife too early. With only the ticking of the long-case clock for company she prepared herself to wait. Nelly slept in the little semi-basement room that adjoined the front area. The servant had grown up in a big family and had a little experience of what occurred in childbirth.

'You know more than I do,' Eliza had laughed. She would call Nelly before troubling anyone else.

Another hour passed, the slow minutes measured out by the clock's ticking. As the fingers crept on towards four o'clock, a rectangle of grey light glimmered in the window overlooking the garden. As the first notes of birdsong sounded Eliza could not help opening her mouth on a low moan. She waited again until the pain released her and she was able to creep to Nelly's door.

'Missis! What are you about, down here? You should be in your bed.' The little servant's eyes were heavy with sleep. 'Come on, now. Let us walk you back up the stairs.'

They climbed slowly. Eliza grunted with each step. She began to feel that her body slipped the constraints of her will and took itself off to a place beyond her control. Devil appeared in the doorway naked to the waist, and Nelly stared before turning her head aside.

He called, 'What's this? Eliza?'

'The baby is coming.'

'Missis needs to lie down.'

They put her in the bed. Sweat glued her hair to her face and she tried to claw it from her mouth and eyes. Nelly wiped her lips with a folded cloth.

'I'll get the woman to come, shall I?' Devil asked, meaning the midwife. He put on his shirt and loomed over her as he did up the buttons. Apprehension showed in his face. He was not confident in this arena, and he needed Eliza's guidance even though she looked to him for comfort. But what man, other than a doctor, would be at home at this moment? Even Matthew

Shaw had gone out of the house, leaving the work to the women.

'Not yet.'

She knew instinctively that she would have to bear this for hours.

'I will be downstairs,' Devil said.

Nelly did her best to make Eliza comfortable. For a while she managed better, thinking of the pains as a series of obstacles to be climbed, each one bringing her closer to her baby. But the intervals between them grew shorter, and the pains more racking. Nelly tried to rub her back. Eliza heard herself screaming from a distance as the pains wrung her body.

'I will do it,' she gasped when the turmoil allowed her. Faith had been through this three times over. Even their stepmother had done it. Why had nobody warned her this was how it would be?

'I'll send Mr Wix with the message now,' Nelly said. 'And your sister should come too.'

Eliza heard the front door slam as Devil left the house to fetch the midwife. She wanted to go away herself. If only she could escape from here. She longed to slide into the lost reverie. Dipping beneath the waves, into the cool blues of the sea picture. Peace.

There was no choosing now. The reveries would never come back. Loss and panic made her rear up in a sweat-soaked coil of bedclothes. She fell back on to all fours and screamed again. The sun beamed through the window as if there was nothing amiss.

'There now', said the midwife as Nelly hurried her into the room. 'I could hear you from down the street. Let's have you lying down.'

The woman lowered the blind and rolled up her sleeves. When she had finished the examination she covered Eliza up. Through pursed lips she said, 'I'm sending for the doctor.'

Time had become a long chasm of agony. When the doctor at last appeared Eliza caught sight of Devil behind his shoulder.

She didn't want her husband to witness any of this, nor any of what was to come.

'Faith is on her way,' he promised. He was clearly shocked at what he saw.

'*Leave me*,' Eliza howled.

The doctor did what he had to and the pain only intensified. It had become a battle that no part of her anatomy could hope to win. She wanted nothing but to die, because that was the only way the agony would end.

The man snapped open a black case with the silvery sections of an instrument nested in velvet within it. She caught only a glimpse but it was too much like the interior of Lucie's trunk. She screamed hoarsely as vivid memory fragments from that night slid out of a dark place and coalesced with the present ordeal.

'I'm here to deliver you, Mrs Wix. Don't make it difficult for us.'

The doctor was fitting together the pieces of a surgical implement. Inside her head she could hear the whirring of Heinrich's terrible influence machine. She writhed in her efforts to escape until the midwife placed a bolster to block her view.

'We're going to help your baby out, dear.'

The pain had been bad before, but compared with what followed as the doctor inserted and engaged the forceps she had felt nothing at all. There was one more scream before a curt order from the doctor brought the midwife with a rubber mask to press over Eliza's mouth and nose.

A sweet, rotting smell. Familiar.

Heinrich.

When she opened her eyes Eliza saw her sister's face.

Terrible chloroform dreams had barely released her, but she found she was not after all trapped in the workshop with the dismembered dolls. She was at home in her own bed. Relief shivered through her.

Faith's hand held hers. Eliza clasped it.

'The baby?'

'He is alive. A big boy. The cord was twisted about his neck and at first he did not breathe. But your doctor brought him back.'

'Devil?'

'Downstairs.'

'Give the baby to me.'

'Eliza, you have lost blood, the doctor said you must lie completely still until he comes back.'

'Give him to me.'

Faith knew the strength of her sister's will. She lifted a motionless bundle from the crib and laid the baby in Eliza's arms. Eliza turned back the shawl. The face revealed was distorted, and at the left temple there was a gash with a bruise swelling beneath the translucent skin. The infant opened his black eyes and looked into hers.

From somewhere within herself – a deep place unaffected by her swollen tongue and cracked lips, even by the battleground her body had become – a smile flowered.

They named the child Cornelius Hector.

Neither Devil nor Eliza was much concerned about such things, but Faith and Matthew Shaw sent for the parish priest from St Mary's church to baptise the infant. The Shaws stood as godparents. Devil huddled in his shirtsleeves beside the kitchen range, unable or unwilling to acknowledge that his son might not survive the day and that Eliza was close to death. Faith had to tell him to put on his coat like a Christian and lift up the child to be blessed.

'If I must,' he muttered.

The rector dipped his thumb in holy water and sketched a cross on the baby's bruised forehead. Faith and Matthew bent their heads for the prayer but Devil stared straight ahead as if he could keep his family alive by the intensity of his concentration alone.

After the baptism Cornelius was placed beside his mother.

The linen had been changed and the floor washed but the room was still rank with the smell of blood.

'Can you try to nurse him?' Faith whispered.

Eliza attempted to do so, but the baby was too weak.

'Then just rest.'

Faith drew the bedroom curtains against the twilight and Nelly brought up a cup of broth. Faith fed her sister spoonful by spoonful until Eliza begged her to go home to her own children. Devil took her place in the chair beside the bed. Eliza and he held hands, staring at each other as they tried to fathom the differences the day had wrought. The versions of themselves that had woken up in the dawn were gone beyond recovery, and they were not yet acquainted with the new individuals.

After a while the baby stirred, and with a sound that was more a gasp than a cry reminded them that they were no longer two.

'My poor boy,' Devil muttered.

Eliza clawed his hand.

'He will live. He *will*.'

She was haggard but her eyes burned. His wife was strong in a new way that Devil didn't recognise, perhaps because it was a new strength that had only been born with the baby. He could think of nothing hopeful to say. To cover this lack of fluency he kissed her hand.

'He will live,' she repeated.

He wished Faith had stayed.

'You should sleep.'

She only shook her head and worked her hand free in order to touch one finger to the baby's cheek. Although the women had washed him a crust of dried blood still clung behind his ear.

In the end it was Devil who slept, on a blanket and a pillow on the floor. He was reminded of the days of Carlo's illness, the first time Eliza had revealed her strength. Briefly and point-lessly he craved a return to those earlier times. He closed his eyes.

It was a long time since he had seen Gabe – Eliza had changed that for him, too – but tonight the old images rose up at once. He pressed his fingers against his eyelids to rub them away.

When he woke again it was some time in the unmarked middle of the night. Eliza was lying against her pillows with the child in her arms. A strange little smile pulled at her mouth.

'Look. He is nursing.'

In the morning mother and child were fast asleep. The shawls had fallen back from the baby's head, uncovering the huge swelling between the soft plates of the skull where the instrument of delivery had applied force. Devil hastily replaced the knitted folds to hide the damage.

He went downstairs and told Nelly to make breakfast.

It was a bright day, with business going on outside the house. It was important to look beyond the present moment.

My theatre, he thought. The new season was upon them; there was Jerry Cockle's street illusion to manage. The theatre was the machine it had always been, yesterday and the day before, and he was necessary there.

The servant gaped at him, her eyes popping with anxiety.

'How is missis? And the little one?'

'They are both sleeping. You should send for the nurse.'

They had not done so yesterday because they had not believed this baby would linger.

Nelly's face flooded with hope.

'Oh, yes. I'll do that. Right away, I will. The boy can run there in a tick.'

The boy was the son of a laundry woman who lived a little further down the street.

Devil said brusquely, 'I must go to the theatre shortly. I'll send word to Mrs Shaw as well, I'm sure she will come in and sit with her sister for an hour or two.'

Nelly bobbed her head. 'Yes, sir.' She went scurrying up the stairs, ignoring Devil's demand for breakfast.

SEVENTEEN

Against all the expectations except Eliza's, Cornelius did begin to thrive.

A week after the baby's birth Carlo was the first of Eliza's visitors outside her immediate family. He brought her a bunch of cornflowers, brilliant and yet with the dust of summer meadows still on them. She exclaimed in pleasure, glancing towards the window and the pulse of sunlight beyond it as if only now recalling that the wider world did exist.

'Let me see your boy,' Carlo said.

She lifted the baby in his shawl and bonnet, wincing at the dart of pain the small movement gave her.

Carlo saw a moon face, swollen eyelids edged with crescents of dark lashes, loosely parted lips and a silver trail of spittle. The baby seemed troublingly inert until a tiny snore bubbled from his mouth.

'I can see no resemblance to either of you. You are fortunate he doesn't favour his father.'

He had been shocked by Eliza's altered appearance but he glanced casually from her face to the baby's as if there were nothing to remark upon.

'My sister says that neither Rowland nor Edwin looked like any human creature. Now of course they are perfect miniatures

394

of their father. And they are agreed that little Lizzie most resembles me.'

'The child is fortunate indeed.'

She smiled at having squeezed a compliment out of him. Carlo was relieved to catch a glimpse of the old Eliza.

'How do you get on with motherhood?'

'It was hard at first. He was so sickly, and I was very weak. But we shall do well from now on, I'm certain of it.'

Her determination at home was a match for Devil's at the theatre. It gave Carlo no pleasure to acknowledge it but they were well paired.

'And how does the proud father respond?'

Eliza smiled again but the glimmer of brightness faded. She began, 'I believe he feels displaced. My husband does not like to come second to anyone, even his own son.'

There was a tiny room on the same landing as their bedroom, dusty and cluttered with boxes. After the first night Devil retired there because Eliza's hours of waking and sleeping were the same as the child's, broken up into brief intervals when they both dozed and long hours when she held him at her breast. Lying alone after so long, Devil found that he was stricken by the loss of his wife's warmth next to him. He was troubled by visions of dying Gabe, after years when he had believed himself free of them. There were new horrors too, in which Eliza bled to death or succumbed to maternal fever. He began to understand that he would not readily survive without her.

But he could admit none of this weakness to his wife, and so took refuge in masculine carping. He remarked on the discomfort of the sleeping arrangements and mentioned that the general lack of domestic order was becoming increasingly apparent in the rest of the house.

Eliza only frowned and murmured, 'Be patient. We'll be strong soon, won't we?'

She spoke to the infant in her arms, not to him.

When he was not at the theatre Devil sat with his wife and child, although in these intervals he felt edged out by the presence of the businesslike nurse, by Faith, even by Nelly. The damage the birth intervention had inflicted on Eliza's body was hidden from him. The carriage of towels and enamel bowls of water, taken into the room clean and brought out rusty, was discreetly performed by the nurse and Faith. At these moments murmurs were audible behind the closed door of the bedroom, but he was not invited to share their import. The secrecy meant that his speculations tended to the worst. The doctor told him briskly that he would have to allow his wife time to recover from her difficult confinement. To contain his anxieties Devil threw himself more than ever into business at the theatre.

Eliza's attention was centred on Cornelius, and to a lesser extent on her physical ills, and she did not properly follow any of this. All she knew was that she needed reassurance from her husband, and a form of understanding that he did not seem able to provide.

Carlo studied her intently, then said with a touch of sourness, 'I can assure you that Wix does not suffer any displacement at our place of work. He is here, there, in every corner, popping out of trapdoors, waving his arms, giving orders, changing what doesn't need changing, dreaming up more plans, generally imposing his infernal will. For the rest of us it is like being driven through a thunderstorm in a coach and four by a mad coachman on an unmade road.'

He placed the baby in his crib so as to be able to mime this freely and Eliza gave a gasp of unwilling laughter before she doubled up over the pain. Carlo was the last person in whom to confide her fear that her husband might be slipping away from her at a time when they might have hoped to be closer than ever before.

Carlo added, 'Jeremiah Cockle is up there on the box beside him, urging him on to further insanity.'

'I can imagine. Tell me how everyone does?'

'Every soul in the place sends you their warmest wishes. Sylvia Aynscoe would like to call on you. I made it clear to her that *I* was to be the first visitor.'

'Tell her I would love to see her.'

'She has made the boy an entire wardrobe – no, what is her word? – a *layette* of miniature garments. Jasper would also like to call, of course.'

Eliza was pleased. It was several seconds before her eyes were drawn to the crib and she motioned for Carlo to hand her the baby.

When Devil came home she told him, 'I was so happy to see Carlo. He made me laugh.'

'I only wish I could do the same. But I'm glad to hear it.'

Encouraged, he leaned over to kiss the knob of bone at the nape of her neck, unwillingly breathing the sour smell of the baby on her. She tensed and drew up the sheet and this tiny, involuntary recoil made him feel like an instrument of damage. She laughed to cover the awkward moment.

'Carlo said you are driving them all like a mad coachman in a thunderstorm. With Jerry on the box beside you.'

'Did he indeed? I thought you favoured Jerry's ideas.'

'I do. But you will be tactful in how you put them into place, won't you? The others have a say in these matters.'

Devil did not welcome the reminder. He stood up so abruptly that the chair rocked.

'What has Nelly got for dinner?'

The Palmyra company continued to play the street illusion. Devil was in a frenzy of enthusiasm for it, as if determined to promote Eliza's protégé in her absence.

They went out to the Burlington Arcade, where the release of the doves was greeted with the patter of gloved hands and a flutter of parasol ribbons. At the Round Pond in Kensington Gardens they delighted a huge circle of children and nursemaids with perambulators. They went on to the City, to the steps of the Mansion House itself. As Jerry Cockle had promised, photographers came to record these scenes, and reporters jotted descriptions in their shorthand notebooks. Stories and pictures duly appeared in the daily newspapers, and there was further pictorial coverage both in popular magazines and in their society counterparts.

One photograph was of an unnamed small boy, a handsome little fellow in a sailor-collared coat, whose gaze followed the ascent of two white doves from a wicker pannier. His eyes and mouth made three round Os of delight and amazement as he pointed a chubby finger into the sky. With Jerry Cockle as the intermediary, the photographer sold Devil the rights for the unlimited use of this image. At Jerry's further suggestion the picture was printed on postcards and greetings cards under the title *Innocent Pleasures*, with the name of the theatre and the palm tree prominent beneath it. Thousands of these cards were bought and posted and in time the *Palmyra Pleasures* image became almost as famous as Mr Millais's *Bubbles*.

Following the run of press interest there was a brief vogue for betting on where the Palmyra theatre's celebrated illusion would next be performed. After a teasing delay and just one more outing – to Belgrave Square, at which they were almost mobbed – Jerry Cockle announced that the job was done.

'So much work, for a mere handful of performances?' Carlo complained, contrary as ever.

'Keep 'em hungry,' Jerry replied.

'They'll come to the theatre and pay for their seats now,' Devil predicted.

The new show opened and the audiences flocked. The street performances had had the desired effect and Devil and Jerry Cockle were vindicated.

That was when they began to make real money.

Devil rubbed his hands in triumph.

A month after Cornelius's birth the plates of his downy head took on a more normal alignment as the hideous swelling subsided. The bruises faded and the crimson scar on his temple from the forceps cut was the only remaining sign of his birth trauma. He was sleeping for longer intervals, although even now these respites rarely extended beyond an hour or two. He fed with more gusto and he gained weight, seemingly in proportion to his mother's diminishment. The bones stood out beneath Eliza's skin and her wrists appeared fragile enough to snap, but neither this nor the lack of sleep troubled her so long as Cornelius flourished. Faith assured her that the boy would learn to sleep in good time, and that Eliza would quickly regain her full strength and health if she would only consent to employ a wet nurse. Eliza refused even to consider the idea.

The women's real anxiety was over Cornelius's crying. He could scream sometimes for hours at a time, his tiny knees drawn up to his chest and his face red and contorted. There was no pacifying him. The screams would continue until he cried himself into an exhausted sleep.

'Did your babies upset themselves so?' Eliza asked.

Faith shook her head.

The doctor said the infant suffered from colic. He prescribed a tincture, and whenever they fed this to Cornelius he fell into a heavy sleep. On waking he would appear dazed and listless. Eliza refused to give him the medicine unless there seemed to be no other option.

It was six full weeks after the birth before she put on her hat and ventured out into the street. Turning up her face to the blessing of thin October sunshine made her feel so much better that within days she was walking to the market, leaving Cornelius with his nursemaid for half an hour at a time. The stallholders hailed her, and she was glad to see so many different faces. As if fresh air and a little personal freedom was all she had needed, her body began to repair itself. Slowly, steadily, the world expanded until it almost regained its old dimensions.

In November Eliza told Devil that she was ready to think about doing some work. In fact she was longing to be back in the thick of the Palmyra, but at the same time she could not bring herself to leave the baby for longer than an hour. Devil agreed to bring home the theatre's books and accounts for her to look through, and the next evening he returned after the performance with a bulging leather satchel. She swept aside the crumbs of their earlier dinner and tipped the sheaves of bills and receipts on to the kitchen table. Devil placed the big accounts ledgers beside them and she began to go through the figures.

'Jasper would gladly do that,' he said.

'I know. He told me as much himself. But it is my job.'

Eliza was astonished to note how much money was coming in.

She sat for over an hour, scanning and totalling, until Cornelius woke and began to cry. Devil was sitting beside the range, reading the reviews in the theatrical papers. The daily nursemaid they employed for Cornelius had gone home hours ago and it was Nelly's evening off.

She said to him, 'I am busy. Won't you go and attend to your son?'

'Me?' His astonishment was genuine, and this nettled her.

'Who else?'

He got to his feet, hesitated, then laid his hand on her shoulder. She was conscious of the newly sharp bones that met his touch, and the way her bodice strained across her heavy breasts. She felt angry as well as ugly, but even so a hot and surprising surge of longing for her husband swept over her. She reached up and caught his arm. Devil had returned to his wife's bed, although not yet to her body. Since the birth of the child they had barely even embraced. Her body had felt too torn and painful, and in this ruined state she could not think of yielding any piece of it to him.

'Eliza?' he eagerly whispered.

'Yes.' She began, 'Devil, I'm sorry, I have been . . .'

Cornelius screamed. If he were left he would work himself into such a state of shuddering anguish that she feared for his life. Eliza twisted in her husband's arms and slid away.

'I'll go to him.'

Devil gave her his blackest glare. 'We need another servant. You need more help.'

'And where would we put this extra help?'

400

The upstairs box room had been made into Cornelius's nursery. Nelly's cubbyhole was tiny. The Wixes lived in their kitchen, the chilly parlour above it was for occasional use, and the house felt uncomfortably cramped.

He shrugged as if it meant nothing. 'In a bigger place, of course.'

The table was between them, piled with accounts ledgers and sheaves of bills and receipts. Devil tapped the black cover of one of the ledgers.

'We are not paupers,' he said. 'We will buy a house.'

By the beginning of December demand grew for tickets to shows that had long ago sold out, so Devil decided that in addition to the regular Saturday matinees there should also be performances at five o'clock on Wednesdays and Fridays. These extra tickets also sold out almost as soon as they went on sale. A visit to the Palymra, the home of magic and illusion, had become a seasonal treat. At last, they were attracting the right audiences in the proper numbers. Jerry Cockle – who took the view that this success was due entirely to his marketing expertise – was smug. Devil was all smiles as he hurried between the backstage warren and the golden front-of-house. He was working up some new front-of-curtain magic to fill an interval of scene shifting between two bigger illusions, and he was engrossed in teaching Tilly Lacey to play his assistant. Carlo complained that close work was his province, and did Devil plan to take over the world?

'Not immediately,' Devil smirked.

The work of the extra performances took its toll, however. Sylvia developed a persistent cough and Carlo had pains in his back and joints that made his temper worse than ever. The senior Crabbe was heard to complain that he was too old to be scrambling along the gantries high over the stage.

Learning all this at second hand, Eliza grew even more conscious of how long she had been absent from the theatre. Tilly and Sylvia in particular were shouldering tasks that were rightly hers. Cornelius was not a placid infant but he no longer seemed under daily threat. His nursemaid and Nelly were devoted to him and the notion of abandoning him for an evening, even for as much as half a day at a time, no longer seemed impossible. Furthermore, to leave Cornelius would be to partly reclaim the life she had loved and shared with Devil. They would be reunited by the urgent demands of the day's decisions and the night's performance.

'Do you not think I should return properly to the theatre, as we are so busy?' she said to him. 'I don't mean to my stage roles, not yet at least, but to backstage work?'

Devil looked into his wife's intent, eager face.

Eliza was the mother of his son and the mainstay of his home. He had been obliged to accept the changes in her after she had given birth, as he supposed all husbands must. He discovered that he liked going out to his work and coming home to find his wife ensconced at his table amidst an approximation of domestic order, and he believed that he was entitled to this. He also very much liked instructing Tilly Lacey in the principles of stage magic. She listened to him with shining eyes, her lips parted in awe, and he was flattered to have a woman's full attention. This was not regularly offered to him in Islington. It was also a fact that in the confined spaces of the box tricks he appreciated Tilly's firm waist and sweet-scented skin.

'Well?' Eliza said.

Devil acknowledged to himself that he had married Eliza for her spirit, not for her housekeeping. She was not meek with a seam of resentment, like Faith, nor – thank God – was she a pretty, empty chit like Tilly Lacey.

He kissed her. 'Yes. I think you should come back,' he said.

Eliza left Cornelius under the care of the nursemaid and Nelly. She went down to the Strand and was as amazed as any country girl at the colourful lights, the vivid shop windows with their Christmas displays, and the throngs of people. The minute she stepped through the stage door the old smell engulfed her, and with it the nervous excitement of the earliest days of her theatrical infatuation. In the dressing room she found Tilly in a new Charlotte costume and Sylvia kneeling with her pincushion on her wrist. The seamstress struggled to her feet as soon as she saw Eliza.

'I am so happy to see you, dear. Your eyes are bright as stars.'

She did not mention how gaunt her friend had become, or remark on the hollows in her cheeks. Tilly demurely smiled from beneath the brim of Charlotte's bonnet.

Devil was in the office. He looked up from envelopes and piles of coin.

'I am just making up the wages.'

'I can do that for you.'

'Thank you.' He absently kissed her before dashing away.

Sitting beneath the niche that had once housed Mr Wu she made up the pay packets and wrote the entries in the current ledger. The bustle of preparation for curtain-up continued and the noisy flurry of it was exhilarating after her weeks of incarceration. When she was done she sent the new backstage messenger, a boy the same age as Jakey had been in the days of Jacko Grady, to put out the pay call. The players and stagehands filed in and she shook a series of hands – some paint-stained, some in costume, some unfamiliar because they belonged to guest performers she had not met before this evening.

'Evening, Mrs Wix.'

'Welcome back, missis. How's the littl'un doing?'

Devil looked in just before he went onstage. He was sharing the master of ceremonies role with Jasper, and tonight was Devil's turn. He looked startlingly handsome in his white tie and waistcoat. Eliza was putting on her coat but her fingers suddenly seemed to lose their efficiency around the buttons.

'You are not staying for the show?'

'I am going home to our son.'

The messenger passed the open door, ringing his bell for the five-minute call.

She called to her husband as he turned to go, 'Don't be late. I will wait up for you and we can drink a nightcap together.'

Eliza was still thinking about this as she reached home and put her key in the lock. Nelly came running down the stairs to meet her.

'Oh, Mrs Wix.'

'What is it? What has happened?'

Looking to the head of the stairs she saw the nursemaid's frightened face.

'It's the baby, mum. He took a fit.'

Cornelius lay in his crib. He was limp and his skin was a strange colour but he was awake, and he whimpered as soon as he saw her. Eliza gathered him up. The nursemaid tearfully explained that an hour ago he had cried a little, she had gone to him at once and found him in a convulsion.

'He cried just a little? You did not leave him screaming?'

'Yes, ma'am. Not at all.'

Her son turned his head to her breast. Eliza took him into her bed, and she was cradling him there when Devil came home.

She tried not to weep but tears squeezed out beneath her eyelids.

'I should not have gone out and left him.'

Devil rested his head in his hands. 'Eliza, however much you wish it, you cannot watch him for every hour of every single day for the rest of his life.'

Her heart almost stalled. Devil was telling her that whatever it was that ailed their child she could not make it well for him. She must somehow find a way to absorb this unknown into her life, and yet not make it her life. She thought of the memorial tablet to another child, in the graveyard at Stanmore, and bowed her head. This boy at least would not lack for love, and while she lived he would never be abandoned.

The architecture of the life she had planned silently crumbled.

'Come, Con, my son.' Devil lifted the infant out of his mother's arms and laid him in his crib in the next room.

Eliza watched her husband strip off his shirt and undershirt.

'Shall I put out the lamp?' he asked.

She wanted to connect with him, but her damaged flesh inhibited her.

She whispered, 'No. I like to look at you.'

Immediately his hands were on her. She shivered in a place between fear for Cornelius and dread of the future, between physical discomfort and love for her husband, and a renewed desire for the intimacy of body and mind that they had once shared.

Feeling her tremors he whispered, 'Do you fear me?'

'No.'

His hands explored her. She spread her knees and tried not to stiffen or to shudder in anticipation of the pain. He was heavy on top of her. If he felt the difference, if he noticed how her intimate flesh had torn and the muscles had given way before knitting themselves only imperfectly, he was ardent enough not to show it. Eliza bit the inside of her mouth. It will be easier next time, she promised herself.

It was Christmas. They celebrated the best autumn season the theatre had ever had. For Devil and Jasper and Carlo the satisfaction increased when they heard that Haggerston Hall was to be closed down. There had been complaints from members of the audience that they had been duped, and claims by mediums that they had called up the spirits but Jacko Grady had never paid them for their trouble.

'Are there no debt collectors in the spirit world?' Devil crowed.

On Christmas Eve, after the curtain came down on the evening performance, Jasper announced that he had a personal cause for celebration. Miss Hannah Dooley, the flaxen-haired daughter of the coffee-shop owner, had that afternoon consented to be his wife.

Eliza kissed him in high delight.

'Joy to you both, Jasper.'

He looked down into her eyes. He was meaning to say more, but her expression warned him not to reiterate his old feelings. With proper restraint he murmured, 'Thank you. I am a lucky man.'

'Hannah will be a good wife to you.' *As I could never have been*, she added silently.

Devil was in exuberant spirits. He seized Eliza by the waist and waltzed her out on to the empty stage. Because of Cornelius's fit she had not attempted to reclaim even the most insignificant of her roles from Tilly Lacey and now she found herself blinking at the silent rows of empty seats and the yawning shell of the cupola overhead.

'I have a Christmas gift for you.'

Puzzled, she replied, 'I have gifts for you too. Won't we open them tomorrow, at home?'

'I can't wait until tomorrow.'

He made an elaborate pass in the air, and held out his clenched fist. Obediently she tapped the knuckle to make him open his palm.

A large key lay there.

'What is this?'

'A key, darling Eliza.'

His delight was so evident she could not help but laugh with him.

'A key to what, may I ask?'

'A house. Rather a *fine* house.'

'And to whom does this fine house belong?'

'It belongs, as of today, to Mr and Mrs Devil Wix.'

Eliza gasped. It was so like him. He was magnanimous and grandiloquent, and he imposed such control over their affairs that he did not even consult her in the matter of her own home.

On Christmas morning they walked out amongst the other families. They were to go later to Faith and Matthew to eat their Christmas dinner, but this morning was their own. Devil enjoyed strolling out amongst the respectable churchgoers with his wife on his arm and his son under layers of covers in the Shaws' loaned perambulator.

The child had had another fit, this time whilst Eliza was with him. The rigid arch of his spine and jerking of his tiny limbs had terrified her, but it had passed like the first, without apparent ill effects. In a way it was reassuring that the first had not after all been brought on in her absence by some neglect on the part of the nursemaid. The doctor explained that her child was suffering infantile convulsions, and that his susceptibility to these attacks would probably pass in time. Devil and Eliza were learning to accept that Cornelius was not like other children but for now, in his own way, he was well enough.

Most of the people out in the chill air were bound for St Mary's in Upper Street, or for the Union Chapel. Fog damped the Christmas bells and smothered the ends of the street under a pale blanket. The Wixes walked in the opposite direction, to the place where the canal emerged from a tunnel beneath the hill. They paused for a moment to look over the brick parapet into the steel-grey ribbon of water. This channel was usually crowded with cargo barges but today most of the water traffic was stilled to allow the bargemen their holiday. Some of the craft were moored in a broad basin further ahead, from where wood smoke added to the general murk and the smell of fried fish rose into the air. The patient heads of the barge horses were just visible above the half-doors of a low brick-and-thatch stable.

Facing the canal cutting across a quiet road was a row of tall terraced houses. Devil stopped at the steps of the middle house. It was a handsome established residence, built in the second decade of the century. He took the big key out of his pocket.

Eliza was gazing up at the windows. On the raised ground floor there was a pretty balcony of wrought iron.

'This is *ours*?'

'It is. Merry Christmas.'

She gasped. 'How in the name of heaven did you find the money for it? How much did it cost?'

'Don't be a shrew. I wanted to give you a surprise. I know your passion for figures and accounts, my dear, and in due course I will show you how the purchase has been managed. I promise we will not end up in the workhouse, but just for today will you not take pleasure with me in our new home?'

Shamed by her seeming lack of grace she turned up her face and kissed him hard on the lips.

'Yes, I will.'

He ran up the steps to the front door and made a show of unlocking it. Eliza turned the perambulator at the foot of the steps but she did not have a chance to pick up the baby before Devil ran down and scooped her into his arms. He carried her up and over the threshold, twirling her around to demonstrate the breadth of the hallway before setting her down with such vigour and in such a tangle of skirts that she almost overbalanced. They rocked in each other's embrace, laughing and glowing from the cold.

'Welcome home,' Devil murmured.

She looked about her, feeling faintly awed. 'It is beautiful.'

There were three floors above the street, with windows front and back looking on to the canal or to gardens, all with a pleasing airiness and abundance of light. Even below stairs the kitchen and scullery and servant's room were well proportioned. At the top of the house was a little attic room, with a tiny grate under a wooden mantel. Eliza said that it would be perfect for a nursemaid.

All will be well in this house, she told herself.

Her anxieties about Cornelius, her frustration at wanting to work and being prevented from doing so by motherhood, her loss of beloved independence, even the growing fear that Devil and she no longer loved each other in quite the old way, all these fell away and she felt light-headed with happiness.

She carried the baby in her arms as they went through every room. Cornelius looked on equably, without a wail, as if to acknowledge that he would be at home here.

They agreed that the house needed some modern improvements, hot water and electric lighting to the upper storeys and
linoleum for the floors, but all of these could be introduced in
time and without any need to apply to a landlord. They would
need a cleaning woman to help Nelly with the heavy work of
cleaning grates and scrubbing floors, but that they could also
manage.

Finally they stood by the window at the rear of the double
drawing room. There was wainscot panelling in both halves of
the room, and this as well as the doors was painted a forbidding ox-blood red. Eliza looked into the garden where evergreen
leaves of laurel and bay dripped with moisture and back into
the room again.

'Light colours,' she murmured.

She was envisaging the garden full of flowers, and the rooms
done up in cream and pearl to reflect fingers of light reaching
in from outside.

'That is your area, Eliza.'

'No, please. We should do all of it together, the decoration
of the rooms and the management of the accounts, the theatre
and raising our children, and we should never say to each other,
"This is mine and this is yours."'

His black brows rose into peaks. 'Our children? Eliza, is
there something you have not told me?'

She blushed and laughed.

'No.'

In truth this would be an unlikely eventuality. She tried to
pretend that it did not, but to be a wife in the way that Devil
needed still caused her physical pain.

'I thought not.'

'But some day . . .'

'Give Con to me.'

Devil took the baby and paced the length of the room. He
swung back to face her and the child's head wobbled because
he did not support it.

'Be careful.'

'You know, there is one thing I should very much like, if you will agree.'

'What is that?'

'Jasper has been the best of friends to me. Now that we have this house, I think it would be a fine gesture if we gave him and Hannah their wedding party.'

Eliza did not hesitate for one second. 'That is a wonderful idea.'

He caught her hand.

'Good,' Devil said. 'I will put the notion to Jasper.'

Jasper was touched by the offer and gratefully accepted. Eliza and Devil moved into their new home and Eliza immediately threw all her formidable energy into restoring the house and planning the party. There was a scraping and lime-washing and wallpapering almost on a par with the works at the Palmyra, and the house readily emerged from its shroud of dark red and dirty brown into a state of elegant pallor. Devil gave her a free rein in the matter of expense, and although she tried to persuade him, he did not involve himself any more directly in the renovations. He had plenty of other matters to concern him, he told her.

Spring came, and the wedding day itself on a green May morning.

Jasper and Hannah Button came straight from the church, leading their small procession of Jasper's two sisters, Hannah's mother, and her uncle who had given her away. Sammy Hill had that morning built a special bower in the Wixes' garden and Eliza and Faith had fixed to it branches of cherry blossom and sheaves of greenery. The bride and groom posed arm in arm under the arch and the commemorative photograph was taken by one of Jerry Cockle's talkative associates.

Eliza looked on.

She was happy that Jasper was married at last, that the threatened rain had held off for the photographer, and that although her home of just five months was unfinished it was welcoming enough for the guests who were now strewing flower petals over the newlyweds. Yet she could not shake off a sense of heavy disquiet. She had woken that morning with a sense of foreboding and it had been closing in on her ever since.

She looked to where Carlo was standing with his arms folded across his chest. The dwarf had been in a bad mood for many weeks now. He complained that the burden of devising and working up ever more ambitious new illusions fell to him because Devil was too busy borrowing money and manipulating the theatre accounts.

'There is no manipulation. I see all the books,' Eliza protested.

She was uneasily aware that their loans were high in proportion to their revenues. When she asked about it Devil only replied that new acts and the lavish staging to frame them was their business, and why would they be content to rely on old material?

As soon as she reached Carlo's side Eliza realised the dwarf was drunk. They were all aware that he drank even more heavily these days. He claimed that it dulled the constant pain he suffered. His small body took a heavy dose of punishment. Audiences favoured spectacular escape tricks involving locked trunks, handcuffs and chains, suspension from a height above the stage or immersion in tanks of water, and most of these effects depended on Carlo's miniature size and extreme suppleness.

She chose a neutral remark. 'This is a happy day.'

Carlo eyed the line of guests as they paraded after the Buttons and Devil. Jasper's sisters Sophy and Sarah, on an unprecedented excursion to London, gazed about them with shy curiosity.

'Aye.'

The outline of the bottle was conspicuous in his pocket.

'Carlo, would you be kind enough to look after the Misses Button for me? They know no one here.'

'Whatever you wish, Eliza. I shall make sure they receive their cold cuts and fruit cup. It will be their first experience of a dwarf attendant, most likely.'

411

She touched his shoulder. 'You know, I wonder if sometimes you make too much of your stature? Perhaps you might think of yourself as a human creature first, and a dwarf second?'

'I take the world as it takes me.'

He glared at her with yellow eyes before he marched away and planted himself in front of a startled Sarah Button. The girl looked anxiously for her sister's support.

The exchange with Carlo only increased Eliza's unease. She went to look for Jakey, thinking he would be a better protector for Jasper's sisters. Locating Tilly Lacey would once have been a guarantee of finding Jakey, but today the actress was loudly laughing in the window overlooking the garden and Jakey was nowhere to be seen. Eliza eventually discovered him at the foot of the kitchen stairs. His sideways slump against the newel post indicated that he had also been drinking, probably with Carlo. He made an effort to straighten up as Eliza approached.

'This is a very shplendid house, Mrs Wix.'

She knew that Jakey no longer lived in the decay-ripe room overlooking the Market, but she was not sure where he had moved.

'Shplendid,' he repeated. He sounded exactly like one of the young bloods at the stage door who begged Tilly Lacey or one of the acrobats to accompany them to a supper club. Jakey's social agility impressed her, as it always did. This afternoon, however, there was a dull blush on his high cheekbones and his almond-shaped eyes were over-bright. He was avoiding her gaze.

'Is all well with you, Jakey?'

'Yes, ma'am.' Still he did not meet her eye. There was something wrong, over and above the gin, but she could not fathom what it might be.

'I was wondering if you might rescue Jasper's sisters from Carlo. But perhaps not.'

She did not attempt to put warmth into her voice and Jakey's flush deepened.

'Yes, ma'am,' he repeated, glad of a reason to move away.

Dishes of meat and side vegetables and salads were laid out on white tablecloths in the kitchen, and Nelly and two hired girls stood ready to serve. Guests were beginning to flow down the stairs in search of refreshment, so Eliza gave her attention to welcoming them and directing them to the plates and cutlery. She was relieved to see Sophy Button talking to the Palmyra's violinist while Sarah stood to the side and listened to them. Devil was in a bland flurry of hospitality, busying about with the jugs of beer and bottles of wine. Jasper and his sisters took only plain cup, although Hannah had been persuaded to taste a glass of hock.

Devil called for silence as soon as everyone was served. There were toasts and speeches, including a tedious one from the bride's uncle and a witty and graceful one from Devil who spoke as the groom's supporter and his oldest friend. Through all of this Hannah's happiness shone out of her face.

Afterwards the guests began the move upstairs to the drawing room where the Palmyra musicians were tuning their instruments in readiness for the dancing. Sophy had by now overcome her shyness, although she was careful to keep her chapped hands hidden in the folds of her Sunday skirt. Devil held out his arm to escort her upstairs and Jakey mimicked him by offering the same courtesy to Sarah.

Sophy remarked to Devil, 'Mr Wix, I am surprised not to see Jasper's friend today. He came all the way out to the house once, you know, just to give me the message that Jasper was well. It must have been quite an errand for him, what with him being so huge and fat.'

'Indeed? A fat man called on you at your place of work? That would be Mr Grady, I dare say?'

'Yes, sir.'

'Surely you don't need to call Hector Crumhall *sir*, nor *Mr Wix* either? You recall who gave me the name of Devil, Sophy, do you not?'

Her eyes fixed on the floor. 'Yes.'

His expression was thoughtful. 'Of course you do. And we

both remember the night when poor Gabe died. It is a long time ago now, but it is not likely to be forgotten. I expect you mentioned our local tragedy to Mr Grady?'

The violinist drew out the first note and bowed to the newly-weds.

Blushing, Hannah stepped into Jasper's arms and everyone in the room applauded.

Sophy looked frightened. 'I did mention it. Did I do wrong? I thought, with him being Jasper's friend . . .'

Devil smiled down at her. He was at his most relaxed and charming. 'Wrong? No, not at all. It is very sad but it is not a secret. Will you dance, Sophy?'

Later Eliza danced with Jasper. He held her tightly in his arms. The rooms were crowded with family and friends. Edwin and Rowland Shaw ran up and down in a state of overexcitement while little Lizzie perched on her father's knee and shook her pretty ringlets at her admirers. The rain had come with a stiff wind that shredded the blossoms of the garden bower.

'I hope you will be very happy, Jas.'

'Hannah and I shall do well together.' He murmured in her ear, 'As do you and Devil. I think I could not go step for step with you, Eliza, the way he does. Although I loved you from the beginning I am obliged to acknowledge that he is a better match for you.'

'Thank you, Jas.'

Her cheeks reddened. She could not help feeling bereft; his devotion had been securely hers for so long and she was used to the quiet reassurance it provided. She reminded herself now that it was selfish to expect any allegiance beyond friendship from Jasper, when Hannah was able to return his affection in full. They separately concentrated on the dance and when the tune ended they exchanged a solemn bow and a curtsey.

Carlo had fallen asleep in an armchair. His mouth was open and he snored as loudly as a man twice his size, which sent

the children off into fits of giggling. Devil smoked a cigar at
the door into the front area. The hired girls were whispering
with Nelly at the scullery sink and he thought there was no
one else nearby. Rain sluiced from the pipes into the gutter at
his feet and a sharp smell of slaked city dirt rose around him.
The music from the upstairs room grew steadily louder as the
dancing progressed.

When a hand touched his arm he was startled.

Jakey slurred, 'I should like to speak to you.'

Devil collected himself. 'My good fellow. Of course.' He
took a step aside, but it was the wrong manoeuvre. Jakey
thought he was trying to evade him, and his grasp tightened.

'Please,' he begged. 'Please.'

'What is it?'

'Jacko Grady came to see me. He wants me to partner him
in a new theatre. Stage roles for me, management for him. Half
shares all the way.'

Devil could not help laughing. 'Really? What did you tell
him?'

Jakey came so close that Devil could smell the gin on his
breath. The young man's skin was as smooth as a girl's. His
lower lip glinted and he wiped the saliva with the back of
his free hand. He said in a low, rushed murmur, 'Why must you
always laugh at me? Loyalty is not comical. I told him that I
would speak to you. I owe you everything, I . . . I want there
to be no secrets.'

Devil grew serious. 'There are none, at least so far as I am
concerned. Jacko Grady is a cheat and a charlatan, and if you
were starving he would sooner skin you than give you sixpence.
I have better reason than you to know it, but still I wonder
why you would want to have anything to do with such a
person? Even if you had the means to buy into his latest cockeyed venture, I'd advise you against it.'

Jakey tried to summon his dignity, staggering a little as he
drew himself upright.

'I have some means. I have worked hard and saved. And I

415

have my share in the the Palmyra Theatre Partnership. I signed the papers.'

Devil cocked an eyebrow. 'Indeed you did. But who would buy such a questionable commodity?'

In truth there was no need for him to ask the question, or for Jakey to try to frame a reply. The answer was obvious to them both, in the shape of the dwarf. But Devil did not really fear that his star actor might abandon the Palmyra in favour of any enterprise of Jacko Grady's.

In a passion Jakey burst out, 'You don't believe me, I see. But I'd go to Grady just to get away from here. It would be better for me to get away from you. That's the honest truth. I think you can't know how much pain your presence causes me. You have no heart.'

To Devil's horror and dismay, tears collected and spilled down the other's reddened cheeks. Jakey pulled away and wiped his face on his coat sleeve.

'I love you,' he wept.

His confession did not come as a surprise to Devil, but this did not make the moment any less painful.

'Jacob, you are thoroughly lushed. You know that's not the way it is with me. If you prefer such activity there are a dozen houses within a mile of the Palmyra where you can be acquainted with your own kind. Will you do me the favour now of walking up to the Angel and taking the first omnibus home? I have had more than a glass myself, and I think I won't remember a word of this conversation in the morning.'

A hopeless sob tore out of Jakey's throat.

Devil threw aside the stub of his cigar and turned his back on the young man. He hoped that Nelly had not overheard any of this.

After Jasper, Eliza had danced with Crabbe father and son and with the two Dickinsons. She was thinking it was time for her husband to come and claim her when she saw Cornelius's nursemaid beckoning from the doorway.

The nursery was lit only by a dim night light. The child

thrashed and jerked and his eyes were rolled back in his head.

Eliza had learned not to scoop him into her arms at these times. All she could do was make sure that he did not choke, and cushion anything hard or sharp that lay within reach of his flailing body. She rested her hand on his rigid back and whispered words of reassurance. The nursemaid hovered in the shadows as they waited, listening to the baby's sucking, gasping breaths and the rain pounding on the attic slates. The music and laughter rose from downstairs.

Only when the fit had passed could she lift him up. She kissed his heavy head and sponged the spittle and mucus from his face.

'I am here. I love you,' she whispered to him.

Cornelius did not yet sit unsupported, nor could he hold his spoon, but he never failed to turn his head to the sound of his mother's voice.

Eliza did not know how long it was before her son fell asleep. She had intended to go into her own bedroom on the floor below and tidy her hair before returning to the guests who still lingered downstairs, but as she descended from the nursery she felt a movement in the shadows on the lower landing. This was followed by a low gurgle of laughter. She knew whose laugh this was, and the murmur that followed it was even more familiar. Two people were covertly embracing in the angle of the stairwell. One of them was Tilly Lacey and the other was Devil.

The foreboding that had dogged her all day, and for weeks before this moment, broke around her like a colossal thunderclap.

She swept down the stairs to the lovers' niche and they instantly sprang apart.

Ignoring Devil she said to Tilly, 'I think you should leave my house now.'

The girl faltered, 'There's no harm, Eliza. There's nothing for you to take objection to, I swear.'

Devil tried for a winning smile. 'It's a wedding party. A little kiss. No more than that.'

'Get out of my house, Tilly.'

Eliza did not look back at them as she made her way on down the stairs.

Faith was drawing on her gloves in the hallway.

'Lizzie is fast asleep. Matthew is going to carry her. That was a memorable party, my dearest.'

'It was,' Eliza agreed. Faith saw her sister's face.

'What is wrong? Tell me, quickly.'

'I have just seen my husband embracing the actress.'

'Oh, my dear. How foolish of him. He has been drinking steadily, you know, while you were attending to Con. Shall I speak to him? Or perhaps a rebuke would be better coming from Matthew?'

'I shall deal with it,' Eliza said through bloodless lips.

Faith knew better than to say any more. The sisters kissed each other and the Shaws took their children away.

Eliza was painfully weary. Carlo was still snoring; there was now no sign of Jakey. Jasper and Hannah and their family guests were on the point of taking their leave. She quietly explained to them that Cornelius had suffered one of his seizures, and although he was quiet now she must go up to sit with him. The newlyweds thanked her touchingly for her kindness. Sophy and Sarah even bobbed to her as they said their goodbyes, as if she were the mistress of some big house. She felt too distraught even to make a gentle protest at this.

In the nursery, Cornelius was quietly sleeping. His soft face took shape, and she saw that he began to resemble his father.

In her bedroom she stripped off the new dress she had had made for the occasion. When Devil lurched up almost two hours later, having dispatched the last of their guests and locked up the house, he found her apparently asleep.

He did not know how long he slept, but he was woken by an unfamiliar sound. He opened his eyes on darkness. Rain gurgled off the roofs and into the gutters. Still half asleep, he realised that Eliza's side of the bed was empty.

There was another movement, and a darker shape moved in the blackness. A vestige of the old fear stirred, but even as it came upon him a human hand snatched off the bedclothes. He gasped as his nakedness was exposed, and the same hand roughly grasped his private parts. As if they made to wring a hen's neck, the fingers twisted. And then a cold blade nicked his flesh.

He yelled in real fear, 'For God's sake, Eliza.'

The steel dug a fraction deeper and he winced. He was much stronger than she, but he was terrified to move in case her hand slipped.

'Stop it. *Please.*'

'How long have you been bedding Tilly Lacey?' Her voice in his ear was colder than the blade.

'Eliza. I swear—' A yelp of pain followed another nick of the blade. 'Once. *Ouch.* Twice, that's all. I didn't have to persuade her, if that's what you are thinking.'

His wife leaned down until her lips brushed his face.

She whispered, 'If you ever touch her again, I will castrate you.'

'Let go, will you?'

She gave his privates one last vicious twist before releasing him. His eyes stung with tears of pain as he gathered the covers around him. She turned on the electric light that he was so proud to have had installed. Eliza was in her nightgown, her eyes hard with rage and hair falling around her face.

In her hand glinted his cut-throat razor.

'You are insane,' he whispered.

'I mean what I say. If I catch you with that little slut again –' she advanced on him with the razor – 'I will cut off your cock and stuff it in your mouth.'

A spurt of half-admiring laughter broke out of him. 'Eliza Wix, where did you learn such ideas, and such language?'

'In your theatre, where else? Do you understand me?'

'How could I misunderstand, when you express yourself so forcefully?'

419

Her face was dark with fury. The violence of her jealousy excited him.

Softly he added, 'Why are you so surprised that I looked elsewhere? You are my wife, yet I am scarcely allowed to touch you.'

There was a clatter as she flung the razor aside. She wrenched off her cotton nightgown and stood naked in front of him. Her breasts were no longer a girl's, and there were silvery marks netting the loose swell of her belly. Still she was ripely and defiantly beautiful.

'You know what the birth of our child did to me.' Bitterly she gestured at herself. He did know and he had always tried to ignore it.

'Am I to blame for that?'

'Am *I*?'

Unable to stop himself he kicked off the bedclothes and grabbed at her.

Her eyes raked over his body, noting his arousal.

'You merely make yourself a bigger target for the blade,' she taunted.

'Bitch.'

He threw her on to the mattress. She tried to fight him off, writhing as he kissed her. Her resistance only excited him further. He put his hand between her legs.

'Come on. You are as ready for it as I am.'

'What? Didn't you get enough from Tilly Lacey?'

'I did not get anything from Tilly. You interrupted me.'

His wife reared up and bit him hard in the neck. Her teeth drew blood and the pain was such that he threw her down on her face and slapped her backside. He had never laid a finger on her in violence before this moment, and the shock of it made them both gasp.

She cried, 'What do you want from me?'

He couldn't gauge whether she was defiant or submissive. He took her hand and placed it on himself.

'I want to love you. But you don't make it easy for me.'

'Why should I?' she countered. He put his lips to the hollow of her throat.

'Because that is the natural order of things. Come,' he whispered again.

Gently he explored the tender flesh that had been torn, and after a long time had wrongly healed in puckers and painful ridges. 'I will not hurt you.'

Her fury with him was subsiding.

'From now on I will decide what causes me pain,' she said.

She laid the flat of her hand against his chest and pushed him back on to the bed. When he was quite still she straddled him and slowly, with infinite care for her own body and no thought for his – except what she would take from it – she lowered herself on to him.

Devil thought he had never known such an exquisite moment.

Through her cascade of hair she murmured, 'Don't let me catch you with another woman, ever again.'

'Eliza, you mean more to me than any woman I have ever had, or ever will have.' He told the truth.

'Because if I do catch you, I will kill you.'

'After tonight, I shall die happy.'

At that he felt the involuntary quiver of her laughter.

It was the most passionate encounter they had ever had. Devil rejoiced that this time his wife did not wince or tense her muscles as he approached her.

Afterwards they lay with the sweat cooling on their bodies. Her chin found the hollow of his shoulder and her belly rested against his flank. They listened to the last patter of rain.

'I have never seen you so angry, Eliza. I was afraid of you.'

'That was my intention.'

'I see. One terror replaces another, evidently. I have discarded one today, at least.'

She settled her cheek more comfortably against his warm skin.

'How so?'

'Sophy Button told me how it was that Jacko Grady knew

421

enough about my past to fake the Haggerston Hall seance.'

'The man is a crook.'

Devil stared up into the darkness. His mind was in the theatre again.

'A crook, yes. But a resourceful one.'

'Go to sleep,' Eliza whispered.

EIGHTEEN

Mrs Edward Mathieson surveyed the house from the comfort of her armchair at the front of the Palmyra's best box.

The gallery was packed. She could hear the exchange of witticisms and laughter as the last arrivals hurried to take their seats, loud rustlings and clinking indicating that refreshments had been purchased in advance. She was not sufficiently interested in this segment of the audience even to glance upwards.

The stalls were also filling up. She scanned the late arrivals as they settled themselves into the *fauteuils* and studied their tasselled programmes. None of them was dressed for the opera, of course, or even for the first night of a new play at the Haymarket theatre, but there was a good show of jewels and furs. There was no question that the Palmyra was a fashionable place to be seen.

Mrs Mathieson's husband was on her left. On her right sat their friend Mr Tree, the celebrated actor and manager of the Haymarket itself. Mr Tree peered down his long nose at the assembly, and those who recognised him openly stared back. Neither he nor Mrs Mathieson had been to the Palmyra before tonight, but Mr Mathieson had a business interest and had seen the show on more than one occasion. He assured them that they would enjoy the entertainment. They agreed that the elegant house with its pretty lighting and opulent furnishings was highly promising.

'Verena, my dear, I would not bring you or Mr Tree to an upstairs room at a tavern behind Covent Garden Market,' Mr Mathieson laughed.

'Well, one never knows,' she murmured. She gestured with her fan. 'It is a variety hall, is it not, for all the gold leaf and palm leaves and acres of such bright green velvet?'

Mr Tree said good-humouredly, 'There's nothing wrong with the variety. It's a lively tradition. As for magic shows such as this, why not? Illusion is an essential component in all theatre. The suspension of disbelief is a vital prelude to the Ghost in *Hamlet* or the cliff edge in *Lear*. I am eager to learn from our magician counterparts this evening.'

The orchestra began to play and Devil came out to the front of stage. Brushed and barbered, polished and starched in his white tie and wing collar with his watch chain glinting, he looked as distinguished as the banker.

'Good evening, ladies and gentlemen. Welcome to the home of magic and illusion.'

The house lights dimmed. On a drum roll, the curtain swept up.

A handsome young man in an open shirt and laced breeches leaned against a broken classical pillar in the middle of a woodland glade. The verdant branches and the dappled sunlight looked real. The musical trickling of a nearby stream was certainly real, although the water itself was not actually visible.

Mrs Mathieson lifted her glasses, and so did the actor-manager.

'If music be the food of love, play on.'

Mr Tree watched attentively. A diamond ring was borrowed from a décolletée lady in the front row. Duke Orsino and the lady Olivia were the framing for the latest elaborate version of the Vanishing Ring trick. Jakey and Tilly Lacey extracted the maximum value from the illusion, and at the end of a series of sleights the ring was finally borne back to its owner by one of a pair of doves. Mrs Mathieson examined her programme for the name of the young actor who had played Duke Orsino. She discovered that he was a Mr Jake Jones.

The applause had hardly stopped before the curtain swept up again. The stage was now miraculously bare except for a box that seemed to float in mid-air. The lid rose and a young lady sat upright. Her pretty shoulders were left bare by her shift. A dwarf sprang on to the stage, brandishing a giant saw. He banged down the lid, padlocked it and threw the key into the stalls.

Devil knew how to keep his audiences alert. Sawing the lady in half was a deliberate change of style and pace. The contingent that had yawned at the whimsical Shakespeare was delighted by the savagery, whilst the other half blinked at the speed and daring. No sooner had the yellow-haired victim been severed and repaired, and stood up to take her bow with the dwarf, than the next illusion was under way.

Mr Tree leaned back in his seat.

Charlotte and the Chaperone, the perennial favourite, played well. These days Devil did not always put himself onstage but tonight he appeared in the chaperone's bonnet and petticoats, where his tendency to overplay for easy laughs was not misplaced. Tilly and a new young cast member were pretty as the lovers, with Jasper as the father-woodman, but it was the snarling wolf that stole the attention. The moth-eaten old costume had been burned long ago. The latest shaggy pelt was made from a handsome wolfskin, and in the bakery workshop Jasper had created the latest glassy-eyed head with a snapping jaw and slavering tongue as lifelike as anything engineered by Heinrich Bayer.

At the creature's first appearance Mrs Mathieson screamed as loudly as the simplest girl in the gallery, and then laughed so much at the ensuing macabre antics that she had to dab her handkerchief to the corners of her eyes. Her husband patted her hand.

At the interval the Mathiesons and their guest were served

champagne by a footman dressed in the theatre's green-and-gold livery. Eliza and Sylvia had discussed the possibility of putting these attendants in powdered wigs, but had decided that the effect would be too florid. The engraved card that came with the silver ice bucket presented Mr Devil Wix's compliments.

'I thought you would enjoy it, Verena,' the banker said. It was one of his satisfactions always to be right.

'I might not have done,' his wife said briskly. 'It might have been vulgar. But it is charming, and quite clever.'

'What's your opinion, Herbert?'

The actor-manager tapped his knee.

'You have done well to invest. I might have done so myself, had you not got in first.'

Edward Mathieson thoughtfully sipped his champagne.

After the curtain came down Carlo pulled off the crimson coat he had worn in the final sequence. He winced because he was in pain that would not respond to any treatment, even the imbibing of too much gin. His body hurt until he drank himself into oblivion, and pain stabbed him as soon as he returned to reluctant consciousness.

He hesitated on the threshold of the dressing room and surveyed the melee. Every member of the cast wanted to scramble into their street clothes and quit the theatre as quickly as possible. The front of house had benefited from Devil's borrowings and spendings, but back here nothing had changed. There was barely room to wriggle, or clean air to breathe or a shred of privacy. In the midst of it Sylvia Aynscoe retrieved costumes from underfoot and looked them over for rips and missing fastenings before hanging them in their designated places on the clothes rail.

'You don't look well,' she said to Carlo.

He made a face, but not an unkind one. 'I'll prescribe myself a dose.'

With his back to the room, Jakey unbuttoned his shirt. Carlo squeezed into the square inch of space next to him. He dipped a cloth into a basin of scummy water and wiped a layer of stage paint off his face. Without a word Jakey uncorked a bottle and passed it over.

In the dressing-room doorway appeared a tall footman in his theatre livery. He held a silver tray at shoulder height. Someone whistled, and there were one or two lip-smacking kisses and a mocking murmur. There was no love lost between the front-of-house staff and the performers. The footman ignored them and pushed his way towards Carlo and Jakey. When he reached their corner he presented the silver tray.

Carlo tried to take the card, but the man swooped the tray out of his reach.

'It is for *Mister* Jones,' he said with all the disdain he could muster before giving Jakey a heavy wink.

Jakey studied the card.

Carlo peered over his arm. 'Jacko Grady again? He must want you for his partner pretty badly. Name your terms, is it, eh?' The dwarf cocked his head and beadily eyed his friend.

Jakey held out the card for him to see. It was handsomely engraved.

Mr Herbert Beerbohm Tree, The Haymarket Theatre.

Carlo was dumbfounded. This was not an eventuality he had even considered.

No one saw Devil come in. But suddenly he was amongst them, in the master of ceremonies' tailcoat that he had worn to close the performance. It was as if the might of the City itself had arrived in their midst. A silence fell.

The half-dressed crowd sensed that this was a pivotal moment, even though they did not yet fully understand why. Cold sausage suppers and street coats were laid aside as people waited for what would happen next.

Devil pushed his way to Carlo and Jakey. Carlo shifted his weight to ease the pain in his hip. Jakey was undressed, so he was obliged to conceal the name on the card by placing it face down beside the basin of filthy water. Devil's glance flicked over it before he met Carlo's eye.

'We had important people in tonight,' he said to the dwarf. 'I am pleased it was a good show. Thank you, Carlo. And all of you.'

'Aye.'

Jakey took his undershirt from a hook and slipped it on. His old brown waistcoat went on top, and once that garment was in place he picked up the card and stowed it away. He kept his head down, as if the stained floorboards demanded his attention.

Devil said pleasantly, 'Shall we eat some supper, Carlo? It's a long time since we have been to the Swan or the Old Ports. Will you join us, Jakey? There are matters to discuss, I suppose.'

'No, thanks,' Carlo said.

'Nor me, Mr Wix. Not tonight,' Jakey murmured, not looking up.

'Mr Wix? What's this?' Devil laughed. He glanced around him but no one responded.

The tense silence grew uncomfortable. Carlo cleared his throat and spat the result into the basin before uncorking his bottle. He took a long pull.

Devil turned away. Even Sylvia drew back a little as he passed her. Near the door Jasper and Hannah stood shoulder to shoulder, their expressions troubled. Devil paused and his friend touched his arm, but did not try to follow him. Devil walked alone to the stage door and out into the shadows of the alley.

It was midsummer and the western sky was still soft with the dark blue residue of twilight. Eliza was sitting beside the open window overlooking the garden. She was always happy to hear her husband's key in the lock, and tonight she had a precious piece of news to share with him.

Devil flung himself into the chair opposite her. His head was full of ideas for the future of the Palmyra, for greater triumphs, for earning and spending and accumulating more money. Every member of his theatre company should by rights be with him. And yet it seemed that they were all against him.

He did not even properly understand how this had happened. The night when he had won the theatre from Jacko Grady seemed to belong to another world. He wondered bitterly whether that long-ago triumph would turn out to be the pinnacle of his career instead of the small beginning.

'The little man hates me,' Devil declared.

'It is not only you. He hates his place in the world. He hates himself.'

'I can't change that for him.'

Eliza sighed. 'My dear, can you not paint any picture in which you are not the centre of the canvas?'

She had handed him a whisky in a handsome crystal glass. The scent of honeysuckle wafted from their garden. The elegant room spoke of his wife's good taste and the life they were achieving. On his way home tonight he had passed what remained of the old St Giles rookery. The rancid buildings in their warrens of filthy alleyways were being demolished in favour of new roads and better houses. It seemed that progress and opportunity were everywhere, and it irked him even more deeply that his players did not share his satisfaction.

'Carlo doesn't hate *you*,' he said.

'I am not his competitor.'

'I don't want to compete with him.'

Eliza inclined her head. 'You prefer to lead and for everyone else to do as you command, meek as lambs. But Carlo was not born meek, and with Hannah behind him Jasper wants more for himself. Remember his ambition for the house in South Kensington? Every man and woman at the Palmyra has himself to consider.'

He made an attempt at lightness. 'It's very disobliging of them.'

Eliza's gaze passed over the rosewood piano they had lately acquired although neither of them knew how to play. The portrait of Devil by Mr George Gardiner, recently and expensively restored

429

by the artist, hung over the front mantel even though she hated the memories associated with it. It was a fine picture by a rising portrait artist, and that earned it its prominent position.

Gently she said, 'I think we may have made some mistakes.'

She was proud of Devil, but she knew how overbearing he could be.

Perhaps this house was too large, and their aspirations too plain to see. It had been an honest gesture to give the Buttons their wedding party and she believed that it had been appreciated, but maybe they had also given the company the impression that the Wixes assumed grandeur beyond their status. She was sorry that Jasper's sisters had treated her as a person above them. Jasper believed so fervently in equality, outside the theatre and within it.

Devil was never slow to follow her thoughts, even though he did not always share her opinions.

'What shall we do?'

'We might just . . . stay quiet for a while.'

He gave a shrug. 'What does that mean?'

'Keep the house full, put on the best possible programmes. Look after our people, pay them as much as we can afford, and let them take more rest time. *Not* try to put on a touring show, or a summer season in Brighton.' These last were cherished plans of Devil's. 'And we should tell Jerry Cockle that we won't need him for a year or so.'

'But you brought Jerry in.'

'He has done his work well, and it is done.'

'As for the wages, Eliza, I am not a charity.'

Devil threw himself out of his chair. Standing with his back to her at the open window he took his watch out of his pocket and set it twirling on its chain. Eliza watched him.

'I'll think about what you say,' he conceded at length. She knew him well enough not to try to press the subject further until he had thought about it, and come to the conclusion that the intention was all his.

Devil asked, 'How was Con today?'

Her face glowed. She had been waiting, hoarding this nugget of news.

'He sits up.'

It had been a miraculous moment. She had taken the child out into the garden, in his petticoats and sunbonnet, and set him on a shawl against a heap of cushions. His nursemaid preferred to keep him quietly indoors, fearing that any excitement might bring on a fit, but Eliza insisted that he should enjoy a normal life as far as possible. She pushed him in his perambulator through the clamour of the market, and carried him to the canal towpath so that he might admire the painted barges and the great horses that hauled them. If his nursemaid was necessarily boring, she thought, there was no reason why his mother should be.

Today Cornelius had been entranced by the butterflies darting amongst the garden flowers. He had stretched his hands out to them, and to her surprise Eliza saw that he was balanced on his solid rear. She slipped away his cushions and he still sat there, his mouth wide open and his chubby fingers reaching into the air. It was a minute or more before he tilted sideways on to the grass and lay there with an expression of astonishment. She swung him into her arms with a cry of delight that brought Nelly and the nursemaid running out to see what was wrong.

Devil was equally surprised. 'He does? That is wonderful.'

Eliza replied that it was as she had always believed. Their son was not as quick to learn as his cousins, but he noticed everything.

He would take his place in the world, she said, in good time.

Jakey called on Mr Tree. He reported later to Carlo that he had never expected to get closer to the great man than the cheapest seats at the Haymarket, yet there he was sitting tête-à-tête in a bare chamber that served as a rehearsal room for his actors.

'Were you offered a glass of champagne or a dish of caviar, perhaps?'

431

Jakey allowed himself a pout. 'Not at all. Better than any high-class edibles, I was asked to read for him. The Player King from *Hamlet*, and a role from Mr Wilde's new play.'

'I'd rather have had a good dinner.'

'That would be why you have not been invited to join the Haymarket company.'

'And you have?'

'Yes,' Jakey said.

Carlo stared.

The rickety starved boy who had once hidden amongst the tattered seats in the old Palmyra had made himself into a sought-after actor. It was not just the fortunate alignment of his features that had attracted attention, although the high forehead and aquiline nose and the girlishly full mouth did not put him at a disadvantage. It had come about because Jakey was not content to remain a poor creature. He had developed his natural talents. Carlo knew as well as anyone how long and hard the work had been.

The dwarf sighed. Their paths would diverge now, and his did not tend in the more inviting direction.

'Good for you,' he said. It cost him some effort to be generous.

Jakey shimmered with pleasure. 'I have told no one but you as yet.'

'Wix will not be pleased.' Carlo could take satisfaction in that, at least.

'I think he will be surprised, but in the end he will not grudge me my chance to do the work I'm fit for. He knows that playing Charlotte's lover and throwing a fakery ingot into the air will not do for me for ever.'

'We shall see. All Wix cares for is profit, and you are a mere line in his account book.'

From the moment Jakey told him his news, Carlo began making calculations.

He would not be called to act on Mr Beerbohm Tree's classical stage; he would never play any role other than dwarf magician and contortionist. The memory of the stilt-walking good philosopher came back to him and his mouth set into a line. Devil Wix had first denied and then taken advantage of his partner's singularity. He and his wife set themselves up at the expense of everyone else. Eliza had said to him, '*You make too much of your stature. Perhaps you might think of yourself as a human creature first, and a dwarf second?*' Her condescension still sent darts of anger shooting through him. Who knew what it was like to live as he did?

Well, then.

He did have one ambition that was nothing to do with his stature.

He wanted to defeat Devil Wix. He wanted the manager to suffer humiliation at Carlo Boldoni's hands, because Carlo did not have long legs and black hair and a handsome face, or a wife who could dish out supercilious advice.

'Jakey,' he said softly. 'When you move on to greater things will you sell your share of the Palmyra Partnership to me?'

The flower seller sat on the steps beneath the Earl of Shaftesbury's memorial fountain. The winged angel of Christian charity drew his bow directly over her head, but she paid him no attention. She sat in this place from dawn every morning without the smallest expectation of charity, Christian or otherwise.

'Buy my blooms,' she sang. 'Sweet violets, roses for your love, fine carnations.'

A pair of well-shod feet stepped out of the crowd and she looked up to see a gentleman in a striped coat. Devil considered her wares before pointing down at the fragrant cluster of darkest red carnations. She selected one for him and he dropped his twopence into her lap.

He was fixing the bloom in his buttonhole when a vehicle bowled past.

Newspaper boys, a passing police constable and Devil all gaped in unison as the motorised apparition cut between the horse-drawn omnibuses and fretting hansom cabs. The onlookers drank in every detail of the spruce black coachwork. The machine had swooping mudguards and scarlet wheel spokes and it bounced gently on the latest elliptical springing. At the front there was nothing but a pair of brilliantly polished brass gig lamps and a pigskin valise strapped to the luggage brackets. The driver and his passenger wore tweed caps, caped coats, gauntlets and driving goggles. Noticing Devil's expression, the driver lifted his hand from the steering handle to squeeze the bulb of the motor car's majestic horn. A two-note blast ripped the air.

Devil had seen other motor vehicles but none as perfect and as desirable as this Benz Viktoria touring car. The machine was the incarnation of power and opulence, the beating heart of modernity. His mouth hung open as the vision spun away towards Regent Street. Suddenly he was much less satisfied with his red carnation and his jaunty coat than a moment before. The electric advertisements surrounding the circus seemed merely gaudy, and the shop windows were stuffed with the tawdriest goods. The flower seller shuffled her feet in the bed of straw that kept out a little of the early morning chill. Devil caught the woman's eye as she hunched in her coat of sacking. He put his hand in his pocket and gave her sixpence before making his way on towards Piccadilly, and his appointment with Mr Edward Mathieson.

Carlo stood up on a bench, from which vantage point he could comfortably see all the assembled faces. Devil's absence gave him a useful opportunity to stir up the mutiny.

Nearest to the door of the bakery workshop, Jasper fiddled with a set model for a black art illusion. This called for a room lined entirely in black fabric, like a much bigger version of the old Philosophers cabinet. They were devising a new series of acts that would be physically easier for Carlo to perform. For the black illusions the dwarf need do no more than wear a black costume and hood, and pass white props to Devil clad in a bright white suit. Jasper was currently working on a papier mâché white skeleton, the arms and legs jointed so the invisible assistant could manipulate them in mid-air.

He sighed. There was much to be done, against an atmosphere of strife and uncertainty. He had been making calculations on a scrap of paper. The black art was one of the most expensive of all illusions to stage. If the fabrics and other materials were not of the very best quality the movements of the assistant within the set would be visible.

Ted Dickinson leaned against the door, apparently keeping potential intruders at bay. Sammy Hill's mouth turned down. Sylvia picked at a seam in a costume coat. Everyone who played a role of any significance at the Palmyra was here except for Eliza, and Devil himself. And Jakey, of course, who had lately gone to join Mr Tree's company and whose departure was the indirect cause of this gathering.

'Right,' Carlo said.

It still happened that at moments of high emotion his speech turned northern again. *Reet.*

Propped up against the wall behind him was the coffin lid that they had brought with them from the old workshop in Clerkenwell. After the murder of Margaret Minchin and Heinrich's death Eliza and Sylvia had taken care that the thing was kept hidden away behind some scenery flats. Now it had reappeared in plain view.

The dwarf let a minute tick past, and then another. He was always the master of timing. The company waited.

Carlo spoke at last. 'Matters have not been justly arranged.'

His tone was reasonable, almost silken, where they might have anticipated ranting.

'Who agrees with me?' he asked. 'Let us have a plain show of hands.'

At first no one moved. Then Sammy Hill raised his hand. Sammy's dissatisfaction was no secret. Although the advertising man was not so much in evidence lately, Sammy despised Jerry Cockle. There had been altercations between the two of them, invariably won by Jerry. The carpenter resented the interloper's lofty manner, but most of all he mistrusted his influence over the Wixes.

'I ain't a fool. Whatever some folk may think,' Sammy muttered.

Jasper twisted a shred of black calico between his fingers. Hannah stood only a yard away and he knew that she was waiting and watching to see what he would do. Hannah urged him to be more forceful in putting forward their interests.

'Thank you, Sammy. I am obliged.' Carlo used the same level tone. There were heavy black shadows beneath the dwarf's eyes and his hand rubbed at the constant pain in his hip. But he had command over all of them, even Jasper.

'Who else?' he coaxed.

When no response came he prompted, 'You all know that Jakey made over his shares in the Palmyra Theatre Partnership to me, even though Devil Wix tried to get them for himself?'

Carlo allowed himself a sidelong glance to a rifle that was propped against the end of the bench. He had been cleaning it while he waited for the company to assemble.

Martin Scurr, the new young apprentice, was the next to put up his hand. Devil had auditioned him and he was glad of his place in the Palmyra company, but he could see which way the tide was running.

The dwarf prowled along the bench.

'Excellent, Martin. Representing those people who have done the work over the years and make the money hereabouts, we have myself, with the added weight of Jakey's shares, and Sammy Hill. Against us –' here Carlo gave a bitter honk of laughter – 'are Devil and Eliza Wix.'

The dwarf stabbed his finger at them. There was a dramatic pause. 'The balance is therefore held by *you*, Jasper Button.'

Hannah had joined the company after her marriage. Now she quietly waited for her husband's response. Jasper loved his wife, partly because the quiet range of her ambitions matched his own. When he held her in his arms she whispered to him, 'It's you and me now, Jasper. It's *us* that matters.'

For a man with Jasper's history, *us* was a seductive notion.

He had long ago quit Camden Town. The young couple now

436

lived with her mother in the maze of streets that lay along the south bank of the river. The tiny house was close to the stinking tanneries and leather works that dominated the area. Only this morning he had found a rat browsing in their kitchen. He seized the broom and chased it over the back step. Devil and Eliza lived in a tall airy house. They had two servants and a piano, and the master's portrait by a famous artist hung over the mantel.

Carlo's voice became even smoother and softer. 'While Jasper takes his time to consider the matter, who else is with us?'

None of the company knew how much open water now lay between what they were variously paid and how much the theatre brought in, but all of them were ready to believe that this profit must represent a long day's outing in a pleasure cruiser. A little ripple passed through the crowd, gathering force like a wind presaging bad weather.

The Dickinson brothers raised their hands.

Roger Crabbe nudged his father, and two more hands showed.

Tilly Lacey followed suit, although she was enough of an actress to look as if doing so caused her profound sorrow. The musicians did the same, and one by one all the other permanent members of the company until only Sylvia, Jasper and Hannah were left.

Sylvia's thin face was eloquent of her unhappiness. 'Can we not consult Eliza? She is generous and a good friend to us all—'

Carlo cut her short. 'Who would try to come between a man and his wife?'

No one looked at Tilly Lacey.

Jasper enquired, 'What will you do, Carlo, with this new power of yours?'

The dwarf leaned over the hand that cupped his hip.

'My power, Jasper? You read me quite wrong. The choices will not be mine but *ours*. We shall choose our new illusions, and not have a programme thrust upon us regardless of risk and difficulty. But most importantly –' here he paused, examining each of them in turn as if to see how they measured up – 'we will share equally the profits from our work.'

Hannah put up her hand. Jasper could not help but meet her intent blue gaze. She looked meek, but he knew she was not. Reluctantly he raised his arm, with the shred of black rag still wound between his fingers.

Only Sylvia Aynscoe shook her head. She was white to the lips.

Carlo shrugged. He had won the support he needed.

'Very good. Jasper and I will tell Devil Wix what we have decided.'

Sylvia burst out, 'Devil owns the theatre. What use is any of us without a stage?'

Carlo's smile was no more than a gash. 'You might ask what use there is in a stage without a company to perform on it.'

Martin Scurr ventured, 'He can get himself another company, easy enough.'

'But he cannot get another dwarf.'

It was the truth, Jasper wearily reflected. Devil had everything else, but he would never command Carlo's skill. Jealousy was at the root of all the trouble between them. He was tired of interceding between two implacable and forever opposing forces. The collision must come, sooner or later.

'What do you want?' he asked Carlo.

There was not a second's hesitation.

'I want to defeat him.'

The dwarf's nose and chin seemed to reach out for each other. Bright red spots showed on his cheekbones and his eyes sank deeper into the shadowed sockets. Framed by the coffin lid he looked for the moment exactly like the malevolent Mr Punch in a street performer's flimsy booth.

The performers and stagehands shuffled and muttered. Only Sylvia sat silent.

Carlo caressed the barrel of the rifle.

438

'We shall begin our new era by putting on the Bullet trick,' he announced.

Everyone had heard him talk about it, usually when he was drunk, but they had not believed he would actually try to bring the notorious illusion to the stage.

'Who will perform it?' Jasper asked heavily.

'It takes one man to fire the bullet, and one to catch it.'

'Not me,' Martin Scurr shouted. 'Too dangerous.'

'No, not you,' Carlo silkily agreed.

Suddenly he seemed to slip into a new, jovial mood. Clapping his hands he declared, 'We must tell our audiences. Let it be known that we are not afraid to stage the most daring illusion, and they will clamour for tickets. Who will do Jerry Cockle's job?'

The only answer was more silence.

'Sammy, perhaps?'

Sammy Hill shook his head. Carlo's mouth twisted, pinching the smile into a slit and then into nothing.

'Very well. I will do it myself'.

Devil let himself in at the stage door and passed through the network of passages to the wings and out on to the stage. The dim auditorium was lanced by shafts of light from the high windows in the cupola, picking up a slice of gilding and a slash of bright colour. He walked forward to the footlights and filled his lungs with the close air. At this point, on the divide between front of house and backstage, the scent of perfumed women and hair oil and furniture polish mingled with the working tang of sweat and warm dust.

Devil closed his eyes. He no longer felt romantic love for his theatre. It was a long time since he had caressed one of the carved pillars as if it were a woman's thigh, but his passion went deeper because of the struggles that had intervened. There had been so many performances on these boards. The magician's arts of disguise and misdirection, the springing of traps

439

and the intricate applications of science, the physical contortions and the carpentry and the hours of painful practice, all employed to coax applause from an audience.

It occurred to him that these days he did not dwell sufficiently on *wonder*.

The longing for it had brought him here from Stanmore village through the tatty portal of an itinerant conjuror's booth. And now he was obliged to think overmuch about money, and fickle audiences, and roof repairs. Devil longed to be rich, and to own a Benz Viktoria touring car identical to the one he had seen this morning. It irked him to have to acknowledge that he was still poor, but in the temporary peace of the theatre he knew that money was not the only currency. He was wealthy in other respects. Devil's anger at the morning's events drained away. He flexed his fingers, thinking he should practise some sleights. Enjoy the discipline of magic again. He wondered if this moment of reflection on the silent stage was reality, and everything else in his life a mere illusion.

Someone pushed aside the velvet curtains over the doors to the foyer.

Devil's eyes snapped open and he saw Carlo. On his back the dwarf was carrying a gun case as tall as himself.

'The workshop must be busy this morning,' Devil said, consulting his gold watch.

'Aye.'

'I was expecting to see Jasper.'

'You see me instead.'

'Evidently. I had expected to work with Jasper on the black art.'

'We will put aside the black art.'

Carlo swung the gun case off his back and laid it in the centre of the aisle. He grinned evilly. 'We'll begin rehearsing the Bullet trick instead.'

It took a moment for Devil to catch the full meaning of his words. Then, as clearly as if a finger had pressed the switch to illuminate the theatre, he knew what must have happened.

'Who is with you?' he asked.

To meet Devil's eyes high up on the stage the dwarf had to tilt his head until it seemed his neck might snap.

'Everyone.'

Devil froze. 'Eliza?'

'No. Nor Sylvia Aynscoe. But everyone else.'

'I see.'

As long as Eliza was still with him he could continue. Devil briefly pondered loyalty as just another illusion.

The open gun case lay between them. Devil strolled down to examine the weapon.

'It is the popular decision, is it, to put on the Bullet trick?'

Versions of the trick had been seen in America and on one or two stages in England, but it had a reputation for being too dangerous as well as profoundly difficult to perform.

Carlo puffed out his chest. 'It is my decision. I told the rest of them we'd be doing it.'

Devil had to laugh. 'And your main objection to my management, I believe, is that it is too autocratic and does not allow every member of the Partnership and the company to make their thoughts known?'

'Yes.'

Carlo was amused too. It did not escape either man that they were as much alike as opposed.

'Every army needs a general,' Devil said softly. 'Tell me, since you are now promoted, who is to stage the trick?'

'You and I.'

'You'll retain my services? That is welcome news. And am I to fire the gun or catch the bullet?'

Carlo grinned even more broadly. It was because he was so much thinner that his smiling face resembled Mr Punch.

'I think it would be fair if we took turns.'

'Hmm. And if I refuse to take part at all?'

The two ends of the grin threatened to meet at the back of the dwarf's head. 'Oh, you can refuse. But I don't think you will.'

Devil understood that Carlo had a plan. The little man had calculated that he would never refuse his challenge, any more than he could walk away from the theatre in which his authority had been overturned.

He considered his options as if they were stage moves waiting to be plotted. The process did not take long. The Bullet trick was a wondrous illusion and it would play well.

'So we had better begin,' he said. 'What is your intended method?'

'Ah. As you can see, this is an ordinary weapon.'

Devil examined it before sighting along the barrel. It was a percussion muzzle loader, out of date but still serviceable. Carlo was pacing rapidly up the aisle and back again, measuring out steps, volubly talking. Devil listened to him. This was the way they had always worked, sketching out ideas to each other and improving on one another's suggestions.

Outwardly it was as if nothing had changed.

At the end Devil said, 'Yes. I see how it can be done.'

The dwarf waited. 'Is that all?'

'Concerning your illusion, yes. As to the other matter – if you are to take over the running of the Palmyra, perhaps you had better come with me.'

They walked the familiar route in silence. In the narrow office overlooked by Mr Wu's niche Devil unlocked the theatre's account books and laid them in front of Carlo. He picked up a sheaf of letters and a large envelope marked '*Mathieson and Co.*' and placed these beside the ledgers. He took the key to the old safe off his watch chain and laid it on top.

Carlo was suspicious.

'What's this?'

Devil's black brows drew together. 'You will manage the company, I assume? And the borrowings? Mr Mathieson would like to hear from you. Or is Jasper to take that role? In either case I shall probably continue to lease the building to you, for the time being at least, on the same terms as ever. Now,' he added with a smile, 'I am going home. I shall be back tomorrow, ready to begin rehearsals for your new programme, but I will take today as a holiday.'

Behind the stage door, Ted Dickinson was in his cubbyhole. 'Morning, Ted,' Devil said affably as he passed.

Sylvia had hurried from the bakery straight to Islington.

Eliza led her into the garden where it was chilly enough for them to be glad of their coats and hats. Nelly was turning out the drawing room, a frenzied business involving clanking of buckets and flailings of the carpet beater, and in the kitchen Eliza had allowed a pan to catch on the range so the room was unpleasantly smoky. In any case Cornelius enjoyed investigating the garden. He could move now under his own propulsion and he crawled or squirmed from tree trunk to bench leg, poking his fingers into the soil before turning to his mother with a questioning pout. He was so much slower than pert Lizzie or either of her brothers had been, but Eliza swore that each day he made new progress. She watched her son with half an eye as she listened to Sylvia's account of the morning.

'Everyone, you say? Jasper and Hannah?'

Sylvia nodded and mopped her eyes. 'I'm so sorry, Eliza. The ingratitude, after all Mr Wix has done.'

Eliza knew Devil's uncompromising ways and the edge of his sarcasm better than anyone, and she understood how the lesser members of the company might believe he did not consider them. But it was a shock to discover that Jasper as well as Carlo had turned against him. The responsibility was partly hers, for failing to mediate between the two forces. She had seen the necessity for it, and she had always intended to act as a buffer between Devil and the others, but it was impossible to play the role of conciliator when she was too rarely at the theatre. She was wretchedly shackled by domesticity, and it had been a mistake to believe that Jasper would deputise in her absence. Jasper's loyalty was to Hannah now. Eliza knew it, but somehow she had overlooked what this meant.

She frowned. It was too difficult.

If only she had had the good fortune to have been born a man.

Cornelius had found an earthworm. His stubby fingers pinched it out of the ground and he held up the squirming thing for his mother's attention. Sylvia gave a faint cry as Eliza caught the child's wrist and prised the worm out of his grasp. She was trying to stop him from pushing the same fingers into his mouth when the front door slammed. Nelly stuck her head out of an upper window.

'Mr Wix is home, mum.'

As soon as his father emerged into the garden Cornelius made for him, calling out, 'Pappy, Pappy.' This was one of his few intelligible words.

'Oh, dear,' Sylvia muttered.

Devil strode down the path. He swung Cornelius over one shoulder to make the boy crow with laughter, and came straight to put his arm around his wife's waist.

'You have heard the news, then.'

'Sylvia was good enough to come straight here.'

Sylvia looked frightened and then embarrassed, but Devil merely deposited his son on the grass and put his other arm around the seamstress.

'Thank you for your loyalty,' he said to her. 'How fortunate I am to have two such strong women to support me.'

Sylvia's pleasure at this tribute looked as if it might over-whelm her. Eliza was less flattered. She asked quite sharply, 'What does this rebellion mean?'

Devil seemed to consider. Eliza could see past the armour of his bravado, assumed for Sylvia's benefit, to the humiliation of having been rejected by the men he worked with. And then underpinning all of this, like a girder of steel, lay the unshake-able self-confidence and the relish for a fight that made him the man he was.

Devil's mouth curled. 'It means Carlo and Jasper will have a good deal to learn in a short time. They will discover that the Palmyra does not manage itself and that money does not stream from the box office directly into anyone's pockets, mine or theirs. In the end, I hope, we shall return to a cordial working arrangement.'

Her husband kissed her cheek.

'We shall discuss it, my dear. Sylvia, I promise that none of this unfortunate business will affect you in the slightest degree.'

The other woman shook her head. 'I'm not important enough to matter. It is one of the advantages of being a small person, you know, that you are thought capable of doing no damage.'

'You are very important,' Eliza insisted.

Devil swept on. 'Carlo's first introduction to the programme is to be the Bullet trick. He and I are to perform it, turn and turn about.'

Cornelius was still poking in the soil for his misplaced worm. The declining angle of the sun warned them all that late autumn would soon shift into winter. Eliza felt a shiver that was only partly to do with the chill of the afternoon.

'You will be careful?'

Devil agreed that care was always advisable when handling guns and live ammunition.

After Sylvia had gone the Wixes stayed in the garden. A bench in a little arbour faced the rear of the house, and they sheltered under festoons of ivy. Eliza held out a pebble and a feather to Cornelius. She told him the words and the child tried to mimic her.

'Pebber, fevrow,' he babbled, his lips wobbling.

Devil beamed. 'That's my boy. Lord Salisbury had better look to his declamatory laurels, don't you think?'

He was inclined to agree with Eliza, nowadays, that their son made distinct progress.

Eliza was thinking how pleasant it was, in spite of the circumstances, to have her husband all to herself in the afternoon.

'I forgot to ask. What did Mr Mathieson say?'

'Mr Mathieson would like his loan to be repaid.'

Eliza stared. 'But . . . we can't do that. He can't just call in the loan, can he?'

Devil looked up at the narrow house. The rear windows of their drawing room stood open and Nelly had hung the mats out to air. Cornelius sat at their knees and crooned over his pebble. The house seemed to loom over them, tilting as if the foundations had cracked and set the roof rocking against the pearly sky.

'Bankers can do as they think fit. We will have to do what we must, Eliza. I won't let the Palmyra go. If I need another company, I shall audition. If we urgently need money, we may have to sell this house.'

There was a silence, threaded by the twitter of birds, the steady thudding of a workman's mallet from somewhere nearby.

Eliza said, 'I see.'

She did see. In a moment of clarity she understood that this was how their life always would be – lived precariously, because wedded to a precarious profession. Devil looked so dispirited that she took his hand, hoping to make light of their predicament at least for tonight.

Mustering all possible conviction she said, 'A house is only bricks and mortar. We can live anywhere so long as we are together. I was going to say, the three of us, but I was thinking before Sylvia came that perhaps it might be time for Cornelius to have a brother.'

'Eliza? Another soul brought into the world? Is that what you want?'

She said quickly, 'Not until the matter of the company is resolved, and the loan. We will do that together. But some day, I mean. Before too long. Don't you want it?'

He disengaged his hand from hers and ran his fingers through his son's curls.

'Perhaps,' Devil sighed.

After a little while it grew too cold in the garden so they went inside. Eliza handed Cornelius over to his nursemaid, to be given his supper and made ready for bed. Devil wrote columns of figures on a sheet of paper and continued at the work until she placed a glass and jug of beer at his elbow with a plate of hot beef and potatoes.

'I thought you had awarded yourself a day's holiday.'

He looked up. 'I did, didn't I?'

He put his work aside and pulled her on to his lap.

NINETEEN

Jeremiah Cockle would no doubt have devised some elaborate game to tease the public, but all Carlo did was to take out press advertisements and distribute handbills. These read:

A Man will Catch a Bullet Fired into his Mouth.
See the Impossible made Real.
On Stage at the Palmyra Theatre.

Eliza and Devil joked in private about the overturning of all their attempts to lure a sophisticated and discerning audience, but they were obliged to change their tune when every ticket for the promised spectacle sold out well in advance.

Devil and Carlo tossed a coin for which of them would take which role on the first night. It fell to Carlo to fire the shot.

When the time came, Eliza was seated in the audience. She slipped into her seat just before the Bullet trick itself, the show's finale. She claimed that she wanted to see it as an ordinary member of the public would. But the truth was that she could not bear to look on from the wings when the dwarf raised the rifle and took aim at Devil. To have remained at home in complete ignorance of events was unthinkable for the same reason.

The audience had been unusually noisy and restless, but as

soon as the lights were dimmed for the final illusion they edged forward in their seats.

Carlo and Devil came out on to the empty stage. They wore matching military coats of red melton wool, brass-buttoned and with gold cording at the shoulders and cuffs. Carlo had wanted to set the trick within an elaborate story, perhaps of a deserter and a firing squad, or an Indian uprising, but Devil had insisted that any embellishment would only diminish the impact.

'You shoot a man point blank and yet he lives. Is that not powerful enough to command attention?'

The absence of fashionable set dressing was noted as soon as the curtain rose. An expectant hush spread from the *fauteuil* seats to the back of the gallery.

As that evening's target, Devil was also to be the illusion's presenter. As his stage assistant Tilly Lacey was costumed in a daringly short dress of silver tissue. Carlo the marksman waited quietly to one side while Devil came to the footlights and spoke to the rows of faces.

'Is there any gentleman present who has served or is serving in the British Army?'

In the stalls a white-haired man stood up. 'I have had that honour.'

'If you will do us the honour in turn, sir, of coming up on to the stage to verify that there is no trickery with the gun or the bullets?'

Under the lights the old soldier's straight back and drooping white moustaches presented the picture of military dignity. He examined the gun before declaring that he had very often fired a similar weapon when he was with the 33rd. Devil thanked him and Tilly offered up a silver tray on which lay half a dozen bullets.

'Would you choose one of these, sir, and tell the audience if you find it to be regular ammunition?'

The old soldier did so, and at Devil's request he next took the sharp knife that was given to him and carved a mark into the lead of his chosen bullet.

'And if you would load the weapon for me?'

The flask was brought by Tilly Lacey and the soldier let the measure of powder fall into the barrel. He held up the marked bullet for all to see, and then dropped it into the barrel.

From the audience there was not a sound or a flutter of movement. In the wings the whole company was silently gathered. The Crabbes perched unseen amongst the lights. Sylvia Aynscoe's thumbs prickled from the memory of the hours she had spent stitching invisible pockets in two pairs of gold-laced cuffs.

Eliza also knew the subtle mechanics. She understood that there was no real danger, but even so her heart pounded in her chest.

As if to echo it a slow drumbeat started up from the orchestra.

With a formal bow Devil took the gun back from the soldier. The steady drumbeat grew louder as Tilly passed him a rod and he rammed the bullet home. Everyone's attention was caught by the silver swirl of Tilly's skirts as she led the soldier to centre stage. Devil withdrew the rod, returned it to Tilly and lifted the half-cocked rifle in his two hands for all to see.

'One more favour, sir.'

The soldier obediently placed the percussion cap in position and fully cocked the weapon. Devil bowed again.

'Thank you. Now we are ready.'

The dwarf stepped into the spotlight. He took the rifle directly from the soldier and mounted the steps of a black podium.

Tilly led Devil to the rear of the stage. She locked his wrists into a pair of handcuffs and positioned him against a black-painted circular target. His red coat was like a beacon. He was visibly sweating so the girl took out a silk handkerchief and mopped his face for him. Finally she secured a black blindfold over his eyes.

Eliza would have covered her own eyes had she been able to move. She sat like a statue with her gaze fixed on her husband's blindfolded face.

Tilly's final task was to position a small black metal frame

450

enclosing a sheet of glass between the target and the shooter. She and the soldier withdrew to a position out of harm's way. While all this happened there had been a double drumbeat, like the slow ticking of a clock, but now even that ceased.

Carlo waited in the tense stillness. He raised the rifle and spoke for the first time.

'Ladies and gentlemen. The bullet will shatter the glass as it passes through.'

He took aim, and silent seconds ticked by. Then he pulled the trigger.

There was a flash from the muzzle. The glass exploded into shards. Devil's body pitched backwards, leaving the black paper circle in tatters. Several ladies in the audience failed to stifle their cries of horror. For a second nothing moved on the stage. Carlo stood with the rifle at his side.

Then Devil stirred. He lurched to his knees and raised his cuffed wrists in triumph. A crash of astonished applause and cheering burst out.

Eliza was not aware she had been holding her breath but now she found herself swallowing a great gulp of air.

Tilly unlocked the cuffs and removed Devil's blindfold. Standing upright in a tight circle of light he parted his lips to show that something was held between his teeth. He spat the object into the palm of his hand and extended the hand to the old soldier.

'Is this your marked bullet, sir?'

The old man examined it.

'It is,' he cried in amazement.

'Magnificent,' declared the man in the seat next to Eliza's. 'He caught it in his mouth. I saw it with my own eyes.'

The Old Cinque Ports was packed to the doors. As ever, a noisy group was gathered around the piano and the singing washed over the heads of the crowd. Carlo and Devil and Jasper were seated up close to the gleaming mahogany bar, a mere two yards from where Devil had first caught sight of

Carlo dipping pockets. They had come in after the evening's performance of the Bullet trick.

Jasper took soda water; the other two were drinking hard.

They had executed the trick half a dozen times now, alternating the roles each time. They did not perform it every night and successful repetitions did not diminish the tension caused by preparing and staging it. The irregularity of the routine seemed to have a particularly malign effect on Carlo. He declared the need to get thoroughly drunk after each occasion.

'So long as he does so after and not before,' was Devil's only comment. He seemed to take a perverse satisfaction these days in deferring to Carlo's every whim, sober or otherwise.

The Bullet trick had gathered a formidable reputation. Queues for tickets stretched along the Strand and the Palmyra was as buoyant as it had been in the best of times. Under the new regime every necessary outgoing payment had so far been met and there had even been a small repayment on the outstanding principal, acknowledged on the bank's cream laid paper by Mr Mathieson himself.

Each member of the company did what was required. If the atmosphere grew heavier and duller each day, the mood in the theatre was not an item that could be written into the profit and loss.

'You see, Wix?' the dwarf had sneered.

'I do see,' Devil replied. 'You do very well. It is as if you were born to theatre management.'

He did not say that it was all very well to oil a machine that was already running smoothly. The difficulty was in constantly looking to the future, to the time when machinery would wear out and need replacement.

Carlo grew still thinner, and the rings around his eyes darkened. He seemed to derive less satisfaction from commanding the company than might have been predicted. His concentration was unnatural. However much he drank after the night's performance the next day his attention was as precise as ever. In the bakery workshop he cleaned and oiled the old muzzle loader

452

with the greatest care. Jasper and he cast the lead bullets for the trick themselves, each one with an iron core, and they cooked up the sugar solution with which to renew the sugar glass in the black frame. In another pot they heated the wax to make substitute bullets. Thanks to the skill of Devil, Tilly and Carlo himself in palming these, the public never caught a glimpse of them.

Carlo slammed his pot on the bar. His stool was between Devil's and Jasper's.

'I want another,' he shouted. His voice was slurred.

'It's time for bed,' Jasper told him.

'I am not going to bed. Do you think I am a child?'

The dwarf's voice rose to a fretful bellow. The bar attendant put down his filthy cloth and came over to them.

'Take your friend home,' he ordered Devil.

Carlo slammed his pot harder.

'Give me another bloody pint.'

'We might go across to the Cellars,' Devil murmured. He and Jasper hoisted the dwarf to his feet and between them they propelled him out into the cold air. Here he staggered alarmingly and would have fallen if they had not supported him. They had done so before, and they knew this would not be the last time.

Jasper had still never taken a drink. He looked over Carlo's head at Devil.

'I am going home now. Hannah expects me.'

Devil only continued with the business of steering the dwarf through the dirt of the New Road to the tall buildings rising around the margins of St Giles's churchyard. The graveyard itself was a slice of blackness between the city lights. Carlo peered about him.

'Where do we go now? Men who have defied death and eaten a bullet deserve some comfort, eh?'

Jasper repeated his intention but Devil caught him by the collar. With their faces almost touching he muttered, 'The man wants a drink and some company. Do you think he doesn't deserve it? Come with us, Jas. I think you owe me that much.'

Since he had joined forces with Carlo, Jasper and Devil had continued to do their necessary work together but the old friendship of their boyhood seemed to have foundered.

Jasper was silent, shadowing the unsteady progress of his two companions until they reached an unmarked door in a brick-lined alley. A shutter slid open in response to Devil's knock and they were admitted into the Crystal Cellars. This was a new drinking and gaming establishment quite unlike the fading Ports. A man who had money in his pocket and did not make too much of a disturbance about it could purchase anything he wanted.

The room was decorated with ornate plasterwork and many glass-shaded lamps; the booths lined in red leather were only the anterooms to more private areas. Devil and his companions were shown to a corner and whisky was ordered. A strikingly pretty girl brought the bottle and crystal glasses and leaned forward to pour their drinks. As she presented her breasts Carlo's upper lip lifted to bare his teeth. Pearly drops of sweat glimmered between his eyebrows.

'You can stay here with us, my lovely.'

She gave him a black-eyed smile but her glance flicked to Devil before she withdrew. She had a slim waist and fine ankles. Carlo drank down the contents of his glass and refilled it. He squinted at the light refracted through the cut glass. Jasper wearily rested his head against the red leather padding and Devil stared into the smoky recesses of the room. It had been a hard day, culminating in a performance of the Bullet trick. Now instead of companionably relaxing the three of them seemed triangulated by mutual dislike. They were yoked by their obligations to the Palmyra, where they had once been connected.

Carlo suddenly swung up on to his haunches to bring his face to the same level as his companions.

'A toast,' he proposed. Devil raised an eyebrow and Carlo stuck out his jaw. 'To Heinrich Bayer.'

The glass that had been poured for Jasper remained untouched. Now Devil shoved it across the table.

'Drink to the memory of a dead man, Jas. Or do you really consider yourself above such things?'

The music and low talk and laughter in the room seemed to fade into silence as Devil and Carlo waited for his reaction.

Jasper reached out for the glass.

'To Heinrich Bayer,' he repeated.

He looked as if he sipped bile. Devil wiped his mouth with the back of his hand and loudly laughed. Carlo only drank deeper.

'May I ask why we drink to Heinrich tonight?' Jasper said.

Carlo belched. The waxy flesh of his face was drawn tight over the bones.

'Because he is *dead.*'

Jasper was not enlightened. Heinrich had been dead for a long time.

'Who is for cards?' Devil yawned and nodded to the tables at the back of the room.

'Not me,' Jasper said.

'You are as prudish as an old spinster, Jasper, with your pursed lips. You might as well go back to Stanmore.'

There was a long, ugly pause.

'Perhaps I shall,' Jasper softly replied.

Carlo flung back his head. It was hard to gauge how drunk he was.

'I don't want cards. I want a woman.'

'Take your pick,' Devil shrugged.

Carlo looked over at the black-eyed girl. 'That one.'

'She'll have her price, no doubt. Shall I ask the madam what it is?'

Carlo's arm swept the table, sending a glass smashing to the floor. His fist closed tight on Devil's groin and viciously twisted.

'I may be a dwarf but you don't talk down to me, Wix.'

Caught by surprise and skewered by the pain Devil could only gasp. 'Jesus. I said I'd ask her price, that's all.'

An older woman, tightly laced, came to the table. Carlo released his grip and slumped back against the red leather cushions. Devil apologised for the broken glass and murmured a question in the woman's ear. There was an inaudible exchange before a sum of money discreetly changed hands and their hostess withdrew.

Carlo's eyes were screwed up but it was clear that he was weeping. Angrily he pressed the heels of his hands into the bruise-dark sockets.

'Carlo?' Devil murmured.

The two women were threading their way back to the table. The elder's hips swayed under the satin of her gown, but the younger was slim and straight. Her mouth was already shaped into her professional smile.

The dwarf said something in a low voice. Devil could not be sure, but it might have been, 'I want a woman of my own.'

The younger woman held out her slim white hand to Carlo. 'Come with me.'

Obediently the dwarf let her lead him from the table. He stumbled a little, like a tired child.

Jasper pushed away his barely tasted whisky.

'Why is he so unhappy?'

Devil frowned. 'Why is any man unhappy?'

'Did you pay the whore for him?'

The girl and Carlo had disappeared.

Another shrug. 'Yes.'

Jasper nodded. He watched his old friend drinking. It was too late now to undo any of the past events at the theatre, or outside it. In any case he believed that given the men involved, matters would always have run a similar course. For this reason Hannah and he were laying plans for a future that did not involve the Palmyra.

'I'm sorry,' he said at length.

Devil looked up. 'Thank you. I'm sorry too, Jas.'

* * *

456

Another full house, another performance of the Bullet trick.

The double drumbeat seemed to tap endlessly within Eliza's head. She wished it would stop, but there was no doubt that it marvellously heightened the tension in the last seconds before the gun was fired. The audiences always loved this build-up. Tonight she was watching from the wings, and from her vantage point she could see a segment of rapt faces rising all the way from the boxes to the last row of the gallery. Every eye was on the two red coats, or perhaps on the daring flash of Tilly Lacey's exposed calves.

The blindfold was secured, and the glass sheet placed in position.

'The bullet will shatter the glass as it passes through.'

The drumbeat was finally stilled and the last seconds ticked away. Eliza felt rather than saw the rifle lifted. The red coat was poised against the black target.

There was a bang, a spray of shattered sugar glass and a red-coated body pitched backwards.

Already the applause had broken out but at the same time there was a cry of agony she had never heard before.

A hoarse voice shouted, 'Something has happened. Bring down the curtain, for God's sake.'

She caught a glimpse of Ted Dickinson's horrified face as she ran on to the stage. The handcuffed and blindfolded body lay where it had fallen.

Eliza knelt. The blood spread in a great stain across the red breast of the coat and trickled on to the boards. Gently she undid the blindfold and he looked up into her eyes. As she gathered him up she felt how tiny and light Carlo's body was.

She whispered his name and he tried to smile at her.

There was blood on her clothes, on her hands, in her hair. She fumbled with the gilt buttons, trying to undo them so she could staunch the bleeding. Tilly was here, her silvery skirts streaked with gore, and the shocked sergeant of the yeomanry who had been tonight's stage witness. This man helped them by pressing a folded cloth into the sopping darkness inside Carlo's coat.

Eliza stroked the dwarf's face. His mouth opened and a great torrent of blood gushed out.

His body gave a last shudder, and he died in her arms.

Tilly began to sob and screech. Eliza looked over the girl's head to see Devil. In the circle of stunned faces her husband stared at the blood and Carlo's lifeless body. He was still holding the gun in his hands.

From the other side of the green velvet curtains the shocked murmuring of the audience sounded like a greedy sea. Jasper signalled to Roger Crabbe to bring up the house lights. He stepped out front to explain that there had been an accident and they should make their way home because tonight's show was over. His face must have told an even more serious story because there was not a word of query or complaint.

Devil gave the gun into the keeping of the yeomanry sergeant. He knelt down next to Eliza and lifted Carlo's wrist. His fingers probed inside the tiny pocket that Sylvia had constructed within the cuff. There was no wax pellet concealed there, which meant the usual substitution must surely have taken place.

Devil uncomprehendingly shook his head. 'I shot him with the wax bullet, didn't I? I don't understand.'

Ted Dickinson came now with a coarse blanket. He laid it over the body.

Tilly began to wail more loudly, her bloodied skirts caught in her clenched fists.

'He lifted the real bullet out on the end of the ramrod and gave it to me, and I slipped it in his mouth when I blindfolded him, just like always. I swear it, before God. I did nothing wrong, did I?'

Eliza could not lift her eyes from the tiny huddled body, and Devil was staring into the depths of nowhere. It fell to Jasper to pat her shoulder and try to reassure her.

'It is a matter for the police now. Roger Crabbe has gone for the constable.'

The soldier coughed and came forward until the toes of his boots almost touched the blanket. Then he picked up something from the blood-soaked stage. It seemed to Eliza that blood had washed all reason away. Her fingers were sticky, stiffening with it as it dried. Carlo's was such a small body to have contained such a volume of blood.

The soldier held up the recovered bullet. Carlo and Jasper had cast these bullets with an iron core for the magnet. It seemed that this one had been flushed out of Carlo's mouth by the last gush of blood. It was marked with a roughly scored X.

Nobody spoke.

There were voices offstage and Roger Crabbe emerged, accompanied by two constables of the Metropolitan Police. These men peered into the flies and the slips before one of them casually lifted the blanket to expose the dwarf's face.

There was a gasp. In death Carlo had become the wax effigy of his decapitated head, as modelled long ago by Jasper Button for the Philosophers illusion.

Eliza let out a single dry sob.

Moving as stiffly as an old man, Devil put his hand out to her.

One of the policemen produced a notebook.

'Right,' he said. He was not a local man. Every member of the Palmyra company heard Carlo's voice in his mouth.

Reet.

Sylvia Aynscoe appeared, white as a spectre. She came to Eliza's side.

'This was beside his clothes in the dressing room.'

Eliza took the envelope, addressed to her in Carlo's hand. The letter was short.

Eliza my love, I am told that my disease will claim me in a few months at most, and you have nursed me once already. I am not a brave man. I know this is the coward's way, but it appeals to me greatly to make Devil Wix the instrument of my death. Nor could Mr Cockle himself devise a finer publicity stunt than a real fatality from the Bullet trick. You are my love now and

always, dearest Eliza. Until we meet again, I am with our Sallie.
Your admirer, Little Charlie Morris. (Carlo Boldoni was only
an unsatisfactory illusion.)

Devil shook his head in agonised disbelief. 'He planned this?
He plotted it all?'

Jasper unlaced his hand from his wife's grasp and came to
the centre of the group.

'Did anyone know that he was mortally ill?'

It seemed that no one did.

Eliza wept. One of the policemen prised the letter from her
bloodied hand.

Devil and Eliza lay in their bed. It was the darkest time of the
night but there was no hope of sleep. Eliza had scrubbed herself
until her skin felt raw but she could still smell blood. Her
husband lay on his back, staring upwards. His flanks were
cold, and he shivered even as she tried to warm him with her
body.

'How did he do it?'

'I don't know for certain. I lifted the marked bullet with
the ramrod magnet and passed it to Tilly, just as always. She
slipped it into his mouth when she blindfolded him. I replaced
the real bullet with the wax replica, to shatter the sugar glass.
Carlo always cleaned and oiled the weapon, you know. I can
only think that he loaded an ordinary bullet before the
preamble began, with no iron core so the magnet did not
affect it. He intended exactly what happened, which was to
die and to lay his death at my door.' Devil groaned. 'There's
too much death. It follows us, lies in wait, then pounces and
makes a mockery of all our little concerns. Illusion, tricks,
magic? What pitiful vanity it is, Eliza, to try to create wonder
out of this sad world.'

She too could feel and hear death. The draught and rustle
of black wings stirred in the room with them.

If she did not keep it at bay, she feared, if she did not stake out her ownership of hope and the future, this latest tragedy might consume them all.

She put her mouth to her husband's ear, consciously breathing her warm life into him.

'I saw the people watching tonight. For those few moments before the shot, not one of them was thinking of his debts or her disappointments. They were transported out of themselves. That's enough for us to do, Devil. We'll keep the Palmyra alive. We are not going to die, not for a long time. Not you or me or Con.'

He was listening to her, so she went on talking into the darkness.

She told him that Carlo had done what he wanted, and he had made his exit in the way he desired. All Devil had done was to take aim and pull the trigger.

It had happened and it could not now be undone.

'Look forwards,' she ordered.

She told him the story of their future lives, inventing their prosperous middle and wise old age, describing how they would grow fat and then weary together, in the end to be naturally supplanted and finally mourned by their children and grand-children. Wix and Sons.

'We shall have many, many years,' she whispered, growing hoarse with the effort of words, almost believing her own inventions.

Devil turned to her so they lay in each other's arms.

'He made us drink a toast, you know, Jasper and me. He made us drink to Heinrich Bayer. He said, "Because he is dead."'

'Poor Carlo. And poor Heinrich.'

'I have killed two men now, and watched another kill himself.'

'No. They died. You did not kill them.' She hesitated. 'Devil, tell me, is he there?'

His wife meant, did he fear that Carlo would haunt him, in the way that Gabe had done?

Devil felt the kick of the rifle in his shoulder, saw the flash

461

from the muzzle and smelled the powder. Facing him the little red coat framed in a black circle. Eyes blindfolded. Will unquenchable.

He did not think Carlo would linger. Gabe was gone; even poor Gabe. Stanmore churchyard was a quiet place.

'No, he is not here.'

There were only the two of them, in their bed, in the house that was theirs for now and for as long as Devil could hold off his creditors. He could do *that*; it was almost too easy.

Fierce longing for life surged through him. He pulled his wife closer, locking her body against his.

'I love you,' he said.

TWENTY

London, 22 June 1897

The weather in the early hours of the day had not been promising, but as the Queen's Diamond Jubilee procession left Buckingham Palace at fifteen minutes after eleven in the morning, the sky brightened. At last the sun came out and shone on the gathered crowds.

The first part of the six-mile route lay up Constitution Hill to Hyde Park Corner, and from there via St James's Street and Trafalgar Square to St Martin's Lane and the Strand. The entire way was lined with a military guard of honour, drawn from every regiment and all corners of the Empire, and in the procession itself under the command of Field Marshal Lord Roberts VC marched or rode men from such diverse and exotic troops as the Natal Carabiniers, Zaptiehs from Cyprus in red fez and sash, the Trinidad Field Artillery and the proud Indian Army cavalrymen, as well as the sailors of the Royal Navy, men of the Household Cavalry, and the British mounted and foot regiments.

The total number of men employed was said to be more than forty-five thousand.

The spectacle was of a vast river of scarlet and gold flowing under the trees. There were lancers with pennons fluttering, dragoons followed by artillery and artillery followed by hussars, batteries of guns and troops of horses, red, white and black dancing plumes, glittering breastplates and cuirasses, swords, pennants and flags, all passing to the music of the massed bands, the booming of guns in Hyde Park and the clamour of bells from St Paul's Cathedral. White handkerchiefs waved by the crowds were as thick as blown blossom.

Following the troops, and the foreign envoys, and a cavalcade of English and foreign princes came the sixteen carriages of the Royal procession, a stately parade of Princesses and Dukes preceding Her Majesty's carriage. This last was drawn by eight cream-coloured horses ridden by postilions, each with a red-coated running footman at his side.

From his position beside the cupola on the Palmyra's roof, Devil had been watching the passing spectacle for more than an hour before he heard the cheers of hundreds of thousands of voices rising in one great roar as the Queen herself came into view. She was a small figure in black and silver under a white lace parasol, escorted on horseback by the Prince of Wales and the Dukes of Connaught and Cambridge.

Devil stood to a proud salute.

The Queen's head turned as she acknowledged her people, and he was convinced that she was admiring his theatre decorated in her honour. Every shop, theatre and restaurant in the Strand was ornamented too, with festoons of flowers, banners, lights and loyal messages, but he had seen to it that the Palmyra looked the finest. Standing the full height of the building, a palm tree outlined in hundreds of white and green electric bulbs on a shaped wooden frame would not be illuminated until dusk, but for daylight he had had Sammy Hill make up a huge scroll with the painted legend '*VRI 1837–1897, God Bless Our Gracious Majesty*'. Beneath it the entire frontage of the theatre was a mass of palm leaves and Union flags, bunched against green-and-gold hangings designed and made by Sylvia Aynscoe.

Through all the clamour of bells and brass bands Devil could clearly hear Carlo's voice.

'Very fine,' he would have said, his top lip drawing up in

his characteristic sneer. The dwarf had never been an admirer of the monarchy. But still, Devil thought, he would have enjoyed standing up here to admire the procession and take pride in the Palmyra's decorative pre-eminence. Devil smiled at this fond notion and also at the regularity with which his thoughts turned to his late partner.

The bullet that killed the dwarf had been found at the post-mortem lodged in his left lung. It was not one of those cast at the bakery workshop, but an ordinary piece of ammunition. The clinical examination also revealed that cancerous tumours had spread from Carlo's lungs into his bones.

It was not the first death of an illusionist by the Bullet trick nor was it likely to be the last, although it would never again be risked on the Palmyra stage. Devil had closed the theatre in respect to Carlo for a week, and when it reopened the infamous trick was withdrawn without comment. The macabre curiosity of the public meant that for months afterwards people still flocked to see exactly where the fatal shooting had taken place, but Devil refused to make any further capital out of the tragedy. Jerry Cockle had been disappointed in him.

They did not know if any of his family remained, so Devil and Jasper Button had arranged for Carlo to be buried in the green seclusion of Stanmore churchyard. That funeral had been one of their last acts of collaboration. Not very long afterwards Jasper and Hannah gave up Jasper's share of the Palmyra Theatre Partnership to Eliza and left the theatre. Six months later they emigrated with Hannah's mother to Canada. Devil and Eliza were left in sole ownership of the company, and of the theatre itself.

The outstanding debts were always a matter for concern, but it was Devil's talent to juggle those. Not to be obliged to defer to, or even give consideration to the views of any partners, suited him better than the old federation had done – but it was also true that his work did not give him the same sharp happiness as in the hard old days with Carlo and Jasper and poor Heinrich Bayer.

Devil lowered his arm. He told himself that the loyal salute had been as much on behalf of his one-time partners as his own. The great Jubilee procession was brought up at the rear by the 2nd Life Guards bearing the Royal Standard, followed by the Royal Irish Constabulary and the Squadron of the Royal Horse Guards. Everyone craned to watch and to give a final cheer as the last men marched out of sight. The theatre windows overlooking the Strand and the steps in front were crowded with members of the company and their families, representing every person connected with both front of house and backstage work, with the single exception of Eliza.

Eliza was this very morning confined at home in Islington. Her sister Faith, the loyal Nelly and the midwife were with her.

Devil did not linger to watch the tail end of the procession, but nor did he join his employees or even set out for home. Instead he slipped out into the alley and by linking back streets and short cuts behind Fleet Street and Ludgate Circus he made his way towards St Paul's. He overtook Her Majesty's carriage while she paused to receive the pearl sword from the Lord Mayor at the entrance to the City of London, and by the time she was passing under the draped bridge at Ludgate Hill he had reached the source of his second great enterprise of the day.

Mr Wix of the Palmyra Theatre was well known for the ingenuity of his mechanical constructions for the stage. When he made an application to erect a Jubilee ceremony public viewing stand overlooking the steps of the Cathedral, this reputation had been taken into account and permission was granted.

Working with Sammy Hill and a team of carpenters, Devil designed and built a stand four tiers high on the north side of the steps leading up to the west doors. The front of the stand was made to resemble the tiers of boxes at the Palmyra. The wood was painted to look like gilding, the seats were tricked out in the theatre's green-and-gold colours, and the whole structure was ornamented with palm trees wherever it was possible to fix one. At the top was a sign that read:

On the Palmyra Theatre and
On Her Empire the Sun Never Sets

Her Majesty's advanced age and her lameness meant that she was not able to walk up the steps and pass into the cathedral for the service of thanksgiving for her long reign. The state carriage drew up at the west front, where the Archbishop and prelates waited for her under the eyes of all the people who had been lucky enough and sufficiently deep of pocket to buy tickets in the Palmyra stand. Pushing his way through the less fortunate onlookers who were obliged to stand on tiptoe for a glimpse of the proceedings, Devil was gratified by the sight of his theatre – that was what it looked like – filled with a huge bouquet of ladies in their festive outfits. He slipped into his own reserved seat at the centre front of the stand as the outdoor service began. Next to him was Eliza's empty chair.

Barely two miles away, just at the moment when the choirs and the prelates and massed crowds began to sing the 'Old Hundredth', Eliza gave a long wail of triumph. The baby was born.

All people that on earth do dwell,
Sing to the Lord with cheerful voice.

It was a big, lusty girl. The infant filled her lungs with the first breath of her life and howled as if she would join in the singing. Faith sponged her sister's face, and cried a little with the emotion of the moment.

'Eliza, we have a dear little friend for Lizzie.'

The midwife did her work and passed the swaddled infant to her mother.

'You had an easy time with this one, dear. Look at her. She's a fine, healthy creature, that's for certain.'

Eliza studied her daughter. The baby's tiny fists clenched.

She had been yelling in outrage but as soon as her mother stroked her cheek her eyes opened and her cries subsided. Her face was round and crimson as an apple and she had a thatch of black hair. The eyes were dark blue at present, but they promised to turn as black as Devil's.

'Dear me. She does look exactly like her father,' Faith declared.

Eliza smiled. Relief that the birth was over and the baby's emergence had not ripped her mother's body apart swelled into immense gratitude. In the wake of gratitude came happiness, a deep joy that knitted itself into every fibre of her exhausted body. Happiness seemed to throb with every beat of her heart. She kissed the top of the baby's wet black head.

'Your daddy has gone to see the Queen. He will soon be here to meet you.'

At the conclusion of the short service the procession moved on, crossing London Bridge and passing through the streets south of the Thames to allow as many of Her Majesty's subjects as possible to offer their congratulations on the sixtieth anniversary of her reign.

Devil did not follow. He lingered at the tiers of seats, bowing and nodding to his acquaintances and receiving congratulations for the Royal proximity and comfort offered by the accommodation. He shook hands with Mr Edward Mathieson and bowed to the banker's regal wife. In conversation with a less refined person (a cousin of Sammy Hill's, who had found much lucrative business in shaping metal gas piping for the commemorative lighting displays) he allowed himself to boast that he did not see Mr Irving or Mr Tree with stands so patriotically and adroitly linking *their* theatres to the matter of the day.

'No indeed, Mr Wix,' this gentleman agreed. 'The Palmyra is the name of the Jubilee, as far as theatres go.'

Devil also did a quick reckoning of how much money he had made on the venture, advertising value apart.

It was a substantial sum.

468

The Royal procession was returning along Pall Mall to Buckingham Palace by the time Devil began his walk through the holiday crowds towards Islington.

He was a little in fear of what might be waiting for him.

He found the house filled with the intimate bustle and scents of new birth. Faith came dancing down the stairs and held out her arms to him.

'A little girl. Such a beauty. Eliza is quite well, and resting.'

Cornelius and his nursemaid had just returned from their walk. Devil swung his four-year-old son off his feet.

'Come, Con, my boy. Shall we go up and see your mother and sister?'

Eliza was propped up in fresh bed linen, dressed in a lace wrap with her hair neatly swept up in combs. The spectacle could not have been more different from the carnage following Cornelius's birth.

Devil congratulated his wife and peered down at the infant in the crib.

'Faith says she looks like me.'

'We have all remarked on it.'

'I can see nothing but a ripe Kentish apple.'

Eliza laughed and Cornelius peeped down from his father's shoulder.

'He is very little.'

Cornelius was a quiet child except for when he was overtaken by one of his inexplicable tantrums, but even these rages passed quickly. He still suffered from fits but they came rarely. He was tall for his age, thin and lacking in coordination. His size and ungainliness made him clumsy, and prone to knocking over ornaments or mistakenly batting others or himself, but his nature was generally sweet. He was not a talkative boy, but he was observant of what went on around him, and sometimes he came out with quaint opinions that surprised them all.

'*She*. She is very small,' Eliza gently corrected him. She asked him if he would like to give his sister a kiss, and with a grave expression he touched his lips to the frill on the baby's bonnet.

'What do you think to call her?' asked Faith. She had brought in a tea tray laid with Eliza's forget-me-not china.

'Her name is Zenobia,' Devil announced.

The sisters stared at him in such dismay that he had to add, 'Zenobia was the Palmyrene queen, you know. The great sovereign of Araby. What could be more appropriate? "Tonight, on stage, Miss Zenobia Wix of the Palmyra Theatre." We might add Diamond, don't you think, as a tribute to the day?'

Eliza said, 'I would like to call her Nancy. You may add Diamond, if you insist.'

Devil gave her a cup of tea and carried his to the window. Even the barges along the canal were decorated with red, white and blue bunting and the huge horses wore flags draped on their traces. He smiled at his sister-in-law.

'What does a name matter? All that signifies is her life, and Eliza's. We have lived through the day when you and Matthew sent for the priest to baptise Cornelius.'

At the sound of his name the boy ran to the window. He admired a horse of particular splendour, and then began breathing on the glass to create a mist in which to draw patterns.

The June twilight was luminous. As darkness gathered Eliza fell asleep and the nursemaid quietly attended to the baby.

The skies over the City of London and further to the west sparkled with the silver and gold plumes of countless fireworks. Thousands of beacons were burning along the length of the country. Devil was gripped by restlessness. He went into Cornelius's bedroom and gently shook him awake. The child made no complaint, allowing his father to dress him in a cap and warm coat before he was carried downstairs.

'We two shall go out and see the sights together, eh? Wix and Son.'

Devil smiled at a memory but he did not find everything amusing, even on this night of celebration.

Cornelius perched on his father's shoulders, his small heels drumming against his father's chest as they moved rapidly south and east into the City. Quite soon they were amongst the grand buildings and offices of commerce and banking, all of them dressed for the celebration in sheaths and chains of brilliant gas or electric light. The throng carried them along, every person struck almost into silence by so much colour and opulence. The Mansion House lay at the heart of the spectacle. The classical pillars were thickly twined with green and amber lamps and a huge crystal star glittered between rows of flaring flambeaux. The City arms glowed at the centre of the display and beams of crimson light darted out over the crowds from a City crown.

'God save the Queen,' Cornelius said.

A woman in front of Devil turned and grinned, showing her missing teeth.

'Goo' boy,' she crooned. "E'll remember this night, wun 'ee?'

When they had absorbed as much dazzle as their eyes could bear Devil and his son moved onwards, to where the dome of St Paul's was outlined against the light-bloomed sky. The dome itself had not been outlined in glow-lamps, because of the risk of fire. Instead, searchlights mounted on the surrounding roofs were positioned to play on it from a distance. As father and son stood in the shadows of the empty Palmyra stand, the first light beamed on the golden cross that surmounted the ball on the summit of the cathedral. The cross gleamed out of the darkness, and then more lights flared up and swept over the whole dome. The old lead that sheathed it stayed dim, but the stone shone out bright and clear to make a lovely skeleton out of the ancient structure.

Cornelius was growing drowsy and his head lolled against his father's. Devil tightened his hold on the child's legs. As he did so, one of the operators invisibly perched on a high roof slid his light beam away from the building and directed it into the crowd. He shone it first on a group of laughing girls, and then on a shy couple who at once unlinked their hands.

Then he brought it to rest on Devil and his son. Cornelius jerked and sleepily rubbed his eyes. Devil stood still, blinded by the intensity of the beam, knowing that they stood out to all the throng massed on the steps and spilling down Ludgate Hill.

The good-natured laughter and cheering continued as the beam swept on, picking a family or a child or a woman in its bright shaft before leaving them to the darkness again.